Praise for Craig Johnson's

"Like the greatest crime novelists, Joh
Walt Longmire is strong but fallible, a
masks a heightened sensitivity to t
traditional genre novelists who obsess
Johnson's books are also preoccupied with the mystery of his characters' psyches."
—*Los Angeles Times*

"Craig Johnson's fourth Walt Longmire mystery, *Another Man's Moccasins*, reveals a writer who's really hit his stride and has a blue-ribbon win on his hands."
—*The Denver Post*

"Johnson seamlessly blends Longmire's memories of a wartime murder investigation with modern-day issues, culminating in a breathtaking conclusion. Final word: Another satisfying entry in this excellent series."
—*The Rocky Mountain News*

**Praise for Craig Johnson's Walt Longmire Mysteries**

"Johnson has continued a series that should become a must-read."
—*The Denver Post*

"The characters talk straight from the hip and the Wyoming landscape is its own kind of eloquence."
—*The New York Times*

"As always, Johnson does it at a can't-look-away pace, beguiling you from page to page late into the night until you emerge bleary eyed, feeling sun drugged and wind seared, your brain and heart seduced . . . by the lush world he creates."
—*The Oregonian*

"There's a convincing feel to the whole package: a sense that you're viewing this territory through the eyes of someone who knows it as adoring lover and skeptical onlooker at the same time."
—*The Washington Post*

"Johnson vividly explores the wide-open spaces of Wyoming, from the lovely landscape to a claustrophobic ghost town. Heroes stand tall . . . from the rugged, intelligent Walt to his longtime friend Cheyenne Indian Henry Standing Bear."
—*Sun Sentinel* (Fort Lauderdale)

"Johnson introduces a vulnerable character who instantly wins your admiration with his humility, integrity, and humor. [His] sense of place and people drive a story in which you don't necessarily care who the killer might turn out to be; you just don't want the ride to end."

—*Daily Camera* (Boulder, CO)

"Johnson evokes the rugged landscape with reverential prose, lending a heady atmosphere to his story." —*The Philadelphia Inquirer*

"If you want a well-written mystery . . . this is your book."

—*Lincoln Journal Star*

"Johnson crafts great, imaginative mysteries with lots of twists, turns and misdirections . . . [and] the author skillfully seasons his books with humor too often missing in this genre." —*Billings Gazette*

"Pile on the thermal underwear, fire up the four-wheel drive and head for Durant. Walt and his idiosyncratic crew are terrific company—droll, sassy and surprisingly tenderhearted." —*Kirkus Reviews* (starred review)

"[Johnson has] a sure-handed touch for jolting both his characters and his readers out of their comfort zones and deep into harm's way. It's hard to ask for more in a literary mystery." —*Booklist* (starred review)

"Johnson weaves together city and country, Anglo and Indian, art snob and proud philistine and creates a laugh-out-loud, hard-to-put-down mystery." —Book Sense

"There's genuine emotion and care in these pages, with humor and humanity to balance its undertone of imminent violence."

—*Mystery Scene*

A PENGUIN MYSTERY

# ANOTHER MAN'S MOCCASINS

Craig Johnson is the *New York Times* bestselling author of the Longmire mystery novels, the basis for the Netflix original series *Longmire*. He is the recipient of the Western Writers of America Spur Award for fiction, the Mountains and Plains Booksellers Award for fiction, the Nouvel Observateur Prix du Roman Noir, and the 2015 SNCF Prix du Polar. His novella, *Spirit of Steamboat*, was the first One Book Wyoming selection. He lives in Ucross, Wyoming, population twenty-five.

## The Longmire Series

The Cold Dish

Death Without Company

Kindness Goes Unpunished

The Dark Horse

Junkyard Dogs

Hell Is Empty

As the Crow Flies

A Serpent's Tooth

Any Other Name

Dry Bones

## *Also by Craig Johnson*

Spirit of Steamboat

Wait for Signs

# CRAIG JOHNSON

# ANOTHER MAN'S MOCCASINS

PENGUIN BOOKS

**For Bill Bower and all those crazy bastards who flew off the USS *Hornet* and into those cold, gray skies on the morning of April 18, 1942—and everybody who ever threw a salute before and after.**

PENGUIN BOOKS
An imprint of Penguin Random House LLC
375 Hudson Street
New York, New York 10014
penguin.com

First published in the United States of America by Viking Penguin,
an imprint of Penguin Random House LLC, 2008
Published in Penguin Books 2009
This edition published in 2015



THE LIBRARY OF CONGRESS HAS CATALOGED THE HARDCOVER EDITION AS FOLLOWS:
Johnson, Craig, ———
Another man's moccasins : a Walt Longmire mystery / Craig Johnson.
p. cm.
ISBN 978-0-670-01861-1 (hc.)
ISBN 978-0-14-310932-7 (pbk.)
1. Longmire, Walt (Fictitious character)—Fiction. 2. Sheriffs—Fiction.
3. Vietnamese—United States—Fiction. 4. Wyoming—Fiction. I. Title.
PS3610.O325A56 2008
813'.6—dc22 2007029979

Printed in the United States of America
1 3 5 7 9 10 8 6 4 2

Printed in the United States of America
Set in Dante
Designed by Alissa Amell

# ACKNOWLEDGMENTS

A writer, like a sheriff, is the embodiment of a group of people and without their support both are in a tight spot. I have been blessed with a close order of family, friends, and associates who have made this book possible. This book is a work of fiction, and as such it's important to point out that the guys at the 377th Security Police Squadron were top-notch law enforcement personnel.

I would like to thank Kara Newcomer, historian for the United States Marine Corps History Division, and the folks down at Willow Creek Ranch. Janet Hubbard-Brown and Astrid Latapie for helping out with handling the French at the Indo-Chinese fire drill, and the staff and doctors at the VA Medical Center over at Fort Mackenzie in Sheridan, including Hollis W. Hackman and Chuck Guilford.

Thanks to my chiefs of staff, Gail Hochman, Kathryn Court, Alexis Washam, and Ali Bothwell Mancini; to my officer in charge of logistics, Sonya Cheuse; and to Susan Fain, my military council. Thanks to Marcus Red Thunder for taking the muffler off the jeep to convince the enemy that we had tanks. Kudos to Eric Boss for requisitioning everything I needed, including the beer. A big thanks to James Crumley for the canteen and to Curt Wendelboe and Rob Kresge for leaning over and pointing out that it was quiet—too quiet.

And to the person I enjoy sharing my foxhole with most, my wife, Judy.

*Great Spirit, grant that I may not criticize my neighbor until I have walked a mile in his moccasins.*

Old Indian Prayer

# 1

"Two more."

Cady looked at me but didn't say anything.

It had been like this for the last week. We'd reached a plateau, and she was satisfied with the progress she'd made. I wasn't. The physical therapist at University of Pennsylvania Hospital in Philadelphia had warned me that this might happen. It wasn't that my daughter was weak or lazy; it was far worse than that—she was bored.

"Two more?"

"I heard you. . . ." She plucked at her shorts and avoided my eyes. "Your voice; it carries."

I placed an elbow on my knee, chin on fist, sat farther back on the sit-up bench, and glanced around. We weren't alone. There was a kid in a Durant Quarterback Club T-shirt who was trying to bulk up his 145-pound frame at one of the Universal machines. I'm not sure why he was up here—there were no televisions, and it wasn't as fancy as the main gym downstairs. I understood all the machines up here—you didn't have to plug any of them in—but I wondered about him; it could be that he was here because of Cady.

"Two more."

"Piss off."

The kid snickered, and I looked at him. I glanced back at my daughter. This was good; anger sometimes got her to finish up, even if it cost me the luxury of conversation for the rest of the evening. It didn't matter tonight; she had a dinner date and then had to be home for an important phone call. I had zip. I had all the time in the world.

She had cut her auburn hair short to match the spot where they had made the U-shaped incision that had allowed her swelling brain to survive. Only a small scar was visible at the hairline. She was beautiful, and the pain in the ass was that she knew it.

It got her pretty much whatever she wanted. Beauty was life's E-ZPass. I was lucky I got to ride on the shoulder.

"Two more?"

She picked up her water bottle and squeezed out a gulp, leveling the cool eyes back on me. We sat there looking at each other, both of us dressed in gray. She stretched a finger out and pulled the band of my T-shirt down, grazing a fingernail on my exposed collarbone. "That one?"

Just because she was beautiful didn't mean she wasn't smart. Diversion was another of her tactics. I had enough scars to divert the entire First Division. She had known this scar and had seen it on numerous occasions. Her question was a symptom of the memory loss that Dr. Rissman had mentioned.

She continued to poke my shoulder with the finger. "That one."

"Two more."

"That one?"

Cady never gave up.

It was a family trait, and in our tiny family, stories were the coinage of choice, a bartering in the aesthetic of information and the athletics of emotion, so I answered her. "Tet."

She set her water bottle down on the rubber-padded floor. "When?"

"Before you were born."

She lowered her head and looked at me through her lashes, one cheek pulled up in a half smile. "Things happened before I was born?"

"Well, nothing really important."

She took a deep breath, gripped the sides of the bench, and put all her effort into straightening the lever action of thirty pounds at her legs. Slowly, the weights lifted to the limit of the movement and then, just as slowly, dropped back. After a moment, she caught her breath. "Marine inspector, right?"

I nodded. "Yep."

"Why Marines?"

"It was Vietnam, and I was gonna be drafted, so it was a choice." I was consistently amazed at what her damaged brain chose to remember.

"What was Vietnam like?"

"Confusing, but I got to meet Martha Raye."

Unsatisfied with my response, she continued to study my scar. "You don't have any tattoos."

"No." I sighed, just to let her know that her tactics weren't working.

"I have a tattoo."

"You have two." I cleared my throat in an attempt to end the conversation. She pulled up the cap sleeve of her Philadelphia City Sports T-shirt, exposing the faded, Cheyenne turtle totem on her shoulder. She was probably unaware that she'd been having treatments to have it removed; it had been the ex-boyfriend's idea, all before the accident. "The other one's on your butt, but we don't have to look for it now."

The kid snickered again. I turned and stared at him with a little more emphasis this time.

"Bear was in Vietnam with you, right?"

She was smiling as I turned back to her. All the women in my life smiled when they talked about Henry Standing Bear. It was a bit annoying, but Henry was my best and lifelong friend, so I got over it. He owned the Red Pony, a bar on the edge of the Northern Cheyenne Reservation, only a mile from my cabin, and he was the one who was taking Cady to dinner. I wasn't invited. He and my daughter were in cahoots. They had pretty much been in cahoots since she had been born.

"Henry was in-country, Special Operations Group; we didn't serve together."

"What was he like back then?"

I thought about it. "He's mellowed, a little." It was a frightening thought. "Two more?"

Her gray eyes flashed. "One more."

I smiled. "One more."

Cady's slender hands returned to the sides of the bench, and I watched as the toned legs once again levitated and lowered the thirty pounds. I waited a moment, then lumbered up and placed a kiss at the horseshoe-shaped scar and helped her stand. The physical progress was moving ahead swimmingly, mostly due to the advantages of her stellar conditioning and youth, but the afternoon workouts took their toll, and she was usually a little unsteady by the time we finished.

I held her hand and picked up her water and tried not to concentrate on the fact that my daughter had been a fast-track, hotshot lawyer back in Philly only two months earlier and that now she was here in Wyoming and was trying to remember that she had tattoos and how to walk without assistance.

We made our way toward the stairwell and the downstairs

showers. As we passed the kid at the machine, he looked at Cady admiringly and then at me. "Hey, Sheriff?"

I paused for a moment and steadied Cady on my arm. "Yep?"

"J.P. said you once bench-pressed six plates."

I continued looking down at him. "What?"

He gestured toward the steel plates on the rack at the wall. "Jerry Pilch? The football coach? He said senior year, before you went to USC, you bench-pressed six plates." He continued to stare at me. "That's over three hundred pounds."

"Yep, well." I winked. "Jerry's always had a tendency to exaggerate."

"I thought so."

I nodded to the kid and helped Cady down the steps. It'd been eight plates, actually, but that had been a long time ago.

My shower was less complicated than Cady's, so I usually got out before her and waited on the bench beside the Clear Creek bridge. I placed my summer-wear palm-leaf hat on my head, slipped on my ten-year-old Ray-Bans, and shrugged the workout bag's strap farther onto my shoulder so that it didn't press my Absaroka County sheriff's star into my chest. I pushed open the glass door and stepped into the perfect fading glory of a high-plains summer afternoon. It was vacation season, creeping up on rodeo weekend, and the streets were full of people from somewhere else.

I took a left and started toward the bridge and the bench. I sat next to the large man with the ponytail and placed the gym bag between us. "How come I wasn't invited to dinner?"

The Cheyenne Nation kept his head tilted back, eyes closed, taking in the last warmth of the afternoon sun. "We have discussed this."

"It's Saturday night, and I don't have anything to do."

"You will find something." He took a deep breath, the only sign that he wasn't made of wood and selling cigars. "Where is Vic?"

"Firearms recertification in Douglas."

"Damn."

I thought about my scary undersheriff from Philadelphia; how she could outshoot, outdrink, and outswear every cop I knew, and how she was now representing the county at the Wyoming Law Enforcement Academy. I was unsure if that was a positive thing. "Yep, not a safe weekend to be in Douglas."

He nodded, almost imperceptibly. "How is all that going?"

I took a moment to discern what "all that" might mean. "I'm not really sure." He raised an eyelid and studied me in a myopic fashion. "We seem to be having a problem getting in sync." The eyelid closed, and we sat there as a silence passed. "Where are you going to dinner?"

"I am not going to tell you."

"C'mon."

His face remained impassive. "We have discussed this."

We had—it was true. The Bear had expressed the opinion that for both of our mental healths, it might be best if Cady and I didn't spend every waking hour in each other's company. It was difficult, but I was going to have to let her out of my sight sometime. "In town or over in Sheridan?"

"I am not going to tell you."

I was disconcerted by the flash of a camera and turned to see a woman from somewhere else smile and continue down the sidewalk toward the Busy Bee Café, where I would likely be having my dinner, alone. I turned to look at Henry Standing Bear's striking profile. "You should sit with me more often; I'm photogenic."

"They were taking photographs with a greater frequency before you arrived."

I ignored him. "She's allergic to plums."

"Yes."

"I'm not sure if she'll remember that."

"I do."

"No alcohol."

"Yes."

I thought about that advisory and came clean. "I let her have a glass of red wine last weekend."

"I know."

I turned and looked at him. "She told you?"

"Yes."

Cahoots. I had a jealous inkling that the Bear was making more progress in drawing all of Cady back to us than I was.

I stretched my legs and crossed my boots; they were still badly in need of a little attention. I adjusted my gun belt so that the hammer of my .45 wasn't digging into my side. "We still on for the Rotary thing on Friday?"

"Yes."

Rotary was sponsoring a debate between me and prosecuting attorney Kyle Straub; we were the two candidates for the position of Absaroka County sheriff. After five elections and twenty-four sworn years, I usually did pretty well at debates but felt a little hometown support might be handy, so I had asked Henry to come. "Think of it as a public service—most Rotarians have never even met a Native American."

That finally got the one eye to open again, and he turned toward me. "Would you like me to wear a feather?"

"No, I'll just introduce you as an Injun."

Cady placed her hand on my shoulder and leaned over to allow the Cheyenne Nation to bestow a kiss on her cheek. She was wearing blue jeans and a tank top with, I was pleased to see, the fringed, concho-studded leather jacket I'd bought for her years ago. It could still turn brisk on July nights along the foothills of the Bighorn Mountains.

She jostled the hat on my head and dropped her gym bag on top of mine. She turned to Henry. "Ready?"

He opened his other eye. "Ready."

He rose effortlessly, and I thought if I got it in quick that maybe I'd get an answer. "Where you going?"

She smiled as the Bear came around the back of the bench and took her elbow. "I'm not allowed to tell you."

Cady's current love interest, Vic's younger brother, was supposed to be flying in from Philadelphia on Tuesday for a Wild West vacation. I still hadn't gotten a straight answer as to with whom he was staying. "Don't forget that Michael is calling."

She shook her head as they walked past me, pausing to lift my hat and plant a kiss on the crown of my head. "I know when he's calling, Daddy. I'll be home long before then." She shoved my hat down, hard.

I readjusted and watched as they crossed the sidewalk, where Henry helped her into Lola, his powder-blue '59 T-Bird convertible. The damage I'd done to the classic automobile was completely invisible due to the craftsmanship of the body men in South Philly, and I watched as the Wyoming sun glistened on the Thunderbird's flanks. I had a moment of hope that they wouldn't get going when the starter continued to grind, but the aged Y-Block caught and blew a slight fantail of carbon into the street. He slipped her into gear, and they were gone.

As usual, I got the gym bags, and he got the girl.

I considered my options. There was the plastic-wrapped burrito at the Kum-and-Go, the stuffed peppers at the Durant

Home for Assisted Living, a potpie from the kitchenette back at the jail, or the Busy Bee Café. I gathered up my collection of bags and hustled across the bridge over Clear Creek before Dorothy Caldwell changed her mind and turned the sign, written in cursive, hanging on her door.

"Not the usual?"

"No."

She poured my iced tea and looked at me, fist on hip. "You didn't like it last time?"

I struggled to remember but gave up. "I don't remember what it was last time."

"Is Cady's condition contagious?"

I ignored the comment and tried to decide what to order. "I'm feeling experimental. Are you still offering your Weekend Cuisines of the World?" It was an attempt on her part to broaden the culinary experience of our little corner of the high plains.

"I am."

"Where, in the world, are we?"

"Vietnam."

It didn't take me long to respond. "I'll pass."

"It's really good."

I weaved my fingers and rested my elbows on the counter. "What is it?"

"Chicken with lemongrass." She continued to look at me.

"Henry's dish?"

"That's where I got the recipe."

I withered under her continued gaze. "All right."

She busied herself in the preparation of the entree, and I sipped my tea. I glanced around at the five other people in the homey café but didn't recognize anyone. I must have been thirsty from watching Cady work out, because a third of the glass was gone in two gulps. I set it back on the Formica, and Dorothy refilled it immediately. "You don't talk about it much."

"What?"

"The war."

I nodded as she put the tan plastic pitcher on the counter next to me. I turned my glass in the circular imprint of its condensation. "It's funny, but it came up earlier this afternoon." I met her eyes under the silver hair. "Cady asked about the scar on my collarbone, the one from Tet."

She nodded slightly. "Surely she's seen that before?"

"Yep."

Dorothy took a deep breath. "It's okay, she's doing better every day." She reached out and squeezed my shoulder just at said scar. "But, be careful. . . ." She looked concerned.

I looked up at her. "Why?"

"Visitations like those tend to come in threes."

I watched as she took the tea and refilled some of the other customers. I thought about Vietnam, thought about the smell, the heat, and the dead.

**Tan Son Nhut, Vietnam: 1967**

I had flown in with them.

A spec 4 on the helicopter ride had asked where I was going and watched as I'd tried not to throw up on the dead that were stacked in the cargo area of the Huey. I wasn't sick because of the bodies; I'd seen a lot of those. I just didn't like helicopters. The men had been in a mortared helicopter that had been waved off to an area outside the defense perimeter—firebase support in the DMZ for Khe Sanh. They were wrapped in plastic ponchos because the army had run out of body bags. They had run out of food, ammo, and medicine, too—the dead were one of the few things of which there always seemed to be plenty. The young corpsman smiled at me, his thin lips grinning like a death's head, and told me not to worry. He said that if I got hurt, they could have me in a base-camp hospital in twenty minutes, critical and they would have me in Yokosuka, Japan, in twelve hours. He had gestured to the plastic-wrapped bundles behind him. Like them, who gives a shit.

Later, I studied the chromate green interior of the Quonset hut as a lean air force investigative operations officer squinted up at me through his thick glasses and the sweat. He was studying my utility cap, so I yanked it off my head and returned to attention. I was sweating, too. Specifically, we were there to win over hearts and minds, but mostly what we did was sweat. I had been fighting the feeling that, since arriving in Vietnam coming up on six months earlier, I was melting.

He made me wait the commensurate amount of time to let me know that I had performed a breach of military decorum with my cover and that the major was not pleased. "What the hell am I supposed to do with you?"

The majority of the humidity in my body was draining between my shoulder blades and soaking the waistband of my fatigues. "Not sure, sir."

"What the hell is a MOS 0111?"

"Marine police, sir. Investigator."

He continued to shake his head. "Yeah. I got the directive from MAF. Your papers cleared the provost marshal at Chu Lai, so I guess battalion headquarters has decided that you're my problem now." He looked up at me. He had the look, the look I'd seen a thousand times in the short period I'd been in-country. He was old—an age that had snuck up on him in the place would stay with him for the rest of his life. The event had him, the war was his religion, and his youth was gone with his eyes. "Marine inspector?"

I remained silent and focused on the corrugated wall in an

attempt not to stare at the photo of DeDe Lind, *Playboy*'s Miss August 1967, that was hung there.

It was December.

The major looked back at my duty papers, rustling them in disbelief. "Inspect? Hell, I didn't even know you jarheads could read." He flipped the page, and I figured the real trouble was about to begin. His eyes came up slowly. "English major?"

"Ball, sir." I'd found it best to downplay higher education in the armed forces, and football was always a quick and successful diversionary tactic.

He blinked behind the glasses and frowned an acceptance that I might not be the complete wastrel he'd first imagined. "What'd you play?"

"Offensive tackle, sir."

"The trenches? Outstanding. I played a little in high school."

With a leather helmet, I figured. "Is that right, sir?"

"Halfback."

"Yes, sir." Backup, no doubt.

He studied my papers some more. "I didn't play much." I didn't know what to say to that, so I just stood there with my mouth shut, another method I'd learned in dealing with military hierarchy. "Look, somebody owes somebody a favor and that's why you're here." He leaned back in his green metallic chair, which almost matched the chromate walls, and finally remembered that I was still at attention. "At ease." He dropped my papers and concentrated on me as I took a quarter step to the side and placed my hands behind my back. I was still holding my hat. "We've got a little drug smuggling problem on the base, but nothing big. We've already got some very good men working on the situation. I'm only guessing, but I'd say the provost marshal wants one of his brand-new MOS 0111s to get his feet wet."

He continued to consider me, and I guessed that he wanted a response. "Yes, sir."

"Why mother-green-and-her-mean-machine can't police her own messes, of which there are plenty, is a mystery to me, but you're here and we'll just have to make the best of things." He glanced back at the papers on his desk. "You are new, and it won't take long for everyone to figure out why you're here. So the best thing you can do is keep your mouth shut and do what you're told. You got me?"

"Yes, sir."

"All of the work you've done in the past has been under the direct supervision of navy investigators; now, however, you will be working with air force security personnel and central intelligence detachment, who, I am sure, you will find infinitely more capable than the swabos."

"Yes, sir."

"I'm putting you with Mendoza, who is our own 377th, and Baranski of Central Intelligence Division. They've been working the case for about five weeks, and you will provide the muscle."

"Yes, sir." If he belched, I was going to yes-sir it.

"They're first louies, and you will follow every order they give you. Understood?"

"Yes, sir."

"They're class of '66." He slipped my papers back in the folder and handed them to me. "That means there's one of you butter bars left; gives great hope to the war effort."

"Yes, sir."

"Dismissed."

When I got to the outer office and handed my folder to the airman, there were two first lieutenants leaning against the doorway. One was short and dark; the other was a tall bon vivant with an Errol Flynn mustache. The tall one had blond hair, air-force-blue eyes, and army fatigues. He stuck his hand out, and I shook it, taking in the casual, self-assured swagger of a man very content with himself. "You our new pet Marine?"

"Yep."

He lit a Camel cigarette and swiveled his head to look at his partner, who now extended his hand. I shook his as well. He spoke with a strong Texas accent. "Mendoza. This here is Baranski."

I had already read their names above their right pockets, just as I was sure they'd already read mine, but it was now a different protocol. I slipped my hat back on. "Longmire."

"Sheriff Longmire?"

I turned and looked up at Rosey Wayman, one of the few females in the Wyoming Highway Patrol. She'd been transferred up from the Elk Mountain detachment about six months ago and had been causing quite a stir here in the Bighorns. "Well, if it isn't the sweetheart of I-two-five." I watched as the trademark grin showed bright white teeth, and her blue eyes sparked.

Maybe my evening was looking up. I wondered when Vic would be back.

"I'm sorry to bother you, Walt, but we got a call in, and Ruby said this would be where you were."

"What've we got?"

"Some ranchers found a body down on Lone Bear Road near Route 249."

Maybe my evening wasn't looking up.

That was near Powder Junction. It was July, and it didn't take much deduction to figure out why the locals were out on that desolate part of the county road system. "Swathers or balers?"

"Balers. They supposedly swathed last week."

No square hectare of grass went unshorn in a Wyoming

summer. The Department of Transportation usually subcontracted the cutting of grass along its motorways to the lowest-bidding local ranchers, which allowed the state grass to become a private commodity commonly known as beer-can hay.

I poked a thumb toward the blond patrolperson as Dorothy returned with the dish full of chicken and lemongrass. "Can I get that to go?"

No matter what aspect of law enforcement with which you might be involved, there's always one job you dread. I'm sure at the more complicated venues it's the terrorists, it's serial killers, or it's gang-related, but for the western sheriff it's always been the body dump. To the north, Sheridan County has two unsolved, and Natrona County to the south has five; up until twenty-eight minutes ago, we'd had none. There you stand by some numbered roadway with a victim, no ID, no crime scene, no suspects, nothing.

I got out of Rosey's cruiser and nodded to Chuck Frymyer and Double Tough, my two deputies from the southern part of the county. "Walt. She's down over the hill."

We headed toward the giant balers at the edge of a large culvert. Lieutenant Cox, the highway patrol division commander, was standing halfway down the hill toward the barrow ditch with two more of his men, still writing in their duty books. It was near their highway, but it was my county. "Hey, Karl."

"Walt." He nodded at one of the pieces of equipment where two elderly cowboys sat, one in a beaten straw hat and the other wearing a Rocking D Ranch ball cap. "You know these gentlemen?"

"Yep." The two got up when they noticed me. Den and James Dunnigan were a couple of hardscrabble ranchers from out near Bailey. James was a little wifty, and Den was just plain mean. "How you doin', James?"

Den squinted and started in. "We swathed two days ago, and she wasn't here. . . ."

James cut him off. "Hey, Walt."

"What'a we got?" I figured the HPs had already gotten a statement from them, but I thought I'd give the brothers another shot at the story before we went any further.

"Already told 'em." Den gestured toward the HPs. It had probably been a long day, it was late on a Saturday afternoon, and he evidently felt they had been detained long enough.

"Tell me." I remained conversational but made sure it wasn't a question. Frymyer had his notebook out and was scribbling.

James continued in a soft voice and did his best to focus on the conversation at hand. "We was balin' and come up onto her."

"What'd you do?"

He shrugged. "Shut 'er down and called 911."

"Go near the body?"

"Nope, I didn't."

"You're sure?"

"Yep."

I glanced at Den, who was blinking too much. "Den?"

He shrugged. "I went over to the edge of the culvert and yelled at her." He blinked again. "I thought she might be asleep. Then I saw she wasn't breathin'."

I had Den show me the exact route that he had taken, and then I retreated to the top of the culvert with my two deputies, where it was unlikely anybody had been. I squatted down in a hunter's crouch and listened as Cox dismissed the Dunnigan brothers.

I turned to Chuck. "You know how to open a baler?"

The sandy Vandyke smiled back. "Born to it."

"Go crack that one open and check the contents and then split the last two bales northbound. If she was walking or running from somebody, then she might've dropped her purse or something along the way." Frymyer paused for a moment, and I looked at him. "You need help?"

He glanced back at the one-ton bales. "Yes."

I looked at Double Tough, and he started off with Chuck.

There was still a lot of light—it was like that in the summer this far north—and you could plainly see where the young woman had played out the last moments of her life. She was provocatively dressed, inappropriate for the surroundings. She had on a short skirt, a pink halter top, and no shoes. Her long, dark hair was tangled with the grasses; it had been blown by the ever prevalent Wyoming wind, and you could see her delicate bone structure. The eyes were closed, and you might've thought she was asleep but for the blue coloring in her face and a swollen eye, and the fact that, from the angle, it was apparent that her neck had been broken.

I listened as Cox came up and squatted down beside me. "You losing weight?"

"Yep, I'm in the gym with Cady every day."

He nodded. "How's she doing?"

"She's good, Karl. Thank you for asking. Hey, speaking of Cady, could I get you to have Rosey call into our dispatch and ask them to tell her I won't be coming home tonight?"

"You bet." He tipped his campaign hat back. "DCI's on the way. I think you got the wicked witch of the west herself." I nodded. T. J. Sherwin was always looking for a reason to come up to the mountains in the summertime. The division lieutenant plucked a piece of the prairie and placed the harvested end in his mouth. "We checked all the way back to Casper, Walt, but no abandoned vehicles." He glanced after my deputies. "Your guys gonna check the baler?"

"Yep."

"Good. My guys wouldn't know which end to look in." He studied the body of the dead girl and then looked up at me. "I've got men checking all the Chinese restaurants in Sheridan, Casper, and Gillette to see if anybody's missing. . . ."

"Don't bother." I ran my hand over my face. "She's Vietnamese."

# 2

"She wasn't walking, not without shoes." T. J. Sherwin watched as the technicians zipped up the black plastic bag and carefully placed the Asian woman's body onto a gurney under the constant racket of the generators. The flat, yellow shine of the emergency lights made even the living look jaundiced.

I closed my eyes. "Fresh?"

It was getting late, and the warmth of the sun was long gone, replaced by the stars and the clear, cool air creeping down from the Bighorn Mountains. It hadn't rained in more than a month.

She hugged herself. "Less than twelve hours." I put my arm around her because I wanted to keep her warm and because I wanted to. She'd been the chief forensic pathologist for Wyoming's Division of Criminal Investigation for half of my tenure in Absaroka County. She'd thought me antiquated, but in seventeen years I'd grown on her. "She wasn't killed here. Preliminary says asphyxiation, manual strangulation by someone very powerful. Whoever it was, they started by strangling her and then broke her neck."

"They didn't do a very good job of hiding the body."

I could feel her eyes on me. "No, they didn't."

I took a quick look ahead to the county road, toward the

highway. "There's an exit only a mile up." I looked at the uncut grass on the other side of the culvert. "We'll have to look for drag marks or footprints farther north. We're going to need to check the roadside back to 249 and down to 246 at the south fork of the Powder." She shivered and snuggled closer under my arm. "My guys about through with the bales?"

She snickered. "They're gonna love you."

"Yep." I watched as the bag boys loaded the dead woman into the Suburban for transport to Cheyenne. "So, you're not going to stick around?"

"Too much to do." She left my protection and started back up the slope toward the emergency vehicles splaying their revolving blue, red, and yellow lights across the wildflowers that were blooming under the sage.

I started to follow but stopped, sighed to myself, and called after her. "Anybody check that thing yet?"

She turned back to me. "The tunnel? No, I think they were going to wait until daylight."

"You wan' company?" Double Tough gave me his Maglite.

I took half an egg sandwich and shook my head. "Nope." The food had just arrived, and I knew they were hungry; I figured I could prowl around on my own. "But I'll take one of those cups of coffee."

It was a clear night, and the full moon and thick swath of the Milky Way gave plenty of illumination on the area surrounding the tunnel, if not the hole itself. I threw a leg over a guardrail and started down the embankment to the entrance on the other side of Lone Bear Road. I wasn't expecting to find a culprit shivering at the mouth of the thing; I figured that whoever had killed the young woman had walked back to his vehicle and driven away, but it never hurt to look.

I opened the Styrofoam cup, shook off the lid and stuffed it in my back jeans pocket in an attempt to keep Absaroka County clean, and stepped down into the three-quarter inch of Murphy Creek.

I sipped the coffee, listened to the distant sound of the eighteen-wheel trucks on I-25, and shone the beam of the four-cell flashlight into the black opening of the drainage tunnel; there was something blocking a complete view of the other side. I took a step and listened to it resound off the hardened walls of the concrete. In the most likely scenario, it was a yearling that had followed the creek bed and gotten stuck or confused; few things in the natural world are as easily confused as a heifer—just ask any cowboy.

There were some rabbit carcasses and a few deer bones a little farther into the tunnel, and I could see that there were some broken pieces of two-by-fours and truck skids piled at one side with a collection of blankets, tarps, and cardboard boxes gathered on them. It was possibly the regular flotsam and jetsam of Murphy Creek, but I didn't think the water flow was that strong.

I thought I'd seen a small movement, but it was probably the shadows of the flashlight. The refuse pile smelled like something dead and got worse as I leaned in closer and nudged one of the blanket layers of the sofa-sized bundle—more cardboard. Something must have been using the blockage as a nest, and the stench made my eyes water.

An old warning bell went off, so I transferred my cup of coffee to the flashlight hand and pulled the Colt 1911 out and to the right, cocked and locked. I clicked off the safety and stooped down as close as I dared, recognizing the quilt as a packing blanket from a rental truck place.

I had pulled my sidearm on a pile of trash.

I started to resafety and reholster my weapon when something in the pile shifted, and the entire collection of blankets, cardboard, and smell exploded straight at me, lifting me completely off the ground and against the far side of the tunnel. The flashlight disappeared, coffee went everywhere, and the .45 in my hand fired as my fingers contracted on impact with the cement wall. The compressed sound of the big Colt plugged my ears like a set of fingers. All the air in my body hung there as I fell forward.

Whatever it was, it was bigger than me, and hairy, and it caught me by my chest and pushed me back. It was roaring in my face as it slapped me, the Colt splashing into the water.

My head felt like it was coming apart, but I thrashed at whatever it was, bringing my arms forward and kicking with my legs. It pressed against me with the force of a front-end loader. My only hope was to get away from the thing before it sunk its claws into me or took off half my face in one bite.

I got a lucky punch at its head, but it still threw me sideways, where I slid along in the muck. The thought of being mauled to death or eaten alive in the darkness of an irrigation tunnel renewed my fortitude for fighting; I leveraged a fist loose and brought it forward with all the force my clumsy position would allow. There was a bit of a lull, and I took advantage and raised my head, but it was back on me in an instant.

I shouldn't have exposed my throat because it started to choke me. I flailed with both fists, but I might as well have been striking the concrete floor. I kicked, but the weight of the thing held me solid, and I was just beginning to feel the blood vessels in my head explode and my vision fail.

I could see flashes of light where there were none, and I could see faces in the flashes; women, they were all women. I could see my mother on a grassy hillside, the summer sun shining through the sides of her pale blue eyes. I saw my wife, the first time I asked her to dance, and the gentle way her fingers first reached for mine. I saw Victoria Moretti, lowering her face to me with her bathrobe undone. I saw my daughter, her determined look in the weight room, and could only think, *Ish okay, Daddy.*

There was splashing, and there were other voices above the roaring of whatever had me and whatever I had. I made one last struggle to bury my thumbs into the front of its throat and could just feel my fingers making headway into the fragile, egg-carton-like cartilage of its larynx, a method I'd used to stay alive in Khe Sanh.

If I was going to die, something was going with me.

I heard a loud crack and felt a shift in the thing's weight as it toppled to one side, just before the women's faces disappeared and it all faded to black.

I sat there on the bank of the hillside as the EMTs worked on the back of my head. I continued to clear my throat and massaged my forefinger and thumb into my eye sockets in an attempt to replace the stars in my eyes with real ones.

Double Tough stood by as T.J. handed me another cup of coffee. I wasn't sure I could swallow it, but it was reassuring just to be able to hold it. We all watched the faint glow of the sunrise on the horizon toward Pumpkin Buttes and Thunder Basin. I nodded thanks and cleared my throat, still unable to speak.

T.J. glanced back at the EMTs, who were finishing up the job. "I assume he's going to be okay?"

Cathi leaned around and looked at the front of me as she finished doctoring the back of my head. "The long arm of the law's gonna have a lump, but we've patched him up before."

Double Tough smiled his slow grin and looked across the grassland to the wall of red rocks. "Lord Almighty, you see the size'a that son-of-a-bitch?"

I swallowed and tried a sip; it tasted pretty good but set off another coughing attack. "What did you use to get him off me?" My voice sounded rough and wheezy.

"One'a them pieces'a two-by-four." He thought about it as Cathi and Chris gathered up the rest of their equipment to change venue. "I think ya surprised him."

"Not as much as he surprised me."

The creature from the cave was as big as a grizzly, and it took four men to carry him out of the tunnel. I noticed they used ankle bracelets at his wrists because the handcuffs would've been too small. He was an Indian, Crow from what we could make of him.

I started to get up but felt a little dizzy and sat back down. T.J. placed a hand on my shoulder and held me there. "Easy."

I sighed. "He still alive?"

Double Tough snorted. "Yeah. I hit him hard enough to fell a mule, but he's still breathin'."

I watched as Chris, Chuck, and two HPs carried the now unconscious man up the hillside, his hair trailing all the way to the grass, snagging here and there as if it were trying to stay the progress. It was as if his hair, like the Vietnamese girl's, had wanted to remain here until all the questions had been answered. He was wearing an old army field jacket, torn and ragged, with the remnants of a denim shirt and a wool sweater underneath. His legs were swathed in tatters of plaid-lined overalls. Everything was frayed and filthy except the intricately beaded moccasins that were on his gigantic feet. They were a design I'd never seen.

I tried to stand again, and this time succeeded, and I staggered up the hill with Double Tough's help. "Anybody checking all that stuff in the tunnel?"

"They're gonna, but they're not gonna be happy about it. The place smells bad enough to gag a maggot off a gut wagon."

I nodded toward the giant. "What about him?"

"He's goin' to the hospital, and then he's most likely gonna be in our jail."

"Find anything in the tunnel to connect him with the Vietnamese woman?"

He shook his head at me. "Not yet, but we figured tryin' ta choke the life out of the sheriff was good enough reason to hold 'im."

We watched as they loaded the gurney into the EMT van, the rear suspension compressing with the weight of one woman, four men, and one very large Indian. "You guys knock him out with something?"

Double Tough gave a halfhearted laugh. "We didn't have to. You jus' about collapsed his larynx, and I pretty much battered his head in."

They closed the van doors and departed toward Durant Memorial Hospital. After the sirens died down, he spoke in a soft voice. "That is one FBI."

I didn't bother to translate the acronym, but I knew he didn't mean Federal Bureau of Investigation.

T.J. had left with her DCI crew and said she'd be in touch as soon as they knew anything, so Rosey gave me a ride back to the office. It was still early morning, and the darkness was slow to release its grip on the county. Ruby, my dispatcher, was always first in, but she was Dog-sitting and hadn't gotten there yet. My dog, Dog, still didn't have a name and after calling him Dog for the better part of a year I was concerned that he would be confused if

I gave him a real name or maybe I was concerned about confusing myself.

I took advantage of the situation to go back to the holding cells to catch a quick nap on one of the bunks. I tried sleeping on my back, but the damage to the muscles in my throat made me feel like I was strangling, and the little yarmulke of bandages at the back of my head made that position even more uncomfortable, so I rolled over on my side and stared at the bars.

Where did he come from, and what was he doing there?

If he had killed the woman, why would he have left her in such a conspicuous spot? Why wouldn't he have just dragged her into the tunnel with him?

Besides, what the hell was a Vietnamese woman doing in northern Wyoming, especially dead alongside Lone Bear Road?

Maybe I'd know more when T.J. called with the official report.

I thought about the girl's face, the cyanosis discoloration, the hemorrhaging of the skin around the eyes. I guessed there would be small, linear abrasions at the throat, either from the perpetrator or from her attempts to dislodge the attacker's arm or hands.

I thought about her bone structure, which was the big tip-off as to her nationality. If you spend any time in Southeast Asia, you pick up the basic differences pretty quickly, and I sure had spent time in Vietnam.

**Tan Son Nhut, Vietnam: 1967**

"No beau-coups, you scat riki-tiki baby-san. He a Marine and they no boom-boom. He a Marine and they no boom-boom, just kill." Baranski laughed, enjoying his own charm, elegance, and immense style.

I smiled, shrugged at the young woman, and took another swig of my Tiger beer, her image swimming in the blown-out sweat and strangeness. She shook her head and placed a provocative leg forward to test the theory. "He no killa."

Archie Bell and the Drells' "Tighten Up" pounded the room as the tiny Vietnamese woman swayed to the driving rhythm. Baranski crossed his ankles on the chair in front of him and belched loud enough to rattle the windows in the Boy-Howdy Beau-Coups Good Times Lounge, if it'd had any—windows, that is. The lounge was just outside Gate 055 near the old French fort known simply as Hotel California. I had been in California a short while earlier and, from my perspective, I could not see the resemblance.

The concrete walls of the old fort were twenty feet high and three feet thick, forming a whitewashed rectangle. Each of the archways had solid iron gates, and I expected Franchot Tone and his troop of French legionnaires to march through at any minute. There was an Army of the Republic of Vietnam company posted to the fort, but the real action was just outside the lounge, where there was a civilian mortuary and a cemetery with thousands of white grave markers. It was strange, having the local bar next to the cemetery, but I'd seen stranger things since arriving in Vietnam. Boy howdy.

"Little sister, you *sabe* specialists in Uncle Sam's fighting forces?" Baranski gestured toward me. "This numba one killer."

She smiled at him and then reconsidered me, but not her opinion. Her eyes were hard, but her smile was dazzling; good teeth, something you didn't see much over here. "What your name, numba one killa?"

I ambled to a six-and-almost-a-half-foot standing position as quickly as the heat and eight Tiger beers would allow, all my mother's lessons moving past the alcohol and to the fore. "Lieutenant Walt Longmire, ma'am, from the great state of Wyoming."

Baranski lit another Camel and smiled. "Killer, hell, he's a cowboy."

Mendoza raised his head just long enough to make one statement. "Bullshit, I'm from Texas, man, I'm the cowboy."

Baranski removed the cigarette from his mouth and spoke with absolute authority. "You're a beaner, asshole."

Mendoza's voice was muffled against the sticky surface of the table. "What'a you know, you fuckin' Hoosier?"

I turned back to the girl as she snapped a finger and pointed it at me, practiced at diverting conflict. "Cowboy better than killa. USA, numba one."

I smiled back. "You bet." She laughed a short burst and sought more monetarily advantageous pursuits at the bar, or the row of powder-blue fifty-five-gallon fuel drums and plywood that made up the bar. "Hey?"

She glanced back with a lascivious wink. Her voice was husky. "You change mind, cowboy?"

"No, miss. I just want to know your name."

Her eyes softened, and she turned completely around to make a formal introduction of herself. "Mai Kim, I am please to make acquaintance." Her head bowed, and I suddenly felt like a visiting dignitary instead of a Marine investigator making the outrageous sum of $479.80 a month.

"The pleasure is mine, Mai Kim." She paused there for a moment, considered the surroundings and her situation, her eyelids slowly blinking in shame, then turned and walked away. She didn't strut.

I looked at the landscape of empty bottles to allow her an unstudied retreat and noticed that there was an old broken-down upright piano beside the bar.

"Tell 'em to turn down that spook music while you're over there, Mai Kim!" Baranski shouted as he took another sip of his 33 Export. "Damn, I been here for almost two months an' never knew her name."

I continued to study the piano as a few of the black airmen stared at our table. I set my beer bottle down and looked at Baranski and decided to go right up the middle. "So, what is the local drug problem?"

He smiled. "Not enough drugs, that's the problem." I didn't smile back, so he felt compelled to continue. "What have you heard?"

"A lot of personnel are passing through here and turning up self-medicated."

He shook his head and sighed. "That's the provost marshal's view?"

I peeled the label of my beer with my thumbnail. "Yep."

It was silent at the table for a minute. "Look, this country is crawling with drugs, and a lot of the shit comes from our very own CIA. There's *bhanj* growing all over the place, opium in the highlands, and *ma thuyi* heroin is the cottage industry of choice." He lifted his beer and tipped mine in a toast. "Pick your poison. Hell, watch this."

He motioned to an ARVN captain, who disengaged from a group at the far end of the bar and promenaded over in polished boots, a sky-blue flight suit, and an honest-to-God white silk scarf. As adjuncts to the USAF, the Vietnamese flyers were allowed a certain amount of freedom in assembling their uniforms, most of which were, well, flamboyant.

He smiled and inclined his head to Baranski as the matinee idol turned to me. "Lieutenant Longmire, this is Hollywood Hoang." The small man extended a hand, and I shook it; his nails were clean, clipped, and polished, his skin lotioned smooth—I figured him for quite the dandy. "Hollywood here can get you anything you need." He grinned at the helicopter pilot. "Hollywood, I need to score a pound of legendary Montagnard grass. How much?"

"One carton Marlboro." His accent had just a touch of French and was remarkably cultured even with the lack of prepositions. He glanced at me. "This for you, Lieutenant?"

"No."

Baranski was laughing. "You get my point?"

The flyboy interrupted. "Half carton."

"That's okay, thanks."

"Half carton is very good price."

"I'm sure, but I'm really not interested."

He gave a slight shrug and smiled. "If anything you need, I get for you."

I watched him swagger back to the bar and glanced at Baranski. "What's that supposed to mean?"

"Anything. Anything you want, he can get. He was Central Office of South Vietnam when they were fighting the French, but now he's got ties to the CIA, so whatever you want he can get it." He watched me as I scraped the rest of the palm tree off my beer label and stared at the table. "Hey, don't make the long face, Longmire. Battalion headquarters don't know shit. Do you have any idea how many personnel we have going in and out of here every day?" He leaned back in his chair, waved his cigarette in the air, and laughed. "This air base is roughly the size of LaGuardia Airport back in the states. We got air force, navy, and army personnel, not to mention you grunts; we got South Vietnamese, Cambodians, Thais, Laotians, and the odd NVA running through this place every day. Now, do you think we have any idea what they've got with them when they get here, what they have when they leave, or what they might've left here once they are gone?"

I looked up. "Tough job."

"Impossible is more like it." He took a deep breath and leaned in, placing his elbows on the table and looking at me over the empties. "The shit is everywhere, and if you go around asking a bunch of stupid questions and causing a lot of trouble, you're going to end up dead; that's your business." He pointed a finger at his most recent partner, still passed out on the table. "But you might get us killed, too, and that shit is a no-go. You *sabe*?"

I looked at him blankly, still trying to figure it all out.

"Look, fucking new guy. I was sent up here six weeks ago; I drink too much, smoke too much, bird-dog a few *ao dai*..." He glanced around and then leaned in even closer. "And then I got with the program. I'm an investigator with CID. And then along comes Second Lieutenant Walter Longmire and we've got a new sheriff in town? Fuck you." We sat there in silence, looking past each other, listening to the music and the idle chatter at the bar. "Why don't you tell me what it is that's got the bug up battalion's ass, and I'll try to narrow our field of operations."

"U.S. Marine PFC James Tuley, of Toledo, Ohio."

Baranski thought about it. "Never met him." The horn section in "Rescue Me" started up from the jukebox as the blond man shouted, "Damn it, I said no more splib music!"

A few more of the black soldiers glared at us as I slowly started to stand. "Well, you missed your chance. He died of a heroin overdose in-flight from this air base about two weeks ago."

He shook his head and motioned for two more beers. "So let me guess; there's a Governor Tuley, or a Senator Tuley back in O-hi-O that wants to know why his little boy died of a drug overdose in sunny South Vietnam?"

I didn't say anything. I didn't say anything about how James Tuley's father was neither a senator nor a governor, but a night watchman at an automobile parts plant. I didn't say anything about a Marine investigator who took an interest when he read that a copy of *To Kill a Mockingbird* was found on the body of the young man from the wrong side of the Toledo tracks.

I took my beer from the passing waitress and moved toward the battered upright alongside the bar. More than a few faces watched my approach. It was time to introduce the Boy-Howdy Beau-Coups Good Times Lounge inhabitants to live music and to the wonders of

James P. Johnson, Fats Waller, Joe Turner, Art Tatum, and the Harlem Stride.

Real soul music.

"Rise and shine, buttercup."

I raised my hat from the side of my head, just far enough to see two handcrafted Paul Bond boots and two knees, one real, the other artificial. I lowered my hat, effectively blocking the view. "Go away."

He kicked the underside of my bunk. "Get up, we got work to do."

Lucian Connally had been sheriff of Absaroka County the twenty-four years previous to my administration; he was a rough old cob who had lost his leg to Basque bootleggers back in the fifties, the prosthetic of which I was preparing to twist off and use to beat him to death. "I worked all night, old man, now go away."

"Yeah, well, you didn't do too good of a job 'cause yer Indian's over at Durant Memorial, takin' the place apart."

I raised my hat again. "What?"

"He come to, and he's over there payin' 'em back for Sand Creek."

I hustled off the bunk. "He's Crow, not Cheyenne."

"He's one pissed-off Indian, is what he is."

It was a disaster.

The ER staff, assuming that the EMTs had given the wounded man a sedative, had rolled him into an examination area and left him until an overworked internist could get to him. A child with an ear infection, an elderly man with chest pains, and a woman going into premature labor had distracted the doctor.

In the meantime, the slumbering giant had awakened.

Luckily, Double Tough and two of the HPs were still at the hospital when the excitement began. He had thrown the gurney and then began yanking very expensive machinery to throw next. They had charged him en masse, only to be plucked off one by one like the gurney and the pricey machinery. The tide shifted when Frymyer joined the fray, and the four men were able to get the Indian down long enough for the internist to pump enough Thorazine into him to knock out a buffalo.

The two HPs who had participated in the newest melee were sitting on the hood of one of their cruisers—Ben Helton's nose was still bleeding, and Jim Thomas was nursing a hand that was wrapped up to the elbow.

Lucian nudged me as we stood there; he couldn't help but give them the needle. "How you doin', girls?"

Ben, the older of the two and the one with the broken nose, spoke through the assembled cotton and gauze with a muffled, nasal voice; he was going to have two black-eye beauties. "Piss on you, old man. Where the hell have you two been?"

Lucian said it like it was manifestly obvious: "Why, safely out of harm's way."

Jim, the other wounded trooper, nodded. "He wakes up again, you call game and fish and tell 'em to bring a dart gun."

We continued into the emergency room, where Frymyer was seated on the floor of the hallway. His hands were bloody, his uniform was torn, and one ripped sleeve draped down over his elbow, which was in a sling, showing a more than prodigious bicep. The entire side of his face was bruised, from the eye socket to the jawline, and the eye that looked up at us was almost closed shut.

"You all right?"

He nodded and then gently touched the swelling at his face. "But Double Tough's arm is dislocated."

Lucian glanced at me. "Maybe he ain't as double tough as we thought."

Frymyer started to stand, but I lowered myself down to his level instead. I pulled the remainder of his sleeve back up his arm. It was a shame that it was ruined since he'd just gotten his Absaroka County patch set and had sewn them on himself. "I asked how *you* are?"

"I guess I'm okay." He probed the inside of his mouth with his tongue. "Except I think I've got some teeth loose."

I took a closer look at him and his ruined shirt, noticing the name bar on his chest, which read FRYMIRE. "You spell your name with an 'I' and not a 'Y'?"

He stretched his jaw. "Yeah, like yours." He tried to smile but quickly regretted it. "It's okay, they still cash the checks." He paused and looked down the hallway to where the Durant Memorial Massacre had taken place. "The internist says they can't handle anything like this guy, and as soon as they get him patched up, we have to take him."

# 3

I wandered back to the holding cells and watched the big Indian sleep.

They had carted him over from the hospital, and he seemed to be, as the nurses would say, resting comfortably. The term barrel-chested did not apply to him—he was more like refrigerator-chested. He cleared his throat and swallowed a few times; I watched as the muscles bunched and relaxed under the bandages.

The report from Durant Memorial indicated hemorrhaging of the short strap muscles of the neck surrounding the thyroid gland in front of the larynx, with a slight fracture of the hyoid bone and possible damage to the esophagus and trachea.

I thought about the Vietnamese woman. If he had been anywhere near normal, I would have killed him but, for now, I was glad that I hadn't.

They had cleaned him up and supplied him with clothing from the hospital laundry—one of those show-me-your-ass gowns that they stick on everybody. It must have been an XXXXL, but it still strained across the width of his shoulders. I had a thought and retrieved a pair of gigantic sweatpants from my office that read Chugwater Athletic Department, a joke gift from Vic, and hung them on the bars. If I woke up in like situation, the first thing I'd want would be a pair of pants.

They had pulled his hair back, and it was the first time I'd gotten a really good look at his face. It was broad, almost as if it had been stretched to fit his oversized skull, with a strong brow, a very prominent nose, and a mouth that was wide with full lips. There was a dramatic, caved-in spot at his left brow and a lot of scar tissue. It wasn't what you could call a handsome face, but it was certainly full of history, hard-fought history. The creases in it were deep and, even though it was sometimes hard to judge the exact age of Indians, I figured he and I were pretty close.

The hospital had sent over his clothes, which rested in a Hefty bag on the kitchenette counter. I figured I'd fish out the moccasins and put them in the cell for him and then thought there was no time like the present to go through his things.

I put on my latex gloves.

The moccasins were on top; they were intricately beaded in a pattern unlike the other Crow work I'd seen. It was Crow, there was no doubt, but a variation on a theme. The soles were still damp from our altercation in the tunnel, and there was a little bit of dried mud on the edges, but that was the only wear that I could find on them. Whatever else the giant's habits were, the moccasins were something important. I placed them inside the cell and continued my search.

There were a few personal items that had been placed in a ziplock. I pulled the plastic bag out and looked at the contents. There was a bandana, a book of matches from the Wild Bunch Bar down in Powder Junction, and an old KA-BAR knife that looked to be of Vietnam War vintage—one of the good ones, with a separate pouch for a whetstone. I opened the bag and pulled out the knife; it was roughly eight inches long. I slid the blade from the worn sheath and felt the keen edge, then slipped it back in the case and placed it on the counter for the property drawer.

Under the bandana there was a pink plastic photo wallet, the kind a little girl would have had. It had gimp plastic whip-stitching along the sides, and the clear vinyl that held the photos was clouded and brittle. There were only two photographs in the wallet.

The first one was of a woman staring off to the right; it was the kind of strip photo you got at an arcade in sets of four, black and white, the emulsion fading just a little at the edges. She had dark hair, part of it draping across her face, half hiding the smile that was there. She was quite beautiful in a simple, matter-of-fact way.

The other was of the same woman seated at a bus station, the kind you see dotting the high plains, usually attached to a Dairy Queen or small café. She was seated on a bench with two young children, a boy and a girl. She wore the same smile, but her hair was pulled back in a ponytail in this photo, so her face was not hidden. She looked straight at the camera as she tickled the two children, who looked up with eyes closed and mouths open in laughing ecstasy.

The sun must have been behind the photographer, because there was a very large shadow of the man who was taking the photograph, and it didn't take much imagination to figure out who it might be. At the back of the laughing little family was a tin RC Cola sign with a chalkboard hung below that was sloppily hand lettered and read *Powder River bus Lines, Hardin 12:05*, and in smaller print, *Indians must Wait* OUTSIDE. I read along the foxed edge of the photo and could just make out the date, August 6, 1968. I closed the wallet and set it aside.

Well, he was definitely Crow.

There was also a hand-stitched medicine bag in the ziplock, with a few straggling ends of fringe left. It was beaded in a primitive pattern that looked like an animal of some sort with a wavy line through its body. It might have been either a bear or a buffalo, as they were the only animals who could have a heart line. I put it and the wallet inside the bars, alongside the moccasins.

The field jacket was regular issue, but it came as no surprise that there were no identification marks. It was in rough shape and smelled bad, but there was a design on the back of a war shield and the words RED POWER were painted in now-faded crimson.

I needed my expert.

I folded the rest of the clothes and returned them to the properties bag, popped the knife in, and carried the collection out to Ruby in the front office. I sat on the corner of her desk and threw my gloves in the wastebasket. Dog looked at them, but I told him no and reached down to pet his head. "Thanks for coming in on a Sunday."

She smiled. "I had things to do on the computer anyway."

"We may have to call the Ferg."

"He's floating the Big Horn. You're not going to be able to get him until tomorrow, if at all."

I sighed. "Still no word from Saizarbitoria?"

She shook her head no, looking past me at the unconscious ex-sheriff asleep on the bench behind me. "There's Lucian."

"Uh huh. How about Double Tough and Frymire?"

"Repaired to their respective lairs, to lick their collective wounds."

I nodded. "Any word from DCI or the HPs?"

She looked like she was tired of answering my questions. "No."

Ruby didn't have to work weekends, but nine times out of ten she'd be here, answering the phone and keeping the machinery of Absaroka County's law enforcement juggernaut staggering forward. I reached out and gave her a playful poke on the shoulder. "Hey, did you hear about my fight?"

She batted the neon-blue eyes in all innocence. "I hear he wiped the floor with you."

"He did."

"Aren't you getting a little mature for that kind of foolishness?"

I felt the bandage patch and the knot at the back of my head. "He was fighting; I was just trying to escape with my life." She shook her head at me, and I decided to change the subject. "How about my daughter and the Cheyenne Nation?"

"As of an hour ago, they were finishing up lunch and going to work out."

I made a face. "That's my job."

"They thought you might be busy."

"I am, but that doesn't mean I can't continue with my responsibilities." I stood, feeling out of the loop, so I changed the subject again. "I guess we should start by checking the VA here in Durant and the one over in Sheridan; maybe they've heard of the guy. An Indian this big is going to be hard to miss."

She studied the sad resolution in my eyes. "What's the matter?"

I avoided the highly calibrated, direct, blue lie detectors that reflected up at me. "Maybe I should just go see if she's all right."

She covered her smile with a hand and turned back to her computer, all mock seriousness. "Maybe you should."

I stood there, valiantly attempting to cover the ground where I stood. "Henry doesn't know her workout schedule."

She still didn't look at me. "Right."

"I think I'll go down there."

She nodded. "You do that."

Having set everybody straight, I headed down the crumbling steps behind the courthouse, past the Uptown Barbershop and the Owen Wister Hotel, and went in the alley entrance of Durant Physical Therapy. I was almost halfway up the steps to the old gym when I heard Henry's voice, patient but persistent. "Two more . . ."

**Tan Son Nhut, Vietnam: 1967**

"No."

She looked at me, hurt and not understanding, recrossed her legs under the silk *yukata*, and smoothed the *Stars and Stripes* on her lap. The military newspaper had become her version of *See Spot Run*.

It was early at the Boy-Howdy Beau-Coups Good Times Lounge, and we were the only ones there. The bartender, Le Khang, would come in a little after six and make coffee but would quickly depart when he figured there was no profit margin in my custom. The last three mornings he hadn't shown up at all, leaving the coffee making to Mai Kim. She was always in the bar when I was there, always anxious for another English lesson. She had dragged a stool over from the bar and sat there, perched in anticipation.

She took a sip of her coffee; she didn't like coffee but felt that drinking it advanced her cause in becoming American. She cocked her head. "More lesson, yes?"

"No." I blew a breath from my distended cheeks and tripped my fingers along the piano keys, abusing Rachmaninoff's Concerto no. 2

in C Minor, which matched my mood in the key of melancholy. It was the *Adagio sostenuto* that my mother had imprinted into my soft head, evening after evening. Somehow, the Harlem Stride didn't mesh with the quiet mornings just off Tan Son Nhut's Gate 055.

Not dissuaded, she unfolded the wrinkled and yellowed copy of *Stars and Stripes*. I had been doing my part for the winning of hearts and minds by working with her on her English. She had settled on an article warning against using C-4 explosives as a field-cooking implement and was miffed that I'd shown little enthusiasm for her presentation. She cleared her throat and sat up straight. "Cookie with fire..."

I automatically corrected her. "Cooking, not cookie."

"Cooking with fire..."

"Mai Kim, I really don't feel like doing this this morning."

She straightened her paper with a brisk gesture to let me know she wasn't pleased with my interruption. "What matter with you?"

"Nothing. I just don't want to do this right now."

She watched me over the newspaper as I sipped the coffee she'd left for me on the corner of the piano. "Battalion command has issy-ued a dire-connected..."

"Issued a directive."

She looked hurt. "That what I say."

"No, it wasn't."

She was reading again. "Con-cern-a-ring the use of C-4 plascatic espelosove..."

"Plastic explosive."

She nodded and studied the paper as if it had tried to trick her. "Plastic explosive."

She was an excellent mimic and a pretty good student. "Mai, please?"

"Resydoo may result in C-4 poisonee, an' fumes from encoseded quarter..."

"Enclosed quarters."

"Enclosed quarters, that what I say."

"No, it wasn't."

She ignored me and continued. "Can be etremelousely dangerous. Wepeaon Speshulist Mack Brown report that atatempie to stamp-out C-4 can produss explosion. . . ." She turned to me, looked over the rim of her cup, and winked. "I get that one right, yes?"

"Close enough."

She saw the uninterested look on my face and continued to study me. "You no like coffee, cowboy?"

"No, your coffee is fine." I continued poking at Rachmaninoff with an extended forefinger. "You ever have a shitty job that you didn't enjoy doing?" I glanced up at the tiny prostitute sitting there in the Boy-Howdy Beau-Coups Good Times Lounge. "Forget I asked that."

Mai Kim's story was not a unique one in the rural villages of Vietnam; when she was eleven, she had been sold. She was fifteen now, and the four years of use in the world's oldest profession had aged her like the major who had greeted me upon my arrival. Maybe it was the place; youth could not be maintained without innocence.

She blinked and folded the paper in her lap. "You no like here?"

I swiveled on the beat-up piano bench and rested the coffee cup on my knee, finally giving her my undivided attention. I could hear in the distance, but approaching, a group of Kingbees tipping their motors and flying over for a morning patrol. I'd learned that the H-34s, with their thirty-two-cylinder radial engines that sat right under the cockpit, were slower than the UH-1s but treasured for the large chunk of metal between the pilots and whoever might be shooting up at them. "It's not that."

She folded her arms. "What it, then?"

"Then what is it."

"Then what is it?"

I smiled at her Wyoming accent.

Baranski and Mendoza had become irritated with my hardheaded naiveté and had begun spending more time on other investigations, leaving me with hours to sit and contemplate what I wasn't getting done. Just as the major had intimated, the locals had quickly made me, and simply being observed talking with me had become reason for suspicion. But the hookers still talked to me; at least Mai Kim did.

I looked into the face of what seemed like the only friend I had in the place and wondered how long she'd keep talking to me if I didn't start holding up my end. "You know about the drugs." She nodded her head with concentration. "There was a young man who died after visiting the air base."

"Lot of men die after visiting air base."

I looked up at her. "This one was different."

Henry studied the sleeping Indian.

"Different than what I know."

"Crow?" I leaned against the counter.

He took a deep breath. "Yes, but not River or Mountain Band. He is something else."

I pointed toward the moccasins. "The bead pattern is one I've never seen; it's geometric, but not the Crow that I know."

He knelt by the bars and examined the medicine bag and moccasins, though I noticed he touched neither, and nodded. "Kicked-in-the-Belly."

I waited a moment. "You mind telling a heathen devil white man what that is?"

He pivoted and sat on the floor with his back to the cell, which Dog took as an invitation and joined him. "*Eelalapi'io*, a shunned band, one of thirteen exogamous maternal clans; fourth clan, grouped with *ackya'pkawi'a*, or Bad War Honors." I watched as he thought about it, first categorizing the information and then translating it so that it would be relatable to me linguistically and culturally. "Seventeen-twenty-seven, or thereabouts, there was a Crow war party led by Young White Buffalo that raided the Fat River country and came back with a very strange animal. This animal was as large as the elk but with rounded hooves, a long tail, and mane; it had no antlers, and the tribe was very interested in this new thing. A brave got too close to the rear of the animal and touched it. The creature struck the man as quick as lightning, knocking him to the dirt, where he rolled and clutched his midriff."

"A horse, hence, Kicked-in-the-Belly?" I plucked the olive-drab field jacket from the top of the bag, crossed the room, and sat in the chair with my arms folded over the backrest. "It doesn't make any sense. I mean, unless he's got a hiding place out there that my guys couldn't find."

"Nothing on him?" Henry continued to pet Dog.

"Just the matches, knife, photo wallet, and medicine bag, but Saizarbitoria is down there now going through the stuff in the tunnel." I could see Henry was having the same doubts I was. "Why would he leave her lying out there where anybody could see her?"

He stopped petting Dog and playfully pulled at one of his long ears. Dog opened his eyes but nothing else. "I understand he is not a reasonable individual?"

"He's tried to kill everybody he's come in contact with so far, if that's what you mean." He nodded and, as I thought about the story, I connected it to the owner/operator of White Buffalo's Sinclair Station up on the Rez. "Is the young White Buffalo in that story an ancestor of Brandon White Buffalo?"

"Probably."

I glanced toward the cell. "Is Brandon related to this one?"

The Cheyenne Nation turned his head and looked at the

Crow in the holding cell. "I know most of Brandon's family. Brandon's father is Cheyenne, but the White Buffalo are Crow, and it is possible that some of them adopted the relatives of the mother." He shook his head and turned back to me. "I do not know this man, but I am unfamiliar with some of the Crow bands, especially Kicked-in-the-Belly." He raised a thumb to the cell behind him. "He resembles Brandon."

"You mean in raw tonnage?"

Henry snorted a soft response. "I can make some phone calls and check the tribal rolls." He stayed motionless for a moment, and I knew there was more.

"What?"

"The medicine bag is warrior society—Crazy Dogs and Crooked Staff." Dog looked up at his name, but Henry scratched behind his ears, and he settled his broad head back onto the Indian's lap.

"Big deal?"

He nodded in a barely perceptible manner. "Great warriors."

I lifted the back of my hat and felt the bandaged lump again. "Myself, a deputy, two HPs, and a couple of hospital orderlies can attest to that."

"Crazy Dogs are the fifth and least structured of the warrior societies—they committed themselves to death in battle."

I had heard of such things. "Kamikazes?"

"In a sense. The death is not to be foolish or useless; it is to be beneficial in the battle as it is fought." He paused for a moment. "It is said that these individuals are known to become very reckless in their lifestyle."

I nodded along with the solemnity. "And Crooked Staff?"

He took a breath and looked back at me. "Every spring the leaders of the war societies would give out four staffs to the newest members. These young men were to plant their staffs upon meeting the enemy and tie themselves to them, essentially fighting to the death. This provided a rear guard to any action and supplied further impetus to the war party to rally and come to the young warrior's assistance."

I unfolded my arms and tossed him the field jacket. "What do you make of that?"

He turned to one side, so as not to disturb Dog, and opened the jacket as I had. He flipped the snap-buttons back and examined them, something I hadn't thought to do. "Scovill Manufacturing, tropical issue; no liner buttons on the inside." He looked up. "He looks to be our age."

"Yep."

"Army surplus, or..." He let the sentence hang there between us.

"Or what?"

The dark hands smoothed the broad back of the threadbare field jacket. He looked at the horned medicine shield and the words RED POWER. "Or... he is one of us."

Henry Standing Bear didn't mean Indian.

Santiago Saizarbitoria had had a rough morning; he hadn't gotten beat up by the Indian like the rest of us, but he had to go through the things in the tunnel. I wasn't sure which was worse. Saizarbitoria was the Basque contingency of our little department and my second bid to keep our median age under fifty. He'd transferred up from Rawlins where he had worked in the high-risk division of the state's maximum-security correction facility, or what we used to call prison in the old days, and Vic had nicknamed him Sancho before they had even met. He was lowest on the proverbial totem pole here in town, so he usually worked Sundays because he had to and because he had a wife with a child upcoming and needed the overtime. He was sitting on the bench in the outer office drinking a cup of coffee and flirting with Ruby. Henry continued making his phone calls.

Dog kept nosing one of the garbage sacks at Sancho's boots, but he kept pushing the beast's muzzle away. Dog didn't take it personally and plopped down beside the bench to wait for the deputy to open the bags. Santiago motioned to one of them. "There was a lot of dead stuff in his belongings."

I glanced at the bag that was tied-off. "Dead stuff?"

"Skulls, hooves, and things like that. I don't think we should open this one indoors, especially since it's kind of hot."

"Granted. And the other?"

He looked a little dejected. "You're not going to like this." He reached in and took out a small, cheap black purse that he had put in a ziplock.

"Where did you find it?"

"About a third of the way back in the tunnel."

I got up with a sense of finality as Santiago followed me to the holding-cell counter. We donned our de rigeur, disposable latex gloves and began the preliminary. Dog followed us and the second bag.

The pocketbook was covered with mud only on one side and was waterlogged where the water of Murphy Creek had entered the unzipped cavity. We began by opening the main compartment. There was an imitation silk scarf, which I carefully allowed to unfold toward the floor. "Doesn't look expensive."

Saizarbitoria nodded and continued to write on the property roster attached to the clipboard at his lap. "Except for the mud, the pocketbook looks new."

"Yep." I dropped the scarf into an evidence bag and reached in again, pulling out a set of keys on a remote. "GM."

My deputy looked at the fob. "Yeah."

There were some other keys but they had no manufacture or code numbers. I dropped them into another bag and set them aside.

There was a romance novel with a bodice-ripper cover of a young woman standing on a cliff with an ocean below her. It was in French and dog-eared about a quarter of the way through, but there was nothing else peculiar other than a zippered pouch that matched the purse, which was filled with about eighteen dollars, all in quarters.

I picked up the pocketbook and started thinking about the young woman who had owned it. It was possible that she was a dust child—a child of a Vietnamese mother and an American father. One generation removed, she still looked Vietnamese to me. "Sancho?" He looked up. "Get the car keys checked."

He scribbled on the margins of his legal pad. "Got it."

There was a side compartment on the purse. I unzipped it, and there was a photograph plastered against the inside in a crease where, if you weren't looking, you'd never find it. I turned and looked at Santiago. "No money except for the quarters, no ID, and a book in French. Doesn't that strike you as strange?"

"Yes." He looked up from the clipboard. "What'd you find on him?"

I glanced at the sleeping giant in cell one. "There was a child's wallet with some photographs but nothing really incriminating and nothing current except a matchbook from the Wild Bunch Bar."

"You want me to head back down to Powder Junction?"

"Yep, please. I'm afraid Double Tough and Frymire are going to be laid up for a while, and I still haven't heard from the Ferg."

I pulled the photo from the damp insides of the purse lining and flipped it over to look at it. It was old and sun-faded, curled at the edges where the water had soaked the paper. It was a snapshot of an Asian woman on a barstool. She was reading a newspaper with a man seated at a piano to her right with his back to the camera. He was wearing fatigues, and his face was partially turned. He was big, young, and heavily muscled with a baby face and a blond crew cut.

And he was me.

# 4

My daughter held my hand. Ruby and Henry sat at the reception desk and looked at me, Henry with the receiver still at his ear.

Saizarbitoria had put our set of photographs of the young woman's body on Ruby's desk, and they lay scattered beside the battered snapshot. I had sent Sancho to Powder Junction to ask some questions at the Wild Bunch Bar, and Lucian lay on the entryway bench, still thankfully sound asleep.

"Daddy?" She was nuzzled up close, standing right next to me with her arms trailing down mine and her chin at the scar tissue on my clavicle. "Daddy, is it possible . . . ?"

I looked at her, and it was almost as if she wanted it to be true. "No."

"Then why would she be here?"

"I have no idea."

Ruby looked again, studying the photos with renewed vigor. I faced the blue yonder in her eyes, and she nodded. "Walt, they could be related."

I compared their faces. There was a resemblance, but with the swelling and discoloration of the victim in our photos, it was hard to make the leap.

Or I simply didn't want to.

Henry began speaking into the phone in Cheyenne; I could understand the references to Brandon White Buffalo, but that was about it.

She was smiling at the camera, and she had great teeth, just as I'd remembered. There was a nervousness in the smile, though, a wayward tension that showed that she wasn't used to having her photograph taken.

I thought about the body of the dead young woman by the highway and tried to connect it with the smiling woman in the old photo and to the one in my memory. I reached down and turned one of our photographs so that the profile of the woman matched the snapshot. Some of the bone structure was the same.

I glanced at Henry, and it looked like he was on hold again. He nodded toward the pictures. "It is possible."

I crossed to the bench beside the stairwell and sat, careful to avoid Lucian's boots; the last thing I needed was for him to wake up. I sat there thinking and looked at the streaming patterns of sunlight on the hardwood floor. Thinking about Vietnam, about Tan Son Nhut and Mai Kim—remembering the heat, the strange light, and the moral ambiguity.

"Who was she?"

I was startled by Cady's voice and looked back up. I thought about all the wayward memories that had been harassing me lately, the recrimination, doubt, injured pride, guilt, and all the bitterness of the moral debate over a long-dead war. I sat there with the same feeling I'd had in the tunnel when the big Indian had tried to choke me. I was choking now on a returning past that left me uneasy, restless, and unmoored.

I chewed at the skin in the inside of my mouth and stared

at the floor. "She was a bar girl at an air force base where I was sent on an investigation." I glanced up at Henry. "You met her, when you came down."

He nodded. "Before Tet."

"Yep." My eyes went back to the sun-scoured pattern at our feet, and I watched the dust that floated in and out of a sunshine that seemed far away.

**Tan Son Nhut, Vietnam: 1967**

Gusts of dust, pebbles, and dirt scoured the airfield as the two rotors of the big Chinook forced everyone to crouch and look away. The wind from the blades was enough to knock me down and lift tarmac sections of over a hundred pounds. I kept my eyes closed and waited for the stinging to stop. The big helicopter landed, the gun crew relaxed, and the .50 caliber machine guns went limp as if the will to fight had left the aircraft.

It had.

I felt a hand on my shoulder as someone gripped me and shoved me away from the swirling, filthy air. "*Ya-tah-hey,* white boy!"

I had gotten a message from battalion headquarters indicating priority one from Special Operations Group, Military Assistance Command. Everyone in the communications shack wanted to know what it was about, but I'd quietly taken the closed paper into the street outside to open and read the short note. "Hue and Dong Ha in last twenty-four. Stopping in for R & R tomorrow night, eighteen hundred. *Nah-kohe.*"

When I could see again, we were standing at the edge of the airstrip, and I noticed that the Bear was loaded for bear—unsecured weapons hung around him like casually prepared death. The Cheyenne Nation, RT One-Zero, Recon Team Wyoming, wore a claymore mine in a canvas satchel, with a homemade detonation device in his chest pocket, a string of the golf-ball-sized V-40 minigrenades, a CAR-15, and a sawed-off M79. He was weighed down with every ammunition pouch I knew of, along with a Special Forces tomahawk at his back. I tapped a finger on the explosive device at his chest. "You better disconnect the blooper on that thing; we've got a lot of loose radio frequency around here, and you're liable to go off to the happy hunting ground."

He didn't move.

I shook my head and looked at him. "Did you think you were going to have to fight your way in?"

It was a tight, flat smile. "In or out; it makes little difference."

He wasn't traveling alone; beside him stood a recon Montagnard, as the French had named them. About half my height, the little guy was a fierce-looking individual issuing sullen looks from under his pith helmet. He also carried the cut-down version of the M16, as well as a suppressed .22 caliber High Standard, a 60 mm minimortar with ammo, and a Special Forces Randall Model 14 Bowie knife.

"Walt, this is Babysan Quang Sang."

I stuck out my hand. "Glad to meet you." He looked at my hand as if he'd never seen one. I waited a moment and then dropped it. "C'mon, I'll buy you guys a beer."

As we turned to go, Henry stepped into a lieutenant colonel who was headed the other way. The Bear's movements slowed until he was absolutely still. "Watch where you are going."

The light colonel stood there for a moment looking at the collective armament and at the tall Indian with the carved bone amulet in the image of a horse at his throat, the recon patch, and the ID bar that read STANDING BEAR. The half-bird then looked at the indig who in turn looked ready to pull his knife and leap for the officer's throat. It took a moment for the colonel to respond, but when he did, he smiled. "That's watch where you're going, *sir*."

It promised to be a stimulating forty-eight hours.

Action at the Boy-Howdy Beau-Coups Good Times Lounge was well under way when we arrived, and there were no tables available, so we sidled up to the bar like a threesome of fur trappers from the great northwest. I ordered three Tiger beers, turned to toast my best friend in the world, and yelled to be heard over the crowd. "Good to see you alive!"

"Good to be alive!" He looked behind him and saw that the tiny Montagnard was being ingested by the crowd. Henry set his beer down, turned to pick Babysan up, and placed him on the bar between us. Quang Sang smiled as if this were an everyday occurrence and drank his beer in one breath. Le Khang gave me a warning look from the other side of the bar but quickly went back to polishing the glassware when Henry took off his cap and rested it between them. "So, this is where you have been spending the war?"

"I sometimes reconnoiter to the piano." He nodded his head, knowing full well I was lying. "Henry, they cut your hair."

He smiled. "They cut yours, too."

It was quiet for a moment, and I felt compelled to ask, "Where to next?"

He looked around but figured there weren't any VC in the immediate vicinity. "Hill 861 and then back over the fence to Laos!"

"I didn't know they were in the war."

He shrugged and sipped his beer. "They are not."

I nodded. "What's on Hill 861?"

"Cong." He smiled. "But there will be a lot less in twenty-four hours!" He nudged the Montagnard. "Powder River!"

The tiny bushman screamed out in a voice as high-pitched as those of most of the women in the bar. "Powder River! Mile-wiye an inch-deep letter buck!"

The Cheyenne Nation stood there, illuminating pride. "I figured if he was going to be on Recon Team Wyoming, he should know the history."

"Boy howdy."

"Would you like to hear his rendition of 'Cowboy Joe'?"

I shook my head and looked back at Henry. "You've gone native."

He smiled, but it was all teeth. "I have always been native." He tipped his beer up and downed it in three swallows, slamming it down alongside Quang Sang's knee. The tiny man followed suit, so I slammed mine and held up three fingers.

He flipped a thumb toward Babysan. "Do you know the story on these people?"

"A little."

He leaned in close, and our more reasonably projected conversation took place over Babysan's knees as I handed them their beers. "They're a combination of Malay tribesmen, Chinese Han, Polynesians, and Mongols." He smiled again, and again it was all teeth. "Did you know that the Mongols used to ride 250 miles a day?"

I made a face.

"Made the Pony Express look like pikers." He took a sip of his beer. "They do not get along with the rest of the Vietnamese. They figure they are a bunch of effete snobs that wouldn't last twenty minutes out in the bush. The lowlanders call them . . . ," he looked around, and his eyes dismissed the other southern Vietnamese in the loud room, ". . . savages."

I nodded along with him. "I get the point."

"They make fun of them because their skin is darker and their pronunciation is different, but they routinely whip the VC with bows and arrows."

"I got it."

"They have a jungle economy, so money does not mean anything to them. The French used to pay them in beads. . . ."

"Got it."

"Uncle Sam pays Quang Sang sixty bucks a month, and he's the highest-paid yard in his tribe." I stopped saying anything. "These people have one of the strongest warrior ethics of anyone I have ever met." Even though we were close, his voice had risen to the previous level. "They have been abused by the Vietnamese, the Communists, the French, and now by us. And when this criminal war is over, I can guarantee you that they will pay the highest price."

I took a breath and waited as the all-around radical calmed back down. Henry had always been a hothead, but it seemed as if his temper had gotten worse in the last few years; maybe it was the war, maybe it was the times. "I guess that 'native' remark got you a little angry."

He took another swallow of his beer, reset his jaw, and looked at me some more. "Yes."

"I'm sorry. I sometimes think I'm funny." I watched him continue to watch me as I sipped my beer, a little slower now.

It was well into the witching hour. I had introduced Mai Kim to Henry and Babysan. We had transferred the party to the piano bench, and Henry and I watched as the two of them slowly danced to "Hurt So Bad." I was accompanying Little Anthony and the Imperials with a one-finger melody. It was a big piano bench, which was good, because the Cheyenne Nation and I pretty much filled it up. He was turned toward the dance floor, while I was drunkenly focused on the piano keys.

Henry Standing Bear swayed with the music but broke the rhythm by bumping my shoulder. I turned to look at him, and he gestured with his beer toward the dance floor. I half turned on the bench and looked at the pair. They were the only dancers still out there, and they swayed in the green and red glow of the dim Christmas lights and in the shadows of the floods from the air force base.

After a few turns, Babysan Quang Sang gave me the thumbs-up. "I think he likes me."

Henry smiled. "I think he likes her better. He was negotiating true love, but I told him you were paying for her services. I arranged it with the pilot over there."

I shook my head and looked back toward the bar. Hollywood Hoang raised a glass of what looked like champagne to seal the deal, and I looked back at Mai Kim. "She's a good kid."

I could feel him studying the side of my face and turned back to the piano. He continued to watch me. "You get some?" I shrugged and shook my head no. "Why not?" He took a sip of his beer, I took a sip of mine, and we sat there in silence longer than sober people would. "You still dating that blonde back in Durant?"

As near as I could remember, Henry had only met Martha once at the county rodeo dance, but the Cheyenne Nation didn't miss much. "I don't know if I'd call it dating. I haven't heard anything from her in about a month and a half."

He snorted. "Walter..." He always called me Walter when he was going to drop a load of philosophical crap on me, as though the shorter version of my name couldn't withstand the strain. "It is a war."

"Even here, I noticed."

"There is a certain suspension of the normal rules of engagement."

"We're not engaged."

"You might as well be. Shit, Walt, you shake hands with a woman and you feel like you have to be true to her for the rest of your life." I didn't say anything but kept plinking, and the silence returned to our voices.

The USO had a piano tuner, of all things, who was touring Southeast Asia, but since the Boy-Howdy Beau-Coups Good Times Lounge was off base, they hadn't come here. I moved up an octave, but it was only marginally better.

"I am sorry."

I wasn't sure I'd heard him and turned. "What?"

He continued gazing at the dancers. "For yelling at you, I am sorry."

"It's not important."

"Yes, it is."

He was silent again.

The Bear didn't make statements like this lightly, and I'd learned to pay attention to him when he spoke in this tone of voice. "I am not so sure that I am going to make it through this war, and I would not have you think poorly of me."

I sat there staring at him and tried to think which part I wanted to argue with first, finally settling on the most important. "Of course you're going to make it through this war." He still didn't say anything. "One day we're going to be old, fat guys, and we're going to sit around and drink beer and talk about getting me laid." It sounded flat, even to me, so I stopped. "I know it's hard out there. . . ."

"It is not hard out there." His head turned, but he didn't look at me. "I like the night; I see my ancestors in the dark, a thousand footsteps, deadly quiet. The ghosts are with me, and I see them, but it was different the last time I was out on recon-ops." His eyes came around like searchlights. "I saw myself."

I waited.

"But it was okay, because I didn't see me. As long as my ghost is behind me, like a shadow, then I am safe."

I continued to wait.

"If he does ever see me, it will be bad."

"It is really too bad."

I took my eyes off the road and glanced at him. "What?" Due to DCI's slow response, the VA administrative staff not being available till tomorrow morning, Brandon White Buffalo not returning our calls, and my inability to sit still, we had decided to take a drive down to Powder Junction and talk to the bartender at the Wild Bunch Bar.

"For the young woman to have come so far seeking a relative. . . ."

"We're not related."

He smiled. "I believe you." He gestured toward Cady. "If it were not for what sits between us, I would be willing to swear that you have never had sex in your life."

She ignored Henry. "Evidently, she thought you were related, or why would she come all the way to Wyoming?"

"And how else would she know who you are or, more importantly, where you are?" He looked out the window at the passing landscape and the trailing edge of the Bighorn Mountains. "Who knew you from back then and could provide that kind of information now?"

I thought about it, and the thought was depressing. "You really think that she thought she was related to me and came all the way from Vietnam?"

"It is the worst-case scenario."

I shook my head. "Why wouldn't she have written or made a phone call?"

"Perhaps her circumstance did not allow for it."

The radio interrupted the philosophical debate. Static. "Unit one, we got the report from DCI, and Saizarbitoria says to tell you he forgot and took the personal property packet for them and says that he'll give it to you when you get there. He wants your 10-40. Over."

I tried to pluck the mic from the dash, but Cady was faster. She had always liked pushing buttons. "Roger that, base. Our 10-40 is . . ." She looked at me.

"You started it, now finish."

Henry's voice rumbled in his chest. "Mile marker 255."

She stuck her tongue out at me and rekeyed the mic. "Mile marker 255, about a mile north of Powder Junction."

I leaned over and added my part. "We're a minute away. Tell him to keep his badge on."

We pulled off the highway, drove through the underpass, and saw two young boys, who looked like brothers, standing at the corner of a day care and jumping up and down in unison with their hands above their heads. They waved.

I waved back, figuring there probably wasn't a lot to do in the southern part of the county.

I turned right onto Main Street into the slanted parking spot alongside Sancho's unit. There was a motorcycle with a cover partially over it and with Illinois temporary plates that was parked on the sidewalk; there was a battered maroon Buick, which had California plates, that was clumsily parked at the curb at the far end of the boardwalk; and there was a forest-green Land Rover with the words DEFENDER 90 across the side parked next to it—didn't see many of those, even during tourist season. We got out and walked down the wood planking, and I noticed that the Land Rover was from California, too.

The Wild Bunch Bar wasn't too different from any other bar along the high plains; it was a rambling affair with three pool tables and a connected café, although there were a few things that made it stand out a bit in comparison with some of the others in the county. Reflecting the influence of the Australian and New Zealand sheepshearers, there was an All-Blacks rugby poster by the door and a tattered Aussie flag over the jukebox.

There was a flat-screen television at the far end of the bar, certainly a new addition, and a dark-haired man in a leather jacket and sunglasses was seated under it; he was actively watching the Rockies being pummeled by the Dodgers. He smiled, cried out, and raised a fist as L.A. loaded the bases. There were no other customers in the café.

The bar was along the left-hand side of the room, and

Saizarbitoria was seated on the stool closest to the door; he was having a cup of coffee with the bartender, a stringy-looking young man with flame tattoos and a shaved head. Thirty, maybe. "'Sup, Sheriff? Can I get you folks something?"

I looked at my daughter, who in turn looked at him. "Diet Coke."

I motioned to Henry and me. "Iced teas."

I sat on the stool next to Sancho and pulled his written report from under the personal property bag at his fingers. The bartender's name was Phillip Maynard, and he had a local address but had only moved here a week earlier from Chicago. He came back with our drinks, and his eyes lingered on Cady. "You new around here?"

She slid the can closer to her. "No."

I folded my arms on the bar and got his attention. "Are you?"

He looked at me and quickly made the familial connection. "Uh huh."

I sipped my tea. "So, there was an Asian woman in here night before last?"

"Yeah."

I nodded toward Saizarbitoria. "He show you the photograph?"

"Yeah."

"Same woman?"

He put his hands behind his back and tried to look at the report. "It was kind of hard to tell, but the clothes were the same."

I nodded. "You get a lot of Asian women in here?"

He paused for a second. "I don't know, I started less than a week ago—they could come in here in droves. I don't know."

"When did she come in?"

"Friday afternoon, before the after-work rush."

"Right. And what time is that?"

He thought about it and shrugged. "She was gone by four-thirty. She wasn't here for very long." I finished my drink and looked at Henry, who had yet to touch his. I followed his eyes as they traveled to the man with the sunglasses in the corner, who smiled a worried smile and then returned his attention to the National League West.

"What'd she have?"

Maynard refilled my glass. "I think she just had some wine." He thought about it. "And a bag of pretzels."

"She say anything?"

He reached around and took a sip of the beer that he had stored on the counter behind the bar. "Nope." His eyes went back to Cady.

I studied the report. "It says here she arrived around noon?"

"Yeah."

"Four and a half hours?" I looked at him. "You don't consider that to be very long?"

The blood was rising in his face. "Well, I mean... some people stay in here all day."

"And for four and a half hours she didn't say anything?"

"Nothing in English, just French and a little Vietnamese."

I gave him a look. "Vietnamese?"

He nodded. "I washed dishes in a Vietnamese restaurant in Chicago. I don't speak the language, but I can recognize it."

"Who did she talk to?"

"Herself."

"Was there anybody else here?"

He studied the bar. "There were a couple of ranchers that came in to get out of the sun."

"You know their names?"

"No."

"Ever see them in here before?"

He shook his head no. "Like I said, I been here less than a week."

I glanced at Henry, who was still watching the man in the corner who still appeared to be enjoying the ball game. "What'd they look like?"

"Working ranchers—locals, not the fly-in type."

I thought that the description fit the Dunnigan brothers who had been haying the roadside along Lone Bear Road. "About sixty-something? One of them wearing a straw hat, the other in a ball cap with a ranch brand on it, had a squint?"

He started nodding before he answered. "Yeah, that was them."

"They talk to her?"

"A little, yeah."

"Catch any of the conversation?"

He shrugged. "They were tryin' to hit on her. I mean, she was good-looking."

"They leave together?"

"No, she left before they did." He paused for a second, and I knew he was thinking about changing this part of the story. "You know . . ."

The trick in these types of situations is to assure the subject that you know there's more to the story and to let them tell it. "Yep?"

"They did leave just a little after she went out." He partially closed one eye and bobbed his head. "They really were hitting on her pretty hard, now that I come to think about it."

I nodded. "Anything else? It's a homicide investigation, so don't feel as if you have to hold back."

"She paid in quarters."

"Quarters?"

"Yeah."

I continued to look at him. "That's odd."

He nodded, quick to agree. "I thought so, too."

"You're not going anywhere, are you?" I handed the report back to Santiago and stood. "I'm assuming that we can contact you here or at the address my deputy's got on the report?"

"Yeah, I'm here all summer. I don't have a phone yet, but I'm workin' on it." He pulled a thin, black cellular from his back pocket. "I've got this, but it only works at the parking spot outside the veterinary office." He nodded up the road. "They've got painted rocks to mark the spot, and a sign that says 'telephone booth.'"

"Welcome to Wyoming."

He was suddenly talkative. "They supposedly have WiFi down at the motel, but I have yet to find it."

I stood, anxious to end the interrogation and work the rest of the room. "Okay. Let us know, would you?" I walked behind Cady and toward the dark-haired man with the sunglasses, who still seemed completely absorbed in the baseball game. I noticed it was in commercial. "Hello."

He looked from the television to me and stood, dropping his sunglasses with an index finger to peer his almond-shaped eyes over the top. "I'm good, Sheriff. How about yourself?"

I was a little taken aback by his friendliness, not to mention the non sequitur, but you get used to this kind of reaction when you wear a badge. "Fine, thanks. Is that your Land Rover out there with the California plates?"

"Yes, sir." He looked about fifty, perhaps a little older, and appeared to be in very good shape. "Is there a problem, Officer?"

"Just passing through?"

He paused when I didn't answer his question. "I have a

piece of property I'm taking a look at in anticipation of retirement."

"Here in the area?"

"Yes, sir."

"And what do you do, Mr. . . . ?"

He extended his hand, and his grip was strong. "Tuyen. I'm in the motion picture industry, in the distribution of Asian-market films in the United States."

"Mind if I see some ID?" He immediately trolled in his back pocket, brought out a black leather wallet, which he held close, pulled out his driver's license, and handed it to me. He waited. His name was Tran Van Tuyen, and he was out of Riverside, California. Even in the photo, he was smiling. Fifty-seven. I memorized the license number and handed it back to him. "Thank you."

"Have I done something?"

"No, we've just had an incident concerning a young woman who might've been from out of state, so we're simply checking everyone." He stopped smiling, just a bit. "Mr. Tuyen, are you Vietnamese?"

He blinked, and I felt guilty for even asking. "Yes." He didn't say anything else.

"The reason I ask is that the girl I mentioned is Vietnamese."

He stared at the bar stool between us. "I see."

"You wouldn't know anything about that, would you?"

"What did this young woman look like, if you don't mind me asking?"

"Long black hair, midtwenties, dressed in a pink top with a black skirt."

It appeared that he was thinking about it and seemed sad that I was asking. "No, Sheriff, I'm afraid not." I watched what looked like a flood of emotions in him, a mixture of sorrow, loss, and then suspicion. "What has happened to this young woman?"

"I'm afraid it's an ongoing investigation, and I'm not in a position to divulge that sort of information at this time." I listened as the training kicked in and thought about how I sounded like a recording and that maybe after the statement, I should have beeped. I had had this feeling before. "Are you going to be in the area long, Mr. Tuyen?"

He seemed preoccupied but answered with the same practiced smile. "Yes, the property I am looking at is near the town of Bailey, which is nearby?"

"Just up the way, off county road 192. What's the name of the property?"

"Excuse me?"

I leaned on the bar and tried to get a read on him. "The property you're thinking of buying, Mr. Tuyen."

He pulled what looked to be a fax from one of the realty offices in Durant. I studied it. "The Red Fork Ranch—that's a nice place." I handed the paper back to him and noted it was dated yesterday. "Richard Whitehead moving?"

"I'm afraid I do not know; I only know that the property is for sale." He returned the paper to his pocket, his license to his wallet, slipped a ten from it, and then stood and placed the billfold into his jacket. He was about five feet nine, tall for a Vietnamese, thick of wrist, and his movements were very precise.

"Mind if I ask where you're staying?"

"The Hole in the Wall Motel, in room number three." He picked up the empty bottle and set it on the inside of the bar. "I'm going to look at the property after I leave here. You're not going to pull me over a mile up the road, are you?" He sighed. "Because if you are, I'll just take the Breathalyzer test now."

I inclined my head toward him. "I get the feeling I've

offended you, Mr. Tuyen." He didn't say anything. "If I have, I certainly didn't mean to. I'm sorry to say that we don't get too many Vietnamese here in Wyoming, and you'll have to excuse me if I find it odd that we should suddenly have two." I continued to look at the man and was conflicted with my own mix of feelings. It was possible that I was bordering on racial profiling.

He smiled, just enough so that you weren't sure if he'd done it at all. He took a card from his breast pocket and handed it to me. His head dropped, and he headed for the door. He looked back when I followed him and paused for a moment with his head still down. The smile was gone. He pushed the door open and disappeared.

Santiago stood and laid a five on the bar. "If you think of anything, here's my card, give me a call?"

Phillip Maynard palmed the fin and the card. He called after us, but mostly to Cady. "Come on back anytime."

The glass door bumped unevenly behind us. Tran Van Tuyen was driving west in the Land Rover, which looked like a passing emerald in a backdrop of overexposed sepia as it rolled down the Main Street of Powder Junction.

It was an absolutely gorgeous summer afternoon, and I took a deep breath like I always did when I remembered it was the pay-off time of the year; and felt like crap.

Cady pulled my arm, always reading the fine print of emotion when I was attempting to appear unruffled. She hugged me. "What's the matter?"

"What's WiFi?"

"Daddy . . ."

I took a deep breath and hitched a thumb in my gun belt. "I'm afraid I may have just engaged in a bit of profiling." I watched as Tuyen faced straight ahead and the shiny green utility vehicle made the turn on 192 and then under the overpass of I-25. I squeezed her arm back. "You were popular in there." I plucked a pen from my deputy and scribbled Tuyen's license plate number on the envelope of the dead Vietnamese woman's personal property packet. I read his card—Trung Sisters Distributing, with an address in Culver City and three phone numbers. I glanced at the Cheyenne Nation as I handed Saizarbitoria back his pen. "What do you think?"

Henry took a breath. "Yes, Walter, you are deeply prejudiced, and I have long been meaning to discuss this with you."

I nodded and dug into the property envelope as they all watched me. "Only against Injuns."

He nodded. "It is to be expected."

I plucked out the plastic bag I wanted and handed the larger one back to Sancho, who was smiling and shaking his head at our banter. "You didn't ask him about the Indians and the matches, boss."

"No, I didn't . . . Call those two numbers in to Ruby and see what she comes up with, then check the Hole in the Wall to see if he's registered and alert the HPs just in case he decides to go somewhere."

"Got it." He disappeared into his unit and left us standing on Powder Junction's old west boardwalk.

The Cheyenne Nation and my daughter watched as I searched the ziplock. She tugged at the short hair near the scar. "What are you doing, Daddy?"

I didn't answer her but held up the key fob, still in the plastic, and pushed the button. The lights flashed, and the doors unlocked on the maroon Buick junker at the end of the row.

# 5

The car had been stolen from a not so small community in Southern California called Westminster, which was, according to the dispatcher at the Orange County Sheriff's Department, better known as Little Saigon. Ruby said she'd spoken with a charming young man who'd confirmed the not so grand theft auto. He said that the vehicle had been stolen from a recycler's lot and that the former owner, Lee Nguyen, had stated that he'd donated the Buick to charity but that the organization must have decided the car wasn't worth the trouble.

We'd done as much physical investigation of the automobile as our limited abilities would allow, so we loaded the rusty sedan onto a flatbed and shipped it off to Cheyenne. The fingerprints we'd lifted from the vehicle were probably female, judging from their size, or possibly from a child, and the tread deposits were from the immediate vicinity. There was nothing in the trunk, and the only thing in the glove compartment was a receipt for a new water pump that had been replaced in Nephi, Utah, only three days earlier.

I sent Henry and Cady back to Durant in my truck since Cady was looking a little tired and hitched a ride with Saizarbitoria over to the sheriff's substation. We drove with the windows down, since the Suburban didn't have air-conditioning.

Santiago spoke over the heated wind and the monster motor that got about eight miles to the gallon. "The bartender didn't seem genuinely surprised about the Buick."

We'd gone back in and questioned the guy again; he said he'd noticed the car there, but that he didn't think it was a big deal. He said that even in the short time he'd been here, he'd noticed a lot of people got ripped and left their cars and trucks on the street rather than be harassed by us. I had asked him if a lot of them came from California, to which he'd responded that he hadn't noticed the license plates. "Did he seem more nervous the first time we questioned him?"

The Basquo thought about it. "Yes, he did."

"Why do you suppose that is?"

"The guy in the corner, Tuyen?"

"I think so, too." We parked in front of the WYDOT annex where we had a small office. "I'll call Ruby and see if she's got anything on this Tuyen guy or heard anything from DCI. You check on the repair bill in Nephi." I handed him the plastic bag which had the receipt in it.

He looked at me, a little worried. "I think they only have one phone down here."

Powder Junction was going to take a little getting used to.

"Then I'll call her on the radio." I plucked the mic from the dash and stopped him as he started to close the door of the unit. "Hey? Call Maynard in about an hour and tell him that we need him to come and talk to us tomorrow morning here at the office."

Santiago smiled. "What time?"

"Make it early."

He continued to smile and adjusted his sunglasses like a movie star, and it wasn't hard to imagine the gascon with a beret, feather, and sword. "Does this mean I'm being promoted to chief undersheriff of the Powder Junction Detachment of the Absaroka County Sheriff's Department?"

"Acting CUSPJD of the ACSD. Sounds impressive, doesn't it? I'll look into getting you a second phone line." As Saizarbitoria went into the office, I keyed the mic and sang, "Oooooh Ruuuuuubeeee, don't take your love to town. . . ."

Static. "Stop that. Over."

"So, you have any news?"

Static. "I've got information on the guy from California."

"I'm all tin ears."

Static. "Tran Van Tuyen became an American citizen in 1982, which is when he obtained an operator's license. He doesn't have so much as a parking ticket to his name."

"Well, it was worth a try."

Static. "You're not going to start singing again, are you?"

I keyed the mic and ignored her. "Keep digging. He said he was here looking at some property, the Red Fork Ranch. Get a hold of Bee Bee and see if she's ever heard of the guy, then call Ned Tanen at the L.A. County Sheriff's Department and see if he can come up with anything."

Static. "Roger that."

"Anything from DCI?"

Static. "They just faxed up the report." There was a pause, and I listened to the silence of the radio. "They got an ID on the young woman."

"Who was she?"

Static. "Her name was Ho Thi Paquet. Turns out she was a Vietnamese illegal who was picked up on prostitution charges in L.A. six weeks ago. She was scheduled for deportation, but I haven't gotten any straight answers about what she might have been doing in Wyoming."

"Ask Ned to talk to his friends in the Orange County Sheriff's Department and to throw that name around along with Lee Nguyen and Tran Van Tuyen; see if they can come up with something down in Little Saigon. Anything else?"

Static. "I'll just let you read the report. When are you coming back up?"

"I'm going to run out and talk to the Dunnigan brothers, and then I'll have Saizarbitoria give me a ride back. I figure I can let him have one more night with his wife before banishing him to Powder Junction. How's Dog?"

Static. "He's fine."

"Thanks, Ruby." I paused. "Cady and Henry make it back?"

Static. "Yes, and they're planning on having dinner later."

"They say where?"

Static. "I'm not allowed to say."

Cahoots.

Static. "I have a Methodist women's meeting at seven o'clock, so can you make it by six-thirty?"

I pulled my pocket watch from my jeans and flipped it around. "Easily."

Static. "I'm holding you to that."

After talking to Santiago, I commandeered our only vehicle and drove out toward the Rocking D and the ghost town of Bailey. The two kids who had been standing in the fenced-in yard were still there. It took me a minute to find the appropriate switches on the unfamiliar Chevrolet, but I tapped the siren and lights and watched as they jumped up and down, this time in counterpoint, both of them continuing to wave as I made the turn and headed west.

Small joys.

There had once been a coal mine near the town, but with the caprice of geology and with the disaster that had claimed the lives of seventeen miners just after the turn of the century, the last one, Bailey had bailed. All that was left of the settlement were a few buildings clinging to the trailing end of the Bighorn Mountain range and a cemetery.

I slowed to look at the abandoned buildings in the late afternoon sun, vertical structures attempting to join the horizontal landscape. There were only six—a few were wood frame and a few were stone, a couple had storefronts, and only one was worthy of a second story. The old grayed walkway was twisted, and the wood was pulled from its substructure, but the rough-cut two-by-eights were still there, waiting for the ringing sound of silent boots.

There was a union hall and a tipple at the end of the street, with an assortment of roofless shacks that had been built along the stone cliffs that rose at the end of the abandoned town; the weedy graveyard was on the far side. Seventeen markers had been placed where there were no bodies. The disaster had happened when the unfortunate miners had hit a gas pocket, and the resulting explosion had shaken the ground all the way back to Powder Junction almost twenty miles distant.

None of the bodies were recovered, and I always felt strange driving by the lonely little spot of abandoned civilization.

There weren't many ghost towns left in the state; most had been packed away and carted off to amusement parks and tourist destinations along I-80. I guess it would be for the good of the county if we got rid of the fire hazard, but it would be sad to see the place go. One of the buildings had already partially burned when some kids had come up from Casper, had drunk too much beer chased with too many shots, and had decided to see how quickly hundred-year-old buildings would burn. We were lucky in that it was winter, and the snow had isolated the damage to one collapsed wall, one DUI, and three minors in possession.

I doubted many tourists came up 190 to the gravel Bailey Mountain Road, and those that did probably mistook what they saw for the real Hole in the Wall of Butch-Cassidy-and-the-Sundance-Kid fame. Through a side canyon, the road leaves the river and the formation of stunning red sandstone with a passage just large enough to allow the entry of a single wagon. A handful of men at this location could hold off an army of sheriffs, but they'd never had to, the Wild Bunch's reputation doing their fighting for them.

Fiction writers would have you believe that this spectacular location was the Hole in the Wall of western fame; it was in reality a cinematic fabrication at best and an uninformed lie at worst. The actual Hole in the Wall was a good thirty miles south and barely noticeable as a slight break in the cliffs, allowing just enough slope for a man on horseback to pass. It had been described by my father to me as the least memorable historic spot in Wyoming.

It was now private land on the Willow Creek Ranch, and the Ferg had been pestering me for years about getting him on the place to do a little fishing at the rustler's settlement, where Buffalo Creek tumbled out of the canyon and into a perfect triangular pasture. The dozen or so log cabins that Butch, Sundance, and the Wild Bunch had used were all gone, the last having been hauled over to Cody and the Buffalo Bill Museum.

I continued on my way and drove past the Bailey public school, which was a one-room schoolhouse, a last bastion of public education with, at last count, two students. It troubled me to think about the school closing, the cabins disassembled, and the ghost towns being flattened; it reminded me that the majority of my life had passed. I had started my education in a school very much like the one here and had spent my childhood in a town a lot like Bailey would have been if there had not been the mining disaster.

I thought about Cady as I drove; about Michael, who was due to arrive imminently; about Vic; then about the upcoming election in November and the debate on Friday.

I tried to stop thinking and propped my hat over the big eyelet hook that was anchored on the dash. We had a lot of DUIs in Powder Junction, and I guess Double Tough had improvised this way to secure drunken drivers to the vehicle.

The road was rough—it obviously hadn't been graded since early spring—and the ruts and bumps kept me from getting the twenty-five-year-old unit above thirty. The clouds of dust obscured my view to the rear as I took a right and continued up through the lodgepole pines and scattered cottonwoods that grew along the draws. It was as if life had chosen to run away and hide in the ragged crevices of the harsh country and forgotten to come back out.

I trailed along a small ravine where swallows cartwheeled in the thermals of the russet cliffs, and glanced over the edge to where the creek still carried the snowmelt of the Bighorn Mountains. It looked like pretty good fishing on the Dunnigan place, but I'd also noted the NO HUNTING signs, and figured that the fish, like everything else, were something the brothers didn't give away.

They were both handsome old bachelors; I figured that they hadn't married because they were too tightfisted to consider a wife. To hear Lucian tell it, their father, Sean Dunnigan, had been like that as well, except that back in the dirty thirties he had had no choice but to marry Eileen if he wanted to eat—he was that broke. Hence Den and James.

Eileen had been known to play her violin from the porch

of the ranch house, a lone and plying sound that had echoed from the canyon. She'd never grown used to the isolation of the place, had grown senile on the ranch, and had died in the late seventies, rapidly followed by Sean, who had evidently grown used to the music of the only woman he'd known.

The brothers were good hands and tough old boys, tough enough to outlast all their neighbors, and they had slowly bought up the surrounding land and the water and mineral rights until the Dunnigans pretty much owned the Beaver Creek Draw.

James was the eldest and had inherited the ranch, even though he'd been kicked in the head by a cantankerous mare when he was a teenager and wasn't "quite right," as the locals had put it.

Den had known that James would inherit, had been pissed off at this rule of succession, but had accepted his lot and consequently taken a job in corrections up in Deer Lodge, Montana. He had even been engaged to a woman, but when the engagement entered its second decade she took exception. Den had returned at his father's request when it became clear that James could not run the ranch by himself and that Sean had gotten too old to be much of a help.

My professional interaction with the Dunnigans was mostly with Den. There had been an incident where he had almost killed another rancher with a shovel in an altercation over water rights and another where he'd broken a bottle off on the bar in town and threatened to perform an amateur tracheotomy on a rodeo cowboy, but other than that, we'd been limited to the instances when Den would call in a lost James. He did this on a periodic basis. A couple of years earlier, during hunting season and an early snow, we'd responded, along with the highway patrol and the county search and rescue, only to find James seated at the Hole in the Wall Bar, adamant that he had phoned his mother and explained that he was safe and spending the night in town.

The problem was that his mother had been dead for a quarter of a century.

I rolled across the cattle guard and parked beside a turquoise and white '76 Ford Highboy; the motor was running, but nobody was in it. The ranch house was simple, sided horizontally with a low-slung roof, and there was a metal shop nearby that was four times the size of the house.

By the time I got to the sidewalk, Den was coming out the front door. His eyes widened beyond his usual squint and then settled into a general dissatisfaction at seeing me. He had on a clean, white straw hat, hard like plastic, with a black, braided horsehair band, and was dressed in a freshly pressed shirt and creased jeans that cut the air as he walked. There was a red and white cotton bandana at his neck, and he'd even polished his boots. "I guess I need to turn off my goddamned truck."

I stopped at the single step leading into the house. "Sorry, Den, but I need to speak with you and James."

He stood there for another moment looking at me and then hobbled past on bowlegs, which approached a full circle, to the parking area where he reached into the side window of the old Ford and shut off the motor. A rifle rack cradling a beaten .30-30 Winchester showed through the rear window.

Den came back down the poured concrete walk, and I could smell the beer on his breath as he scuffled past. I followed him into the house without a word or invitation.

The tawny light of early evening was spreading across the Powder River landscape, and it settled a comfortable glow inside the kitchen. James was seated at a Formica table with a shot glass and a bottle of Bryer's Blackberry Brandy, which I assumed was dinner. There was an empty bottle of Busch with more than a few bottle caps pinched together and scattered across the table where I assumed Den must have been sitting before my arrival. The walls were paneled in knotty pine, and all the appliances were what they had called golden harvest in the fifties. I was sure that nothing in the kitchen had been changed since their mother had died.

The heat was oppressive, even with the industrial-type box fan that was propped in one of the windows. The older of the two brothers stood when I entered, wiping his palms on his jeans and sticking out his hand. He seemed embarrassed that I'd found him drinking in his own home. "Hello, Walt. Would you like some coffee? Mother makes it in the morning for us."

I withheld comment. "No, thanks. Mind if I sit down, James?" He pulled out a chair for me and glanced at his brother, who stood by the door with his arms folded and his hat still on. "I suppose you know why I'm here?"

James sat back down and laid an arm along the table. "It's about that girl we found?"

"Yep."

He nodded and then trapped his lips between his teeth. "About the bar?"

"Yep."

"We did see her there."

I took my hat off and set it on the orange vinyl seat of the chair beside me. "That's what I understand."

James looked at the surface of the table. "Well, we . . ."

"We don't have to tell you a God-damned thing. We didn't do nothin' to that girl."

I turned toward Den, but his eyes were fixed on the linoleum. "I'm not aware of anyone having said you did."

He folded his arms a little tighter and continued to look at the floor. "But that's why you're here, ain't it?"

"There are some questions I wanted to ask you and your brother." I waited a moment. "Why don't you have a seat, and we'll talk." He sat on a fold-out stool by the refrigerator. I turned back to James. "You want to tell me about the bar?"

It took him a while to speak, and he didn't answer my question but instead gestured toward the bottle on the table. "Would you like a little, Walt? I'll git you a clean glass."

"No, thank you." I waited and started getting the feeling that there might be something more to this than I had at first anticipated.

James licked his lips and poured himself another shot of the sugary liquor. "It was hot on Friday, so we took a little break about one or two in the afternoon. You know, duck in for a cool one." I noticed his hands were shaking as he put the bottle back down. "She was in there, sittin' at the end of the bar. So, Den and I sat a couple'a stools away." He looked up and smiled sadly. "She was a good-lookin' young woman, and she kept glancin' over at us." His eyes turned to the full shot glass. "We're just a couple of old hands, Walt. We're not used to a good-lookin' young woman payin' us much attention."

"You talk to her?"

Den interrupted. "Hell, we thought she was a Jap. She didn't speak no English."

I waited, and James started again. "We tried to buy her a couple of drinks, but she wouldn't take 'em. After a while she got up and waved a little wave at us and left."

"Bartender can tell you that."

I looked at Den. "Then what?" He clammed up, sullen again, but James cleared his throat, and I turned back to watch him down his shot. It seemed to me his face was redder than it ought to have been.

"We went out and started to get in the truck, and she was standin' by her car like she was waitin' for us."

Den interrupted again. "She was damn well waitin' for us."

I tried to keep the conversation moving. "Then what?"

James cleared his throat again and looked as if all the blood in his body was rising in his face. "She needed gas money. . . ." His face continued to grow redder, and if I hadn't known any better, I'd have said that both of the Dunnigan brothers were about to implode of embarrassment. "And she . . . she wanted to couple with us."

I sat there for a moment to make sure I'd heard what I heard. "I thought you said she didn't speak any English?"

James seemed to be on the edge of a cardiac arrest. "She didn't. She didn't, but . . ."

"Then how could you tell that?"

Den yanked off his straw hat and threw it against the kitchen cabinets. "She grabbed James's crank and pointed toward the gas cap. That good enough for you, God-damnit!?"

I stopped at the top of the office stairs and stood there glancing around the reception area and listened to the continuing ring of the phone. It was late, but the lights were all on and Ruby's purse sat in her chair along with her sweater.

I stumbled forward and ran to get the phone, but as I reached for it, it stopped. I stared at the red light that had stopped blinking but stayed steady; someone had gotten it, someone in the building.

Dog was gone, too. I walked down the hallway and past my darkened office where I looked for any Post-its on the door jamb—Post-its were our prose form of communication—but there was only one and it was from Cady. I held the yellow square up to the light and read, "Daddy, we're at the Winchester—come join us." Ruby had marked the time at 6:17 P.M. Four hours ago.

There was a noise from the back of the building, so I continued to the end of the hall where I could see the lights on in the holding cells and the kitchenette.

I stopped in the doorway and watched as Ruby stepped away from the phone on the adjacent wall and sat down on one of our metal folding chairs to pet Dog and resume what looked like knitting.

I leaned against the wall and spoke. "Ruby?" She didn't hear me, even though Dog looked up and wagged. "Ruby!"

She glanced up and looked stern. "I missed my Methodist women's meeting." Her eyes shifted to the holding cell, and I leaned around the corner for a peek at our only inmate.

He was eating with his fingers, and there was a carefully stacked pile of potpie containers near the door of the cell. He didn't look up when I stepped around the wall to get a better look at him. His hair hung down around his face and to his knees, but he had on the sweatpants I'd provided, and the moccasins. "I guess he woke up."

"And he was hungry."

I glanced at the assembled cartons at the big Indian's feet. "How many has he eaten?"

"Eight, at last count. That, and three Diet Cokes."

"I guess his throat wasn't hurt that bad." He continued chewing as I crossed to stand by Ruby's chair. "He say anything?"

"No."

"How did you know he was hungry?"

She looked up at me. "I made the assumption that since he had been living in a culvert under Lone Bear Road . . ."

The giant deftly placed the empty tubs on the top of the others but didn't move from the bunk. "Does that mean he wants another?"

"It has eight times now."

I dug into the minifreezer and pulled out the last of our potpies, removing it from the box and tossing it into the microwave. I punched the requisite buttons I'd memorized from my own gracious dining and turned to stand by my dispatcher. "Why are you still here?" I folded my arms. "You knew I was coming back."

She picked up her knitting and ignored my question.

I looked into the holding cell—the big Indian still hadn't moved. "Where's Lucian?"

"He decided to go home." The microwave dinged, and I pulled out the freeze-du-jour, quickly resting it on the counter and out of my burning fingers.

"Let it cool or he eats it still cooking."

I nodded, pulled a plastic spork from the drawer, and rested it on the rim of the potpie. "DCI's report?"

"On your desk." She continued knitting.

I turned and started back to my office to retrieve the report. I held my daughter's Post-it so that Ruby could see it. "She go home?"

"That was her on the phone just as you came in, and in answer to your question, she's in bed, where all sane people should be."

I stopped. "Well, since you're answering questions, do you mind answering why it is you're still here?"

She stopped knitting and looked back at me. "Would you like to see why?" She stood and stuffed the needles and yarn into her oversized canvas bag. "Would you like me to show you why I'm still here?"

I recognized a loaded question when I heard one but just nodded my head and gave her the strange look I gave crazy people that asked the sheriff those kinds of questions. She calmly walked past me and down the hall out of view. Dog had started after her but stopped when he reached the doorway. I stooped down and ruffled the fur behind his ears. "What?"

Ruby had turned to look back at me. "Come here."

I shrugged and walked over to her, the three of us standing there as Ruby listened for something. After a moment, I asked again. "What?"

She held up an index finger. "Just a minute."

We all listened, but the only thing I could hear was the air-conditioning of the building and the hum of Ruby's computer on the reception desk. "What?"

There was a sudden thunder of sound and impact, and I would've sworn a truck had hit the building. I actually stuck a hand out to the wall to steady myself. Not much time went by before the noise and vibration were repeated, and I would've sworn that the truck had backed up and taken another run at the building. "What the . . . !"

The roar and impact seemed to come from the holding cell, and I stumbled over a barking Dog as I rushed back into the room and watched as the big Indian launched himself into the bars with all his considerable force and with a sound I'd never heard come from anything human.

A private contractor had set the bars back in the fifties, when Lucian had inherited the old Carnegie building from the Absaroka County Library after they'd moved a block away. I hadn't thought about the quality of the job in more than a quarter of a century, but it was foremost on my mind as I watched the monster back up to the opposite wall of the cell and prepare for another charge.

"Hey!"

I subconsciously backed against the counter, knocking the

potpie into the sink, and watched as about 350 pounds of bull muscle slammed against the bars.

I could've sworn they moved.

"Hey!" I stepped forward, placed my hand on my sidearm, and thought about how bad it was going to hurt if he and the bars landed on me. "Hey!"

The giant had just started backing up for another run when he heard me and noticed that I was standing there only six feet away. His head rose, and I have to admit that it was a strange feeling, having someone look down on me. His hair had parted a little, and I could see one eye beneath the scar tissue as his hands came forward and rested lightly on the bars. He wore a silver ring with what looked like alternating coral and turquoise wolves running around it, and I was pretty sure I could've gotten it over my big toe.

I put my own hands up to show I didn't mean any harm, even if I had been capable, and stood there looking into that one eye. "It's okay. It's okay . . . I'm not going anywhere."

He stood there for a moment and then slowly lowered himself back to a sitting position on the bunk. He was breathing heavily from the exertion of trying to tear the jail down, and I stood there listening to the wheezing of his breath from behind the bandages at his throat.

After a moment, Dog stopped barking, and I noticed that he and Ruby were peering around the doorway. Some backup. I pulled the palm of my hand across my face and looked at her, still a little breathless myself. "You couldn't have just told me?"

**Tan Son Nhut, Vietnam: 1968**

He shook his head. "No, it is classified."

Babysan Quang Sang had never seen a hamburger before and

poked with a finger to lift the bun as if it were booby-trapped; it was water boo, or water buffalo, and the local *viande du jour.* He turned and looked at Henry, who picked up his own hamburger and took a bite. A few seconds later the Montagnard picked up his own sandwich and took a bite, chewing quietly and watching Henry for more pointers. *"Il ne gout pas comme le jambon."*

Henry laughed. "He says that it does not taste like ham."

We watched Babysan try to figure out the fries, and I studied the tall Indian who would have been more at home scalping white men on a sunny afternoon along the Little Big Horn River. "I'm going to say something I never thought I would."

He picked a fry up from Babysan's plate, dipped it in the ketchup, and stuck it in his mouth as an object lesson. He turned back and leaned in close. "What?"

Babysan ate part of a fry and then dropped the remainder back on his plate. It was possible that the Vietnamese had had enough of all things French. "I envy you." The exhale of his laugh was as if I'd punched him, and he sat there only inches away with a look a shade past indescribable. "I envy the clarity of what you're doing."

He laughed again and thought about it. The pause was so long you could've said the pledge of allegiance in it, but for the Northern Cheyenne, it was nothing. "What, exactly, are you doing here?"

I took a long pause of my own. "Not a lot. I got sent up from BHQ to investigate a drug overdose, but nobody's talking." I looked into a set of eyes that saw the world the way it really was and felt the shame of my duty. I thought about what I was doing and whether it was making any difference. "This place is such a mess. . . ."

Henry took another fry from Babysan. "That may be the understatement of the century."

My next words were out before the thought was fully formed. "Take me with you to Khe Sanh."

He looked back at me and laughed, but he realized that I was serious and so became very serious in turn. "Are you insane? Everybody, including every Marine in Vietnam, the general staff, and LBJ are trying to get out of there, and you want to go in?"

"Yep."

He looked around as if the guys in the white jackets with butterfly nets might be hovering nearby. He was silent and then lowered his head as if I hadn't said what I'd said, his eyes just visible below his boonie hat. "Walt, you can get killed up there."

"Better there than dying of boredom here."

"Walter…"

"Look, I've got a three-day at China Beach, and that is not where I intend to be."

I read the report with my hand on my chin.

She had been unconscious within seconds, although her heart had probably continued to beat for another fifteen to twenty minutes. As was assumed, the manual strangulation applied by the forearm indicated an assailant much stronger than the victim.

There were small linear abrasions on the neck, but these had been caused by the decedent's fingernails as she had attempted to dislodge the arm around her throat. The flesh under her nails had been tested and, as I'd surmised, it had turned out to be her own.

Fracture of the hyoid bone and other cartilage was evident, as was hemorrhaging of the thyroid gland in front of the larynx. I read the thing again, from the beginning, and looked up at the man lying in the cell.

It didn't make sense. Why would a man this size, and with this much strength, use his forearm in a chokehold strangulation when he could've practically snapped the tiny woman's neck with a thumb and forefinger?

The giant had finished the last potpie hours earlier, had carefully replaced the unused spork, and put the empty plastic tray in the others, slipping it forward, halfway through the bars. He was dead asleep now, and his whispery snores provided a steady beat to the conversation Sancho and I were having.

Saizarbitoria had spent a night at home with his wife while I stayed on duty for both Durant and Powder Junction. He'd called the Hole in the Wall Motel and had ascertained that Tran Van Tuyen was actually staying there through Wednesday. He sipped his coffee and then added more sugar from the container on the counter, just like Vic. I sipped my own coffee and pulled the sleeping bag a little closer to the wall where I'd eased my aching back. I yawned and looked at my well-rested deputy. "What about the Veterans Administration?"

He retested his coffee and found it to his liking; he came over and sat on the chair that Ruby had occupied last night. "The administrative staffs don't work much on Sunday nights, so we might want to call around again." I nodded and continued to sip my coffee. "But I can tell you one thing..."

"What?"

He gestured with his mug toward the stacked pie pans at the bars with the lone utensil handle pointed out. "He's been inside."

"How so?"

"We used to have them get rid of their dinnerware in just that fashion in the extreme-risk unit of the high security ward."

The Basquo had done two years in Rawlins and knew more about corrections than I ever wanted to. "He look familiar?"

"No, and it's not as if he's somebody you're likely to forget." The young man tipped his hat back and stroked his musketeer goatee. "If I was guessing, I'd say federal."

"The hospital was going to send his prints down to DCI. Check it."

"I will."

I sipped my coffee and watched the big Indian sleep. "You ever have anybody respond the way I described he did when we left him alone?"

He nodded. "Once or twice."

"What'd you do with them?"

"Straight to Evanston."

The state psychiatric hospital. "Check that, too."

"Okay."

"We're going to have to keep somebody in here at all times." I turned and looked at him. "Otherwise, I don't think our jail will be able to take it." He got up and started out. "Vic or Ruby make it in yet?"

He called back from the hall. "Nope."

I yelled after him as I glanced in the cell. "Call and tell them to pick up more potpies."

# 6

"That is one Fucking Big Indian."

She reaffirmed what FBI really stood for.

Vic was back from her sabbatical in Douglas, but it hadn't broadened her vocabulary. She sipped her coffee and looked at me; I was trying to decide what all I needed to take with me to Powder Junction, since that appeared to be where I was going to be spending my day. Her feet were propped up on my desk where she had put the shooting trophy she'd won over the weekend.

"You out-quick-drew the entire Wyoming Sheriff's Association?"

"Yeah, including that ten-gallon ass-hat Sandy Sandberg and that butt-cheek Joe Ganns."

Sandy was the sheriff over in neighboring Campbell County, and Joe Ganns was the controversial brand inspector who was reputed to be the fastest gun in the West. "Oh, I bet that made you popular."

My diminutive deputy from Philadelphia shrugged, and I tried not to notice the muscles of her bare arms in her sleeveless uniform. "Kinda frosted his flakes, but shit, Walt, what is he, a hundred and three?"

It was quiet in the room as I tossed the shooting bag on my

seat and piled a couple of hand radios in along with two large bottles of water, the reports from Illinois, and my thermos, a mottled green monstrosity made by Aladdin with a copper pipe handle and worn sticker that read DRINKING FUEL. She finally spoke again. "So, you get to go play in Powder Junction, and I get to talk to all the VAs on the high plains?"

"You wanna trade jobs?"

She thought about it. "No."

"Call Sheridan first; they've got a psychiatric unit in ward five. See if they ever had this guy."

She made a face, and then the eyes balanced on me like a knife. "How do you know where the psychiatric unit is in Sheridan?"

I looked at the collection in the duffel. "I visited with a fellow over there back in '72; Quincy Morton, the PTSD coordinator."

"Post-traumatic stress disorder?"

"Yep."

She studied me. "What were you doing, having flashbacks?"

I sighed and zipped up the shooting bag. "It was different back then; nobody wanted to discuss that stuff, so I'd go over to the VA once a month and drink a beer and talk with Quincy at closing time on Friday afternoons. It helped."

"Nineteen seventy-two?"

"Yep."

She continued to study me. "That's when you came back, got married, and started with the Sheriff's Department?"

"Yep."

"I got a question." It was pretty obvious where she was headed. "You got out in '70, but you didn't show back up here until '72." I waited. "What'd you do for the two years in between?"

I threw the strap of the duffel over my shoulder, walked to the doorway, and looked down at her. "Who can speak broader than that has no house to put his head in?"

The eyebrow arched in its trademark position. "What the hell is that from?"

"*Timon of Athens*, Varro's Second Servant."

She nodded. "Oh, how could I forget." She reached over and slipped a forefinger in the pocket of my jeans. "You really are a dark horse." She pulled, and I shifted my weight toward her. She looked up at me, the tarnished gold pupils softly feathered by the long dark lashes. "So, you gonna have any free time when my brother gets here and reinstitutes the courting ritual with your daughter?"

"I'm hoping."

The carnivore smile returned. "Maybe we could double date."

I took a moment to take in all that she was giving me, thinking about that night in Philadelphia, thinking about the parts of her I hadn't seen since then. There were about a half-million things I wanted to say, starting with the part about when I looked at her or thought about her, about that night; that I felt like something inside of me took flight and I wasn't sure if I'd come back to earth yet. Then I thought about the years between us, how they would never go away. How the distance would only grow greater, and how even if everything went right, there were so many ways it could still go wrong.

Her gaze flicked across my face, and it was like my thoughts were leaking out of me and into those iridescent Mediterranean eyes. "What?"

I tried to breathe and then looked at the worn marble floor; it was easier. "Look..."

"No." She sat there for a moment and then stood, both of

us aware that her finger was still in my pocket. She was close now and was standing next to my arm and slightly behind me where I could feel her breath on my shoulder. "I'm not looking for hearth and home."

"Yep."

It was silent in the room, but I could still hear Ruby typing at the receptionist's desk in the front. "You are so fucked up, and you're carrying so much shit . . ." I felt her chin on my tricep. "But I just like being around you, okay?"

"Yep."

Her breathing continued on my arm, and even that felt good. "That's all I need." I nodded and didn't say yep again, because I knew she'd hit me. After another moment, she pulled away, and I felt the finger leave my pocket with one last tug. "What about Henry? Does he have any leads in the big case?"

I nodded and tried to get my mouth to work in complete sentences. "There might be a family connection with Brandon White Buffalo."

Her voice continued to come from behind me. "Another FBI."

"Henry's working out with Cady this morning, and then he said he'd run up to the Rez and try to track Brandon down." I adjusted the bag, leaned against the doorway, and played with the hole in my door where I'd yet to replace the knob—still not meeting her eyes. "You've got Frymire back there Indian-sitting, but I don't think you're going to get anything else out of him or Double Tough, so call the Ferg again and tell him to get his butt in here."

"Aye-aye, Captain." She saluted. "What about the guy in the Land Rover, Tran Van Tuyen?"

I looked at her and tried to think about it; about anything else. "I might go by the Hole in the Wall and check him out."

"You want me to come down to PJ later?"

I thought about that, too. "Somebody's got to work the rest of the county."

She nodded. "I can take your daughter to lunch." She smiled, her eyes igniting again, and I thought about Philadelphia. "We can talk about your wartime indiscretions."

"Uh huh." I walked ahead of her, but she followed close behind me into the hallway.

"Ol' love-'em-and-leave-'em Longmire..." She was still talking as we got to Ruby's desk. "Suckee-fuckee, fi-dollah..."

Fortunately, Ruby was fussing with the computer and not paying any attention to us. She was going through the graymail, trashing unwanted messages, of which we'd had a rash last night. I decided to quickly take the conversation in another direction. "Are we still getting all that gobbledygook?"

"Yes." She continued to hold the delete button down, and I watched as the words marched up the screen and disappeared. "Seventy-two since yesterday."

"Any idea where they're coming from?" She moved the mouse, and I watched as she clicked it a few times and gestured for me to have a look. The setting read Absaroka County School District: BPS. "I guess the school board is out to get me before the debate."

She ignored me and looked at one of the messages. "It's just a random mess; they started late last night and stopped early this morning."

Vic leaned in, and I could smell her shampoo. "So it's not automated."

"No."

I looked up at the wall clock and figured I'd better get going if I was going to make it to Powder Junction for our meet with the bartender. "Any word from Bee Bee over at Durant Realty or Ned in L.A.?"

Ruby's big blues looked up at me in irritation. "It's a quarter till eight."

I glanced at the two of them and nodded. "Right."

"Which means it's a quarter till seven on the coast."

I was about halfway down the stairs when Vic called after me in a singsong voice. "You come back soon soldier-boy, me so horneeeeeeee . . . !"

**Tan Son Nhut, Vietnam: 1968**

"Fifty dollars?!"

Hollywood Hoang stood there on the tarmac in the late afternoon under a pan-fried, tropical sun as the big Kingbee warmed up. He was waiting for his money with his arms folded over his powder-blue flight suit. We were shouting at the top, bottom, and middle of our lungs even though our faces were only about six inches apart. "He with her all night. I like you, Lieutenant, and that why you get half discount rate!"

I looked past Hoang to where Henry was carrying Babysan Quang Sang into the cargo hold. "Fifty dollars is the discount?!"

He smiled. "It extra for girls to sleep with Montagnard tribesmen, so that remove discount! I happy to take greenbacks or MPC; no dong."

I pulled out my wallet and gave him the five tens. "She sure didn't seem to mind last night. . . ."

"She world-class entertainer!" He slapped me on the shoulder and drew me toward the slow-moving rotors as he turned to where Baranski stood on the flight line. The inspector from CID and Mendoza had told me that this particular idea was a bad one but had relented when I'd remained obstinate. Baranski motioned for Hoang and gave him a messenger satchel. He waved one last time as the pilot followed me and we climbed in the cargo hold of the helicopter, the slight Vietnamese man carefully slipping the satchel behind the copilot seat.

It was dark in the Kingbee even with the cargo doors open. I pushed my steel pot further down on my head and waited for my eyes to adjust. There wasn't much room with all the supplies that were going into Khe Sanh, so the flight personnel consisted of the Bear, Babysan Quang Sang, two navy corpsmen, and me. I pulled at my flak vest, stiff from nonuse, and felt it constricting my chest as the big machine began to rise; at least I hoped it was the flak jacket.

By chance, it was the same helicopter I'd flown in on, the one with the dead. I wasn't sure if Hollywood Hoang had been the pilot, but we'd had a conversation about hauling them. He said that once the *ma,* or spirits of the dead, had ridden with you, they were always there, riding along. Flamboyant and dramatic, the flight crews were a superstitious lot who had tapped into that resonance, and they knew death, like suicide, was catching.

Babysan was propped up asleep against the bulkhead, with a cargo net partially wrapped around him and secured with some nylon webbing, just in case we were to make any unexpected turns. Henry was checking the magazines on his assortment of weaponry and looked over to see how I was doing. It was going to be a long flight, and he knew about my stomach's stance on helicopters.

"How are you feeling?"

I nodded but kept my head straight, where I wouldn't see the passing countryside as we sped north at a hundred and twenty miles an hour, willing it to grow darker so that I wouldn't be able to see anything.

"Do not puke in here."

"I won't."

"The one thing you must do..."

"Yep?"

"When this thing lands, you run like hell."

I glanced at him but quickly averted my eyes so that I wouldn't see any of the smoke from the lower hells we were flying over—the whispering gray smoke from the burned rice paddies of strike-free zones, the alabaster of the phosphorus smoke, and the smudged black smoke and gasoline smell of the napalm. I hoped I would see the purple landing zone smoke that would mean the ride was over.

The medics always offered you Dexies when you went out at night. I never took them, because I was so wired I was afraid that with the extra stimulant I'd fry my wiring and go stiff. I tried to hand the pills to the Bear, but he just shook his head and smiled, his teeth glowing like river stones in the gloom of the cargo hold. "I do not need them; you?"

I leaned over and felt his shoulder against mine. "Right now, you couldn't pull a needle out of my ass with a tractor."

He laughed, and as we flew, the light died.

No grunt ever called Khe Sanh the western anchor of our defense, but a lot of other people did. The heroic image of besieged Marines holding out against unimaginable odds had captured the imagination of the public, enough so that Lyndon Johnson called in the boys of the Joint Chiefs of Staff to sign a statement to "encourage public reassurance" that Khe Sanh would be held at all costs.

Khe Sanh was a holding of hands by the high command and a rousing rendition of "Kumbaya."

Within the rolling hills, astride an old French-built road that ran from the Vietnamese coast to the Mekong Delta's Laotian market towns, Khe Sanh began as a Special Forces encampment built to recruit and train local tribesmen. Now, it was an uneasy fort with U.S. intelligence reports stating that four North Vietnamese infantry divisions, two artillery regiments, and assorted armored units were converging on that wide spot on Route 9.

It was déjà vu and Dien Bien Phu all over again.

It was the Little Big Horn.

I wasn't sure what I thought I was going to do once I got there, but I figured something would turn up. More than eight thousand personnel were there, more than three times the size of my hometown, and I guess they had caught my attention, too. They were Marines in trouble, and I didn't want to have had the chance to go and then have to say that I didn't. I couldn't say that my head was the clearest it'd ever been, but sitting at Tan Son Nhut and enjoying the sunsets was driving me crazy, and I knew I had to get out.

I studied the canvas webbing of the jump seat and then the black plastic surface of the M16A1 that seemed to absorb what light there was. In basic, they'd given us honest-to-God comic books to tell us how to operate and maintain the rifle—it made the M16 seem even more like a toy. There was even a shapely cartoon blonde who told you important things like you should never close the upper and lower receivers with the selector lever in the auto position, or how to apply LSA, which stood for Lube oil, Semifluid, Automatic weapons. I thought of another blonde, a night at the Absaroka County Fair and Rodeo, about a slow dance that had ended with a soft kiss. That was the thought I settled on for the remainder of the flight, until the buffet of air currents reminded me what I was doing and where I was going.

I glanced over at the navy corpsman and read his name patch, MORTON. When I glanced at his face, he was looking at me. "Quincy Morton, Detroit, Michigan."

I took the hand. "Walt Longmire, Durant, Wyoming."

He smiled. "The crazy Indian a friend of yours?"

"Yep."

He nodded his head. "He's got that shit right; when this thing touches Mother Earth, it's *di di mau, di di* mother-fuckin' *mau*."

I nodded as we flew over the tortured ground and thought about a raw recruit that had asked about foxholes and remembered a sunny sergeant in a very quiet classroom, who told us that a Marine didn't dig in.

But they had at Khe Sanh.

As we approached in zero-zero, you could see that the fortifications were slapped together in a haphazard manner, with sandbags and tanglefoot wire stretching to the dusty, smoky hillsides and the mist of the night. The landing zone, only a short distance ahead, had circuitous roads and makeshift buildings; it looked like we were landing in a Southeast Asian junkyard.

The ground was shaking, the hills were shaking, and the air was shaking, which meant the chopper was shaking. I could see Henry leaning over the piles of cargo; holding on to a handset and screaming into it as Babysan Quang Sang's lips puckered and his eyes focused into the darkness from under his pith helmet. The Bear fell back against the quilted bulkhead, turned his face to me, and smiled a stiff smile.

I shifted in the seat. "What?"

He took a breath and then expulsed the words as if he were eager to rid them from his body. "We are backed up. They are bringing in reinforcements, so we have been shuttled off to the garrison."

"Where's that?"

"Khesanville." His eyes widened. "Outside the wire." I nodded my head, or I thought I did. He leaned in again, and his voice was the most intense I'd ever heard. "Listen to me, when this thing hits the ground, you run. You run and you do not stop for anything, do you hear me?" This time I was sure I nodded. "They are going to be targeting this chopper like a tin bear in a shooting gallery, so you run like you have never run before. Run for the slit trenches, run for the sandbags, but make sure you run till you get to something far from this helicopter."

*"Di di mau?"*

The Bear smiled, and Corpsman Morton gave me the thumbs-up.

After a moment, Henry leaned back and pulled the CAR-16 closer to his chest, along with the claymore with the detonating device.

He pulled out the horse-head amulet and ran his thumb across the smooth surface of the bone.

I dropped the clip on my own Colt rifle and checked the safety. "What about the supplies?"

It took him a moment to respond and when he did, he wasn't smiling. "We are not in the supplies business anymore."

I poured him a cup from my thermos and looked around. There might've been more depressing places than the sheriff's substation in Powder Junction, but I couldn't think of any.

I'd been here back in the dark ages, when I'd first made the grade with Lucian. The standard used to be a trial period of duty in PJ before being transferred to Durant and the Sheriff's Department proper. Santiago Saizarbitoria had sidestepped the process, and it appeared that he now realized how lucky he'd been. There was a metal desk, three chairs, a filing cabinet, a plastic clock, one phone, a collection of quad sheets encompassing the entirety of the county, an NOAA radio, and that was about it.

I poured myself a cup and sat in the chair in front of the desk, which allowed Sancho to sit in the command chair. He sipped his coffee but seemed dissatisfied. "Got any sugar?"

I shook my head. "No."

"Any objections if I go over to the mercantile and get some more supplies for the duration?"

"Nope." I felt like I should be making some effort, so I tried to continue the conversation. "Did I tell you about James Dunnigan?"

"What about him?"

"He thinks his mother makes coffee for him in the mornings."

Sancho nodded, a little puzzled. "That's nice."

"She's been dead for almost thirty years." I sipped from my chrome cap-cup. "Den told me that he bought one of those coffeemakers with a timer and that he explains it to James every day, but every morning James thinks his dead mother makes the coffee."

A moment passed. "You think he's dangerous?"

I smiled at the Basquo; he was so serious. "No, I was just making conversation."

"Oh." He set his mug on the desk and leaned in. "After Maynard, we go over to the Hole in the Wall Motel and check out Tran Van Tuyen?"

"Yep."

"I just got the skinny on the Utah receipt. I think you're going to find this interesting." I glanced up at the clock and figured we had an easy five minutes for more conversation before the bartender arrived, if he got here on time. "There's no telephone number on the receipt, so I called up the Juab County Sheriff's Department, faxed a copy, and got a deputy to run over there and see what she can find out. She called me back and reported that it's not actually a repair shop, but more of a private junkyard alongside the highway. She said when she got there and found the mobile home in this maze of junk, after being chased around the place by assorted dogs, goats, and a mule..."

"Okay."

"...there's a guy standing outside the trailer, and a woman throwing what appears to be all his stuff at him. The deputy asked him what was going on, and he said that he doesn't know, that she's just crazy. The deputy showed him the fax of the receipt, and he said he'd never seen it before. Now, along with most of this guy's worldly possessions that have come flying out the door was a checkbook, which the deputy picked up and casually compared with the handwriting on the receipt. Dead match. She showed it to the guy as they're dodging the next salvo, and he admitted that he might just remember the girl. He described our victim and said she rolled up to his gate with a busted water pump and that he fixed it and sent her on her way.

"Sounds plausible."

"Now, I'd told the deputy about the quarters and that the girl probably didn't have much money, so she asked him how the Vietnamese woman paid for the repair . . ."

"She had sex with him."

The Basquo stopped and looked at me. "How did you know?"

"She used the same morally casual bartering system with the Dunnigan brothers."

He studied me for a second more. "Well, that certainly establishes a pattern."

There was the sound of a motorcycle and a knock at the glass pane, and Santiago got up to get it. He opened the door, Phillip Maynard came in, and Saizarbitoria gestured toward the empty seat to my left. The bartender sat, and he looked like he needed it. He looked like he had been up all night.

"How are you, Phillip?"

He sniffed and readjusted in his seat. "I'm good, a little tired. . . . What is all this about?"

"Phillip, I made some phone calls back to Chicago and got some information relating to some incidents that involved you on Maxwell Street, where you're originally from?"

He looked at the manila folder lying on the edge of the desk. "Uh huh."

I nodded toward the envelope. "I don't have to tell you what's in this, but we both know how seriously some of the charges could be interpreted—two cases of unlawful entry, larceny, one domestic charge, and a restraining order that's still being enforced."

"Look, that was a bullshit deal and . . ."

I held up a hand. "Phillip, hold on a second." I allowed my hand to rest on the file. "To be honest, I don't care about any of this. It tells me that you're no Eagle Scout, but as long as you keep your nose clean in my county, we'll get along fine. But we do have a problem." I let that one sit there for a moment. "I think you might've lied to me yesterday, or at least you didn't tell me everything you know. Now, is that the case?"

He shifted in his chair. "Yeah."

"So, why would you do that?"

He shrugged and sat there, silent for a while. "He paid me."

"Who did?"

"The guy."

I could feel Saizarbitoria watching me as I questioned Maynard. "Tran Van Tuyen?"

"Yeah, him; the Oriental guy at the bar."

"Asian, Vietnamese to be exact. What did he say?"

"He asked about the girl the day before yesterday, then came back in and gave me a hundred bucks to not mention his name."

I glanced up at Sancho, who snagged his keys from the desk and quickly went out the door. "What kinds of questions did he ask?"

"Just if I'd seen this girl or heard anything about her. He had a photograph of her."

"Did he call her by name?"

"Yeah, it was something like Packet."

"Did he say anything else?"

Maynard thought and then shook his head. "Just that he

knew the car was hers and that she'd run away and he was looking for her."

"Nothing else?"

He shook his head again. "Nothing, and that's the truth, Sheriff."

I walked him out, stood there by my truck, and warned him that if he ever lied again that I'd find a place for him under the jail. He nodded and threw a leg over the Harley and rode off toward the rows of shanty housing at the south end of town.

I was still standing there when the Suburban came reeling around the corner; Saizarbitoria stood on the brakes and ground to a stop in front of me. He started to reach across and roll down the window, but I saved him the grief by opening the door. "Tuyen's gone."

I nodded. "What'd they say?"

"They said that he came into the office, paid his bill, hopped in the Land Rover, and took off."

"How long?"

"About twenty minutes ago. I already called it in to the HPs."

I thought about it. "You take 192 out to the Powder River, do the loop up toward Durant, and then circle back on 196. I'll take 191 and 190 toward the mountains."

He disappeared east, and I headed west.

I was about to make the turn at the underpass of I-25 when I saw the same two kids who had waved at me the day before and noticed that one was wearing a Shelby Cobra T-shirt. They were leaning on the same fence like regular eight-year-old town criers—well, one eight, the other maybe six. I had a thought and pulled onto the gravel. I pushed the button to roll my window down, but before I could say anything, the taller one with the glasses spoke. "Are you the sheriff?"

"Yep. I don't suppose . . ."

He grinned and grabbed the younger boy by the shoulder. "I'm Ethan, this is my brother Devin."

"Good to meet you. I don't . . ."

The smaller one piped up. "Are you looking for bad guys?"

I nodded. "Yes. You didn't happen to see a green Land Rover go by here about fifteen minutes ago, did you?"

They both nodded. "Yes, sir. DEFENDER 90 . . ."

The older boy continued. "Coniston green with the convertible top, the ARB brush/grill guard, and front wing diamond plating."

I sat there for a second looking at him, wondering what to say after that description, and then fell back on an old western favorite. "Which way did he go?" They both pointed toward I-25. "Did he get on the highway?"

The blond one answered. "No, he went under it."

"Get on the highway on the other side?"

The one with darker hair responded this time. "Nope. Hey, can we have a ride?"

"Not right now, maybe later." I saluted them and hit the lights and siren, but this time I left them on, thanking the powers that be for the American male's preoccupation with all things vehicular. I thought of the Red Fork Ranch and called Saizarbitoria to tell him to turn around and take the 191 leg of the west side of the highway, and that I'd take 190.

The next call I made was to Ruby, who still sounded irritated, and that was without me singing. "What's the matter?"

Static. "It's another flood of these e-mails, and I'm getting tired of deleting them."

I keyed the mic. "Any word from L.A. or Bee Bee?"

Static. "Nothing from L.A., but Bee Bee called and said that this Tuyen fellow inquired about the Red Fork Saturday, so if he was interested in the property, it was a sudden interest."

"Well, I'm not sure how, but this guy is involved."

Static. "Have you got him?"

"No, but I'm working on it."

I hung the mic back on the dash and made the gradual ascent through the red wall country and broke onto the gravel road leading past the ghost town. I had just topped the hill when I noticed the flash of something reflective and slowed. I shut off the lights and siren, threw the truck into reverse, and backed down to where I could get a look into the canyon at Bailey's ramshackle and only street. The Coniston green Land Rover sat parked along the boardwalk at the far end. I turned the big three-quarter-ton around and pulled off and into the ghost town.

In Bailey's heyday, it had had a peak population of close to six hundred. The town had had a bank, hotel, hospital, post office, and something you rarely saw in high plains ghost towns: a large union hall, which stood at the top of the rise beside the road leading to the mine.

I drove slowly down the short street, looked back and forth among the buildings, and pulled my truck in front of Tuyen's vehicle. I got out and walked over to the Land Rover; it was locked and unoccupied. Tuyen's bags were in the back, along with a solid case that looked like the kind that might hold a computer.

I looked around the street again and unsnapped the strap on my Colt.

Nothing.

I stepped up onto the warped boardwalk and started down one side of the street. I tried to be quiet, but my boots resonated off the planks like I was starring in some B-movie western.

Most of the windows in the buildings were broken and

boarded up, but between the cracks I could see the gloom of the interiors; the floors in most of them had held up. The buildings were dusty and dirty, but they were solid, and only Zarling's Dry Goods, which was at the end of the street and had been the one with the fire damage, looked as if it might fall over.

There was a stone wall at Bailey's far end; it was partially collapsed and provided a large, picture-framed view of the hillside that led to the mine, the weed-filled graveyard and, above the overhang, the union hall.

There was a wrought-iron fence around the old graveyard, a token of condolence from a company that hadn't bothered to try to retrieve the bodies of the seventeen dead miners. Tran Van Tuyen sat on one of the thick iron rails beside the gate, with his back to me.

I walked the rest of the length of the boardwalk and down the stairs to the dry, cracked earth of the roadway and began walking up the hillside to the cemetery. The trail was overgrown with purple thistle and burdock, and the only thing you could smell was the heat. As I approached, Tuyen didn't move even though I was sure that he'd heard my truck and me in the street below.

I stopped at the gate and looked over at him. He was sitting with his hands laced in his lap, his head drooping a little in the flat morning sun. He had the same light, black leather jacket he'd had on in the bar draped over his knee, and the sunglasses. It was hot and getting hotter with every second, but he wasn't sweating.

After a minute, I saw his back rise and fall. "All of them died on the same day."

I continued to watch him as the cicadas buzzed in the high

grass, and I thought about rattlesnakes. "It was a mining accident, back in 1903."

"A terrible thing."

"Yep."

He paused again. "Do you believe in an afterlife, Sheriff?"

It wasn't the line I thought the conversation would take. "I'm not sure."

"What do you believe in?"

"My work."

He nodded. "It is good to have work, something you can devote your life to."

Something wasn't right. "Mr. Tuyen, I need to speak with you."

"Yes?"

"It's about the young woman."

He nodded. "I assumed as much."

"We questioned the bartender at the Wild Bunch Bar, and he said you were asking questions about this Ho Thi Paquet, and that you paid him some money."

His hand moved, and I found mine on the .45 at my hip. He had been holding something in his hands, and he extended it toward me. It was a photograph of the same young woman, perhaps younger, wearing a dance outfit, a snapshot of her in a crowd; she had turned her head and was smiling.

He took a deep breath and let it out slowly. "This was taken when she graduated from a dance school in Thailand when her mother came to see her perform." I thought he was done speaking, but the next words barely escaped him. "She was our only grandchild."

# 7

We sat in the office. Tuyen was holding his coffee cup, the contents of which he had doctored using the supplies that Saizarbitoria had procured from the Powder River Mercantile. He must not have liked the nondairy substitute, because he had yet to take a sip.

"I have another business; a group that unites Vietnamese children with their American relations—*bui doi,* which translates to 'dust child' in English." He stared at the floor. "Children of the Dust is a nonprofit organization, and I became active in their efforts two years ago."

"Working with the Vietnamese Amerasian Homecoming Act?" Santiago looked at me, and I shrugged.

"Exactly." Tuyen glanced at Saizarbitoria. "Since 1987 we have assisted twenty-three thousand Amerasians and sixty-seven thousand of their relatives in immigrating to this country."

I sipped my coffee. "Must be rewarding work."

"Very."

I nodded and made the mental note to ask Ned to check the organization from California. "What's all this about Trung Sisters Distributing?" I thumbed his card from the folder on the desk.

He looked up. "It is another of my businesses, and the one

that makes a profit." He pulled another card from his jacket pocket and handed it to me; this one was emblazoned with the words CHILDREN OF THE DUST and had an address the same as the one for the film office, with the same three phone numbers. "I sometimes find it more advantageous to be in film distribution than an individual tracking down men who may have illegitimate children."

I nodded. "Especially men in my age range who might've been in Vietnam?"

"It can be rather shocking, and sometimes responses are not particularly positive."

"I can imagine." I put my coffee cup on the desk. I had had enough of the stuff. I looked at Saizarbitoria, who seemed to be studying me. I turned back to Tuyen. "What about the Red Fork Ranch?"

"I am genuinely interested in the property."

"But that's not why you're here."

His face lowered. "No."

"Mr. Tuyen, I'm really sorry to be insensitive, but I need to know about your granddaughter." He placed his still untouched coffee on the desk, and I wasn't happy about what I had to do next. "I'm assuming her married name was Paquet?"

"Yes, she was briefly enjoined to a young man, here in the U.S."

"And that would be in California?"

"Yes. Orange County, Westminster."

"Little Saigon."

He looked up and smiled sadly. "I am not used to people referring to the area in that manner outside of Southern California."

"Mr. Tuyen, do you have any idea why your granddaughter might've stolen a car and then run all the way to Wyoming?"

"A number of them, actually."

"She obviously didn't want you involved, so how was it you were able to find her?"

"She acquired one of my credit cards, a gas card. She also, well, borrowed a valuable laptop computer, some jewelry, and a few other items, but it was through the credit card I was able to follow her."

I watched him for a moment. "We didn't find any credit cards on your granddaughter's person."

"The card was left at a Flying J truck stop in Casper. I recovered it there."

"So you figured she was heading north and drove to Powder Junction?"

"Yes, it was as good a guess as any other."

"Did it occur to you to contact any law enforcement agencies to see if they could find her?"

He laced his fingers in his lap and stared at them. "My granddaughter... Ho Thi had some unfortunate incidents, which I thought might color a more official response to her disappearance."

I looked at the planing light on the side of his face and then plunged ahead. "That would have to do with the troubles of a month and a half ago?"

It took a commensurate amount of time for him to respond. "Yes."

"So you figured with your experience in working with Children of the Dust, you would find her yourself?"

"Yes."

"These incidents you referred to concerning Mrs. Paquet: We got some information from the Orange County Sheriff's Department concerning some charges?"

He looked at me with a sharpness that he couldn't or didn't want to hide. "I don't see how that is..."

"I'm just trying to get a clearer idea as to her situation, and how and why it is she ended up here the way she did."

His eyes stayed steady with mine. "I understand you have a man in custody?"

I knew he was upset, but I needed answers. "The prostitution charges?"

He took a deep breath. "It was the young man she was married to; he was party to a number of illegal ventures and got her involved."

"In prostitution?"

"Human trafficking." He picked up his cup but only looked into it. "There is an underlying problem with the Vietnamese Amerasian Homecoming Act in that a number of corrupt Vietnamese staffers in the U.S. consulate, along with human brokers who acquire these mules who assist them, are—what is the colloquialism?—piggybacking illegals into the United States. Visas are granted as long as they are prepared to take their new, well, family, one can say, along with them. These human brokers make close to twenty thousand dollars for each accompanying visa."

"And this man, Paquet?"

"Rene Philippe Paquet."

"He's involved with this?"

"Was. He died in Los Angeles."

"How did he die?"

Tuyen swallowed, as if the words were leaving a bad taste in his mouth. "He was also involved in the drugs and found dead in his apartment."

I got up and walked over to the only window, which was in the top of the only door, and looked through the curling and sun-faded decal of the Absaroka County Sheriff's Department at the overexposed light baking the empty playground of the elementary school across the street. "I guess I'm a little confused, Mr. Tuyen. How did Ho Thi, whom I'm assuming was a United States citizen, get involved with Paquet?"

From the sound of his voice, I could tell he had turned toward me. "I'm afraid you may not understand the complications of my relationship with my granddaughter, Sheriff."

I leaned on the door facing with my back still to the desk and waited.

"Perhaps, Sheriff, I should tell you my own story first?"

"You were in the war?"

"Yes."

A rusty, half-ton pickup chugged by on the otherwise empty roadway. "You speak English very well."

He took a deep breath. "Yes. I was drafted from a small village in the Lang Son Province and, because of my ease with acquiring languages, was sent from the South Vietnamese Army to the Rangers. I spoke English especially well, along with French, Chinese, and Russian, and so they conscripted me in conjunction with the American Special Forces and the Short Term Road Watch and Target Acquisition program."

"Black Tigers and STRATA?"

"Yes. I was twice wounded and received a battle citation before being transferred to the American Embassy in Saigon. As the war worsened, I was given the opportunity to expatriate myself to the United States, but not with my wife and son. I stayed, and we survived through my bureaucratic skills until I was able to take my family on a vacation to Taiwan, where we escaped to France and then here. With my contacts in the embassy, I was able to procure a job in film distribution and six years ago was finally able to open my own business."

Santiago poured himself another coffee. "Sounds like the American dream come true."

I kept looking out the window. "I notice you didn't mention a granddaughter?"

"Yes." Something in the way he said it caused me to turn my head and look at him. "It is sometimes difficult to explain the abandonment of wartime to those who have not experienced it. You were in the American war, Sheriff?"

"I was."

He studied me awhile. "Then perhaps you will understand. There was a woman whom I spent time with in Saigon, both during and after the war; not my wife."

I nodded, abandoned the playground, and came back to sit on the corner of the metal desk. "Your participation with Children of the Dust came from your personal experience?"

"Yes, and then my granddaughter arrived over a year ago, and it was obvious that she had not had an easy life which, as she grew older, exhibited itself in numerous ways." He took another breath. "She did not speak English and made no attempts to learn the language after arriving. She was trenchant and rebellious toward us and began spending more and more time with the young man I mentioned." I watched as he examined his laced fingers. "She was arrested for solicitation six weeks ago."

"I think I'm getting a clearer picture as to why she would want to run away, but do you have any idea why it is that she would come to Wyoming?"

"None."

Saizarbitoria was still watching me as I reached over the desk and into the Cordura shooting duffel. I slipped the photograph, still in the plastic bag, from one of the folders and handed it to Tuyen. "Do you know this woman?"

He took the photograph and studied it, finally looking up at me. "No." His eyes stayed on me for a moment, went to the photo again, and then back to me. "And this is you?"

"Yes."

"When was this picture taken, if I might presume to ask?"

"The end of '67, just before Tet." He studied the photograph again, and I could hear the years clicking in his head like abacus beads. I leaned forward. "Third generation; is it possible that this is Ho Thi's grandmother?"

"It is not the woman I knew. . . ."

"Then possibly her great-grandmother? This woman in the photograph, her name was Mai Kim and she died in 1968."

He stared into the black-and-white, memorizing the woman's face and comparing it with his granddaughter. "It is possible. Did you know her well, Sheriff?"

"Not in the personal sense, but she was a bar girl at the Boy-Howdy Beau-Coups Good Times Lounge just outside Tan Son Nhut air force base, where I was sent as a Marine inspector."

"You were a police officer then, too?"

"Yes."

He thought about it some more. "You think it is possible that Ho Thi received this photograph from her mother or another woman within the family and mistakenly believed that she was related to you?"

"Right now, it's all I've got to go on and the only connection to Wyoming that I have."

"I see."

"Mr. Tuyen, I'm going to need you to look at some photographs of your granddaughter for purposes of recognition, see some identification that she was, indeed, your granddaughter, and then we can make arrangements with the Division of Criminal Investigation to have the body shipped back to California."

"Yes, of course."

"Were you planning on heading back anytime soon?"

He was still looking at the photo in the plastic bag and possibly thinking of other things in other plastic bags. "I had intended to leave today, but I didn't seem to have the energy once I'd gotten in my vehicle."

I stuck my hand out for the black-and-white, but he misinterpreted and shook it, so I took the photograph back with my other hand. "That's perfectly understandable. I can appreciate it if you need some time alone, but if you'd rather look at those things this afternoon, you'll have to come up to my office in Durant."

"I'm not sure if I will be up to that this afternoon, but perhaps I will go back and check into my room again and see how I feel later today." He stood.

"That'll be fine. Tomorrow morning is just as good. You still have my card?"

"I do." He stopped at the door and looked back at us. "And you have my granddaughter's belongings?"

"Yes."

"I would like to pick up those things."

"I'm sure we can release them as soon as we get all the information back from Cheyenne, and I get some documentation on you and your granddaughter."

"I will see to it." He still stood there, and I knew what was next. "I am reticent to ask again, but I understand you have arrested a man for the murder of Ho Thi?"

I crossed my arms. "We have a man who is being held under reasonable suspicion in connection with her death. However, there is not conclusive evidence against him."

In the backlight of the glass-paned door, Tuyen's outline was dark and featureless. "This man was living under the highway?"

"I'm afraid so."

I could see the outline of his chest rise and fall. "It is difficult to remember that things like this can happen, even here."

He turned the knob, pushed open the door, and was gone.

"Jeez, Boss..."

Saizarbitoria had followed me out the door to the playground where I stood with my boot propped up on the jungle gym. I looked out at the flat grasslands leading to the Powder River. There was a low rise to the east of town before the breaks of the northbound water crumpled the plains like an unmade bed. Everything was a dried-out watercolor, and it looked like if you touched anything, it would crumble and blow away. We needed rain.

"What did you say?"

He stood next to me, his hand wrapped around one of the bars for an instant, then he yanked it away from the cooking metal. He blew on his fingers. "Kind of rough on a guy who just lost his granddaughter."

"He didn't find her that long ago."

"Jesus." He barely said it, but I still heard him.

I was having a hard enough time thinking about the things I needed to think about without the weight of his judgment. "Call up Jim Craft down in Natrona County and get him to go check out the Flying J, see what they say about the stolen card."

He cleared his throat, adjusted his wraparound sunglasses, and stuffed his hands into his pockets. "All right."

"And then ask DCI if there was anything in Ho Thi indicating drug use." The brim of my hat hung across my brow, so I pushed it back and continued to look at the horizon for clouds that weren't there.

He stiffened a little. "Why?"

"Because Paquet was and, most likely, if she was involved in prostitution she was involved in drugs." I took my boot off the rung and stood there looking at him. He was a handsome kid, and there wasn't any back-down in him, especially with me, and that's why I liked him so much. I turned and started toward my truck. "You'd be amazed at what you'd do if you were desperate."

**Khe Sanh, Vietnam: 1968**

The NVA had found the range of the helicopter pretty quickly, and the mortar fire was singing around us like roman candles in the monsoon wet.

I ducked against the bulkhead and forced air in and out of my lungs, unsure if the whistling I heard was my breath or the enemy rounds. I looked over and saw Henry disconnecting Babysan Quang Sang from the webbing and the cargo net in anticipation of the Indo-Chinese fire drill from the helicopter.

He looked at me only once. "Run, and do not stop until you reach something."

The generators along with the Willie Petes, or illumination rounds, from inside the wire lit up the area with a blinding sideways glare that threw dramatic contrasting shadows on the wet, rain-slicked surface of everything—as if the situation needed it.

We were coming in hot, and the big Kingbee followed the contours of the valley as we made the final approach, skimming in about six feet off the hard ground and stalling our movement at the LZ, with the gigantic circles of water imitating the interlocking revolution of the rotors.

Everybody moved at once. Hollywood Hoang gunned the engine with a roar as we piled off on one side, the two corpsmen following Henry and Babysan Quang Sang out of the helicopter's side door and into the pouring rain and incandescent night.

I came out of a crouch and shot after the receding images of the running men; the two corpsmen had slanted right, toward the burned-out hulk of an M47 tank, and Henry and Babysan disappeared into a trench about fifty yards away.

I felt like a buffalo chasing antelope.

As my foot came off what pretended to be the landing strip, I felt the chopper begin its hurried ascent like it was falling from the earth instead of rising. Hoang had given us all the time he could and was now on his way out. I ran the first twenty or so yards from the helicopter when something pushed me to the red slime with a tremendous outburst of air and an immediate loss of oxygen, along with an explosion much louder than the rest. The impact of the overpressure forced my helmet onto my nose and pushed me forward, and I slid diagonally in the raw scarred mud.

I was pretty sure I was burning. It wasn't that I felt like I was on fire, but the smell was so close that it had to be me. I couldn't hear anything, just the sound of my breath and the coursing blood in my temples. When I moved, it was as if I were viewing myself in slow motion; even my head pivoted like it was on some long boom.

I forced myself to get up but fell to one side in the muck, and I half turned toward all the light. My eyes closed with the fury of it but, when I half opened one, I could see someone lying in the distance. The fire backlit the outline of a hand, and then an arm reached out into the night air. I stumbled up through the smoke and slanted sheets of rain.

There was wreckage everywhere, and the acrid taste of the fire filled my throat and pushed itself back out from my body. I gagged but staggered forward, looking for the arm that had reached out to me. I fell over smoking debris and could make out part of the helicopter's fuselage as the drops sizzled on the superheated metal.

Hollywood Hoang's uniform was singed but still mostly powder blue. I reached down and grabbed him, fell back, but held on, still trying to get my ears to clear the shrieking.

He didn't weigh much, so I carried him, slowly pulling him the distance toward the trench and wondering what had happened to everyone else.

That's when I saw the other bodies.

One of the corpsmen hadn't made it. For some reason, the majority of the explosion had blown to the left and had taken him with it. The rotors, the engine, or just the sheer ferocity of the blast had caught him, and he lay there in three pieces. The other was crawling through the burning oil and was screaming. At least I assumed he was screaming since his mouth was open.

I got to the man, picked him up by the front of his flak jacket, and leveraged him onto one of my muddy knees. I grabbed again and got a better hold of him as his face rolled up toward mine. "Don't leave me."

I lifted Quincy Morton from Detroit, Michigan, put Hoang over my shoulder, and turned, starting toward the trench again. The smoke enveloped everything, and it was as if we had disappeared. I slogged forward into the darkness; the heat pressed against my back like a steam iron, and the weight of the two bodies slowed me down to a crawl in the mud that collected under my combat boots.

I remembered the blocking sleds at USC and the grueling two-a-days under the California sun, squared my shoulders, put my head down, and pulled.

I had taken a good seven steps when somebody ran into me. He bounced off and must have fallen to the ground, so I released the swabo corpsman only for a second to try and help whoever had fallen, but the swabo misinterpreted the movement and grabbed my arm just as I saw the barrel of the AK-47 rising up and into my face. It didn't matter. I didn't have my rifle.

He fired, the cicada sound of the machine gun coming unwound as I fell with the whistling rush of the bullets flying beside me; I came down on him hard and could feel him trying to get the automatic loose from under me, but I'd yanked a hand free and could feel his throat. Everything was wet, and we slithered there against each other.

He was kicking, but the weight of all three of us didn't allow for much movement. I tightened my grip on his larynx and felt the cartilage begin to give as his voice box collapsed and pressed into the air cavity of his esophagus. I couldn't hear anything since the explosion, but I could imagine that I could still hear the spittle. He must have gargled like a baby working itself up for a full-blooded scream.

It never came.

He wasn't moving and wasn't breathing, but I still wasn't sure if he was dead.

I lay there on top of him, retching, coughing, and finally vomiting.

I spit and cleared my mouth and felt for the two men who lay beside me, feeling the corpsman's hands grabbing my arm. I got to my knees and then my feet, picked them up again, and staggered forward into the smothering rain. I gathered momentum, realizing that if we stayed out there in the open for much longer, we were dead.

The NVA had overrun the garrison and were headed for the wire; we were only a few steps ahead of them. I could feel my boots digging into the goose-shit ground, and what adrenaline I had left propelled me as we blew through the swirls of the remaining smoke- and mist-clogged night.

I continued to push off with each stride growing just a little bit longer, and with the mantra *I will not die like this... I will not die like this... I will not die like this....*

Men rose up ahead, but I didn't have time to fight them all so I just continued on, blasting forward and taking them with me. The biggest was at point and tried to shrug down like a running back looking for a hole in the line, but I was too much weight with the two bodies I carried and took him as I lost my footing and carried us over the edge of a flat world.

We fell, and I could finally hear the weapons firing around me and the curse words, thankfully, in English. I opened my eyes but could only see the reddish rainwater that filtered between the stacks of soggy sandbags and Henry. He was cradling his brow with blood filtering through his fingers as he laughed and shook his head with that bitter secret-survivor smile.

He spoke out of the side of his mouth as he fired the CAR-16 over the lip of the trench, the flame from the 5.56's barrel extending from the black metal like the eyes of some deflated jack-o'-lantern. The blood was still seeping from his head where I'd hit him, when he looked at me.

"When I said run till you reach something, I did not mean me."

She tossed part of a crust to Dog, who was sitting in the hallway to my left. We watched as the beast took the baked dough and swallowed it in two bites.

"Because it's your turn, and there isn't anybody else." She didn't look satisfied with my answer, but she was relatively happy that I'd brought dinner before I headed back to the ranch to check on Cady.

Vic sipped her Rainier beer and watched as the giant folded the last slice of his pizza, stuffing it into his mouth behind the impenetrable curtain of black hair, and chewed. He had eaten all of his own pie and all but the one slice Vic had picked at and the three slices I'd devoured of another. He'd chugged the liter of pop that we'd provided and finally lay back on the bunk and covered his eyes with his arm.

Vic studied him for a moment and then spoke. "So the one night I'm going to sleep in the jail, you're going home?" I didn't say anything. She watched me as I took a sip of my beer. "Sure you don't want to stick around?"

"One of us can't leave this room." I glanced at the prisoner, now snoring softly. "And under the circumstances..."

She shrugged. "This is the shittiest pizza I've ever eaten."

I continued to watch the Indian. "He seemed to like it."

"He lives under the highway; I'm not so sure his culinary sensibilities are all that refined."

I peeled the *R* on the label of my beer bottle with my thumbnail. "Saizarbitoria thinks I'm a racist."

"That's okay. I think you're a slave driver." She pushed her ball cap back; the hat was a sign that she was having a bad hair day—something that I had learned not to mention. "Why?"

"I was kind of hard on this Tuyen fellow today."

"Really?"

"Yep." I looked at the glue strip where the label had peeled away. "I don't know, maybe it is prejudice. He was in the Black Tigers and STRATA."

She stared at me. "And for those of us who weren't born until after the Age of Aquarius, what the fuck does that mean?"

"Black Tigers were the South Vietnamese version of our Special Forces, and STRATA was a program that dropped these guys behind enemy lines. There were, I think, about a hundred of them and about a third never made it back."

"So this guy's one bad motor scooter?"

"Could be." I took a deep breath. "His English is good, better than any Vietnamese speaker I've ever heard...." It was silent too long, so I changed the subject. "Anything from Quincy, over at the VA?" She lowered her beer bottle and looked at me as I stood and gathered the detritus, setting the two empty pizza boxes and bottles on the counter.

"He's on vacation in the garden spot of garden spots, Detroit, and won't be back until first thing tomorrow. I told them somebody would be by."

"Did you ask them if they were missing a seven-foot Indian?"

"I did, but the twit I was talking to didn't really come forth with much."

"You want to ride over to Sheridan with me tomorrow morning?"

"No." She stood, considering me as I stopped in the doorway and then leaned back against the minifridge door. "Not after sleeping on the jail floor all night... alone." I watched her as she approached me—the way the uniform hung in all the right places, the lush, hanging-gardens-of-Babylon quality of her general physique. "It's the uniform, right?"

"No, it's not the uniform."

"I mean... because it's okay. I mean some guys are freaky, and they like a woman in uniform, but you're not."

We were standing in the doorway, just out of the giant's line of sight, and somehow the conversation we'd been meaning to have was even worse here. "Not what?"

"Freaky."

"No, I'm not." She was standing close, and my back was against the wall in more ways than one. She put a hand out and touched my sleeve, running her fingers up my arm and feeling the embroidery at the sheriff's patch. Those eyes turned up to me. I could smell her, all of her, and started remembering that night in Philadelphia again. "Look..."

Her face was about eight inches from mine. "What?"

"I just... I don't know if..."

In the dim light of the hall, her eyes shone, and I found myself studying the haloed glow. "What?"

"What we did, that one time, was out of context and now we're back. . . ."

She slowly went up on tiptoe and her hand trailed to the back of my neck as she pulled, and the distance between our faces decreased. "What'a ya say we slip out of these uniforms and get out of context again?"

I brought my hands up to the small of her back and felt her shiver like a colt.

Contrary to popular belief, the best kisses don't start lip to lip. This one started at the scar at my collarbone, nibbled its way up the muscles at the side of my neck, and paused at my jaw. I was having trouble breathing when I heard her moan, and it sounded as if it were coming from somewhere else, somewhere east and not so long ago. I turned my face to allow our lips to meet, but she'd frozen and had turned her head toward the holding cells.

We both stood there breathing, and her voice caught. "I think the prisoner is waking up."

I nodded and watched as her arm and face slipped away. I caught her and pulled her in with one hand, placing the tip of my chin on top of her head and holding her there for just a moment, not talking. I felt her sigh and then loosened my grip.

"I guess I better get back in sight."

I watched as she moved the folding chair and sat in plain view of the Indian, who immediately quieted down.

"If it makes you feel any better, I was thinking about asking you out on a date."

Her head rose, and the dark gold of her eyes shone again, the lengthy canine tooth exposed like an ivory warning flare. "A what?"

I could feel my courage heading for the hills. "That's what we used to call it back in the old days—dating."

"Really?"

"Yep." I'm pretty sure my face was taking on a little color, but I braved it through and went back to pick up the trash from the counter. "What do they call it now?"

The half-smile smirk stalled there like a cat playing with a mouse as she looked up at me. "Sport fucking."

I lingered beside her for a moment and then glanced at the big Indian before heading out. It just seemed like our timing was never right. She waited till I was halfway down the hall before calling after me. "You sure you go? Me love you looooooooong time. . . ."

I took Cady with me to make the sixty-six-mile loop over to Sheridan after we'd worked out in the morning. We were just passing Lake DeSmet along I-90 with Dog seated between us. She had her sandals kicked off and her legs folded up on the seat the way she always did.

I noticed she'd dressed for Michael's arrival later that day in a bright turquoise broomstick skirt and a black-sequined, cap-sleeved T-shirt. She was wearing a stylish straw cowboy hat with a leather strap adorned with conchos and lots of feathers on top of her auburn hair. Her earrings matched her skirt. Biker/cowgirl haute couture. She glanced up at me and continued to pet Dog. "Don't make fun of my hat."

"I haven't said a word."

"You were thinking about it."

I set the cruise control and settled back in my seat. "It's a very nice hat."

"Don't."

I glanced at her. "What?"

"You were going to try and be funny." She took a deep breath and looked out her window and back down the Piney Creek valley.

This is the point where as a father you're supposed to say something—the right thing—and I wondered what that might be. She was obviously nervous about Michael's arrival, and it was my duty to assuage some of the anxiety. "You look great."

Her head dropped, and I waited. "I'm wearing the hat because of the scar."

"Oh, honey . . ."

"I just thought at first . . ." She was silent for a moment, but it wasn't because there was nothing to say. "My hair is too short; I haven't gotten enough sun. . . ."

"You look great, honest." I passed an eighteen-wheel truck and steered back in our lane. "It means a lot to you, this visit?"

She reached out and adjusted the air-conditioning vent, then readjusted it back to the same position. "Yes."

There was something I'd been meaning to talk with her about, and this was the closest to an opening I'd gotten. I'd decided that as a parent I would adopt a relationship with my little redheaded, large-eyed daughter that was based on an unrelenting truth, and it had become the only language we both understood. "Well, this'll be a good opportunity for the two of you to spend some time really getting to know each other even if it's just a couple of days."

I was hoping it sounded better to her than it did to me.

"What's that supposed to mean?"

It hadn't.

"I just think it'll be a good visit; before, you had these roles—he was a police officer, and you were a victim. . . ." I glanced over and then quickly returned my eyes to the road. "It was a hospital, and then it's been phone calls. I just think this'll be a good opportunity for the two of you to be in a more natural setting and really get to know each other."

"That's the second time you've used the word 'really,' meaning we don't know each other now?"

"That's not what I said."

"Really?"

It seemed to me her mind was rapidly getting better. I tried my last hope, the authoritarian patrician voice of reason. "Cady . . ."

"I don't want to talk about it."

We drove the next twenty minutes in silence as I took the second Sheridan exit, turned off Main, and made the gradual ascent to the Veterans Administration. The VA had taken over Fort Mackenzie, and it was in a gorgeous spot on a plateau just north of town with vast, feathering cottonwoods and solid, redbrick buildings. We passed the unmanned guard shack and the rows of conifers stretching shadows across the pavement, and she decided to talk to me again. "So how come I never met this Quincy Morton guy?"

"He was before your time."

"More stuff that happened before I was born?" She glanced around as I wound my way through the fortlike buildings. "So, you had a hard time after the war?"

I thought about it. "I don't know if I'd call it a hard time. . . . It was a confusing time, and I was looking for some answers. Quincy wrote me and said he was transferring to Sheridan from Detroit."

She watched me. "Did Mom help?"

"Yes, but she wasn't in Vietnam, and I think I needed somebody who had been."

"What about Bear?"

I shrugged. "He wasn't around."

I could feel those composed, gray eyes on the side of my face. "It doesn't seem to have affected you."

I parked the Bullet under the shade of a tree and left the windows partially down for Dog. I thought of the contract I'd made with her. "Well, it did."

When we got out of the truck, I noticed she left the hat on her seat.

The Sheridan founding fathers had lobbied for Fort Mackenzie as protection against hostile Indians. The fact that there were only 23,133 Indians spread over an area roughly the size of Europe; that this count included men, women, and children; or that it was 1898 and the director of the U.S. Census Bureau had stated plainly that the frontier was dead, didn't appear much in the argument.

Pretty cagey, those Sheridan politicians—realizing the economic advantages that accrued by having an army post nearby. The market for local goods, especially beef, would increase, and the fort would provide jobs for a burgeoning workforce; it would also supply young West Point cadets to whom the founding mothers could marry off their daughters. One can only imagine the looks on their faces when the first troops of the Tenth Cavalry, Companies G and H, disembarked from the Sheridan trains and were—buffalo soldiers.

Quincy Morton's office was not in the same location; in fact, nothing was. I hadn't been to the VA for a while, and it appeared that the place had gone through quite a growth spurt. It was good to see Quincy again, and when I described the big Indian in my jail, he definitely knew who he was.

"You realize I'm under no obligation to give you any information without the proper authorization?"

"I am and, if it makes you uncomfortable, I can go over to Chuck Guilford and get the avalanche of paperwork sliding, but that's not going to help this man I've got sitting in my holding cell."

I watched as Quincy twisted his fingers into his wooly beard, which was now curlicued with a gray that I didn't remember. It was easy to see how the plains Indians had made the association between the soldiers' hair and the coats of the roaming herds. He adjusted his glasses, glanced at Cady, and then crossed to a large oak file cabinet and knelt down. I noticed the drawer he pulled out was the bottom one, W–Z.

White Buffalo. Had to be.

He pulled a thick file from the hanger and came back over, setting the folder on the edge of his desk; I noticed he didn't sit. "I'm taking this lovely lady over to the dayroom in ward five, which has mediocre coffee but a glass solarium with incredible views of the mountains." He hooked his elbow out to Cady, and she smiled and joined him at the door with her turquoise skirt twirling. He plucked an ID off the navy blazer on his coat rack. "The file stays in my office, and I will expect you in fifteen minutes. It's a voluntary lockdown ward, but just tell them you're with me and they'll let you in."

He shut the door.

I pulled Quincy's chair closer to the desk and looked around the room; I guess I was avoiding the file. The therapist had a framed poster from the Buffalo Bill Museum in Cody of the Tenth Cavalry buffalo soldiers on the wall, a couple of unopened Meals-Ready-to-Eat on his bookshelf, and a fake hand grenade on his desk with a small plaque that read, IN CASE OF COMPLAINTS—PULL PIN. At least I assumed it was a fake grenade.

There was a white adhesive label on the cover of the file that read VIRGIL WHITE BUFFALO.

Virgil.

I thought about the author of *The Aeneid* and Dante's supposed guide through hell. I studied the folder and hoped his travels had been more pleasant. They hadn't.

It had taken the full fifteen minutes to get through the file, and since I'd left Quincy's office on my way over, my mind repeated only one word.

God.

It was a cloudless day, if hot, and I took a deep breath and smelled the pungent fragrance of cut grass. I thought about what I'd read as I walked across the trimmed sidewalks leading to ward 5. I stopped at the double-paned Plexiglas doors and watched as the officer came over. I mentioned Quincy's name, and he told me to go down the hall to the second right and to just keep going.

They were sitting at a small round table on which were three thick-handled coffee mugs and a white plastic carafe. I sat and listened as they continued their conversation, which was mostly about Michael's impending visit and Cady's plans to return to Philadelphia after Labor Day.

I sat and gazed out at the mountains and thought some more about what I had read back in the doctor's office.

God.

Cady slid me a mug of coffee. "Quincy says you saved his life."

I turned my head and looked at her. "Yep? Well, he's delusional and that's why they keep him in a place like this."

Figuring that she wasn't likely to get the story out of me, she turned to Quincy, who told her a tale that made me sound like *Sgt. Fury and His Howling Commandos*. He said that I'd talked so much about Wyoming that when a job came up in the Veteran's Administration in Sheridan for a post-traumatic stress disorder coordinator, he and his wife, Tamblyn, had made the jump and never looked back.

"We had only three black people in Wyoming at the time, and I was in charge of trying to achieve a racial balance."

Quincy shook his head, patted Cady's arm, and pointed to another set of double Plexiglas doors leading outside to a grass field so green it looked chartreuse. "There's a walkway through there that leads to another walkway that surrounds the parade ground and then to a big mansion that used to be the fort commander's residence. There's a ballroom upstairs with a hardwood floor and bay windows that look out on the mountains." He waited a moment. "You should see it."

Cady, used to being dismissed from my more indelicate law enforcement conversations, nodded and squeezed my shoulder as she passed, looking back at Quincy. "If you decide to keep him, you can't; we need him too much."

The Doc smiled. "He's too smart; the smart ones are always trouble." We watched as an attendant pushed the door open, and she slipped off her sandals to walk across the parade ground barefoot. "My God, Walter. What an amazing young woman. . . ."

I watched her pick her way across the field, periodically skimming a foot across the blades of soft grass, before walking on. "She's a punk."

He turned to me, and his concern was palpable. "She told me about the problems in Philadelphia." I nodded but didn't say anything, wondering exactly how much she'd told. "It appears as if she's progressing magnificently."

"I hope so."

He studied me. "What's worrying you?"

I groaned. "That she's pushing too hard, that she's not

pushing hard enough, that we're doing too much physical and not enough intellectual, that we're doing too much intellectual and not enough physical. . . ."

He laughed. "You haven't changed, Walter."

I took a deep breath and tried to strain my anxiety through my lungs. "I'm not so sure that's a good thing, Doc."

"It is." He sipped his coffee. "You read the file."

"I did."

"And?"

I looked into my cup and a past that made my coffee appear transparent.

"And if I ever labor under the supposition that I've had a hard life, I'm going to think of Virgil White Buffalo."

He set his mug down and pulled in his chair. He listened to the story of Ho Thi Paquet and nodded gently at the smooth surface of the table without interrupting—a ritual I'd remembered. When I finished, he looked up at me. "Do you think he did it?"

I took another breath. "I didn't until I read that damn file."

We sat there in the comfortable silence we'd cultivated from long ago before he spoke again. "I just went back there."

"Where?"

"Vietnam."

"Why?"

He laughed. "It sounds like you've still got some issues."

"Issues, hell; I've got volumes."

I poured him some more coffee as he continued to laugh. "I took Tamblyn and we went back just last year, stayed at the Morin Hotel in Hue. We're sitting there having breakfast and drinking *Buon me Thuot*–style coffee and watching the nuts fall off the bang trees like incoming . . ." He took a sip.

I nodded. "What was it like, other than nuts?"

He smiled. "Everybody's trying to sell you something." He glanced back up at me. "We took Route 1 through Da Nang to this old fishing town, Hoi An—motor scooters all over the place and not a single water buffalo. Shops everywhere with paintings, jewelry, and T-shirts. The nightclubs in Hue have names like Apocalypse New and M16. I showed Tamblyn Red Beach 1 and Red Beach 2, where we dropped off the first American ground troops." It was a long pause, and it was only then that I figured he was talking to himself. "All in all . . . it was pretty strange."

I sipped my coffee and looked off to the few narrow and melting snowfields on the mountains. "Maybe we won after all."

**Tan Son Nhut, Vietnam: 1968**

The same air force major as before was still the security officer, and DeDe Lind, the *Playboy* playmate, was still on the wall of the Quonset hut and insisting it was August. "I find it strange that you were posted here by the provost marshal to investigate the overdose of a soldier but ended up in Khe Sanh in an exploding helicopter."

"Yes, sir."

He looked back at the folder on his desk, which contained the hospital discharge papers. It'd been almost a week, and they'd tried to send me back to Chu Lai and battalion HQ, but I told them that I wanted to return to Tan Son Nhut. "It says here that the swabos have you up for a Navy Cross and a Silver Star."

"Yes, sir."

"What'd you do up there in Khe Sanh, sink a submarine?"

"Yes, sir."

He looked up through the thick glasses. "What was that?"

"No, sir."

He studied me a good long time with the dead eyes. "Your official investigation was to be four weeks in length, but I'm going to see about getting that rescinded to three and get you out of here early."

"Sir, but my orders from HQ..."

"You mean those orders about an investigation that you ignored because you were out joyriding in Khe Sanh?" I didn't say anything, so he stood up and walked around his desk. He looked at my arm, still in the sling, and the sutured split on my eyebrow where I'd run into Henry. "How's that investigation going, Lieutenant?" I started to speak, but he cut me off. "The job you were sent here to do? How's that going?"

My head hurt, and I figured informing him that drugs were rampant in every part of the country and that I'd been warned off by his own personnel wasn't going to make my situation any better. "Not so good, sir."

He folded his arms and sat on the edge of his desk. "In the remaining time period in which we are to be blessed with your presence, you will confine yourself to this investigation and to this air base." He shook his head at my incompetence. "Do you read me?"

I thought about those comic book manuals for the M16s. "Yes, sir."

"Dismissed."

It was late in the afternoon—that point in the Asian day when the sun seemed like it just wouldn't die. I walked out to Gate 055 and to the Boy-Howdy Beau-Coups Good Times Lounge with the explicit idea of getting epically hammered. There weren't too many people in the place, so I got four beers from the bar and retreated to my weapon of choice. I took off my sling and tossed it on top of the piano, doodled a little in the key of F and then attempted to slide into some Fats Waller.

Mai Kim came over and pulled up a bar stool to watch me play. The *Stars and Stripes* was folded up under her arm, but she didn't ask for a lesson. I guess my mood was evident. She hovered there, though, looking at me. "Hey, Mai Kim."

She smiled and crossed her legs. "Hi, you back?"

"For a little while."

She looked concerned. "You go to America?"

I sipped the first of the second brace of beers. "Eventually, but for now it will just be BHQ in Chu Lai."

She leaned forward to look at my face and the bandages on my forearm. "You hurt?"

I looked up and was struck by the symmetry of her China-doll face, framed by the black silk hair. "Not so bad."

"You sad?"

"A little." I continued to look at her and noticed she seemed down, too. "How 'bout you?"

She smiled a flicker of a smile that died before it could catch. "Tennessee boyfriend, he no write."

"He rotate home?"

"Yes." She nodded. "What you think about?"

"A girl." I thought about the blonde back in Durant and wondered if she was still around.

She seemed even sadder. "American girl?"

"Yep." I continued to vamp the stride piece "A Good Man Is Hard to Find," my left hand alternating between single notes at the lower portion of the keyboard and chords toward middle C.

She made an attempt at brightening, the smile catching a little at the corner of her mouth. "This my favorite song, you play." I kept the title to myself, even though I think she knew it, and continued playing. "You tell me about America?"

"Big subject. . . ."

She reached out and stroked the side of my brow, careful to avoid the stitches. "Tell me favorite place again."

"Back home?"

Her fingers brushed through my hair and then settled on my shoulder. "Yes."

The words flowed like the stream I was thinking of, and I smiled back at her. "There's a spot in the southern part of my county in Wyoming, by the Hole in the Wall down near a place called Powder Junction."

"Hole in the Wall?"

"Yep. I told you, remember? It's a famous spot where the outlaws used to hide out."

"Outlaws."

"Butch Cassidy and the Sundance Kid." She nodded her head in recognition. I thought about how, after serving three-quarters of his sentence, George LeRoy Parker had been brought before Governor William H. Richards and declared that he would never rob another bank in Wyoming. He was released and, true to his word, never robbed another Wyoming bank—nobody said anything about Colorado. "They took cover near where Buffalo Creek spills out of the canyon just as you get to these gigantic red walls that run fifty miles." I thought about the big, wary trout that swam in the sun-sparked cold waters below the narrow-leaved willows. "There's an old ghost town called Bailey, and near there, it's the best fishing in all the Bighorn Mountains."

"Bailey, Bighorn Mountains."

"Yep."

"Mai Kim!" Le Khang's voice called from the other side of the room. She turned and looked at him and at the ready airman with the mustache who stood by the counter.

She looked at me, smiled, and got off her stool. "You go back there?"

I set my bottle back on the piano and stared at the keys. "I don't know. . . ."

She slipped her hand from my shoulder onto my wounded arm and carefully stroked the gauze and bandages that were wrapped there. "This girl, she there?"

I laughed a short exhale. "Yep."

She gave me one last pat on the shoulder before walking away. "You go back."

I drank steadily through the afternoon, the weight of my wounded arm sloping my shoulder farther and farther down until it was all I could do to continue raising my one hand to play.

I'd probably gone through an entire case of beer by the time I noticed it was full night; the crowd was pushing in against me. I'd also noticed that Le Khang hadn't brought any more beer over for a while, a sure sign I had been cut off.

Rescue came in the form of a familiar powder-blue arm, which reached across and placed another beer next to all the empties on the flipped-up cover of the zebra-striped, grained piano.

"How you feelin', Hollywood?"

He smiled and sat on the edge of the bench, and I noticed how little room he took up in comparison to Henry Standing Bear. Hoang had been released only two days after the incident at Khe Sanh, had already been reestablished to active flight duty, and had flown three more missions since the beginning of the week. "I buy you beer."

"Thanks."

He continued to smile at me. "You drunk."

"Stinking." He looked puzzled. "Stinking drunk."

He brightened, always game for another piece of American slang. "Stinking drunk?"

"Stinking. Drunk."

He held his beer up to mine as he chanted the phrase to himself. I picked up the bottle, wet with condensation, and tipped his. The English lesson made me think about Mai Kim, and thoughts of her battered away at the waves of alcohol that kept rolling onto the beaches of my mind. "Where's Mai Kim?"

He looked at me blankly. "She not here."

"Where is she?"

"She gone."

I drank my beer. "Oh."

I scratched my head and watched as my hat slipped off and fell on top of the foot pedals of the piano. Hoang reached down and snagged it and placed it back on my head backwards. "You stinking drunk!"

I pushed back and stood, none too steadily, and waited for the world to stop moving. It was getting late, and I decided to make the long trek back to the other side of the airfield where they'd lodged me in the visitors' barracks. Hoang was next to me and put an arm on mine to help me steady a persistent list. "You go home?"

"Yep." I stuck a hand out to grip the piano, which provided a little more support than the compact pilot. "If I can."

"I help you."

I half tripped over the piano bench and watched as everyone moved away. There was a brief upsurge of nausea, and I belched, which made me feel a little better. "I'm okay."

As I turned and shambled toward the open doorway, Hoang raised one of my arms and slipped under to help me navigate what now appeared to be the pitching deck of the Boy-Howdy Beau-Coups Good Times Lounge. I pulled away and fell down the two wooden steps that led out of the bar.

I rolled over and stared up into the hazy star-filled night. "Ouch."

Hoang's face was above mine. "You fall."

"I guess I could use a little help."

The Vietnamese pilot grabbed an arm and helped me get to my feet. He was surprisingly strong and half led, half supported me as I wavered down the deserted red-dirt road. He nodded his head. "You save my life."

I looked at the ludicrous figure of the tiny man in the powder-blue jumpsuit and white silk scarf. "When?"

"You funny guy."

I stopped and saluted the two air policemen who were stationed at Gate 055. The APs asked Hoang if I was going to make it or should they call a patrol with a jeep or maybe a forklift. Hoang shook his head and explained that we would walk the perimeter to the next gate to give me a chance to sober up. He also explained how I'd saved his life.

They said that was great.

He then explained how I'd saved other people's lives, too.

They said that was great, too.

I puked.

I don't think they thought that was so great.

Hoang supported me as we walked along the fenced boundary and looked at the moonlight casting down on the high whitewashed walls of the old French fort—Hotel California, as the locals referred to it. It didn't look real, or it looked too real, and I felt like I was on some movie set where we would walk behind the structure and see the two-by-four bracings that held up the naked backs of the walls.

The nausea was creeping up in my throat again, and I stopped, leaning against something and sitting on a hard surface. "Hey, Hollywood, you ever see *Beau Geste*?"

"No, but need to talk to you."

"One with Ronald Colman?"

He looked a little worried. "No..."

"Gary Cooper?"

"No."

I looked at Hoang, who was blurred and wavering in the close strangeness of the Vietnamese night. "How about *Gunga Din*, did ya see that?"

"Lieutenant... need to tell you something."

"What?"

He looked around. "Need to tell you something."

I ignored him and started reciting Kipling.

*You may talk o' gin and beer*
*When you're quartered safe out 'ere,*
*An' you're sent to penny-fights an' Aldershot it;*
*But when it comes to slaughter*
*You will do your work on water,*
*An' you'll lick the bloomin' boots of 'im that's got it.*

He edged away. "Lieutenant..."

I shook my head and immediately regretted it. "Doesn't matter."

I looked down and saw that my hand was resting on a cemetery headstone. I focused and saw more of them around me; they stretched into the late-night mist, thousands of them, and with the moonlight it was as if they were glowing like teeth. A dog barked in the distance, the sound rolling toward me like the cutting edge of harsh whispers.

When I looked up, Hoang was gone.

Quincy had gone back to work, and I'd made the march across the VA parade ground with my boots on.

It was Ranald Slidell Mackenzie that the fort was named after, and it was his residence to which the Doc had sent Cady. I thought about him and the history of the place as I crossed the foyer and climbed the steps to the upstairs ballroom. Mackenzie graduated West Point in 1862, number one in a class of twenty-eight. He fought in the Civil War and, before it was over, he'd been wounded four times, received seven brevets, and was a major general in charge of an entire division.

In our part of the country, however, his fame arose from the defeat of Dull Knife, the Cheyenne chief, and his village. On a cold November day in 1876, on the Red Forks of the Powder River, a spot just up the creek from where I'd been the day before, Mackenzie and four hundred men of the Fourth

Cavalry, along with four hundred Indian scouts, took the Cheyenne chief and his 183 lodges by surprise. He destroyed the village and their supplies and effectively ended the nomadic lifestyle of the Northern Cheyenne nation.

Henry Standing Bear liked to remind anyone who would listen that Mackenzie died in his sister's home on Staten Island, New York, in 1882, victim to the later stages of syphilis and, as Lucian would say, crazy as a waltzing pissant. It was, Henry also noted, not an unpleasant enough death.

Cady was standing in front of one of the large casement windows and was looking out at the last thin remains of snow that clung to the shadowed crevasses of the rocky heights. She was still barefoot. She turned and the broomstick skirt swayed as the wide-planked oak floor popped and echoed under my approach.

She raised her arms. "Dance with me?"

I smiled and took her hand. "There isn't any music."

"Sure there is." She placed my other arm behind her back and led me in a fanciful waltz, her face tucked against my shoulder. We wheeled around the empty and silent ballroom, and I thought about Virgil White Buffalo and watched my daughter as her head rose and she smiled. After a full sweep of the dance floor, I bent down to kiss the U-shaped scar at her hairline and attempted to keep time to the counting of my blessings.

# 9

"Forty-two charges of manslaughter?"

"At the least." I could picture the California native, born in the high desert up near Edwards Air Force Base, and sheriff of a county that had eighteen times the populace of my entire state. "They brought 'em in through Long Beach, and we got an anonymous tip from down at the municipal pier; container vessel out of Belgrade, Yugoslavia."

"Why Yugoslavia?"

"The Vietnamese don't need a visa to go there. About 40,000 Chinese go through the place every year, and they can blend. Not everybody can tell the difference, like you can."

I took a breath and played at pulling Dog's ear, his head resting on my knee. "What happened?"

"The traffickers had told the illegals on board the container ship to not make any noise and had packing crates of fruit pushed against the walls to help insulate any sound. The assholes closed the air vents, gave them four five-gallon buckets of water, and told them they'd be transferred in a matter of hours."

I'd met Ned at the National Sheriff's Association meeting in Phoenix, where we'd both avoided the social hour by hiding in the hotel bar and lamenting about our grown daughters.

He liked to fly-fish and had made the trek out to the Bighorns twice in the previous eight years. He was a good man, and I could hear the pain telling the story was causing him, but I needed it all. "Didn't happen?"

"No. They loaded the container onto an eighteen-wheeler and headed up to Compton." I waited. "This jaybird, Paquet, parks the truck in a lot behind his apartment and goes in to have lunch, watch a movie and, while he's at it, shoot a little smack. He misjudges the product and ODs, leaving forty-two people in an airtight container on an asphalt parking lot in Southern California in July at 103 degrees."

I slowly exhaled, and Dog looked at me.

"They stripped down to their underwear, tried drinking the juice from the tomatoes, and tried to pry open the vents." After a moment, he continued. "We figure they started panicking after about six hours and began pulling the cases from the walls and pounding on the doors. I guess there was a lot of screaming and shouting, but nobody came. . . ." There was another pause. "Walt, I've never seen anything like it in my life."

"All of them?"

"All but one. I had a freight supervisor from the DOT, Danny Padilla, with me late that afternoon and we were the first ones in after we got the doors open. He said it was strange that it was a produce truck and not refrigerated; then we got the smell. I shined my flashlight, the floor was covered with bodies, none of them moving; like something out of *Night of the Living Dead*. Then I saw this young girl in the back. She was tapping the side of the container and trying to get our attention. She had to crawl over the bodies to get to us."

"What happened to her?"

"Took her to County General, ran her through INS. Then

she got a sponsorship from some group who deals with that sort of thing."

"What was her name?"

"Not Paquet." I listened to him rustling the papers. "Ngo Loi Kim. The poor kid.... Hell, I thought about adopting her myself."

"Did you say last name Kim?"

"Yeah, ring a bell?"

I stared at the blotter on my desk and watched my hand write the name. "An old one. There was a girl I knew in Vietnam with that last name."

The phone was silent for a second. "Walt, you know what the English translation for Kim is, don't you?"

"Smith?"

He chuckled. "That, or Jones."

Ruby appeared in the doorway, but I held up my hand and she disappeared with Dog trotting after her. "What else did you get on this Paquet?"

"Quite a bit, actually. We seized his phone records, computer, and a bunch of other stuff. There was somebody moving a lot of Vietnamese illegals through L.A. County—child porn and some brothels that were in operation down here—and it turned out he was the kahuna on the deal, or so the California state attorney general's office tells me."

"Big investigation?"

"Whopper. They even wanted to know how you were involved in all this."

"Ever heard of this guy, Tran Van Tuyen?"

"Can't say that I have, but I can make some phone calls from this end."

"That would be great if you could. Thanks, Ned." I could hear someone talking to him in the background and waited.

I looked up at the clock on my office wall and figured Vic would be back from lunch any time now. "What about the prostitution charges on the granddaughter?"

"First-timer, and she had the unfortunate, or fortunate—I guess it all depends on your point of view—experience of having her premier customer turn out to be an Orange County plainclothes deputy." It was silent on the line. "It's hard for some of these people to assimilate into a new culture, and if she was from the wrong side of the tracks..."

I stared at the name I had just printed on my desk blotter. "Hey, Ned?"

"Yeah."

"Can you check and see where this Ngo Loi Kim ended up?"

"I can do that." It was silent again, the way it always was when men talked about things they'd rather not. "What makes you think this big Indian fella didn't do it?"

"Just a hunch."

I could hear him sniff out a laugh on the other end. "Sounds like he did a number on you." I didn't say anything. "You want that information faxed or do you guys have e-mail?"

"I am speaking to you now from a push-button phone and hope you are duly impressed." I transferred him to Ruby, and he called me a dirty name just before I pushed a button, and the coast grew silent.

I sat there and watched the aspen leaves quiver in the slight breeze along Clear Creek; the sky was still cloudless, and we continued to need rain. I was getting that feeling, the one like an itch I couldn't quite reach. There was something going on with all of this, something below the surface, and I had a notion that when I found it, it was going to be something pretty simple.

I got up and walked down the hallway to the holding cells

where the big man lay with an arm over his eyes and where Frymire sat snoring in his chair. My dispatcher/receptionist appeared a moment later with Dog and a notepad. Dog leaned against my leg with all the grace of a pet Kodiak, and Ruby lowered her voice upon seeing that everyone else in the room was asleep. "Henry says that Brandon will be back from Rapid City tomorrow, and Lucian called." I looked at her blankly. "It's Tuesday."

I stared at her for a while longer, then shook my head and gestured toward the holding cell and whispered in return. "Vic and Cady are going to Sheridan to pick up Michael at the airport, so it's my night to sit Virgil."

"He said he'd bring the chessboard over here." She crossed something off of her list and then sighed, making a face at the notepad.

"What?"

"More of these garbled e-mails from the school WiFi system marked BPS."

I pretended like I knew what that meant. "Call the school board."

"I am."

"Anything from Saizarbitoria?"

"No."

"Vic?"

"Court duty, and that's the second time you've asked."

"DCI?"

"No."

"Do me a favor?" She looked up at me, the *Webster's Dictionary* illustration of irritated. "I don't have a computer, or I'd do it myself."

"What?"

"Look up this organization, Children of the Dust, and see

what their connection is with Tuyen." I stood there, looking into the holding cell, unable to tell if the big guy was really asleep. "And let me know when that report from LASD comes through?"

"He called."

"Tuyen?"

She nodded. "It was next on my list. He was asking about his granddaughter's body and her personal effects."

"Did you tell him that's a DCI deal?"

"I did."

"How did he respond?"

She looked up. "Not well, but considering the circumstance . . ."

"Did he mention anything about any official documentation that connects him with Ho Thi Paquet?" I could feel the big blue eyes on me.

"No, but he said that he'd be at the Hole in the Wall Motel, room number five."

I returned her gaze. "He changed rooms?"

"He said the television wasn't working in the other one." She continued to watch me. "Walter, the man lost his granddaughter, and he's sitting in a motel room by himself in Powder Junction." Except for the quiet hum of the minifridge and Frymire's snoring, it was silent in the holding area—her voice carried the extra weight of being whispered. "You don't think that Saizarbitoria should go over and check on him?"

"I'll go down in the morning—Cady will be spending time with Michael." My voice sounded a little harsh, like it always did when I was embarrassed. I stood there for a while longer thinking it was probably time to take a Ruby moral sounding. "Can I ask you a question?"

She folded her arms. "Sure."

"Do you think I'm a racist?"

She smiled and then covered it with a hand. "You?"

"Me." I stuffed my hands in my pockets.

She tipped her head up and considered me, and I felt like I should be wearing a lead vest. "You mean because of your experiences in the war?"

"Yep."

"No."

It was a strong response, and one that didn't leave a lot of room for further discussion. I glanced at her unyielding eyes and shrugged, turning to look back as Virgil's arm moved and he looked at the two of us. "Just wondering."

"You do have one prejudice though." I looked back at her again from under the brim of my hat. "You don't care about the living as much as you do the dead."

**Tan Son Nhut, Vietnam: 1968**

I leaned there on the headstone, but before long gravity and alcohol forced me to slip, and my head jarred with the impact of my ass hitting the ground. I sat there looking at my lap for what seemed like a long time before a streak of red light ricocheted off the thousands of white markers that surrounded me.

There was a movement to my right, and I rolled my head in that direction and rested it against the cool surface of the stone. There was somebody there. She was looking into the distance, standing in the graveyard. It took a while for me to find my voice. "Hey..."

The young woman turned. She was Vietnamese and familiar. She raised a hand and reached out to me, the fingers loose but imploring.

I started to move, but all I could do was swipe a gesture toward her. "Can't, sorry...." I took a few breaths to get my stomach settled.

I remembered her from somewhere but couldn't see clearly through the red shooting stars.

Her fingers were still extended; they looked cool somehow, but they were just out of my grasp. I pushed my weight against the stone and raised myself on one arm, catching the edge of the next grave marker with my fingertips, and stood. I felt like a poleaxed Lazarus and wasn't sure if I was going to make it.

I looked around, but she wasn't there. When I saw her again, she was moving lithely through the stones, her fingers trailing on their surfaces, and I'm sure it was because I was drunk, but each time she touched a grave, I heard music.

I moved forward in her wake. She paused and looked back at me. The red lights flickered again, and there was a slight movement at the corner of her mouth like a smile.

"Wait, miss, please. . . ."

She turned slowly as though dancing, with two fingers whispering back toward me as I stomped forward like a sleepwalker, my head floating on my shoulders.

"*Ma* . . ." Her fingers traced the tops of the markers, and she played the headstones like a piano. She played like me, making the same mistakes, using the same dissonant chords.

I could see the waves of sound ringing from the markers like pebbles striking smooth water. The song was melancholy and sad, and I recognized it and started to sing—"A good man is hard to find / you always get the other kind"—I surged forward, but each time I touched a stone, the note it held was silenced until there was no more melody.

The night mist from the random bamboo stalks and irrigation ditches consumed her, the flickering red light was gone, and it was dark. I crashed against a line of markers and fell, lay there for a moment, breathing, and then finally rolled over again and pushed myself up. I looked for her, wavering a little, but there was no one there. I blinked. Nothing. Then I slowly stumbled forward using the now silent tombstones as crutches.

When I got through daydreaming, the sun was booming through the windows, and even with the air-conditioning it was hot. Frymire was still asleep in his chair with his arm in a cast and sling, his face discolored from his brow to down below the jawline.

I figured if Virgil White Buffalo had hit him any harder, it would've killed him.

The giant was standing by the bars now. He was so tall that he could see through the bars and out the window of the common area to the elementary school across the street. There was no formal school in the summer, but the county ran a day care, and the little citizens were scrambling over the playground like barn swallows. I had been a little unnerved when he'd first started doing it, but since reading his file I understood. Whenever the kids came out for recess, he would stand there with the bars in his hands and watch. When the bell rang and the youngsters went indoors, he would sit back down and the dark hair would once again enclose his face.

I thought about how the guys in Alcatraz could hear the New Year's parties going on across the bay in San Francisco, how the prisoners at Folsom could listen to the passing trains, and wondered what they heard in Leavenworth.

I'd spoken to him, everybody had, but he remained incommunicative. He was scheduled for an examination with the attending physicians later in the week, and I was still trying to figure out how we were going to pull that one off without loss of life, limb, or deputy.

"He had a big lunch." I turned to look at Chuck, who was now awake but was still talking a little funny. "We shared a family-style bucket of chicken from the Busy Bee; I had three pieces and he had thirteen, along with all the coleslaw, baked beans, six biscuits, and four cans of iced tea."

We watched the giant as he continued to study the children. "That may be his plan, to eat his way out."

Frymire stood and stretched, wincing a little when his right arm slipped. "I'm going to make a run to the bathroom, if that's okay?"

I threw a thumb up, sending him out and then crossing to the window for a look at Virgil's world. I watched the kids with him and thought about the boy and girl whose photograph was in the plastic child's wallet, the beautiful woman who was tickling them on the bus stop bench, and about the hateful words scrawled on the chalkboard.

I thought about the file.

God.

The bell rang, and we watched the children flow to the open doors of the primary school as if somebody had pulled a stopper and they were all draining away. After the doors closed, I turned and looked up at Virgil. "Don't worry, they'll be back."

He said nothing, lay down, and crossed his arm over his eyes again.

I watched him for a while before the intercom on the holding cell phone buzzed, and I crossed over and picked it up. "DCI on line one."

I punched the required button. "Longmire."

"No drugs."

I nodded and leaned against the wall and tipped my hat back. "Hi, T.J."

"Walt, this young woman was most likely a prostitute."

"The sheriff of L.A. County pulled her sheet. He said it was a first offense."

"Well, she might have been arrested only once, but the physical evidence indicates a number of vocational eccentricities."

I could feel the old cooling in my face and the stillness in my hands. "Such as?"

"She's been used to excess; internal abscess, ulceration, and thickening of the vaginal walls uncommon in a woman this young." It was quiet on the line. "And she's been modified."

"What?"

"At some point in time, she was sewn up to appear virginal, and the breasts are implants; a poor job."

I took a deep breath and let the dregs of emotion trail out with the exhale, as well as the haunting image of the Vietnamese woman lying along the interstate.

**Tan Son Nhut, Vietnam: 1968**

I looked at her body before the air patrolman stepped into my line of sight. She could have been asleep; it was difficult to tell in the gloom of the early morning. The red revolving lights of the air security patrol's jeep had drawn me from the cemetery.

"Whoa there, chief. Where did you come from?"

He looked like one of the guys from Gate 055. I pointed back at the cemetery, immediately regretting the jarring that traveled from the middle of my back to the fracturing pain in my head. "Over there."

He looked past my shoulder. "The graveyard?"

I stepped to the side and almost fell down. "Is that the girl I was following?"

He tried to block me again, but a voice commanded from behind. "Let him by—he's one of us."

I moved forward, and my eyes focused as Baranski looked up at me; he was sitting on the fender of a jeep and was filling out paperwork as the crimson lights flashed across our faces every two seconds. "Well, what'a ya know. It's the First Division's secret weapon."

I stood there weaving, trying to get some idea of what was going on. "What are you guys doing out here?"

Mendoza stood and stepped in close to me and looked up from the second button of my uniform. "More to the point, man, what are you doing out here?"

I didn't like his tone, so I pushed him. I guess I misjudged my own strength, because he fell backward and bounced off the jeep before falling to the ground. I felt one of the security detail grab my arm, but I threw an elbow at him and he went away. Another guy grabbed my other arm, but I pushed his helmet down and slammed him away, too. I stood there for a second and looked down at the woman who was lying on a collection of sandbags in the crumbled remains of the old bunker.

I recognized her and reached down through the pain in my head. She looked as if she'd fallen, so I thought the only thing to do was help her up.

There was a jarring at the back of my head, and suddenly my eyes wouldn't focus. I could hear loud voices coming through in waves—and the world pitched to the left. I slowly started shifting in the same direction so I tried to correct the problem by transferring my weight, but then my legs collapsed from under me like a weak chair.

I hit the ground and could feel people piling on top of me. I lay there and could see the familiar face now, the stillness of the hand stretching to the arm, and finally Mai Kim's eyes, which did not move.

"It's your move, and it's been your damn move for about three minutes now." Lucian had decided to bring the game to the jail.

I looked at the chessboard again and couldn't remember a single tactic. "Sorry."

I was black and, from all appearances, black was in deep trouble. I reached across and hooked a knight in to take one of his pawns, a move he immediately countered by taking my knight with a rook that had been loitering with intent.

"Damn. . . ."

He shook his head, tipped back his hat, and clutched his chin like a fastball he was preparing to deliver high and inside. "What the hell's the matter with you? You havin' flashbacks or what?"

I half smiled. "I guess I am—daydreams at least. . . ."

"This all about that Viet-nam-ese girl from out on the highway?"

"Yep." I started to bring out my queen but thought better of it. "Her grandfather, the fellow I told you about?"

Lucian peered into the holding cell where Virgil sat slumped on the bunk with his back against the wall. He was staring at the space between us. Lucian nodded. "That Van Heflin character."

Jesus.

Lucian's malapropisms were usually reserved for the Indians, but the Vietnamese had given him a whole new venue.

"Tran Van Tuyen." I explained the situation, along with the ambivalence of my feelings toward the man.

Lucian didn't say anything but studied the board. "They ought'a burn down that ol' ghost town, that or ship it off to Laramie, put in a slicky-slide and a carousel up and charge admission."

I opted for a pawn, and he immediately stymied the move with the same rook. I thought about the old Doolittle Raider and his experience in that Japanese prison camp. "You ever think about the war?"

"Mine?" I nodded, and he took a deep breath and let it out slowly. "Not so much as I used to."

We sat there for a while, sitting on the folding chairs and looking at the chessboard balanced on the wastepaper basket between us. Every once in a while a question hangs in your throat waiting to be asked of the exact wrong person, but I asked it anyway. He laughed hard, fighting to catch his breath. "You?"

I nodded.

He shook his head. "You could do with a dose of prejudice."

It was, after all, the response I expected. I brought my queen out.

He sat there looking at the board as I watched him, the smile slowly fading from his face as his ears plugged with the racket of two radial-cylinder Pratt and Whitney engines roaring him into his past. I listened to the ticking of the clock on the wall and waited.

"We ditched just off the Chinese coast, and the impact pushed my copilot, Frank, through the windshield. We had two men that were wounded so bad that they drowned before we could get to shore. A civil patrol pulled Frank and me out and pretty well beat the shit out of us right there on the boat. I guess that was one of the scary parts; there were so many of 'em that I figured they'd just tear us apart. Near as I could make out, an officer in the Kempeitai pulled 'em off us and claimed us as prisoners of Tojo, and they shipped us off to Shanghai in occupied China."

"They got ten of you, right?"

He worked his jaw, moved his other bishop, and then leaned back in his chair and folded his arms. It was like he'd been compacted there by the memories of his war. His sleeves were rolled up on his thin snap-front shirt, and I watched his Adam's apple as it bobbed the top button a few times before he said anything. "They beat the shit out of us on a regular basis with them little bamboo, kendo swords, *shinai*.... Then they finally got around to shipping us off to Tokyo where they interrogated us for a couple more weeks."

He reached down and picked up his bottle of Rainier, turning it so that the label faced him. It was quiet again, and I wasn't sure if he wanted to go any further. "We don't have to talk about this, if you don't want to."

"I'm trying to tell you something, so shut up and listen."

I smiled at him and watched as the jaw worked some more. He sipped his beer and rested it on his prosthetic knee. "They wanted us to sign these statements sayin' we'd committed crimes against Japo citizens—you know, bombed hospitals, strafed schoolchildren, and shit like that." His mahogany eyes came up and met mine. ". . . Which we didn't."

I moved my queen again. "I'd imagine they asked with all due courtesy?"

"Oh, hell yeah." He leaned back in and examined the board. "They started out pretty easy, you know, not lettin' ya sleep for a couple days, no food, hardly any water. . . ." He took another sip of his beer and wiped his mouth on his sleeve. "Get you good and loopy and then they'd start in with the hard stuff." He took a deep breath and held it, finally letting it out with the words. "They had this one trick where they'd tie a wire around your head and twist it with one of them little kendo swords and they finally did it to Frank for so long that his jaw broke."

I studied the hardness in the old man's eyes as they reflected the light like tiny drops of crude oil.

"Any man that ever tells you that he won't break no matter what they do to him?" We both remained silent until his black eyes blinked. "They shipped us back to Shanghai and decided they were gonna have a trial, not a trial in any sense of justice, since they'd already found us guilty, but they needed to determine what kind of punishment was called for. Frank's jaw was infected, and he was pretty weak by that time, so they'd take the two of us in together. We were in this solitary confinement compound at Kiangwan Prison, and they'd come get me and I'd lead Frank up these concrete steps into this shitty little wooden-slat building and they'd scream and yell about us and at us for a couple of hours, us not understandin' a single word; then they'd take us back out and throw us in our cells until they'd come and get us the next day and do it all over again." A tight little curve appeared at the corner of his mouth. "With the obvious limitations of not bein' able to speak or write Japanese, we threw up a brilliant defense, and do you know them sons-of-bitches still found us guilty?"

"Hard to believe."

He moved a rook, and his hand stayed on the little wooden piece. "October 15, 1942. They gave us pencil and paper to write good-bye notes to our family, and I wrote mine to my mother and asked her to please ask Franklin Delano Roosevelt to bomb these little yellow bastards back into the Stone Age with all due speed." He drank some more. "She never got it, so I guess it got lost in the mail. . . ." The short-lived smile faded again.

"What happened?"

He stared at the chessboard and withdrew his hand from the rook. "They put us all in this concrete bunker with these narrow slit openings and come and got the first three. They took 'em outside and made 'em kneel and tied 'em off to these stubby little crosses, and then they just shot 'em in the back of the head, one by one."

I moved my queen in a disinterested fashion. "They let you live."

He watched me move and then nodded. "I guess they felt like they'd made their point, so the rest of us got life imprisonment."

"What happened to Frank?"

"Died in a camp in occupied China." He reached over to straighten the angle of the wooden board on the trashcan. "So, you asked me if I thought about the war much—an' I guess the honest answer would be, yes, I still think about it a lot. At least I think about Frank. . . ."

*"Check."*

I'd been watching Lucian's face but hadn't seen his lips move. I looked down at the board, and it was true that I'd accidentally positioned my queen for an impending and final victory over Lucian's king. I looked up at the same time he did, a questioning expression on his face as he asked, "Did you just say *check*?"

I shook my head. "No, I thought you did."

We both turned and looked at the big Indian, seated on the bunk and pointing a finger as big as a bratwurst toward the chessboard. The resonance of Virgil's voice rattled through the damage in his throat like a very large and singular exhaust.

*"Check."*

# 10

"What the fuck." She sipped her coffee and then added another sugar to the four she'd already dumped in her mug. "He didn't say anything else?"

I kept my volume low, even though she was still talking in full voice. There were a gaggle of tourists at the other end of the Busy Bee counter, and I saw no reason why they should be privy to the finer points of Virgil White Buffalo's life. "No, but he and Lucian played until about three this morning. Prison chess, fast-moving; twenty-seven games, and Lucian only won five."

"That's why the old pervert's asleep on the floor; he's gathering his strength for another assault." I nodded and took a sip of my own coffee; Dorothy refilled my mug as it touched the counter.

The proprietor of the café put the pot back on the warmer and parked herself within easy ear reach. "Michael make it in okay?"

I nodded. "Yep. Cady picked him up last night, and I haven't heard from them since."

She studied me, then Vic, and then changed the subject. "Any word from up on the Rez?"

Dorothy generally knew more of what was going on in the county than I did, so I figured it wouldn't hurt to have her in on this part of the conversation. "Henry left a message that he and Brandon White Buffalo would be back from South Dakota this morning with a special guest."

They both looked at me, but Vic was the first to respond. "A what?"

"A special guest." I shrugged. "It's Henry."

Vic slipped her hair behind an ear and palmed her chin; evidently, it was a good hair day. "And . . . ?"

"And what?"

My deputy spoke through her muffling hand, the only filter she had. "You said you read the report at the VA over in Sheridan. So, what's the story on the jolly red giant?"

I glanced up at the chief cook and bottle washer. "How's the usual coming?"

She glanced at the manila envelope resting on the counter between Vic and me and then studied my face. "Does this mean you're dismissing me?"

I sighed. "I'm just not so sure that you're going to want to hear all of this."

She nodded and smiled. "Well, it's good enough for me that you'd rather I didn't." She picked up both coffee pots, decaf and regular, from the warmers and retreated toward the tourists. "How are you folks doing?"

I took a deep breath and turned to my undersheriff. "You want the whole dog-and-pony show?" I pushed my elbows on the counter and looked out the doorway toward Clear Creek. Dorothy had the glass door propped open, and I was enjoying the cool from the screen door at my back before the heat of the day. "Virgil was misdiagnosed as mentally deficient by Big Horn County Health because of a speech impediment, but he graduated from Lodge Grass High School in '68 anyway and got culled into Project 100,000."

"What was that?"

"It was supposedly a program for social uplift. Every year, a percentage that scored at the bottom of the military aptitude test were inducted and then shipped off to Vietnam. Some uplift."

I held my mug there, a little away from my mouth. I thought about the file and tried to remember the details. "He showed an aptitude for the art of war and got transferred to the 101st Airborne Division's reconnaissance patrol. They were up in the central highlands north of Dak To looking for VC alongside this river, and they found them. . . ." I sipped my coffee. "About two regiments of 'em."

I placed my mug down and looked at her. "Small-arms fire pinned them down for about eight hours, thirteen dead and twenty-three wounded. Air support finally arrived, and they started driving the North Vietnamese back enough for them to medevac the wounded out with a T-bar." She started to raise her hand like she was in school. "It's a harness and winch system dropped about a hundred feet from a helicopter."

I leaned in, studying the collection of porcelain, plastic, glass, and wooden bees along the shelf above the range hood. "The VC saw that everybody's concentrating on getting the wounded out, so they mounted a counteroffensive. The rest of the platoon hugged dirt and prayed for more support and suddenly this giant came up out of the ditch beside the road and started moving up and down the line firing his 16 in single shots, moving from the high spots to the low, each shot taking out a hostile as he went, firing with absolute purpose and never saying a word."

"Fuck me."

"The report says he went through three clips." I took a breath and continued. "There were less than twenty men left in the platoon, but the battalion commander, safe in one of the helicopters, radioed back for them to attack again and believe it or not, they did. This Lieutenant Shields raised his rifle arm up like he's in some bad Audie Murphy movie and screamed, 'Follow me.' The whole platoon, including Virgil, broke rank and followed this lieutenant straight into an ambush, where six seconds later, twelve more were dead, three were critically wounded, and they're left with only three effectives. . . ."

"One of them being Virgil White Buffalo."

I nodded at the marbled surface of the Formica counter. "The wounded were stuck in this gully, where Virgil made all three trips and dragged each one of them back to the original landing zone, including the lieutenant, who got on the horn and called for extraction but was told by this colonel in the helicopter that they needed to charge this machine gun nest to their right instead."

She ran her fingers through her hair and looked at me in disbelief. "Get the fuck out of here."

"This lieutenant started to get up."

"No way."

"And Virgil smacked him alongside the head with the butt of his M16, knocking him out cold." I watched as she bit her lip to keep from laughing. "Then, just for good measure, Virgil rolled over and threw a few rounds at the battalion commander's helicopter."

She laughed, and the tourists looked at us.

"The colonel said, 'I've got incoming, I've got incoming . . .' and flew off."

I nudged the handle on my mug and noticed the little half-ring on the counter that it left behind. "So there they were without any air support or EVAC, and this lieutenant, Tim Shields, the one that wrote up the report, came to and leaned over to Virgil to say, 'We are going to die.' Virgil told him that they could slip down in the river; that it's only about knee-deep with a four-foot berm on either side so that they could retreat. This lieutenant told Virgil that's a good idea and gave him the M60 and ordered him to provide rear guard as the rest of them retreated a little farther down the river, where they'll wait."

She groaned.

"They left him. So there he sat, alone, with a half-empty M60 machine gun and the better part of a North Vietnamese regiment on the way. The shooting began, and he returned fire and started working his way back down the river for the next three hours, alternately dealing with the mosquitoes, leeches, and the North Vietnamese. He got to an embankment that led to a roadway, where he tossed the empty M60 into the river, pulled out his sidearm, and started jogging into the night. Three clicks down the road, he ran into a patrol."

"Ours?"

I nodded. "Yes."

"Thank God."

"They called in an EVAC, and an hour later Virgil was standing tall in front of the same lieutenant and battalion commander, who were screaming at him for getting lost and losing the M60. Virgil, after enduring sixteen hours of close combat, most of it single-handed, told them to stop yelling at him and that he's going to go take a nap. The lieutenant grabbed Virgil's arm, and Virgil swung around and punched him in the face, breaking his nose and driving the bone shards into his brain, which killed him instantly."

She didn't move. "Manslaughter, at worst."

I looked out the windows at the flickering leaves alternating their light and dark sides. "Not in this man's army. The colonel pushed and got a premeditated murder charge stemming from Virgil having struck his commanding officer while under fire in the field. Nobody stepped forward to say anything, and Virgil gets convicted of second-degree murder with a twenty-two-year hard-labor sentence in Leavenworth."

Vic leaned in. "Twenty-two years?"

"With good behavior, he got out in seventeen." I tapped the manila envelope that I had put on the counter. "I had Ruby check the database and she came up with the rest." I opened the folder and read the small print on the faxed sheets. "On the walk home . . ."

"From Leavenworth, Kansas?"

I nodded. "He was picked up by the Troop E highway patrol and told that he can't hitchhike on the interstate. They dropped him off just outside of Abilene where he got a ride from a fellow by the name of Peter Moore and a young girl, Betty Coleman, who said that they're on their way from East St. Louis and could give him a lift as far as Rapid City. They got up near North Platte, Nebraska, that night, where this Moore says he's tired. Virgil offered to drive, but this guy said that they'll just sleep in the car, the two of them in the front and Virgil in the back. The next morning, Peter Moore was found with his head caved in, and Betty Coleman was picked up by the North Platte Police Department and swore that Virgil did it."

"Drugs?"

I nodded. "Cocaine found on Betty's person and in Peter Moore's bloodstream. Virgil got picked up by the Nebraska Highway Patrol and had one wicked-looking blunt trauma and skull fracture."

"That would explain the scar."

"Virgil stated that Moore attacked him in the night with a claw hammer and that he fought the guy off, but that Moore was alive when he left with Betty Coleman."

"They test Virgil?"

"No, but with an eyewitness and Virgil's record..."

"They print the hammer?"

I sipped my coffee. "Missing."

"She did it, finished this Moore guy off after Virgil split, and then took the drugs."

"Yep, but she was a petite little blonde, and Virgil was a seven-foot Indian, dishonorably discharged and a convicted murderer." I set my empty mug back on the counter. "Ten to twelve."

Dorothy sidled over and motioned with the regular coffee; she knew that the Absaroka County Sheriff's Department ran on heavy fuel. "Can I interrupt long enough for a refill?"

We both slid our mugs forward, and I smiled up at her. "How's the usual coming?"

She studied me some more and then turned toward the grill.

I looked down at the file and, once again, lowered my voice. "The prison psychologist, this Jim McKee at the Nebraska State Pen, got the Native American Defense League to check Virgil's records and neither of them thought he did it, so they started an investigation. Turned out Peter Moore had a record as long as my arm, and they found that there was a warrant on a homicide that occurred back in East St. Louis six weeks before."

She leaned in closer, and I could see the faded freckles at the base of her throat. "Don't spoil it for me. Some other ass-clown was beat to death with a hammer?"

I swallowed, this time without the assistance of coffee. "You got it. The NADL fought the good fight, but Betty Coleman stuck to her story even after being sentenced to fourteen months for possession, after which she commited suicide." I flipped the folder shut. "Virgil did ten, with good behavior, and went to the VA when he got out." I sighed. "Where he just disappeared. No tax records, DMV, nothing. I asked Quincy, but he says it happens a lot with the Indians—they just disappear into the Rez and are never heard from again."

"Seventeen and ten..." She crossed her arms and turned her stool toward me. "You think he's been living under the highway for nine years?"

"I don't know."

Dorothy turned back and put two Denver omelets in front of us. I considered my plate. "This the usual?"

She wrote up a check for the tourists and walked away without looking at me. "Usually."

I am a big man, but with current company I was feeling a little measly. I'm maybe an inch taller than Henry, but the other two men standing in my reception area barely missed hitting their heads on the trim above the entryway as they came up the steps.

The first giant leaned over to pull me in for a one-arm hug, for which I was grateful, since I'd seen Brandon White Buffalo lift Henry Standing Bear with both arms and hold him off the ground till the Bear's face had gone redder. "Lawman, how are you?"

"Still stuck with myself."

The other giant, and Henry's special guest, was maybe in his forties and looked strangely familiar. I smiled and extended my hand. "Walt Longmire; have we met?"

"Eli...Eli White Buffalo." He shook my hand and then stepped back. His hands were large and soft, but capable. "No, we haven't."

He was perhaps a shade shorter than Brandon, but not by much, and wore a freshly starched white dress shirt, jeans with a cowboy crease, a hand-tooled belt with a large turquoise belt buckle, and black alligator boots. His glossy black hair was pulled back in a single ponytail that was held with an elaborate silver and turquoise clasp.

Artist; had to be.

Eli seemed a little nervous, placed his hands in his back pockets, and then glanced toward Ruby, who sat quietly watching the two giants from behind the reception desk. Dog was with her; he stared at us, seemingly noncommittal. Vic studied both men from her perch on Ruby's desk.

Brandon placed a hand on my shoulder, covering it. "You think you have some of my family, lawman?"

"It's possible."

He smiled the great smile and inclined his head. "Let's go see?"

They were on game nine for the morning and, from the look on Lucian's face, I assumed he had yet to beat the colossus. I walked over to the board. "You win one yet?"

He muttered and pulled his unlit pipe from his mouth. "No, and I'm about to get my ass kicked again." He looked at his king on the border, which was completely surrounded by other pieces and a smothered mate. He kept his finger on the black sovereign, finally tipping him over.

The old sheriff turned and looked at the collected force, including the gigantic Indians. "Jesus, just what he needs—reinforcements."

I scooped up the board and transferred it to the counter of the kitchenette. I noticed that Eli remained near the doorway and around the corner with Vic. Lucian stood to the side, but his chair remained in front of the cell. Brandon ignored it and stood in front of the bars. He looked down at Virgil, who was still seated on the bunk. *"Na-ho e-ho ohtse."*

The giant in the cell remained silent, lowering the hand that had held his hair back, the hair once again covering his face and both enormous hands hanging limp over his knees.

Brandon stooped down and looked through the bars. He was speaking Cheyenne. *"Ne-tsehese-nestse-he?"*

Virgil breathed in deeply and let out with a sigh, still saying nothing.

Brandon leaned in and placed a hand on the bars, smoothly shifting from Cheyenne to Lakota. *"Nituwe hwo?"*

The giant's head rose to look at Brandon, but he still said nothing.

*"Tokiya yaunhan hwo?"* Still nothing. *"Taku eniciyapi hwo?"*

The voice erupted, hoarse from no practice, and he spoke in a deep bass. *"Tatankaska . . ."*

Brandon touched his chest and smiled. *"Lila Tatankaska."*

Virgil's head inclined, and he leaned forward, just a little. *"Niyate kin tanyan icage. . . . Canhanp hanska etan maku wo-ptecela onzoge?"*

Brandon choked out a laugh, finally turning to look at us. "This is my uncle, who used to call me Begs-for-Candy-in-Short-Pants." His eyes strayed from Henry and me, and he looked toward Eli, motioning him to step forward so that he could introduce him as he stood and spoke to Virgil again, but this time in Crow. "*Hená de dalockbajak*, Eli?"

As Eli stepped around the corner, Virgil slowly rose, standing almost a full head above the other two. Eli stepped to the bars and looked up into the face of the giant and, to our utter amazement, he spit.

I've been spit on—it's a part of law enforcement that you never get used to, but it hardly ever comes completely unexpectedly. This did, and it was a mouthful.

I stepped forward and put a hand on his shoulder. "Hey, there's no need . . ."

He shrugged me off and lunged at the bars where he got a hold of Virgil's hair and pulled his face into the metal. Virgil offered no resistance, but Brandon grabbed Eli's other arm and pulled it, as the younger man yanked Virgil's head into the bars again. He screamed at him. *"Vasica! Tuktetanhan yau hwo?! Tokel oniglakin kta hwo?! Taku ehe kin, ecel ecanu sni!"*

With Henry and Lucian's help, we got Eli away, but the effort threw all of us off balance and onto the floor in an agitated version of Twister. Eli was the first to stand, and he spit on Virgil again, whose face was bleeding from a busted lip.

Eli stopped as we all scrambled to get up and made a dismissive gesture. *"Le tuwa ta sunka hwo?!"* He slammed his fists against the bars, then turned and strode out of the room and down the hallway. He pushed Vic back as he went. I was the first of the pile to the door and loped after Vic down the hall after Eli.

We found him on the hardwood floor at the bottom of the stairs in a reverse wristlock with Tran Van Tuyen's knee lodged at the small of the Indian's back. Dog was barking from behind Ruby's desk, and she stood with her open mouth covered with her hand.

I looked at the man in the black leather jacket and black slacks, who looked particularly small in comparison with Eli White Buffalo. He smiled a flat smile up at me. "Is this the man who killed my granddaughter?"

I shook my head. "No, it isn't."

The sickly smile faded, and his eyes turned back to the large man he'd incapacitated. "Then, perhaps, I should let him go?"

**Tan Son Nhut, Vietnam: 1968**

Baranski and Mendoza stood away from the bars and watched me impassively. "Why don't you tell us what you were doing out there near the old fort with a dead girl?"

I could feel a cooling in my face, and my hands steadied. The security police had put a pretty good set of lumps on my head and evidently somebody had stood on my hand while they'd cuffed me, because most of the skin on the back of my fingers was gone. There was a metal desk by the doorway leading to the brig, where I was being held. "Let me out of here."

Mendoza sat on the edge of the desk and thumbed the crease in his uniform pants. "Near as we can tell, you left the lounge a little after Mai Kim, and the APs at Gate 055 said you came by there."

"Open. This. Damn. Door." My eyes stayed on them as they looked at each other.

"They said you weren't alone, man."

"Now."

Mendoza sighed and reached behind him and picked up my sidearm, wrapped in the Sam Browne holster, and handed a large ring of keys to Baranski. "The major is getting your papers together; looks like you're headed back, pronto."

I didn't say anything but just stood there looking at them with my hands chiseled into fists; Baranski shook his head and stepped forward, unlocking the bars and stepping back and out of the way as I pushed the cell door open. They followed me out, down the hallway, and through the front door of the security headquarters onto the sunny streets of Tan Son Nhut's miniature city. Mendoza hung back but handed my holstered Colt to Baranski, who quickened his pace to pull up beside me.

"The CO says they would have shipped your ass out today, but with the heightened security and the holiday, they couldn't make arrangements to transport you back to BHQ."

The CID man reached up and grabbed my shoulder, but I slapped his arm away and pulled up short. I grabbed him by the front of his shirt and leveraged him across the dirt street and into a corrugated sheet-metal wall. Mendoza grabbed my arm, but I elbowed him and pushed him out of the way.

I turned back to Baranski and, without my even having time to notice, he had pushed the blunt barrel of my sidearm under my chin. He held it there. He smiled, and I heard the unmistakable sound of the .45 being cocked.

Neither of us blinked. "You better pull that trigger, 'cause that's the only way you're gonna stop me."

I saw his eyes shift, and we both heard the safeties go off of more than one M16, behind me and to the right. A voice I didn't know spoke in a steady and loud tone. "We got a problem here, Lieutenant?"

Baranski's eyes returned to mine and widened just a little. I slowly released him. I could see four security airmen from the 377th, all of them with their automatic weapons trained on my right eye.

Baranski spoke quickly. "Look, there's no need."

One of the security detachment, a captain, swiveled the barrel of his rifle toward the CID man. "You wanna secure that weapon, sir?"

Baranski lowered the .45 just a bit and then carefully used both hands to aim the barrel at the dirt and lowered the hammer, and slowly glided the Colt back into my loose holster, which was wound around his fist. "We're clear."

The airmen lowered their M16s to their hips, still keeping them generally pointed in our direction. The captain was a goofy-looking guy with eyebrows and a smile that sloped down at the sides of his face. "Not too smart having a riot just outside of security headquarters, sir."

Mendoza was still sitting on the ground, but Baranski straightened his collar, smoothed the front of his uniform, and tucked my .45 under his arm. "No riot, Captain—just a little interservice miscommunication."

The captain continued to study me from under his helmet, and it was like a voice coming from a cave. I got the feeling most of his brains were down in his neck, and he probably had the same thoughts about me. "You the Marine who broke the nose on one of my men last night?"

My breath gummed up my throat, but I still got it out. "Coincidentally." I sounded sarcastic, maybe even more than I wanted to.

He watched me and then nodded. "Well, why don't we just take this little party back inside."

"There's no need for that, Captain." Baranski took a step forward and flipped out his ID. "We're with security, too." The captain studied the Central Intelligence Detachment card and badge, looked at Baranski, then at me. He took a step back and fully lowered his weapon. They all did.

"All right, sir."

Baranski smiled, showing the gaps in his front teeth, and stuffed his wallet back in his pants. "Thanks, Cap. I owe you one."

The security detachment backed away from us and continued down the street. Baranski spoke in a soft, friendly voice and continued to smile as the captain glanced back at us one last time. "That's right, keep going, you stupid motherfuckers." One final wave, and he turned to look at me.

I met his eye and thought about how calm he'd been with my pistol under my chin. "I'm not leaving until I find out who killed her." He shook his head and bumped up a smoke from the Camels in his breast pocket. He bit the cigarette and extended the pack to me. "I don't smoke."

He flipped open his Zippo and lit up with a deep inhale, the streams of smoke continuing into his nostrils as he pulled the cigarette away from his mouth. "Maybe you should—it might help calm you down."

"I was hoping that you could assist me in making the arrangements for my granddaughter's body to be transported once it's released?" Tuyen sat in the chair opposite my desk and held the cup of coffee Ruby had given him.

"Certainly."

Tran Van Tuyen was speaking into the mug and had yet to look up. "You may find this strange, but I was actually thinking of a cremation and scattering her ashes near the place she died."

I was a little surprised. "You don't want to take her back to California?"

His head shook slightly. "I don't think her spirit was ever happy there, and I was thinking that she could, perhaps, find peace here."

I nodded and tipped the brim of my hat, which was resting crown down on my desk. I watched as it turned slightly to the left. "Well, with a situation like this, it may be a while before they release Ho Thi, so you'll have a bit of time to think about that." There was no immediate response, and I hoped that he was coming to terms with the loss. "It's a standard procedure with an open homicide investigation. We don't want to miss anything that might lead us to apprehending the individual responsible."

"Yes. I understand."

He didn't say anything else, so I waited. I'd sacrificed lunch with Vic, who had joined Cady and Michael. The Cheyenne Nation and the Crow contingency were having a cooling-off period out on the bench beside the walkway leading to the courthouse. I had told them to wait, that I'd be out as soon as I was through with Tuyen.

I had gotten a washcloth for Virgil, run it under some hot water, and handed it to him. We still had a doctor's examination to contend with, and I wanted to get a closer look at the big man's face, but it was all going to have to wait until I was finished with the dead woman's grandfather.

Tuyen had followed me back to my office, and here we sat. "That was pretty slick out there." His head rose, and he looked at me blankly. "With Eli?"

There was a sudden look of realization, and he sighed a quick laugh. "It is difficult to forget, once you have been properly trained."

"Yep."

After a moment, he spoke again. "Do you think about the war a great deal, Sheriff?"

I touched the brim of my hat with a forefinger in an attempt to straighten it and was relieved that someone else was asking the question. "A lot more, lately, it seems."

"Because of my granddaughter?"

I looked up at him. "Yep, I believe so."

He stood and put the untouched cup of coffee on the corner of my desk, and I thought about offering him tea next time. "Would it be possible for me to see my granddaughter's things?"

It was the third time he'd asked and DCI had returned some of the items, so I nodded and motioned for him to follow me to the basement to our personal belongings cabinets.

Once there, I opened the large drawer and placed the small collection of items on the counter—the purse, the change, the French novel, the scarf, and the keys. The photograph of Mai

Kim and me was being held, along with her clothes and herself. "What would you like to do about the car?"

He looked at the small group of objects. "Excuse me?"

"The car she was driving; I was wondering what you'd like to have done with it?"

"I may want to look at it."

I wondered why. "I can make arrangements for it to be shipped back up here from Cheyenne, if you want."

"Yes, thank you." I waited as he looked at the items on the counter. "And the computer?"

"Excuse me?"

He cleared his throat. "Ho Thi had a computer of mine. It was not with her?"

"No." I studied him, as he continued to look at her things. "Is there something wrong?"

He took a deep breath. "It doesn't seem like a great deal . . . for a lifetime, does it?"

I pushed open the door and walked out to the war council. "How's it going?"

Eli sat on the far side of the bench, his elbows on his knees, and looked as though he was memorizing the cracks in the sidewalk. Brandon stood with his thumbs hitched in the back pockets of his jeans, and Henry watched the side of Eli's face. The Cheyenne Nation turned and looked up at me. "This may take a while."

I beat a slow retreat back to my office. Ruby was holding her phone up to me. "Saizarbitoria."

I came inside and sat on her desk, took the receiver, and reached down to pet Dog. "What's up, Sancho?"

"Jim Craft wants to know if you have any idea how many

credit cards the Flying J truck stop processes in a twenty-four-hour period."

I ruffled Dog's ear, and he mouthed my hand with his big teeth. "Tell him I'll buy him lunch next time I'm through Casper." I wiped the slobber off on my jeans. "What've you got?"

"The manager says that there was a card left at the counter and that they contacted the company, who in turn contacted Tuyen."

"Well, it was worth a try."

"Boss, there's something else. . . ."

His tone froze me. "What?"

"The manager says that he remembered the incident because he was running an inventory that night and got a glimpse of the car as it pulled away."

"Yep?"

"He said the card came back declined and reported stolen, so the woman working the register called it in and they told her to confiscate it. She did and got the manager as the girl ran out of the store with two bottles of water and a large bag of chips. The manager said he saw the suspect jump in and back into a concrete spacer before hitting the accelerator and tearing out onto I-25 headed north."

It was silent on the line, and I noticed I wasn't breathing.

"Walt... he said there were two girls in the car."

# 11

Henry rode with me as we headed south to Powder Junction in an attempt to overtake Tuyen's Land Rover, but we hadn't seen it so far. He looked at a nondescript section of the frontage road, just off I-25. "Who died there?"

Most people didn't like riding with me, and most of my friends and family had learned not to ask when my eyes unfocused on some lonely stretch of prairie or on a desolate part of the road. "Those three kids that turned over that Camaro on the way back up from the Powder Junction Rodeo back in '98."

"Have I ever told you how depressing it is to ride in this county with you?"

I switched on the emergency lights and coaxed the Bullet up past eighty-five. "Well, you never look at the place the same way."

He nodded. "Where is Vic?"

I made a face. "What's that got to do with anything?" He didn't answer, and I glanced at the clock on the radio of my truck. "With Cady and Michael, eating lunch."

He adjusted his signature Fort Smith Big Lip Carp Tournament ball cap and carefully placed his thick ponytail through the adjustable strap. "At the risk of getting my head bitten off, I will ask again. How is that going?"

I watched the road, then readjusted in my seat and propped an elbow on the armrest. "I don't know." I was the picture of annoyance and uncertainty.

The Bear laughed. "You do not know?"

I sighed. "We . . . When we . . . When we were back in Philadelphia?"

"Yes."

"We got really close."

"Yes."

"But that was a different context and now we're back home and it's different."

"Yes."

I started to speak, then stopped, waited another moment, and then continued. "What happened back there between the two of us—I'm not so sure it should've happened. Not so much me, but her." I turned up the air-conditioning as it seemed to be growing even hotter in the cab. Pretty soon, I was going to run out of knobs to play with; maybe it was a family trait. "I just think that she might've done it because she felt sorry for me."

He stared at the side of my face. "There are a multitude of reasons why she might have instigated the . . . intimacy between the two of you. A sense of mortality connected with Cady's accident, strangers in a strange land . . ."

"She was born there."

He stuck out a hand to silence me. "Let me finish?"

"Sorry."

"Perhaps even a competitive response to her mother, but the one I would be willing to believe the most readily is that she deeply cares for you. Not about you, but for you, and there is a difference." He turned back toward the windshield. "That, or it was a mercy fuck." I turned and looked at him, and he shrugged. "To use her terminology." The Bear drummed his long fingers on the dash and changed the subject. "So, you think Tuyen knows something?"

I stared at the road. "I'm not talking to you anymore."

"I was joking."

"It wasn't funny."

He gazed at the rolling prairie. "It was a little funny."

We both escaped into our separate silences and watched the golden-brown grass sweep patterns in the heated wind. We needed rain, soon, or all of Absaroka County would be a tinderbox.

I knew full well that I'd never outlast him, so I started talking again, anxious to pick up another conversational thread. "I'm thinking Tuyen might know if Ho Thi had any friends, or if anyone else is missing." We passed a wide load, carrying two halves of a modular home, and navigated back into the right-hand lane. "I've got calls into the Los Angeles and Orange County Sheriff's Departments to see if they can get me anything, but Tuyen is here and he might be useful."

Henry watched the road. "Did the manager at the Flying J say that the girl was Asian?"

"Jim said the manager was unsure, but that they were both female and had long dark hair."

He shrugged. "Possibly Native . . ."

"Wouldn't be the first time an Indian girl was hitchhiking up I-25, but I'm not betting on it."

"Why do you want this young woman, if she exists, to be Vietnamese?"

I glanced at him. "It would mean that somebody's alive

who knows what's going on." My eyes returned to the road. "Why do you ask that question?"

He continued studying me. "I sometimes wonder if you are trying to come to terms with two mysteries almost four decades apart."

I drove and stared at another patch of the highway where more lives had come to an abrupt halt. I remembered who they were, their names, their family, their friends; these dead weren't the ones I worried about—there were people who would remember them. It was the ones who had died truly alone who concerned me most. If no one remembered them, were they ever really here? I took a deep breath and forced my eyes back to the road. "Ruby says I care about dead people more than the living."

Henry said nothing.

**Tan Son Nhut, Vietnam: 1968**

I wasn't letting him go, and there wasn't anybody else in the Boy-Howdy Beau-Coups Good Times Lounge to save him.

They had all run away.

My hand fit well around his throat, and I was surprised at how little effort it took to hold Le Khang against the wall, a good foot and a half off the floor. "I don't like those answers...."

He squeaked, which I took as an answer of sorts, so I lowered his feet to the plywood. He tried to yank away, but I still had him pinned pretty well. "She no say!"

I started lifting him again, but he shook his head so I put him back down. "She go with customer!"

"Who?"

"No say..." I tightened my hold, but he slapped at my arm and I eased off. "Air force personnel, fly-boy."

"Gimme a name."

"No name." I shrugged and started to pick him up again. "Thunderchief, F-105! He fly F-105 name Jumpin' Jolene!"

I let go of his throat and then threw an index finger in his face. "This better be the straight dope, because if it's not—I'm gonna be back, and brother you do not want that." Mendoza and Baranski stepped aside as I passed between them, and they followed behind me as I headed for Gate 055.

I could hear Baranski's voice over my shoulder. "Look, it's just a question of time before you get shipped off to the Long Bin stockade if you keep..." He caught up and pushed me a little to the side with a shove to my shoulder, and I stopped and squared up to him. "Whoa, whoa... We're not going to do that again." He held his hands up at me. "Just stop for a second, all right?" I waited. "It's one thing if you wanna brace the Slopes or the wing wipers, but you go over to the flight line and start leaning on air force personnel, they will send you back to Chu Lai if they have to do it in a rickshaw."

I stood there in the dirt street and felt the heat waves in my lungs. I was tired, hungover, and pissed, but even with my limited experience in law enforcement, I knew he was right.

Baranski smiled a white and wicked grin, and Mendoza came around to stand next to him, but I noticed they both stayed a good arm's reach away. "You follow us, but you don't do anything and you don't say anything. Got it?"

I followed them back to security headquarters, where we commandeered one of the jeeps. We set out with the two of them in the front and me in the back.

We drove along the flight line on the tarmac where the Imperata grass scrapped the undercarriage and the mud puddles splashed khaki on the jeep's flanks—past the debris and broken fuselages of damaged aircraft. We went by large Quonset hangars, which reminded me of surplus ones that were used by ranchers back in Wyoming. The sight made me homesick and started me thinking about blondes, but I could feel other things overtaking my passions and my hands stilled.

At the flight barracks, I got a clearer view of how the other half lived. On an air force base, pilots are royalty, and fighter pilots are kings.

"He leaves the base all the time." The duty sergeant didn't know where Brian Teaberry was and didn't even look up when we came in. "He's not scheduled for duty until 0800 tomorrow morning."

Baranski leaned on the counter and looked at the top of the sergeant's head. He was an embattled Korean War veteran and was not likely to be overly impressed with our homicide investigation. "This concerns a homicide investigation."

The overworked man finally looked up from the forms he was stapling. "So?" I came around and rested an arm on the corner of the counter as he put the stapler down. "Look, big man, I don't know where he is."

I stapled his right earlobe to his neck.

"Damn it!"

I stapled his left earlobe to his neck.

"Damn it, God... Wait a minute! Christ, get him off me!"

The duty sergeant said that Teaberry was over at passenger service awaiting the arrival of his new fiancée, who was an administrative assistant coming up from Saigon for a visit, and that he was probably playing cards.

There were dark blue buses lined up out front, waiting for passengers from flights in, along with a great number of air force personnel, who were sitting on the ground waiting for both flights in and flights out. I read the two-language sign at the entrance, CLEAR WEAPONS BEFORE ENTERING.

"Stay in the jeep, man."

I looked up and Mendoza motioned to me, like you would a dog. *Stay.*

They were inside for only a few minutes, then returned, fired up the utility vehicle, and pulled us around back to the other side of a wire and lath fence where there was an officers' waiting area. They got out of the jeep, and the Texican motioned to me again to stay put.

I sat there and watched as they went through a gate to our left and crossed the yard where three captains and a first lieutenant were playing cards under a makeshift awning. A few C-123s were warming up on the tarmac only a couple of hundred feet away, the racket from their engines literally shaking the ground.

Baranski and Mendoza ambled up to the card players, and I watched above the noise as they introduced themselves and made some small talk to the seated men. A sizable fellow with sandy hair and a vulpine-looking mustache said something to Mendoza.

Teaberry.

Mendoza said something back. Teaberry said something to both Mendoza and Baranski. Baranski said something to Teaberry who said something again, at which the other men at the table laughed. Mendoza nodded, said something, and then gestured toward me. *Come.*

I stood up.

Teaberry glanced at me and then said something else to the other card players, who laughed. Mendoza smiled and gestured again. *Sic 'em.*

I got out of the jeep.

Teaberry started to stand, but Mendoza pushed him back in his metal folding chair.

I tore the gate off the fence as I entered.

The other two captains and the first lieutenant threw their cards down and disappeared into the passenger service building. Teaberry yanked away from Mendoza and ran to the far side of the yard.

I caught Teaberry at the fence.

He said he didn't know anything about Mai Kim. Mendoza and

Baranski grabbed me, but I held on to Teaberry and told him he was a liar and that if he didn't tell me everything I wanted to know, I was going to strangle him with his own intestines. Teaberry said something, but it wasn't particularly what I wanted to hear, so I threw him into the fence.

Mendoza wrapped his arms around my head and Baranski grabbed my knees, but I was still able to get Teaberry as he tried to scramble away. I fell on him, and the fence collapsed.

Teaberry said that Hollywood Hoang was the one who had set him up, and that for a nominal fee of ten bucks Mai Kim had taken the captain to a sandbag bunker between Gate 055 and Hotel California, where they had had sex, which had been invigorating without being overly lengthy. Then he walked her back to Gate 055, where they parted company. Teaberry said she went toward the Boy-Howdy Beau-Coups Good Times Lounge at about 1:00 A.M. and that that was the last time he'd seen her. The security detail at the gate could vouch for his story.

I let go of him, and Mendoza and Baranski let go of me.

"What's the story on Eli?"

He sighed and pulled the seat belt out from his chest with a thumb. "Blooding the medicine . . ." He released the belt and turned his head but continued watching the road.

I vaguely knew about most of the Cheyenne talismans. "The medicine arrows?"

He took a deep breath. "There are three."

"Arrows?"

"Talismans; the Medicine Arrows, the Sacred Cap, and the Autumn Count are all Cheyenne. I am not sure about the Crow."

"Autumn Count. Is that the one you mentioned in Philadelphia?"

"Yes. The *Tonoeva Wowapi* is the only one I have never seen. It is a sacred hide with many symbols that reveals the history of the people and, if read correctly, can tell the future. It is said that this is the smallest of the medicines it possesses."

These were things that Henry Standing Bear did not take lightly, so I drove silently, waiting for the rest of the explanation. The jaw muscles in his face tightened, but he said nothing, the dark of his eyes reflecting the glare from the windshield. "My half-brother, Lee, has seen it. . . ."

I was curious, not only about the artifact but also about Lee, whom he rarely mentioned. I knew he had just seen him on his way back from Philadelphia, but I hesitated on the personal front, familiar with the frontier between red and white, where there was no pink. "What about the Sacred Cap?"

He seemed pleased to leave the subject of the Autumn Count and Lee. "Matriarchal in nature, the *Issiwun* typifies the buffalo and harvest."

"And the arrows?"

His eyes lowered and stared at the space in the floorboards between us. "Four stone-headed arrows wrapped in a coyote skin. I was a small child and brought by my father to a lodge where they were revealed to me; I remember that my mother waited outside and was not allowed to look upon them. Periodically they are renewed with fresh sinew and feathers. They are kept, like the other items, by an individual who holds the office for life or until it is voluntarily relinquished."

"So, let me guess, the White Buffalo were keepers of the arrows?"

"No, the keeper of the arrows must be full-blood, and to my knowledge the arrows are with the Southern Cheyenne in Oklahoma."

"What about the Sacred Cap?"

He breathed a short laugh. "The cap is adorned with a Crow scalp; it is unlikely that it would be entrusted to a Crow warrior." His face stiffened, and I knew he was thinking of his brother Lee. "The Autumn Count's location is unknown, so the medicine that Eli spoke of must be the medicine bundle that was found with Virgil."

"The one he had around his neck?"

"Yes." He stood. "It would appear that Eli feels his father's actions have tainted his stewardship of a holy item."

"Hence *blooding the medicine*?"

His face was still. "Eli has no doubt that his father has committed these acts."

I sighed. "That's unfortunate."

"Yes."

I thought about the photograph of the boy. "So, Eli is Virgil's son."

"Yes."

I thought about the pink plastic wallet. "What about the rest of the family, the woman and the girl?"

"Sandra and Mara, both dead."

"How?"

The trials of his people wore heavily on the broad shoulders, but he spoke without emotion. "Head-on with a drunk driver. They died in January of '71."

"And Eli survived?"

"I understand there were behavioral problems even then, and he was shuttled off to foster homes. He now has his own gallery over in Hot Springs, South Dakota; Native abstracts, but things are difficult." I nodded and, after a moment, he turned to watch me. "What?"

I took a deep breath and set the cruise control at ninety. "So blooding the medicine is like a curse?"

The Cheyenne Nation frowned. "Yes, I suppose it is."

I felt my face tighten. "Well, it appears to be holding."

I noticed that one of the highway patrolmen had pulled a green vehicle over at the top of a far hill and hit the brakes. I slowed my truck and slid in behind the Dodge as the shapely blonde in mirrored glasses placed a hand on her hip, near the Glock, and looked back at us from the driver's side door of Tran Van Tuyen's Land Rover.

Rosey wore short black search gloves with undone pearl snaps that revealed pale skin at the wrists of her tanned arms. She straightened her campaign hat as she walked toward us with Tuyen's license, registration, and insurance card in her hand.

I liked how she walked and smiled. "How you doin', Troop?"

She tipped her sunglasses down and looked at me. "Have we got some kind of Vietnamese migration going on?"

"He's the grandfather."

Her demeanor changed immediately. "Oh."

I glanced up at Tuyen, who was still calmly seated in his vehicle, but who was adjusting his rearview mirror to look at us. "How fast?"

She leaned an elbow on my truck and glanced back at him. "Borderline, eighty-three."

"Let him go? He's had a rough couple of days." Her eyes came back to mine, and the delicate parchment of the skin at her high cheekbones reminded me of someone else who had been beautiful.

She nodded, and the eyes went down only to come up slow. "You owe me one." She handed me the paperwork and smiled crookedly. I was feeling a little warm, and I don't think it had anything to do with the temperature.

As she strutted back to the black Dodge and climbed

in with one last glance, I turned to Henry. "It's you, right? I mean . . . it's not me."

He frowned. "No, it is you. Some women have very peculiar tastes."

I climbed out and walked up to Tuyen's vehicle as Rosey slipped back onto the highway like a glossy panther looking for prey and disappeared over the hill. Tuyen turned to look at me as I leaned on his door. I noticed that the hard case I'd seen at the ghost town had now gravitated to the passenger floor. I handed him his identification and then looked up and down the empty highway. "Headed back to your motel?"

He stuffed the license back into his wallet and flipped the other papers into the center console. "Yes."

"Mr. Tuyen, would you have any idea if Ho Thi was traveling alone?"

He looked at me, his face unchanged. "What?"

"I got some information that your granddaughter may not have been traveling alone and was wondering if you would have any idea who might've been with her in the car."

I watched as he stared at the steering wheel. "I . . . I have no idea."

I crouched down and placed both arms on the sill. "Do you think you could contact your organization back in California and see if there's anyone else missing?"

"Certainly." He began reaching for his cell phone, which was plugged into his dash.

"That's okay, you're not going to get service till you get down into Powder Junction."

He tried to smile, but his face remained grim. "Outside the veterinary office?"

"Yep."

He took a breath. "You think that Ho Thi might have been traveling with someone?"

"It's possible." I nudged the brim of my hat back.

He nodded. "I will contact Children of the Dust and see if anyone else is missing." He glanced at me and then to the rolling hills that seemed to recede in the distance, a terrain so broad it hurt your eyes. "This is most distressing."

"Yes, it is." I stood and gestured back toward Henry. "My friend and I are going down to Powder Junction and ask a few more questions. Are you going to be in your room?"

"Yes."

"We'll have lunch at around one?" He looked up at me with a questioning expression, and I called back over my shoulder. "There's only one restaurant in Powder Junction. It's the one connected to the bar."

Henry studied the side of my face as I pulled around Tuyen's vehicle and jetted back up to ninety. I glanced at my best friend in the world as I thought it all through, watching as Tran Van Tuyen pulled out after us and followed at a slower speed. "Do you think I'm prejudiced? Really?"

"Yes." I glanced at him, and his smile was sad. "We all are, to a certain point—unfortunate, is it not?"

As he watched me, I watched the green Land Rover recede in my rearview mirror. We were both silent the rest of the way to Powder Junction.

The Dunnigan brothers were easy to find—they were now haying the opposite side of the highway, the giant swathers working like prehistoric insects along the gentle slopes of the barrow ditch. I turned on my light bar emergencies, slowed my truck, and pulled in ahead of the big machines.

Den slowed his swather and stopped only inches from

my rear quarter-panel. I got out and looked up at him, but he didn't move from the glass-enclosed cab of the still-running machine. James was already out of his, had climbed down, and was hustling to get to me. He raised a hand, his thin arm hanging in the frayed cuff of his shirt like a clapper in a bell. I glanced up at Den, who pushed his ball cap back on his head and didn't look at us. James smiled nervously. "Hey, Walt."

Figuring it would unsettle him, I leaned on the front blades of Den's machine. "Hello, James. I've got a few more questions for you and your brother, if that's okay." I watched as he took off his sweat-soaked straw hat, the red clay trapped in the perspiration on his forehead looking dark as bloodstain. James gestured to Den, who reluctantly shut the swather off, threw open the glass door, and walked toward us on the front frame of the machine. I allowed the Dunnigans to assemble before asking my questions.

Den looked down at us; he had pulled out a small cooler from the cab, sat, and started to eat his lunch. "We haven't found any more bodies, if that's why you're here."

I ignored him. "James, when you met Ho Thi Paquet, the young woman in the . . ."

"Was that her name?"

I studied him for a moment. "I'm sorry, James. Yes, it was." He nodded and looked at his scuffed-up ropers, which were wrapped twice with duct tape. "When you met Ho Thi at the bar, was she alone?" They both looked at me, but the only emotion I could read was confusion.

Den unwrapped a sandwich and opened a bottle of Busch, squeezing the cap between his fingers and pitching it into the high grass, before he finally spoke. "In the bar?"

I nodded. "Yes."

"Well, yep. I mean the bartender was there."

"Anybody else?"

They looked at each other, and then James answered in a soft voice. "No."

"When you came outside, was there anyone else in her car?"

Den squinted into the sun and chewed a bite from his sandwich. "No."

I nodded. "Guys, the next question is going to be a little personal. Where did you have sex with her?"

James looked worried and glanced at Henry, who had gotten out of the Bullet and had become more interested in farming equipment than I'd ever seen him. "In the truck."

"Your truck."

"Yep."

I nodded. "Parked where?"

"Out near Bailey."

"She rode with you?"

"Yep."

"Then what?"

James's neck was turning red as he glanced back at the Bear. "Well, I went first . . ."

"No, I mean after." He looked up at me. "After you and Den had sex with her, did you drive her back to her car?"

They replied in unison. "Yes."

"And you didn't see anyone in the car with her?"

They replied in unison again. "No."

"What time was it when you let her off?"

The two brothers looked at each other, and James started to speak before being cut off by Den, who threw the remainder of his sandwich into the open cooler and snapped it shut. "How in the hell should we know what time . . ."

James silenced him with a hand, the other clutching the brim of his hat as he thought. "We stopped cutting at about three, spent a couple of hours with her in the bar; then a little over an hour with her out at Bailey, and then brought her back to town."

"So, six, six-thirty?"

"Yeah."

I nodded. "All right, if you fellas see or hear anything..."

James shifted his weight toward me, and I stopped speaking. His eyes welled up. "Walt, there's somethin' else."

Den's voice exploded as he crouched down between us, still on the front rail of the swather, with the beer bottle dangling from his fingers. "James, God damn it, he don't want to hear that shit!"

I looked back at James as he cleared his throat. "I been havin' some strange things happen, seein' things, I mean."

Den climbed down. "James."

The older rancher worried the corner of his mouth with an index finger. "After we found her on the side of the highway..."

Den yanked off his ball cap. "God damn it!"

James leaned in a little, and I got the first whiff of blackberry brandy. "After you talked to us the first time?"

I nodded. "Yes?"

"And we all knew she was dead?" I waited but said nothing. A few cars passed by on the highway, but James's eyes stayed steady with mine. "Walt... do you believe in ghosts?"

Of all the things I was thinking James Dunnigan might reveal, a steadfast belief in the paranormal might've been close to last. I ignored Henry, who redirected his gaze from James to me. "I'm not sure I understand."

James interrupted, and his voice carried an edge. "It's a pretty simple question—do you think dead people come back?"

I thought about recent circumstances and felt an unease

growing in the tightness of my chest. I thought about seeing Indians on the Bighorn Mountains during a blizzard, whose advice was that it was sometimes better to sleep than to wake. I thought about a battered cabin on the breaks of the Powder River, with floating scarves and brittle paint that flaked away from the whorls of cupped wood like sheet music. I thought about Eagle helmets and ceremonies and cloud ponies. "James..." My voice caught in my throat like a vapor lock and sounded strange, even to me. "To be honest, no, I don't think the dead come back." My voice caught and his head dropped, just a little. "Because I'm not so sure they ever leave."

He looked back up. "I seen her."

"Who?"

"I swear I seen her."

Den erupted again. "God damn it, James! They're gonna put you in a home!"

"Ho Thi, I seen her."

I placed my hand on the old rancher's bony shoulder. "Where, James?"

"Bailey." He looked to the left and a little north, as if somebody might be listening. "In the ghost town."

# 12

I released the button on the microphone again but still heard nothing. The Cheyenne Nation stepped up on the boardwalk out of the sun and pulled the brim of his ball cap down low on his forehead. "Anything?"

I hung the mic back on the dash and shut the door. "No. It must be the rock walls."

He leaned against one of the support posts and looked down the ancient ruts of Bailey's main street and then up to the cliffs hanging over us like red waves. The sun was high, there was no discernible shade, and somehow it seemed even hotter out here. "There are a number of footprints, along with yours, up near the cemetery."

I had canvassed the town while Henry had headed up the rocky outcropping near the union hall. I nodded and hung my Ray-Bans in my uniform pocket to rest the bridge of my nose. "That's where I found Tuyen, at the cemetery."

"There are rattlesnakes up there."

"I figured." There was a cross rail between two of the supports, so I walked over and sat on the outside, continuing to look up and down the dusty, dry, and empty street. "James said he saw her out by the road."

"James says his dead mother makes coffee for him in the morning."

I looked up at him through a squinted eye and immediately regretted taking off my sunglasses. "There's that.... But just in case this mystery girl does exist, he says he saw her out by the road. Now, where else could she be?"

"Making coffee?" I gave him a longer look. "All right; assuming she does exist, we are assuming that she does not wish to be found?"

I looked to the east and then north at the union hall and the scrub pines and scattered cottonwoods along Beaver Creek. It wasn't hard to imagine Bailey as the bustling little town it must have been before the disaster. You could almost see the horses tied off to the railings, the draft wagons, and the narrow-gauge locomotive chugging and steaming to a stop at the mine tipple at the end of the street. "Yep. Assuming she exists, she ran off after her friend was killed and dumped alongside the highway."

He came over and sat on the other end of the railing. "She was not killed in town."

"No, too much of a chance of being spotted."

"And away from the highway."

"Yep."

He nodded, the wooden-nickel-profile looking off toward the cemetery. "Do you think she witnessed the murder?"

"It would go a long way toward explaining why she's hiding." I watched as a red-tailed hawk was chased by two smaller birds, and wondered how Vic, Cady, and Michael were doing.

The Bear turned back and stared at the side of my face as a slight breeze came up, hotter than the still air. "You know, there is something funny about this town...."

"You mean besides the fact that there are no people?" I could be a smart-ass, too.

"Yes, besides that."

"What?"

"There is no church." He glanced up and down the street, perhaps expecting one to appear. "If there was one, it would be up near the cemetery, but there is no foundation, nothing."

I stood, stepped down, and walked into the street, turning to look up at the old mine. "Did you check the union hall while you were up there?"

"No."

"Why not?"

Henry flipped his legs up on the railing and leaned back against the post. He pulled his ponytail loose from above the adjustable strap of his hat, which he put over his face. "I told you, there are rattlesnakes up there."

I stared at the embroidered fish on his hat. "Since when are you afraid of rattlesnakes?"

"I am not, but they told me that no one had been up there since Tuyen and you."

"Oh, right." I put my sunglasses back on. I noticed he wasn't moving. "What are you doing, taking a nap?"

"Yes. I assumed it was the only sensible thing to do while you checked the union hall."

I looked up the street and at the high, razorlike grass leading to the lone building on the hill, past the dark pyramid of the coal tipple—perfect ambush territory for rattlers. "What makes you think I'm gonna go do that?"

The hat remained over his face, muffling his voice. "I knew you would not believe me about the snakes."

Rattlesnakes shed in August. Their eyes become cloudy, and they grow uncomfortable, pissed off, and strike out at anything; contrary to popular belief, they do not always rattle before striking.

Part of the trail leading past the cemetery was still visible to the left of the cliffs, with a few rock steps that turned the corners where hard men descended into the ground to bring up soft fuel. I paused at one corner to see if the Cheyenne Nation had moved, and it hadn't.

Most of the American public had been hoodwinked by the director John Ford in the forties and fifties into believing that the entire West looked exclusively like Monument Valley, where he filmed most of his movies. It was a vista that had become emblematic, and I had to admit that my view of the Hole in the Wall, with its bold crimson palisades and the hazy flux of the horizontal landscape, looked a lot like Monument Valley.

The only tracks were indeed the ones that Tuyen and I had made, but they ended at the cemetery—above that, there were no tracks, no broken grass, nothing to indicate that anyone had been up here in ages. I caught my breath. It was still early, and the heat of the day had yet to push us into triple digits. I didn't want to be up here in a couple of hours, when the sun reached its zenith and Bailey would feel something like the fifth ring of hell.

The union hall was up and to my right, standing alone like a weathered lighthouse amid the storm toss of the rocks.

I leaned on the iron railing surrounding the cemetery, then immediately regretted it, the dark metal feeling as if it had been just pulled from the smelter. I thought of Saizarbitoria at the jungle gym back in Powder Junction and smiled. Maybe the Basquo was learning fast, or was it that I was learning more slowly?

I found myself reading the tombstones, the names, and the single date on seventeen of them, and thought about the survivors walking the path next to the graveyard. I wondered if they saw those dead miners who had been trapped in the dark tunnels beneath my boots.

I thought about the two bottles of water in my shooting bag, which I had left back at the truck, and turned the corner. I'd taken only a dozen steps into the high weeds when I heard the rattling sound, the one that makes westerners freeze and wonder why they didn't wear their high-top leggings.

As Lonnie Little Bird would say, he was a big one, um hmm, yes, it is so; twelve buttons at least and only about ten feet away. Again contrary to popular belief, you can't judge a rattler by his buttons since they shed and accumulate a new pod three or four times a year. It didn't matter, he was big, and neither of us was in a mood for counting.

He was curling in an "S" and backing away from me, the majority of his body as big as my forearm. He had backed himself up against one of the rises on the stone steps, and there was nowhere else to go. He coiled himself tighter and flicked a dark tongue at me as the vibrating tail shook beside his rectangular-shaped head.

"Howdy." I figured now was as good a time as any to test Henry's theory. He didn't respond and stayed compacted, the dark eyes shining like black beads. "You haven't seen anybody come by here lately, have you?" His head dropped a little as I began raising my hand very, very slowly. "That's what I thought."

I could go for my sidearm, but the thought of what the .45 round might do after hitting the stone step gave me more than a little pause, so I continued raising my hand till I got it to the brim of my hat.

The buzzworm's head dropped a little again, and I froze.

It was my fault really, disturbing him as he'd peacefully sunned himself after indulging in a brunch of field mouse or sagebrush lizard. I could have introduced myself as the sheriff and told him about the important case I was working on, but he didn't seem interested and I was more than beginning to doubt Henry's theories on interspecies communication.

I chucked my hat in a tight curveball, low and outside; he hit it in the sweet spot, then disappeared into the rocks that stuck out in shelves to my right.

I took the two steps and picked up my hat as a few rocks kicked loose and joined the scree at the bottom. He probably wasn't alone. "Hey, there's an Indian asleep in front of the dry-goods store, why don't you go bite him?"

I looked at the crown of my hat—there was a scuff and stain where the rattler had hit it. I was about due a new hat, anyway. I tugged the battered palm leaf back on my head and continued up the steps with a more wary eye.

The union hall was a masterful piece of early-twentieth-century architecture, with castellated cornices and a unique second story and balcony. The structure had weathered the century better than the ones below as few people were willing to make the rest of the hike up the hill—that, and the rattlesnakes. There was still glass in the windows and, although the transom above the doorway was cracked, it still shone with the high gloss of old lead. There was a chain padlocked through the door handles, but one end had pulled loose and hung below its match. The damage was old, and there were no marks in the dust that covered everything.

The paneled door rested heavily on the sill, but I lifted it and pushed in and it swung wide with a grating noise from the old hinges. There was an entryway leading to the offices in the back and a stairwell to the right, nothing looking as if it had been disturbed in as far back as the dust remembered. I walked through the empty offices and listened to the soft squeals of the wide-plank floor.

There was a counter to one side, and a bundle of broken chairs huddled in the corner, but there wasn't much else. The stairs to the second floor were about a quarter of the way down and ascended to the middle of a dance hall. When I got up there, I noticed that there was a doorway to the balcony overlooking the cliffs and the town on one side; on the other was a stage and a doorway that led to the wings.

I walked around the railing and stood in the blinding glow of the four windows where the balcony's half-paned door captured the floating motes that hung in the still air. It was stifling on the second floor, and I could feel the sweat streaking down between my shoulder blades. I took off my hat, hung it on the butt of my Colt, and ran my fingers through my hair as I took the three steps to the stage.

There was an old upright piano, which was pushed against the back wall with the bench tucked underneath. I flipped the dust-laden keyboard cover up and touched a chipped F. It was flat but resonated through the silence, raising the thought of ghostly dance steps where there had been no dancers for almost a century.

I thought about the story Lucian had told me that Red Angus, the sheriff before Lucian, had told him and that the sheriff before that had told him. The double murder had occurred on December 31, 1900—New Year's Eve, just a few seconds after midnight, to be exact. There had been a big dance to celebrate the incoming year, and I guess Maxfield Holinshed hadn't liked the unidentified woman who was kissing his father to welcome in 1901, so he pulled a gun right there on the dance floor and shot and killed them both. He was hung in the street below just over two weeks later. Lucian said he still had young Max's journal that recorded the two weeks that had intervened and that someday he'd let me see it, just to raise my hair.

I pulled the bench out, placed my hat on top of the piano, and sat in front of the yellowed-white and grayed-black keys. I tinkered out a one-fingered version of the old cavalry favorite, "The Girl I Left Behind Me."

It was horrible, and any ghosts that might've been in the place I had certainly driven out. Most of the soundboard was dead, what was left was remarkably out of tune, and I had a feeling that there was more than one mouse nest inside the ignored instrument.

I could always go get my friend the rattlesnake and put him to work.

I plinked away, trying to find the live portion of the board, and thought about Ho Thi Paquet, and how abandoned her body looked alongside the highway tunnel; about Tran Van Tuyen, and the look on his face when I had questioned him at the cemetery; and, finally, about Mai Kim. I thought about the photo in the lining of the purse, about who I had been in Vietnam, and the way Virgil White Buffalo watched the children on the playground across the street from the jail.

Even in the heat of the midday, I could feel the ghosts crowding in around me, their hands on my shoulders, their feet tapping to the nonexistent beat. I felt a cold wave pass over my back, which made me shiver in the hundred degrees, and I stopped playing. The palpable feeling of company was as oppressive as the heat, and I knew someone was watching me.

I placed a hand on the piano bench and turned.

Nothing.

The windows were hazed with the dust of full daylight,

the diffused glow stretching across the whitewashed floor like identities. I sat still and listened.

Nothing.

I watched and waited for the motes to swirl in time with the long-dead ghosts of Maxfield Holinshed, his father Horace, and the mysterious woman who had set their lives in desperate motion, but they didn't. The dust hung there, almost motionless. Out of the corner of my eye, I thought I saw movement, but every time I looked, there was nothing. I laughed at myself and wondered if maybe the rattlesnake had made me jumpy, or if I was just getting scary in my middle age. I stood up and closed the piano, scooted the bench back underneath it, and thought about Cady in the ballroom of the VA, where there was no music, but there was.

I walked to the edge of the stage, considered what my two-hundred-and-now-forty-pound frame might do to the hundred-year-old floor up here and then to the one downstairs when I crashed through this one, and crossed to the doorway and took the steps down.

On the way back into town, Henry told me that the Dunnigans' turquoise and white Ford had pulled in at the top of the cut-off leading to Bailey but then had backed out and continued up the road. "Probably looking to get lucky."

I peered at him from above the shooting guard of my sunglasses while I radioed Saizarbitoria to check in on Tuyen. He sounded only mildly disgruntled that he had been watching the green Land Rover outside the Hole in the Wall Motel for the last hour and a half.

Static. "He's probably taking a nap; I wish I was."

I keyed the mic. "We're on our way into town, and he's supposed to have lunch with us."

Static. "You want me to get him?"

"No, just meet us at the bar."

Static. "Roger that; out."

I looked at Henry again as we drove the winding road back toward Powder Junction. "I don't think my staff is completely happy with me." He shrugged as I keyed the mic again. "Base, this is unit one." I didn't wait for a response; instead I sang, "I gotta gal and Ruby is her name. Ruby, Ruby, Ruby baby / She don't love me but I love her just the same. . . ."

Static. "I told you to stop that."

"But I haven't gone through my entire litany of Ruby songs yet."

Static. "Oh, yes, you have."

I keyed the mic. "Any word from the young Philadelphians?"

Static. "They just finished lunch."

"Am I in trouble?"

Static. "Not if you get back up here for dinner."

"How's the sleeping giant?"

Static. "Not sleeping. Double Tough made it in to relieve Frymire, but Lucian is back there again playing chess, so he left." There was a pause. "Please don't sing again; I don't know if my ears can take it."

**Tan Son Nhut, Vietnam: 1968**

He had gotten the staples out of his earlobes, but the duty sergeant wasn't particularly happy to see us again. He was a lot more helpful this time, however, and much more understanding of the severity of a homicide investigation. He said that Hollywood Hoang had gone into Saigon on a three-day.

Mendoza asked if he could be a little more specific about Hoang's exact location, and I picked up the stapler.

He said that Hoang was known to frequent a place in the red-light district on Tu-Do Street. I put the stapler back down.

The three of us stood there in the close humidity of the Southeast Asian night. I stared at the two of them as Baranski tried to make up his mind. "This is a bad idea. We don't have any jurisdiction there, and we're under maximum alert since 0945 this morning and a security condition red since 1730, and we've got just as good a chance of being shot by the good guys as the bad."

Mendoza nodded. "Yeah, but..."

Baranski shoved his hands in his pants pockets and trapped his mustache with his lower lip. "It's going to be like looking for a needle-dick in a Vietnamese haystack."

After a moment, the Texan spoke again. "Yeah, but..."

Baranski pulled out a cigarette without offering one to anybody else and lit up. "Why is this suddenly so fucking important to you?"

Mendoza gestured toward me. "Well, Mother Green here is going to be leavin' on a jet plane tomorrow morning..."

Baranski interrupted him, switching his cigarette to the other hand and sticking out a finger, tapping him in the chest. "No, I said you. Why is this shit so suddenly important to you?"

The shorter man looked up at him, his dark eyes steady. "I don't know, man."

"You don't know?"

I watched the Texican's jaw moving. "Hey, maybe this is it, man. Maybe this is the one thing we'll be able to look back on in this great big shitty mess and be proud of." He turned and studied me. "The cowboy here is short and headed back to the real world—after the shit he's pulled in the last few hours, he ain't gonna be making a career out of the Corps." His eyes stayed on Baranski as he reached under the front seat of the jeep and handed me my sidearm and holster. He finally looked at me. "If we don't take you, you're going to walk into the city, aren't you?"

I nodded. "Yep."

He sighed and glanced back at Baranski. "I thought the zipperheads were on a truce?"

The redheaded man nodded, continuing to smoke his cigarette. "They are, but there have been some bullshit attacks up north."

Mendoza stood there for a minute and then climbed into the jeep, the decision made. "I'm having trouble keeping up with all these damn holidays. What's this one?"

Baranski threw the rest of his smoke onto the ground and himself into the driver's seat as I climbed in the back again. "Lunar New Year."

The Texican looked at the main gate with its guard shack, which would have been more at home at a public pool in Southern California, and down the busy four-and-a-half-mile road that led to Saigon. "Yeah, but what do the Slopes call it?"

Baranski started the jeep. "Tet."

Phillip Maynard was MIA.

We were sitting in the café section of the Wild Bunch Bar, waiting on Tuyen, sipping iced tea, and studying the menus. "He didn't show up for work?"

"No, and this is only his sixth day, so he may end up getting his ass fired." Thinner than the rattler I'd encountered earlier and just about as tolerant, Roberta Porter had bought the bar back in '98 and had had trouble keeping staff ever since. "No call or nothing. I was by his place and didn't see his motorcycle but could hear the TV. I beat on the door, but he didn't answer."

I looked at Henry as he perused the menu, his voice smoothly modulating from behind the single sheet. "Did he work last night?"

"If you'd call it that."

She pulled a pencil from somewhere in the suspiciously

blonde tangle of her sixty-two-year-old hair and yanked a pad from the back pocket of her jeans as I ventured an opinion. "Maybe he's hungover?"

"He has been sampling an awful lot of the product the last couple of days."

"We'll roll by and check in on him." I handed her my menu and followed the Cheyenne Nation's lead, ordering a Butch Cassidy Burger Deluxe with cheese, bacon, grilled onions, and fries.

She scribbled on the pad, glancing at Henry and then back to me. "I heard you picked up that big Indian."

I looked up at her. "Virgil White Buffalo."

"Is that his name?" I nodded. "He's been around here since I had the café. He used to watch the kids play out at Bailey School; made some people nervous." She adjusted the menus under her arm. "You think he killed that girl?"

"Roberta, you got some Tabasco around here somewhere?" She disappeared into the back, not particularly satisfied with the title of chief cook and bottle washer. I turned to Henry. "This Maynard thing seem suspicious to you?"

He leaned back in his metal bentwood chair, which whined its disapproval. "Not enough to miss lunch."

I watched as Saizarbitoria's unit pulled up. The handsome Basquo got out, slapping his hat at the dust on his jeans in an attempt to freshen himself—riding around with the windows down had its disadvantages. He swung the glass door open and came over to stand by our table, his left thumb tucked in his gun belt.

"What's up, Sancho?"

"I waited till one and then went and knocked on Tuyen's door at the motel, but he didn't answer."

"Why'd you do that?"

"I thought I'd give him a ride."

I looked up at my young dandy of a deputy. "It's only a half a block." He shrugged and folded his arms. "You trying to make up for my picking on him?" He didn't say anything more, so I stood and motioned for him to sit. "When Roberta comes back, order up another burger and you take mine."

"Where are you going?"

"I'm going over to check on Tuyen."

"I'll go with you."

I took one last sip of my iced tea. "No, you eat, and I'll go get him. Chances are he's asleep or in the shower." Santiago continued to stand and study me as I scooted my chair back under the table. I stood there looking at him, fighting the urge to laugh. "I promise I won't rough him up."

He kept watching me until Henry pulled out a chair.

It was even hotter, but I decided to walk to the motel. It was just easier. I flipped on my antique sunglasses and started up the boardwalk. The main street was paved, but the side streets and alleyways were dry reddish dirt, with dust as fine as talcum.

We needed rain.

By the time I got to the motel, there was a wide slick of perspiration holding my uniform shirt to my back, and I'd taken my palm-leaf hat off twice to wipe away some of the sweat that continued to flood down and behind my glasses. I was regretting my decision to walk.

The Land Rover was parked out front. As I crossed the dirt and gravel parking strip between the motel rooms and the street, I noticed a set of motorcycle tracks, the mark from the kickstand where it had been parked, and the tracks where it had been backed up and ridden off.

I thought about Phillip Maynard and knocked on the door. "Mr. Tuyen?"

Nothing.

I knocked again, but there was no sound. "Mr. Tuyen, it's Sheriff Longmire."

One kick would do it, but I figured the management might appreciate a more subtle approach. As I walked past the Land Rover, I noticed the doors were locked, but the hard case was missing from the front seat.

"You got a key for room number five?"

A young woman I didn't know—with one earphone connected to a small device in her shirt pocket, the other dangling at her chest—handed me the fob from a hook behind the counter. "Is there some kind of trouble, Sheriff?"

"No, I'm just checking to see if all the mattresses still have their tags." She continued to look at me, and I could hear what passed for music to her in the one loose earbud. "I'm kidding."

She blinked. "Oh."

I palmed the key in my hand and stood there for a moment, enjoying the air-conditioning. "Have you seen Mr. Tuyen this morning?"

She nodded. "Yes, he left pretty early and then came back a couple of hours ago. Is he in trouble?"

I tossed the key in the air and caught it as I swung open the door and faced the wall of heat. "Only if he's taken the labels off." I left her there to wonder if I really was serious this time.

I knocked again and waited, thinking about the missing hard case. "Mr. Tuyen, this is Sheriff Longmire. I got the key from the front desk, and I'm unlocking this door."

I turned the key and swung the door open. There was an entryway to the bathroom on the left, and I could see an open closet where a number of expensive suits hung along with plastic-covered and freshly laundered shirts.

I took a step inside and allowed my eyes to adjust. Tuyen's toiletry and personal items were on the bathroom counter, along with a hand towel, which was saturated with blood, that hung from the lip of the sink, the excess dripping to the tile floor.

I unsnapped the strap from my Colt and pulled it from my holster. I clicked off the safety, looked at the dark spots on the carpeting, and took another step inside.

I raised my sidearm and heard a noise to my left. There were two double beds, with a kidney-shaped pool of blood at the foot of one, and there was more on the far side of the room.

Even with the clattering of the aged air conditioner, I could tell the noise was coming from another room on the far side; it sounded like someone walking and possibly dragging something. I extended the large-frame semiautomatic.

There were some clothes lying on the unslept-in bed and another pair of shoes, but what caught my attention was the phone cord that was stretched taut and led from the nightstand, across the wall, and out the adjoining doorway.

I took another step and silently cursed the creaking floorboards under my boots. The noise from the other room stopped, and the phone cord grew slack and drooped to the carpet.

I held the .45 toward the open doorway and took a deep silent breath before taking another step. I took another and could hear a slight creak and saw a flicker of movement. I swung the Colt around, pointing it at whatever had made the noise. Tran Van Tuyen was holding a tan push-button phone in one hand and a blood-soaked towel to his head in the other.

Even from this distance, I could hear Ruby's voice coming from the receiver of the telephone. "Mr. Tuyen? Mr. Tuyen . . . are you still there?"

The blood from the wound at the side of his head had drained down to his face and stained his smile that half-beamed from across the room. "Sheriff?"

The smile remained as his eyes rolled back in his head, and he slumped against the jamb, streaking a handwide smear of blood down the door and collapsing unconscious onto the carpet.

# 13

"Saizarbitoria thinks you did it."

I listened to the squeal from under the hood as we turned the corner and figured the staff vehicle from the Powder Junction detachment of the Absaroka County Sheriff's Department was going to need a power steering unit and soon. "Really?"

"No, but we had a long talk about race relations." I drove the faded red Suburban to the address Phillip Maynard had given us, as the Bear fiddled with the nonfunctioning vents, finally settling on rolling down his window, which stuck about halfway. "Santiago is a very intelligent young man."

I'd given Sancho my truck after we'd gotten Tuyen stabilized and sent them rocketing off to the hospital back in Durant; I figured a one-way trip in the Bullet was faster than a two-way trip with the EMTs. Even with the vast loss of blood, Tuyen had come to and said that he had no idea what had happened other than that he had entered the motel room and someone had struck him from behind.

"So, we are basing our suspicions on a single set of motorcycle tracks outside the motel?"

"Sort of."

"How sort of?"

I shrugged. "Exclusively."

He sighed. "Why would Phillip Maynard kill Ho Thi Paquet and then try to kill Tuyen?"

"I don't know, but he seems our most likely suspect."

Henry pulled his shoulder belt out, where it hung loose across his chest. "Drive carefully. I question the ability of this belt to keep me from slamming face-first into the dash should we find ourselves in a crash." We were headed for the south side of town near the rodeo grounds. "He is our only suspect." He thought about it some more. "Sometimes living in Wyoming has unexpected benefits."

"Vic says that most of the benefits of living in Wyoming are unexpected."

"She is a modern woman and expects a great deal." I could feel him watching me before he turned back to the road and smiled.

Phillip Maynard's house wasn't really a house; it was more like an upscale chicken shack, which meant that in comparison to the other shacks that sat a little farther toward the banks of the middle fork of the Powder River, it seemed even more uninhabitable.

Henry placed his hands on his hips and stood at the gate. "Where do you suppose the door is?"

"Drawing from my ranch upbringing, I'd say it's on the side." I followed him as he walked around the end of the ramshackle building where we found a hollow-core door that had a tin sign tacked to the surface that read KEEP OUT.

We could hear commercials squawking from a television inside, and I knocked on the door. We waited and listened but heard nothing but the TV. This was getting reminiscent of Tran Van Tuyen's motel room. "Phillip Maynard, this is Sheriff Longmire. Would you mind opening the door?"

Nothing.

We listened and learned how white our teeth and how fresh our breath could be if we would only use Brand-X toothpaste, but nothing from Phillip Maynard. I tried the knob, but the door was locked. I glanced at Henry. "I hope we're not seeing a pattern here."

"Do you want me to kick it down, or do you want to?"

I studied the scaly and cupped surface of the interior door, which had spent at least a winter in the high plains exterior. "I think if we breathe on it, it'll collapse." Testing the theory, I grasped the knob and pressed. The door popped open, taking a little of the jamb with it.

We shrugged at each other. The television was a tiny thirteen-inch sitting on a beanbag chair, and clothes were scattered across the dirty yellow linoleum-tiled floor and exploded from a large backpack that rested on a built-in bunk. Unlike Tuyen's room, it didn't look like anybody had been killed here, anybody besides Mister Clean.

The Bear walked past me, watched Suzanne Rico anchor the news out of Channel 13 in Casper, and then clicked off the TV. There was an open paperback lying on the bed, along with what looked like an old horsehide motorcycle jacket and a number of empty Budweiser bottles, and a full ashtray with a few joints mixed in with the butts. There was another collection of bottles beside the only chair.

Henry crossed back and flipped over the book. "*Zen and the Art of Motorcycle Maintenance.*"

"Appropriate."

He showed me the cover as proof and then gestured toward the bottles by the chair. "It would appear that Phillip has been entertaining."

I kneeled down and looked at the empties, plucked a pen

from my shirt pocket, and tipped one over enough to lift it by the neck. Something rattled at the base, and I saw it was the cap, which had been bent in half. I set the bottle back down and looked up at the Cheyenne Nation. "I guess I'll go check with the owner."

Gladys Dietz had rented her swank chicken shed to Phillip Maynard for the lofty sum of a hundred dollars a month, including utilities, but she was beginning to have second thoughts. I was having second thoughts as she smoked a cigarette with the oxygen tube attached just under her nose, expecting any moment to be blown off the porch.

"The TV is going all the time, and that damn motorcycle makes such a racket." She leaned on her walker one-handed and held the screen door back with the other.

I knew Gladys. She and her husband had owned a commercial fishing lake that my father and I had frequented, and she had gladly told anybody then that she was intent on dying soon.

I had passed more than a half century and was the chief law enforcer in the land, but she still addressed me as if I were eight. I held my hat in my hands. "Mrs. Dietz . . ."

"Your shirt needs ironing, Walter."

I self-consciously smoothed the pockets of my uniform and desperately tried to remember her husband's name. "Yes, ma'am. How's George?"

"Dead."

That's what you got for asking about old people. "I'm sorry to hear that."

She shrugged her silver head and studied my unpolished boots. "I'm not. He was getting pretty cranky toward the end."

I decided to try to keep on track. "Mrs. Dietz, have you seen Phillip Maynard today?"

She glanced toward the shack, where Henry was standing by the gate. "What's that Indian doing out near my chicken shed?"

"He's with me."

She looked up through lenses as thick as the windshield on my truck. "I heard your wife died?"

"Yes, ma'am, a number of years back."

"Was she cranky?"

"No, ma'am."

She nodded her head. "They get like that, you know."

"Yes, ma'am, so they tell me. Now, about Phillip Maynard?"

"Is he in trouble?"

"We just need to talk to him. Have you seen him?"

She continued watching Henry. "I usually don't rent to those motorcycle types."

I sighed and hung my hat on the grip of my sidearm and held the screen door for her. "It's pretty important."

"What is?"

"Phillip Maynard."

"What about him?"

I took that extra second that usually keeps me from strangling my constituency, always important in an election year. "Have you seen him today?"

"No."

I glanced back at Henry. "Well, his motorcycle isn't here."

"He keeps it in the barn."

I turned and looked at her. "I beg your pardon?"

"That fancy new one that he doesn't want to get rained on." She glanced past me and at the cloudless sky, the smoldering cigarette still frighteningly close to the oxygen nozzle under her nose. "Not that it's ever going to do that again."

She watched us as we turned the corner and walked past a

corral toward the Dietz barn with a Dutch-style hip roof. "She thinks you're going to steal her chickens."

"There are no chickens."

"See?"

It was a standard structure, with the roof supported by a number of big, rough-cut eight-by-eights, which had been sided with raw lumber that had long faded to gray. There was a metal handle with a wooden latch on the door, which I pulled, and we stepped back as the big door swung toward us. Up in the loft there was a flutter of barn swallows, sounding like angel's wings might. The Harley sat parked on its side stand, swathed with the same cover that I had seen at the bar. Henry lifted the vinyl shroud and whistled. "What?"

"FLHRS Road King, custom job."

I vaguely remembered Henry having a bike, but he had rarely ridden it. "What's that mean?"

"Expensive. Close to twenty thousand."

I thought about the chicken shed. "Well, he hasn't been spending his money on lodging." I reached down and felt the chrome-bedecked engine, only vaguely warm. "And he hasn't ridden it lately."

I took a step into the barn proper, and let my eyes adjust to the gloom. There was a smell, one that I knew.

I unsnapped the safety strap on my .45, pulled the Colt from my holster, and glanced back over my shoulder at Henry. The main breezeway of the barn was empty except for the motorcycle, but there were two other passageways through the stock stalls. I motioned for the Bear to head right, and I would take the left.

The stalls hadn't been used for their initial purpose for quite some time but had instead been filled with used lumber, broken equipment, and aged firewood. I worked my way through the four of them and met Henry at the far end of the center breezeway.

"Well, he's not hiding in the corn crib."

There was more fluttering, and I noticed the scar tissue under Henry's chin as he studied the rafters. "No, not in the corn crib." He turned in a circle until he was facing back toward the opening where we'd come in. "But it appears he has received a suspended sentence."

I turned and followed his eyes up to the rafters where, from a stout length of hemp rope, hung the dangling body of Phillip Maynard.

"How long?"

T. J. Sherwin was on another call in Otto, so we had Bill McDermott, who was the medical examiner from Billings, Montana. I hadn't seen him since he and Lana Baroja had gone to Guernica together, but it was good to have him back. "Hard to say with the heat, but with rigor and approximate temperature, I'd say it was possibly early this morning or maybe very late last night."

"Suicide?"

"I hate to guess, but if I was a betting man . . ." He looked at Maynard's body. The pressure from the base of Phillip's neck and from the area where the tongue attaches had forced his lower jaw open, and his tongue stuck out from between his teeth in a parody of a naughty child. "There's some additional contusion alongside the trapezoidal muscle, but that could easily be explained by the force of the drop."

I looked back up at the roof beams, which were at least eighteen feet high. "He did a number, didn't he?"

"It takes surprisingly little; you don't even have to be suspended."

"What would you suspect?"

Bill looked like a choirboy, which belied his occupation. He peered up and calculated. "From the loft, I'd say about six-and-a-half feet." He pulled back the body bag to reveal a V-shaped abrasion and furrow at the back of Phillip Maynard's neck, which had been caused by the rope that had slipped up past the thyroid cartilage. "Incomplete circle where the rope pulled away from the subject." He looked at the dead man some more. "He didn't change his mind after the fact."

"Why?"

"No fingernail marks at the neck. I've even seen cases where the fingers are trapped under the rope, but this guy dropped the exact distance, which resulted in a fractured neck, and we'll probably find the break between the third and fourth or fourth and fifth cervical vertebrae." Bill looked up at me. "Was he a bad guy?"

I took a breath and felt the closeness of the barn. The light glowing through the spaces between the slats made stripes as if it were shining through bars. I looked at Phillip Maynard's sightless eyes and at the spot where a blood vessel had burst, clouding and unbalancing the pupil, which was ragged at the edge, unlike you'd expect. "I'm not sure yet."

**Saigon, Vietnam: 1968**

I watched all the people who crammed into the few tiny blocks around Tu-Do Street and thought about all the bars we'd already checked, including the Flower Brothel, Rose's, the assorted steam baths, massage parlors, boom boom rooms, and an honest-to-God

Dairy Queen. Even this early in the morning, the street was in full swing, and I suspected it stayed that way for the full twenty-four hours of the day. It was leaning toward early morning, and I took a deep breath and felt like I was leaking time.

Mendoza laughed. "Oh, come on now, it's not that bad."

Baranski had pulled the jeep half onto the sidewalk, but no one had seemed to notice, not even the two ARVN QCs that we'd almost run over. With their oversized white helmet liners, the Vietnamese military policemen looked like those bobble-headed sports dolls. One of them tried to beg a cigarette from Mendoza, who shook his head and replied, "*Toi khong hut thuoc lo.*"

Baranski, however, sat on the hood of the jeep and handed the two Mice cigarettes, lighting one for himself and then theirs. He paused for a moment and gestured. "*Quels sont vos noms?*"

The two introduced themselves as Bui Tin and Van Bo.

Baranski pointed at me. "*Je suis venu avec quelqu'un d'important, il s'appelle Sammy Davis Jr.*"

The two QCs looked up, so I smiled and raised a fist. "Black power."

Baranski continued. "*Il veut passer un bon moment. Tu vois ce que je veux dire.*"

Bui Tin gestured toward the bustling street. "*Choisissez une des portes.*"

Baranski nodded his head and gestured helplessly with both hands. "*Ouais, mais il aime les cowboys et il voudrait quelque chose qui fasse un peu western.*"

Tin, who seemed to be in charge, pointed to a side street. "*Il y a un club qui s'appelle Western Town un peu plus bas sur ce trottoir.*"

As we walked past them, Van Bo grasped my hand and shook it. "*Je suis tellement heureux de vous rencontrer, Monsieur Davis. J'ai tous vos disques.*"

I followed after Baranski and Mendoza and nodded, completing the conversation with two of the twelve French words I knew. *"Merci beaucoup."*

I caught up with them as they turned the corner. "What'd he say?"

Baranski stopped and looked across the street to where a neon cowgirl's leg kicked up and down in a more than provocative manner and gestured to a hand-painted sign that read WESTERN TOWN. "He said he's got all your albums."

Static. "There are no records with the Chicago Police Department, other than the ones from the reports we've already received."

"No next of kin?"

Static. "There was a mother in Evanston, but that number's been disconnected."

I sighed and stared at the mic in my hand. "All right, pending any further information from the great state of Illinois, we'll file Phillip Maynard with the boys up in Billings. Anybody comes looking for him, and we'll defer to that other great state."

Static. "And what are we?"

I keyed the mic. "Somewhere between. What's the word on Tran Van Tuyen?"

Static. "He lost a lot of blood, but it looks like he'll make it. Isaac Bloomfield says it's a pretty good blunt trauma from a not-so-blunt instrument."

"Meaning?"

Static. "He said something like an angle iron."

"Or a motorcycle part?"

Static. "Possibly, but why didn't he kill Tuyen?"

"Remorse."

Static. "That would explain both crimes, wouldn't it?"

"Roger that." I started to hang up the mic.

Static. "Walt?"

I keyed it again. "Yep?"

Static. "Anything you'd like me to tell Cady?"

"Where are they?"

Static. "They were talking about coming down there."

"Tell them not to. I'll be in Durant soon. I need to talk to Tuyen, but I have to make another stop before I head back."

Static. "Roger that.... Hey, you didn't sing."

I watched Phillip Maynard's body being loaded into a step van. "I guess my heart isn't in it."

Bill came over and joined us as I backed out of the open door of the unit, propped my forearms on the top of the window, and looked at Henry, who had just rolled up the sleeves of his faded blue chambray shirt. He still looked cool and crisp, even in the heat. "Is this what they call an open-and-shut case?"

I nudged my hat back and rested my chin on my forearms. I didn't look cool—didn't feel it, either. "As far as Phillip is concerned, it is." I stared at the shiny glare of chromed reflection in the Harley's air cleaner, wondering where somebody like Maynard would get the money for a twenty-thousand-dollar motorcycle, and then voiced my real concern. "I'm wondering why he would want to kill Ho Thi Paquet, let alone Tuyen."

Henry wrapped his arms over his chest, and I watched the muscles bunch under the dark skin, reminding me of the coiled rattler in the ghost town. "Perhaps she came back into the bar, and things got a little rough."

"There are the charges from Chicago, but I'm just not sure..." I stopped suddenly and thought of the woman on the fax. "Damn." I leaned back in the vehicle and keyed the mic. "Ruby, you there?"

Static. "You ready with your reprise?"

"Find the name of the woman who had the restraining order on Maynard, and see if you can get me a phone number?"

Static. "Roger that."

I straightened back up, and the Cheyenne Nation was beside the door, along with McDermott. "What charges?"

"There was a domestic disturbance, an assault charge, and a restraining order concerning a woman in Chicago—Karol Griffith, I think her name was."

McDermott looked between the two of us. "So this Maynard fellow had a record?"

"Yep, but something about all of this doesn't seem right, and I'd like to talk to somebody who actually knew him before I tag him posthumously with murder in the first and attempted homicide."

Static. "Walt?"

"I'm here."

Static. "It's a work number." I copied it down. "Tattoo You."

"Thanks." I tossed the mic back on the seat as the Bear reached down and pulled out his cell phone from a nifty little leather holster at his belt. "So, do you want to go make a phone call?"

I nodded. "Yep, then we'll go get Tuyen's Land Rover. I figure he'll appreciate us picking up his stuff and bringing his car to him."

Henry smiled. "That, and it will give you another chance to look over his room and the vehicle?"

"There's that."

He nodded. "I'll drive the Land Rover."

We parked by the veterinarian's office, and Henry dialed the number and handed me the phone. Ms. Griffith answered on the second ring—she sounded personable and precise. I told her why I was calling, and she became less personable, but still precise. "He beat up my car."

The reception, even in this key part of Powder Junction, was spotty at best. "He what?"

"He beat up my Charger with a baseball bat, but he paid to have it fixed the next day." There was a pause. I had learned from years of experience to never interrupt the flow. "I'm sorry to hear he's dead. Was it that piece of shit motorcycle?"

"The new one?"

"New, hell; he could hardly keep that ancient piece of crap running."

"We're not really sure." I decided to keep the details to myself. "Ms. Griffith, would you say Mr. Maynard was given to acts of physical violence as a matter of course?"

"No, not really."

I thought about it. "But you say he beat up your car?"

I listened to the silence on the line. "Well, that was kind of my fault."

"In what way?"

"I beat up his motorcycle first." It was quiet on the line again, and I listened to or imagined the thousands of relays, switches, and electric impulses within the cellular system. "He wasn't particularly devoted to our relationship. He had this thing for Asian girls."

It was only a block and a half from anywhere to anywhere in Powder Junction, so rather than suffer the tin can of a Suburban, we parked at the office and walked to the Hole in the Wall Motel. "So, she said he had this constant stream of Asian women he brought in from Canada?"

"Suspicious, considering the circumstances."

"Yes." We walked past Ethan and Devin, the two young

boys who had identified Tuyen's Land Rover. They were dressed in another set of automotive T-shirts. I waved, and they waved back. "And what about Virgil White Buffalo? With the most recent developments, you cannot still be seriously considering him as a suspect."

I took a deep breath and felt the hot afternoon air burnish my lungs. "I don't know what I'm going to do about Virgil."

Henry stepped in front of me. "Let him go."

I pulled up and stared at the dirt street. "I can't do that, and you know it."

His eyes stayed steady on me. "Why not?"

"He's a potential witness to a homicide, and I don't think he can be released on his own recognizance." I took another breath but still found it hard to look at him. "Henry, he fought two highway patrolmen and two deputies to a standstill."

"Trying to stay out of jail for a crime he didn't commit."

I sighed. "Look, we can't be sure . . ."

"He has spent enough time behind bars for one life."

I finally looked at him, because I was getting a little angry. "If he is a potential danger to himself or anyone else, he becomes my responsibility."

He shifted his eyes, and they shone like shards of obsidian. "And where does that responsibility end?"

"It doesn't." We stood there, the echo of my voice coming back at us from the empty street, louder than I'd intended. "It doesn't ever end. Ever." I spoke softly now. "As long as he's in my county, he's my responsibility, and that puts me in line with a lot of other people who might consider leaving a seven-foot sociopath in a culvert under the highway a serious dereliction of duty."

"So, you are going to keep him incarcerated for the common good?"

"Until I can find somewhere for him to go, yes." I started

to walk around him and then stopped. "Henry, I can't let him continue to live under the highway. It's not humane."

"Neither is keeping him caged like an animal."

I took another breath, this one even hotter than the ones before, and held it for a moment. "I am aware of that." I continued on a few steps before turning and looking back at him. "What?"

He stood there for a moment and studied me. "I know you."

"And what's that supposed to mean?" He didn't move. "What?"

"I know that the real reason you are holding Virgil is in an attempt to fix his life, and that is beyond your abilities. You look at him and see experiences and directions similar to yours, but badly taken." He walked toward me. "You cannot correct the path he has chosen; it is his path. The only thing you can do is not punish him for something he has not done."

"I'm not looking to punish him, Henry, but there's got to be something better for the man than living under I-25."

His face remained impassive as he answered. "Perhaps, but that is something for him to discover, not for you to give him."

We walked along. "Well, maybe I can help."

The Bear smiled. "I know. This is not the first set of moccasins in which you have walked."

# 14

The Bear stood up from his hunter's crouch where he'd been studying the motorcycle tracks. "They are the same."

I took the key I'd gotten from the office and unlocked the door to room number 5 and ducked under the SHERIFF'S LINE—DO NOT CROSS tape we'd festooned across the door. At the front desk, I had asked the girl who had one headphone in her ear if she'd heard any motorcycles this morning, but she'd said no.

I asked her if she usually wore both headphones while cleaning.

She said yes, she did.

I asked her if she'd cleaned Tuyen's room this morning.

She said that she would have cleaned the room, but that he hadn't been around and they never entered a room without the occupant's expressed permission.

I asked her if she was kidding.

She said she wasn't.

I asked about the previous night, but she said that they pretty much closed up at nine and always left a number that would reach the owners if there were any problems, that they lived only three-quarters of a mile away.

I told her she could put the other headphone back in now.

---

I had turned Bill McDermott and his crew loose. I figured that the more important crime scene was the Dietz barn and that Henry and I could go over Tuyen's room as a preliminary before calling in the cavalry.

The place was as I'd left it hours before. There was a large bloodstain at the foot of the bed, a smaller one further in, and an intermittent trail that led to the adjoining room and bathroom.

I turned and looked at Henry, who was still standing in the doorway. "If you came through that door and someone was waiting to hit you, where would they stand?"

He looked around the entryway and to his right. "Behind the door."

"Okay, you want to come in and close that?" He did as requested and then joined me in looking at the distance from the door to the first bloodstain. "What'd he do, jump when he got hit?"

"Perhaps the assailant waited until he was farther inside?"

I shook my head. "Doesn't make sense. I mean, if you were planning on getting somebody, would you wait until he closed the door and took three or four steps before you hit him? Especially someone as physically capable as Tuyen?"

"So, you think he knew him?"

I walked toward the bed and kneeled beside the larger of the two stains. "I didn't get much out of him, but he said that someone had struck him from behind, that he had hit the ground, started to get up, failed, and then hit the floor again."

Henry stood by the dresser. "That would explain the first pool of blood, and then he tries to get up and falls where the smaller one is. Did he say he was unconscious before you got there?"

"Off and on."

He squatted down beside me. "Where was the wound?"

"Right side of the head and toward the back, just at the crown."

"Just one?"

"I'm not sure."

Henry looked back toward the door. "Is it possible that he was struck once, and then, when he started to rise, the assailant hit him again? That would explain the two stains."

"It's possible." I studied the spread that had been flung back from the corner of the bed, revealing the end of the angle-iron bed rail and the corner of the mattress, stained with blood.

Henry studied the corner of the bed frame. "So he was struck and then hit the corner?"

"Maybe."

The Cheyenne Nation studied me. "What are you thinking?"

"I'm thinking I want to talk to Tuyen." I stood and noticed that the metal case that was in Tuyen's car was on the dresser. "Under the strictest sense of the law, I'm not really supposed to be going through his personal items."

"No."

I walked over to the bureau and flipped the leather-wrapped handle. "He didn't say anything about missing his wallet and nothing else in the room seems disturbed, which leads me to believe that it wasn't a robbery attempt." I nudged the corner of the case with my finger. "Heavy; possibly a computer. If I was going to steal something in this room, I think I'd start with this."

"Yes."

"That makes this a suspicious item."

"Yes."

"And as a duly appointed law-enforcement official, it would be my responsibility to open it."

"Yes."

"There's only one problem."

"Yes?"

"It's locked."

With a sigh of exasperation, Henry slid the case toward him and flipped it up, looking at the four-digit combination. He paused for a moment and then rolled the thumbwheels until it read 1975. "Fall of Saigon."

Click.

**Saigon, Vietnam: 1968**

I heard the safety go off but wasn't sure where. The bouncer still stood in front of us, big, too big to be Vietnamese—probably Samoan. Our noses were about six inches apart—I was a couple of inches taller, but he probably had me by a good forty pounds. The really disconcerting part was that he was the one wearing a cowboy hat.

Baranski held his badge over my shoulder into the giant's face. "Look, Babu, Criminal Investigation Detachment. We're on a homicide investigation."

That much was true.

"We're working with your own ARVN intelligence sector..."

Not particularly true.

"...And if you don't step aside, I'm going to tell USMC specialist Longmire here to drag you over to the Long Bin stockade and specialize in stomping a puddle in your chest and walkin' the motherfucker dry."

Hopefully true.

He didn't move, but after a few seconds, he turned toward a slick-looking little fellow standing to the side, who disappeared behind the giant and then reappeared. He nodded his head, and the bouncer slipped to the left. I took a step forward but kept my face to him as Baranski and Mendoza passed behind me.

"Fuck you, son-of-bitch."

I slowly smiled my best Powder River grin, the one that would've made Owen Wister proud. "Smile when you call me that."

Western Town's theme was western, but whose was anybody's guess. The ubiquitous dancing girls wore white go-go cowgirl boots and either cheap costume cowboy hats or multicolored war bonnets, the kind that came from the Woolworth's back home. In the dim light, I could see the walls were raggedly festooned with western movie posters that were hand-painted with Vietnamese print or maybe Japanese. I could hardly move with the amount of people in the place; nearly all were locals, but the few servicemen who were mixed in with the mass of civilians were mostly enlisted. It looked like we were the brass, for better and probably worse. Mendoza and Baranski were already scouting the crowd but, from their continued craning, it was pretty clear that they hadn't spotted Hollywood Hoang yet.

Mendoza leaned in and spoke above the music. "You stay here, man, and we'll walk through and see if we can't flush him out."

"What about the back?"

He shook his head. "This your first time to the rodeo? There ain't no back door."

I watched as they disappeared into the crowd. There was a dance floor where Jim Ed Brown's "Pop a Top" warbled through the narrow building and made me homesick. I planted myself against a newel post leading to a stairwell to the basement and a beaded door. I was tired and all I wanted to do was sleep, so I closed my eyes for only a second. When I opened them, there was a teensy Vietnamese woman in a brightly feathered child's war bonnet who was standing on tiptoes to get my attention. "You like dance?"

"No, thanks."

"I give special plice?"

"No, that's okay." It was easy to see over her; only the tips of the feathers were in my line of sight. With the constant flux of people going in and out, it was hard to keep track, but if Hoang was wearing his trademark powder-blue jumpsuit and white silk scarf, I figured he'd be easy to pick out of the crowd.

She stepped in closer and put her hands on my uniform. "Special plivate dance?"

I blew on the feathers to get them away from my face. "No, really..."

"You look for fliend?"

"No..." I glanced down, and her eyes carried a greater intensity than they should have. "What?"

Her voice lowered but still held the same urgency. "You look for fliend?"

I was glancing over her head for either Baranski or Mendoza, neither of whom were in sight. "No, really, I'm a monk."

She stared at me for a moment, looked back into the main part of the room, and then glanced down the stairs leading to the basement. "Onree you."

I stood there looking at the sheen of the Southeast Asian night on her skin and thought of Mai Kim. I was assaulted by the hokey music, and the tumblers fell into place. "Do you know Hoang? Hollywood Hoang?"

Her eyes flicked back over her shoulder and then down the stairs again. "Onree you."

"Is Hoang down there?" Her face remained immobile. "I'm not going to hurt him, but I can't leave this spot unless he's down there."

The feathers bobbed imperceptibly as she nodded. My nod was just as slight. I slipped around the railing and started down the steps and thought about Hoang—how much he'd thanked me for saving his life in Khe Sanh, and how, if he'd really wanted to kill me, he probably would have already. He'd certainly had a bunch of opportunities.

But you never knew.

I unsnapped the strap on my .45 and pulled the hammer back. There was no door, just the beaded curtain, and it was dark. I thought about what a great backlit target I was making, parted the curtain, and stepped through.

The basement was even narrower than the bar. I walked past a dirt shelf that held a bunch of tiny compressors that looked more like gerbil wheels than coolers as they valiantly attempted to keep the upstairs, well, cool. There were boxes to my left, stacked to the ceiling as far as the light from the doorway would allow me to see. Jim Ed Brown had given way to Buck Owens and the Buckaroos upstairs, so I raised my voice a little and rolled the loaded but still holstered dice. "Hoang?"

I thought I could make out the sound of a movement behind me and to my right. I turned slowly and looked into the beer-can barrel of a Type 64, integrally silenced Chinese pistol.

His eyes were wide, and sweat had saturated the powder-blue jumpsuit to a sopped navy. I raised my hands without being bidden. "How are you, Hoang?" He didn't say anything and scanned to the right for anybody who might've been following me. "I'm alone."

His eyes couldn't remain still, and I could see the barrel of the pistol shaking in his hands. "Mai Kim..."

"She's dead."

His eyes welled, and he half swallowed, like there was something in his throat that wouldn't go down. He looked at the ground between us, but the pistol stayed where it was. After a few seconds, his voice wavered. "You know who kill her?"

I lowered my hands a little and he didn't seem to take exception, so I let them drop to my sides and slowly placed the .45 in my duty holster but left the safety off and the leather strap unsnapped. "You know, that's funny—we had a little discussion about that; your name came up."

He shook his head vehemently. "I no kill Mai Kim."

I was developing a hard-fought talent in Vietnam for being able to tell if people were lying to me. He was convincing, and I let the weight of it settle and drift us toward more conversation. "Well, then, who did?"

"I no kill Mai Kim!" The fat barrel faltered a moment then came closer to my face; I turned my palms out and took a half-step back, dropped my gun hand down, and gestured with the other. "All right, all right." He switched the gun to his other hand. "If you didn't kill her, then why are you holding a pistol on me?"

His lips compressed, and he swallowed again, the barrel not moving. "You on up?"

"What?"

"You on up?"

I inclined my head. "You mean the up-and-up?"

He nodded. "Up-up."

I took a breath and sighed. "Yep, I'm on the up-up or else why would I be in a bar basement off Tu-Do Street with my sidearm back in its holster?"

He paused for a moment, took a deep breath that caused his whole body to shudder, and then lowered the pistol. I took another half-step back to show him I'd meant what I'd said, leaned against the dirt shelf, and listened to the rickety compressors and Buck and the Buckaroos. "Hoang, if I wanted you dead, I'd have left you in the mud at Khe Sanh."

His eyes were steadier now, even with the sweat coursing down his face. "No mortar."

"What?"

"No mortar." He said it again, emphasizing each word.

"What's that supposed to mean?"

"At Khe Sanh, no mortar."

I felt cold, and it had nothing to do with the temperature. "You mean the round that hit the helicopter?"

He gestured with the barrel, which came up and to my left. "No mortar. Timer was..."

The shot compressed the confined space, and the spray of blood splattered in my eyes, making me blink. It didn't feel like I was hit, but something was falling against me and I caught it. It was Hoang, choking on his own blood with a sucking wound that made ghastly noises in his chest. He was already covered with blood, and his eyes looked up at me imploringly. I lowered him to the dirt floor as Baranski and Mendoza approached with their guns drawn.

I unzipped the flight suit and looked at the wound, blowing air with his breath, the bubbles flowing with the blood as it drained down Hoang's side. I gently pulled the silk scarf from around his neck and raised him up, wrapping the length of cloth around and under his shoulder to secure the front and rear wounds as best I could.

I looked up at the security officer and the CID investigator. "God damn it, why did you fire?"

Baranski looked incredulous. "Hey, new guy, I just saved your fucking life."

"He wasn't going to shoot."

He looked at Mendoza and then back to me. "He was pointing that bazooka at your head and why do you think he was using a silencer, dumb ass? You were about to become the honored dead."

I ignored him and began picking Hoang up.

"What're you doing?"

I pulled the tiny man against my shoulder, careful to avoid the entry and exit wounds. "I'm taking him to a hospital."

Baranski snorted; the Texan remained silent. "He's dead."

"He's not dead." I glanced down at the little man's eyes and watched as he blinked but didn't seem to be able to focus on my face. "You're not dead, do you hear me? You're hurt pretty bad, but we're gonna get you to a hospital and they'll patch you up. Do you hear me?"

His eyes clinched like they were capturing my words, and I knew he understood. I stepped forward, moving the two men back. "And you can either help me or get out of my way."

It's amazing how fast you can clear a path in a crowded club with guns and a mortally wounded man. I climbed into the back of the jeep and carefully placed Hoang on my lap. His pupils were a little constricted, and I was beginning to suspect that the pilot/drug dealer might've sampled a little of his own product and that it was the only thing that was keeping him alive.

Baranski backed the jeep into the crowded street, swung it in a tight circle, and took a left at the next block. I knew the nearest hospital was in the other direction. I yelled above the shifting gears as the M-1A1A veered around traffic and started north on Highway 1. "Where the hell do you think you're going?"

He yelled back at me over his shoulder. "I'm not taking that little dink to a civilian hospital here in Saigon where he can conveniently disappear. I'm taking him back to Tan Son Nhut."

I looked at Mendoza, who stared straight ahead with an arm braced against the dash.

I looked down at Hoang. "He'll die."

"We've got the best medical care in Southeast Asia only five minutes away, so hold on and shut the hell up." Baranski shifted into third, and the jeep slipped from the traffic and followed its headlights into the glowing dawn at the edge of the war-torn town.

"How are you feeling?"

He smiled and shrugged. "Rather foolish, actually. That, and I have a headache."

"I bet you do." I sat in the mauve-colored chair Durant

Memorial provided for visitors and took off my hat, placing it on Tuyen's metal case at my boots. Santiago Saizarbitoria stood by the door and, like all good flies on the wall, was doing his best to remain inconspicuous. "I hope you're feeling up to answering some questions."

"Oh, yes." He used the electric control to push himself further up on the bed and pulled a pillow down lower. "They're keeping me here overnight for observation, but other than the headache, I feel fine."

"That was quite a hit you took."

"I've had worse." He glanced at the floor. "Is that my case?"

"Yes, it is. I was thinking that you might like to have it."

"Thank you."

We were both aware that I was making no attempt at giving it to him. "Mr. Tuyen, are you sure you don't have any idea who might've attacked you?"

He looked up. "None whatsoever."

"Were you visited by anyone today? I mean before the attack?"

He didn't hesitate in responding. "No."

"You're sure?"

He waited for a moment, perhaps weighing the old adage that when law enforcement officials ask questions, they usually know the answers. He looked down at his hands. "There was someone who came to visit me early this morning."

"And who was that?"

His eyes returned to mine. "The bartender."

"Phillip Maynard?"

"Yes."

I leaned in, placing my elbows on my knees and casually flipping my hat around by the brim. "Do you mind telling me why you lied to me just now?"

"He wanted more money, and I didn't want to get him into trouble. It was a bad thing I did, paying him to be silent, and I did not wish to make the same mistake again."

"Mr. Tuyen, that's twice that you've dissembled when I've asked you a direct question. I'm going to advise you in the strongest terms, no matter what the circumstances, to not do it again."

He nodded. "I'm sorry, I..."

"What did he say?"

He seemed startled at my abruptness.

"He...he said that he could make my life difficult unless I gave him more money."

"Difficult in what way?"

"The conversation didn't go much further than that. I told him that if he threatened me again, I would contact you."

I looked into my hat, knowing full well that none of the answers to my questions were there. "But you didn't. You didn't tell me about Maynard's visit, his attempts at extortion, or anything." It was quiet, and we all listened to the thrum of the air-conditioning. "Did it ever occur to you that Phillip Maynard might've been the one who killed your granddaughter and that withholding this kind of evidence could be seen as an obstruction of justice?"

"I'm very sorry."

I looked at the worn label in the hatband of my hat and then back up to Tuyen's face. "Maynard left?"

"Yes."

"How?"

The questioning look returned. "I'm afraid I don't..."

"When he left, how did he leave, on a pogo stick?"

"On his motorcycle." I continued to watch him and could just see the little bits of anger at the corners of his mouth. "He came and left on his motorcycle."

I nodded. "Mr. Tuyen, were you struck once or twice in your motel room?"

"I believe once, but I could be wrong."

"Mr. Tuyen, I'm getting really tired of your inexactitude."

He clutched the bridge of his nose between his thumb and forefinger. "Sheriff, my granddaughter is dead. . . ."

"Mr. Tuyen, you have yet to provide me with any documentation proving that she was your granddaughter."

He took a breath but kept his eyes shut. "You don't believe that . . ."

"I'm not sure exactly what I believe, but you're not making it any easier for me." I stood, placed my hat back on my head, and picked up his case. "I'm afraid I'm going to have to ask you for a birth certificate, either Vietnamese or American."

He started to interrupt. "Sheriff, surely you understand the red tape involved."

"Papers such as baptismal, school records, or anything that will lead me to believe that Ho Thi was your granddaughter." I continued to hold the case, and we were both very aware of it. "Now, you can provide me with this information or I can contact the probate courts in California and have a deputy from the Orange County Sheriff's Department expedite the information."

He looked up at me and then spoke slowly. "Ho Thi was not adopted; she was my blood granddaughter."

"Then I'll have them contact the Bureau of Vital Statistics in Sacramento."

He nodded, and his lips tightened. "Sheriff, I did not expect to find Ho Thi dead. Any and all of her official papers, including a visa and birth documentation, are in the safe in my office, back in Los Angeles."

"Then you better contact someone and have that information faxed to us, and then I want the originals overnighted, now." I pulled the small 9 mm from the back pocket of my jeans. "And you better have a license for this."

Saizarbitoria followed me to the old Suburban parked next to my truck. I figured I'd take it and give him the Bullet. He deserved a few perks if I was going to make him work Powder Junction—that, and I wasn't sure if the aged vehicle would make it back and forth too many more times. According to how the election turned out this fall, somebody was going to have to requisition the county for a new or relatively new vehicle for the Powder Junction substation.

When I looked up, Santiago stood there by my open window. "Why did you bring the laptop to the hospital?"

I noted the 173,472 miles on the odometer and knew just how it felt. "I thought he might want to know it was being attended to." He kept watching me, the dark of his eyes deepening. "What, Sancho?"

"You mentioned that case a couple of times. Are you sure you didn't just want to see his reaction?"

I shook my head. "You have a sordid and suspicious mind." I sat there continuing to stare at the odometer and wondered what the mileage really might be, since it hadn't worked in years. "We couldn't get past the security software, so I figured I'd just hang on to the case for safekeeping."

"How about not telling him that Maynard was dead?"

I put on the loose seat belt and ground the starter. "He has his little secrets, and I have mine."

His turn to nod. "You really want me to stick around and keep an eye on him?"

The Suburban finally caught and roared. "Yep. Call up Frymire or Double Tough over at the jail and get a replacement for midnight."

He looked at the sun, which was attempting to escape over the Bighorn Mountains, and I didn't blame it or him for wanting to put a little distance between them and what appeared to be going on. "What're you going to do?"

"I'm going to go have dinner with my daughter, her new boyfriend and his sister, and Henry, and then I'm going to sleep at the jail."

His arms rested on the sill of the Suburban. "You really think Tuyen's liable to do something?"

I mused for a moment on how quickly the Basquo was developing and how long he was likely to be satisfied with the job of deputy. "I don't know, but according to you, somebody tried to kill him and you never can tell if they might come back and try to finish the job."

"So you don't think Maynard hit him or murdered the girl?"

I slipped the truck into reverse and waited a full five seconds for it to engage. "At this point in the investigation, I'm not ruling out anyone."

# 15

"Daddy."

It was possible that Tuyen had been attacked, but had he been hit twice or was it a setup?

"Daddy?"

I had pushed him, but had I pushed him enough? Was I pushing the wrong guy?

"Daddy!"

I focused on my daughter, who was giving me hard looks as Henry chuckled and the collective Morettis smiled and continued eating the hors d'oeuvres. "Sorry."

I picked up a stuffed mushroom from the appetizer tray and glanced at Michael for a little backup as he helped himself to another Rocky Mountain oyster. The Philadelphia beat cop came in like a champ with a little mind reading. "So you don' think this Tuyen is on the level?"

I chewed the mushroom, not tasting much of anything, and looked around at the interior of the Winchester Restaurant and the replica antique firearms over the fireplace. "I'm not sure how, or how deep he's involved, but something just doesn't ring true with the guy." I looked at Henry, who I'm sure was reading my mind; for him it had been a lifetime avocation. "What do you think?"

The Cheyenne Nation sighed. "He is spooky; once a spook, always a spook."

I thought about the old term for spies, nodded, and looked at Vic; I was still trying to get used to her in a white, ribbed tank top and a tight, short skirt. "What do you think?" She munched on a fried cheese stick and extended a hand, holding the palm down flat, shaking the turquoise bracelets at her wrist as her manicured hand wavered. Then I watched as she took another breaded steer testicle from the center platter and placed it onto Michael's plate.

I still wasn't sure if he knew what he was eating.

"One of the things that keeps snagging me is the preciseness of the hanging." I caught the eye of an elderly woman at the next table, and Cady glared at me, causing me to lower my voice and lean in. "The hanging was textbook—the drop according to height and weight, and there's only a limited number of people in the common populace who would know how to pull something like that off."

Vic played with the silver dancestick earrings I had gotten her up on the Crow reservation for her birthday. "Would Tuyen?"

"It's possible. Some of the organizations he was cozy with were known to perform these types of executions."

"Who else would know?"

I turned my glass of Rainier in the water ring. "I am loath to say it, but Den Dunnigan did a stint as a corrections officer up in Deer Lodge, Montana, back in the old days when they used to hang people. That and we just saw the Dunnigans' truck pull into the turnoff to Bailey but then continue on."

Michael dipped the high-plains delicacy in cocktail sauce. "He got any kind of record?"

"He has a temper, and once came close to beating a guy to death with a shovel."

Despite her reservations, Cady joined the conversation. "Is that the crazy rancher?"

"He's not crazy."

Henry chimed in. "I am not sure that confusing your mother with the timer on the electric coffeemaker denotes a great deal of mental stability."

I turned back to Cady. "Not James, his brother Den."

My daughter leaned in even more. "He thinks his mother is a coffeepot?"

I looked at all of them. "It's complicated. . . ."

The waitress interrupted. "Are you folks all right?"

Michael looked up at her, still munching on the Rocky Mountain oysters. "These are great; can we get another round?"

I thought about the girl, the missing one. Who was she? More important, where was she? The only thing I could think we might do is knock on doors from ranch to ranch and see if anybody had seen her. It was a long shot but all I could come up with in the rough and expansive country of the Hole in the Wall.

"What about the second girl?" The Bear was mind reading again, and I wasn't sure if I was happy that he had just made my internal monologue the topic of conversation for the group.

"What second girl?" I hadn't had a chance to fill Vic in.

"The manager of the Flying J down in Casper said there were two girls in the car and that both had long dark hair, but I asked Maynard and the Dunnigans, and they all said Ho Thi was traveling alone." I nodded at Henry. "James said that he was having . . . I don't know. What would you call them?"

He smiled. "Visions."

"Anyway, we went out to the ghost town and took a look around but couldn't find anything."

Michael took the last Rocky Mountain oyster. He hadn't noticed that he was the only one eating them. "Ghost town?"

"There's an old settlement to the west of Powder Junction, a mining town that dried up."

Michael stopped chewing and looked at Vic. "You have to take me there."

I looked at them. "There are snakes."

Vic blew a breath between her lipsticked lips. "Fuck that."

Cady smiled and reached a hand out for Michael, who took it. They both turned back to look at me. Cady seemed concerned. "What kind of visions?"

The elderly couple at the next table were leaning in, too, so I lowered my voice. "He said he saw the girl who had been murdered out there in Bailey."

"You mean when they found the body?" Cady's voice was a little too loud, so I gave her a look back.

"After that. James said he was driving home one night—this was after finding Ho Thi's body—and there she was standing on the side of the road."

Cady's voice was just as loud as before. "What'd he do?"

I shrugged. "He said he stopped his truck, but by the time he got out, she was gone."

Henry leaned back and sipped his wine and stared at the elderly couple who suddenly took less interest in our conversation. The Cheyenne Nation returned the glass of red to the surface of the table and, after a moment, spoke. "Den was a prison guard?"

"Yep."

"He seemed defensive."

Cady looked uncertain. "This is the crazy one?"

"His brother, but obviously a certain amount of eccentricity runs in the family." I looked at my neglected beer on the table and continued to lose my taste for it. "However, Den is very protective of James."

Henry nodded. "Yes, but why would Den, or for that matter James, kill Ho Thi, kill Maynard, and attempt to kill Tuyen?"

They were all silent, and this was when my job sucked.

Cady sipped her wine and smiled; always the optimist, she was trying to find the upside to my predicament. "So that means that Virgil White Buffalo is innocent."

"Yep." I watched the tiny bubbles rising in my glass, avoided all their eyes, but especially Henry's.

"So, you're sleeping at the jail again?"

I pulled the Suburban up to Vic's single-wide and slipped the decrepit thing into park. "It's my turn."

"You relieving Frymire?"

"Yep. Then Frymire is supposed to relieve Saizarbitoria at the hospital, because Double Tough didn't look good." Henry had disappeared in the Thunderbird, giving Cady and Michael a lift out to my place, so I had given Vic a ride home. I watched as she pulled a leg onto the bench seat, exposing a little thigh well above her boots.

"What are you going to do about Virgil, Walt?"

"I don't know, maybe call Human Services or try and get hold of somebody in charge of the social programs up on the Rez." She unsnapped her seat belt, turned, and carefully placed the black leather boots that were embroidered with blue roses in my lap. I thumbed the stitching. "Pleurosis. . . ."

"What?"

"Blue roses; it's what Tennessee Williams used to call his sister's pleurosis."

She shook her head, sighed, and considered me. "You are

so fucking weird." She crossed her ankles and made herself comfortable. "You have to let him go."

I thought about the big Indian and placed a hand above the boots on her well-shaped calf, marveling at the smoothness of her skin. "Yep."

She stretched and pushed her heels further into my lap. She curled an arm and propped up her head. The slight breeze from the open window stirred her hair. "What are you going to do about Tuyen?"

I stroked her calf, my hand pausing at the back of her knee as she drew it up, parting the short skirt further. "I figure I'll keep him under house arrest until I get some validation from California."

"The Dunnigans?"

"Well, considering the circumstances, I really don't have any choice but to bring them in for a formal questioning."

She smiled one of her more carnivoristic smiles, the one that displayed the oversize canine tooth to its best advantage. "And what are you going to do about me?"

I tipped my hat back, sighed, and looked at the analog clock—it was practically the only thing on the dash that worked. "I have to be at the jail in ten minutes."

Her golden eyes were enormous, and I tried to focus on them as her skirt slipped even higher. "Your loss."

Boy howdy.

"I'd ask for a rain check, but it doesn't seem to want to rain around here lately."

My handsome deputy shook her head and shifted her body. Like a dervish, she swung her boots down and kneeled on the seat, enjoying her height advantage as she turned, tilted my head back with both hands, and captured my mouth with her own. It was a bandit kiss, hard and fast—designed to leave the victim with a lingering feeling of what could have just been.

She straightened her lipstick with her third finger, slid out, closed the truck door, and turned, strutting away without bothering to pull her skirt down. She called over her shoulder. "You're telling me."

I felt like I'd been hit and run.

Virgil White Buffalo was the only one awake by the time I got to the jail. After snatching a few Post-its off my door facing, I discovered Frymire with Tuyen's computer still in his lap, and snoring again. It was possibly the reason the big Indian wasn't sleeping. He still didn't talk much, but I'd begun making a habit of speaking to him whenever possible, hoping that I could get him in practice. "Hey, Virgil."

He didn't say anything but nodded toward my deputy.

I carefully lifted the computer from Chuck's lap and nudged the young man, and he looked up at me. I put the computer back in the case that was open on the counter and read Ruby's latest missives.

"I guess I dozed off again, huh?"

"Yep, but if Virgil here won't hold up his end of the conversation and you don't play chess, it's to be expected. Anything new?"

"I was playing around with the computer, but the security systems are tough."

"You know about those things?"

"Yeah, I've got a degree in computer science."

"You do?" I thought about it. "I don't remember seeing that on your application."

"I didn't think it mattered—we don't have any computers in Powder Junction." He had a point.

I held one of the Post-its in my hand and read the designation. "ACSS-BPS." I looked up at him. "What the hell is BPS?"

"I have no idea."

I read the yellow square in my hand. "WiFi?"

"Wireless connections for computers; most people use it for laptops. Haven't you seen the signs on the motels out by the highway?"

The next note was about some stolen drilling equipment east of town. "Yep."

He yawned. "It means you can run your computer without hooking to a landline; just open it up and it acquires a signal."

I thought about it. "But what does WiFi actually stand for?"

"Wi is for wireless, and . . ." He paused. "I'm not sure what the Fi stands for."

I stuffed the Post-its in my shirt pocket. "Semper . . ." I wasn't so sure he got it and watched him yawn again.

He caught me glancing at him, and he gestured toward Tuyen's computer. "You want me to take that thing and see what I can come up with?"

It was personal property, but if everything checked out with the Vietnamese man's story, I'd just be hauling it over to the hospital for him anyway. "Sure; maybe it'll help you to stay awake."

I sent him off with his homework and sat in the chair opposite Virgil. I slid the upside-down trash can with the chessboard between us. Virgil White Buffalo, Bad War Honors, Crazy Dog Clan, studied me.

"I'm afraid I'm not going to be much of a challenge in comparison to Lucian."

His voice was still rough but carried like a bass viola,

vibrating the air between us. He turned the board, and I ignored the symbolism as he gave me white and the first move. "Maybe you're better than you think."

I froze my finger on a pawn. "I doubt it."

"You must be worthy. Short-pants told me the Old Ones speak with you." I looked up, and his eyes stayed on mine as we listened to the old Seth Thomas on the wall tick. He gestured through the bars and toward the game. I brought the pawn out to G4 and he countered with another to B5. There was a pause, and I listened to him breathe along with the ticking of the clock. "The Old Ones have never spoken to me."

**Tan Son Nhut, Vietnam: 1968**

"He's dead." I looked at Hoang's eyes and watched as they stared indifferently, his mouth slack in silence and the bubbles no longer struggling through the blood that saturated his chest. I held his head up and supported it against me.

Baranski laid an arm over Mendoza's seat and threw a look back. "What?"

The sunrise oranged the sky, and I desperately tried to contain my anger. "You can slow down now, he's dead."

The CID man peered back at the road and returned his eyes to me through the rearview. "What'd you just say?"

"I said that he's dead, and you can slow down. You accomplished what it was you set out to do."

He looked at Mendoza, who was in the passenger seat and was still staring ahead. If I hadn't known any better, I would have sworn that there were two dead men in the jeep. "Are you accusing me...?"

"He told me about the satchel, the one you gave him to take in the helicopter when we were on our way to Khe Sanh." Even in the gloom of early morning, I could see his eyes as they flicked to the side. "He told me, and I saw you do it. Pretty slick, getting rid of all your bad eggs in one basket."

"Hey, fucking new guy, do you have any idea the shit that you're getting yourself into?"

I ignored him and continued. "It didn't make any sense when the chopper blew to the northeast with Charlie attacking from the same direction. Anything they would have shot at us would've blown the other way." I gestured with the body in my arms. "I guess Hoang didn't know you intended to kill him, too. And then, since that didn't work, you tried to get him to kill me. If I've got it right, Hoang was supposed to get me good and drunk and then take me out to the bunker where you'd already killed Mai Kim and finish me off." I swallowed, my spit catching in my throat. "But I saved Hoang's life in Khe Sanh, and he couldn't shoot me himself or pick me up and drag me over to the murder site where you could finish the job. He didn't even tell you where I was." I looked down at Hoang's dead face. "Turns out, he was a pretty good guy, huh?"

He kept the jeep at close to sixty. "Fuck you, you fucking asshole."

My hand slipped below Hoang's legs, where the safety strap from my .45 was still unsnapped and the safety was not on. "The acceleration in drug trafficking roughly coincided with your arrival here at Tan Son Nhut, and the only thing I'm wondering is whether you knew about the investigation beforehand and were trying to protect your interests, or if you just stumbled onto this mess and made it your own little cottage industry."

He looked at the road through the windshield as if there were something up there. "You don't know shit."

Mendoza suddenly spoke. "Hey..."

I looked over at Baranski. "I think I've got it all pretty much figured out, except for one thing." I studied the back of Mendoza's head. "Is he in on it, too?"

The Texan raised a hand, pointing toward the road. "Hey!"

Baranski looked at the side of his partner's face, and I cleared the big Colt from under Hoang's legs as the Texan grabbed at the steering wheel. Baranski swung back around as we struck something in the road, which sent the jeep in a two-wheeled spiral off to the left. "What the . . . !"

The vehicle didn't quite flip, but the jolt tore Hoang's body from my grip, and I tumbled out the back with the .45 still thankfully in my hands. I hit a dirt pile and carried a lot of it with me into the barrow ditch beside the road. I lay there for a moment, trying to get my breath back, and looked around for Mendoza and Baranski, but the only body visible was Hoang's, lying askew about twenty yards in front of me.

I shook my head and felt some blood dripping down my cheek. I must have picked up road rash from the pavement. I rose up on my skinned elbows and shook my head again in an attempt to clear my vision; it seemed as though the surrounding bushes were approaching Hoang's body and the jeep, which was still lying on its side on the elevated highway. Birnam Wood marching on Dunsinane.

I listened to the pounding that sounded like tanks firing in the back of my brain and wiped some of the dirt and blood from my face with my free hand. I took a deep breath and stood, thinking that I'd better find the CID man and his chum before they found me.

Then the bushes turned and looked at me.

They were wearing black pajamas and flat hats and stood there with gleaming AK-47s. One of the bushes toward the back held a Soviet-made RPG grenade launcher and gestured for the others to help him haul a light machine gun that Hoang's body must have hit when it had been thrown from the jeep.

I raised the .45 as the closest soldier, the one with the RPG, began screaming. I fired, and he slumped backward into a sitting position, the bush camouflage falling to his side. I ran toward the others. It was a dicey proposition, but the range on the Colt was useless against the AKs unless I could get in close. I ran forward as the next bush swung his weapon toward me. I blocked the barrel by grabbing the fore stock, and he fired into the hillside. I pressed the .45 into his midriff, pulled the trigger, and held on to his gun as he fell away.

A spray of gunfire ripped up from the ditch, and I fell to the side of the man I'd just shot, yanked the automatic rifle up, and took a bead on the VC soldier who was shooting. The kick was a little harder than an M16, or maybe it was just the uncomfortable wooden stock, but the other fellow dropped anyway, and I lit up a few more VC as the rest disappeared into the high grass.

Do what you're trained to do and you might get out of this alive. Make the right decisions as if your life depended on them, because it does. Hesitate and you hesitate forever.

I lay there trying not to focus on the multitude of ways I could've died in the last few minutes and listened to the pounding in the back of my head instead. I stretched my jaw muscles and looked down the road where the sappers and Viet Cong squad had been headed. I knew we weren't very far from the west gate of the air base, but the few hooches in the area appeared deserted and there were no civilians on the highway, which was something I'd never seen before. It was then that I noticed the wreckage of an M48 tank. There were bodies sticking out from all the hatches, and it was obvious that the machine was out of action. Beyond it was an M113 armored personnel carrier—the battle-taxi must have run into the back of the Patton when it'd gotten shelled—and there was another body slumped over the .50 caliber machine gun at its commander seat.

Farther down the line, I could see more wreckage where a few more of the APCs had been likewise shelled and were out of commission. Along with the remaining tank, five vehicles were herringboned off the road and firing into an old textile manufacturing building to the west.

It was obvious what had happened. With boots and saddles, the cavalry force must have been dispatched from further north, possibly from Cu Chi, in defense of Tan Son Nhut, and been dry-gulched on Highway 1.

A buddy who had been at the Fort Knox armor training school said they'd shown them what a real firefight was supposed to look like in a display known only as the Mad Minute, but where the tank and machine-gun fire was directed at a target in the display, here and now the thousands of green tracers that were lighting up the quasi-darkness were traveling toward me.

A few streaming bolts of fire from a bazooka caromed off a billboard at the roadside until one found a trajectory that hit the armored personnel carrier that had been the source of the nearest friendly fire. It blew to pieces with a thundering shudder.

A few of the Viet Cong squad that had been disguised as bushes were now throwing hand grenades over the arch of the highway about a hundred yards away. I was unfamiliar with the AK-47, but I finally found the single-shot switch and aimed at the nearest VC. My shot was a little low and to the right, but he fell and the grenade he held exploded, taking him and the two men nearest him.

I stepped back into the bamboo for cover, counted five seconds, then leaned back out and fired again. I had a clean miss on the next, and he began running the other way to join another squad that had come out of the civilian hooches.

There were hundreds of them.

I started rethinking my tactics and thought that perhaps I should try to find somebody on my side who wasn't dead. With a glance at Hoang's body, I struggled to get up the embankment to the burnt-out M48. The footing was pretty good, and I got to one of the dirt berms that had blocked the road. A few enemy rounds ricocheted off the surface. I took some deep breaths and slid around to the east behind another dirt pile to get to the personnel carrier's forward track. The driver was the closest, and it was obvious that he was dead. I glanced up at the commander's cupola and could see that he was dead, too. I decided to check the next APC.

No one was firing from the vehicle, but I could still hear noises from inside. The main hatch was open, and it looked like the majority of the personnel had escaped with only a few dead. I could smell the blood, so sweet it was almost sour, and was about to move on when I noticed a sergeant who was still breathing sitting with his back against the engine housing. I yelled at him. "Gunny, you all right!?"

His head wavered a moment, then he raised his face. His left eye was gone.

I scrambled through the hatch and grabbed his arm, pulling him toward me as another round of AK fire ricocheted off the tough hide of the armored vehicle and flew around the area where I'd just been standing. I had a flickering of anger at the men who had deserted the damaged sergeant as I staggered into the vehicle and placed him against the bulkhead. "On second thought, it might be a little safer in here."

I grabbed a first-aid kit from the steel-plated interior and pulled out a pad and a box of gauze, carefully wrapping it around his head to stanch the bleeding. The round must've entered his eye and then exited at his closest ear, a miracle in itself. Then I slipped out one of the syrettes of morphine and stabbed the one-hitter into his chest.

He started and looked at me with the one eye. "Do you know what day it is?"

He had a thick Appalachian accent, and I studied him, stunned that he could still talk or hear. "What?"

I watched as he tried to speak with one side of his mouth. "Do you know what day it is?"

I swallowed in an attempt to work up some spit, but my tongue still felt like one of those fly strips. "I think it's a Tuesday."

He nodded. "It feels like a Tuesday."

I smiled back at him and placed the sticker from the syrette on his lapel so that the medics would know he'd been dosed. "Yes, it does." He mumbled something else as I checked the rifle's banana-style magazine and found it had only two rounds left.

The attacking soldiers were getting closer, and it was only a short question of time before they hit us with another screaming antitank round or dropped a grenade in the hatch. I laid the almost-spent AK in the sergeant's lap. "Sarge, I need you to sit tight, because if I don't start laying down a little suppression fire, we're about to be overrun."

I saw that one of the M60s had exploded its barrel and that the other one didn't look much better. I was trying to avoid the dead commander, but the .50 caliber machine gun looked like our last chance. I reached up and gently pulled the captain down from his position and set him beside the sergeant. He'd caught at least three rounds in the chest, and his expression was one of profound interest; he didn't look surprised, and it was as if he'd known exactly what was happening to him as it had happened. I looked at the sergeant, who appeared to sink back a little as his one eye closed, and I hoped I could get us a little breathing room before he stopped breathing.

I checked the .50 and could see that it had never been fired. I racked the charging handle, braced my boots, and carefully raised my head up through the hatch. I could hear voices to my left and pivoted to see a number of VC crawling all over the M48 that I had abandoned.

I swung the barrel of the heavy machine gun around and tried to remember the numbers from basic and recalled that the air-cooled M2 would cycle 550 rpm if you let it, but that if you did, it would shoot out the barrel; so I pulled the trigger with just a little restraint—sprayed and prayed.

The weapon did everything it was designed to do, and I hoped that I would never have to see anything like it again.

I pivoted back to the ditch and laid suppression fire along the embankment; those who could crawl or run scattered into the hooches and grass like Wyoming wild turkeys on the third Thursday of November.

If I was going to get the sergeant and myself out of there, now was the time.

I jumped down from the commander's platform and turned around in time to see Baranski. He was perfectly framed in the open back hatch of the armored personnel carrier, and he was smiling.

I stood there for one of those slow-motion frozen seconds as he raised Hoang's Type 64, integrally silenced Chinese pistol at my face and fired.

"Do you want to answer that?" His voice was coarse with enough gravel to fill a five-yard dump truck.

I looked up at Virgil's eyes and tried not to focus on the damage to his left brow. "What?"

He exhaled a slight laugh. "You're playing a very good game, but the phone is ringing."

I looked down at the half-finished chess match and then up to the phone on the holding cell wall. "Thanks. You'll let me know if I win, right?" I walked over and picked up the receiver. "Absaroka County Sheriff's Office?" I didn't sound like I was sure.

"Walt?"

I came back fully when I realized it was Frymire. "Yep?"

"I'm over here at the hospital, but Sancho's not here."

That wasn't like the Basquo. "What about Tuyen?"

"Sleeping like a baby."

"Maybe he went to the bathroom or to get something to eat."

Chuck was sounding a little rattled. "Sheriff, I've been here for a half an hour, and he hasn't shown up. I asked the on-duty nurse, but she said she hadn't seen him since she'd made her rounds at eleven forty-five." I looked up at the clock—forty-five minutes. "You want me to call him at home?"

I thought about Marie and their expected child, and her reaction to a one o'clock in the morning call from the Sheriff's Department concerning the whereabouts of her husband. "No, I'll take the beeper and come over."

I glanced back at Virgil White Buffalo as I hung up the phone and thought about what he would do to the jail when I left him alone. I was going to let him go tomorrow anyway—today, technically, so what could it hurt? I handed him his personal effects from the drawer, including the photo wallet, jacket, and knife. "Virgil, how would you like to go on a little field trip?"

By the time we'd driven through the sulky, high-plains night and gotten to the hospital emergency entrance, the duty nurse, Janine Reynolds, was waiting for us.

She looked up worriedly at Virgil, no doubt remembering his last visit. I glanced up at him. "You're not going to trash the place again, are you?"

His face remained impassive. "No."

Frymire was standing in the hallway next to his chair at Tuyen's door when we approached. He stood, a little unsteadily, and readjusted his shoulder with Tuyen's computer still under his arm. "I haven't seen him, and I've been here for almost an hour."

I turned to Ruby's granddaughter. "Janine?"

She pointed. "When I made my rounds before midnight, he was sitting in that chair."

Frymire tried to interrupt, but I was still looking at Janine. "Tuyen?"

She nodded toward the closed door. "I took his dinner tray away. He was looking out the window when I told him it would be a good idea to turn off the light and rest."

I shrugged as I turned the handle and opened the door. "Well, at least he hasn't been asleep long." Frymire held it open as I entered and flipped on the light. "Mr. Tuyen?" He was rolled up in the sheets and a single polyester blanket and was turned away from us toward the windows. "Mr. Tuyen, I'm sorry to bother you, but . . ."

He didn't answer and, as I got closer, I could see that there was a dark stain on the covers. I leaned over and carefully pulled the sheet back from his face.

"Oh, Sancho."

# 16

He wasn't dead, but damn near.

Tuyen had used the serrated dinner knife from his hospital tray and had utilized the flimsy blade to its worst advantage, planting it deep while twisting it upward and into Saizarbitoria's kidney, then breaking it off, resulting in massive internal hemorrhage and partial paralysis. Fortunately, he had been attacked in the hospital, and we had him in surgery in less than ten minutes. "I'll call Marie, you call everybody else and get an APB out on my truck. He's got Sancho's gun, so make sure they know he's armed, then get over to the office and coordinate."

"Who's everybody else?"

We stood by the swinging doors. "Vic, the Ferg, Ruby, Double Tough, the highway patrol, Natrona County, Campbell County, Sheridan County.... And if there's a Canadian Mountie on duty, I want him on it, too."

"What about Henry?"

I looked up at Frymire, at his battered face and broken arm, still cradling Tuyen's computer. "Especially Henry."

I started toward the emergency room exit and noticed that something continued to block the fluorescent light in the hallway over my shoulder. I turned and looked at Virgil; how had I forgotten about a seven-foot Indian? I pointed at Frymire, who was making his calls from the nursing station. "Virgil, could you go with him?"

He didn't move but studied me and then strained to get the words out. "You need help..."

I stared at him. "I'm about to get a lot of it."

I looked into the haloed reflections in his pupils and could tell that it cost a lot for him to speak. "You need help now."

Other than shoot him, there wasn't a lot I could do to stop him, and maybe I was ashamed that I had him locked up for almost a week with barely any cause, but I didn't have time for this. "Look, I appreciate the offer, but..."

"I know that country."

I looked up and felt like a child arguing with an adult, the medicine bag on his chest at my eye level. "What?"

"You are going to Bailey, the ghost town. I know it better than anyone."

"What makes you think that I'm going..."

"The silver-haired woman, she said the electric messages were coming from the school."

It took me a second to make the connection. "The e-mails?"

"Yes."

I thought about it. "They were coming from the wireless-whatever-it-is of the county school system."

He nodded. "The electric messages from the BPS." His eyes darkened; reflecting everything, showing nothing. "It is the same abbreviation that is on a plaque they have on the outside of the building. I have seen it while watching the children... BPS. Bailey Public School."

It was like I was falling from the earth. It all fit; the random e-mails, the missing computer that was of such interest to Tuyen, the appearance of the second girl—the fact that Ho Thi didn't bear much of a resemblance to Mai Kim. The real great-granddaughter of the woman I knew in Tan Son Nhut was in Bailey and had been desperately trying to get in touch with me the only safe way she knew how.

"She is there, and we must find her before he does."

Once I'd called Marie and asked Doc Bloomfield to update me on Santiago's condition, Virgil and I were in the old Suburban and on the road. I radioed in to give everyone an indication as to our location and destination, and it was Rosey who responded.

Static. "Damn it, I'm I-90, east of Durant, but I'm turning around now. I'll call ahead to the Casper detachment and send them north."

I keyed the mic. "Roger that." Virgil continued to watch the road ahead. I flattened my foot on the accelerator and listened as the big block made like Big Daddy Don Garlits; she was old, but in a straight line the 454 cubic inches was some kind of fierce.

Thirty minutes later, we took the exit at Powder Junction and shot west toward the south tail of the Bighorns and Bailey. Virgil braced a hand that nearly covered the dash as I made the corner before dropping over the hill to where we had a clear view of the abandoned town.

I was hoping to see my truck parked on the main and only drag of the old mining community or at the school just over the hill, but the only vehicle I saw was the turquoise and white Ford that belonged to the Dunnigan brothers.

I stopped the truck and tried to decide if I should continue to the school or head down and see what was up with Den and James. I decided to check on the brothers and turned the wheel.

I pulled up alongside their truck and got out. Virgil opened the passenger-side door and stood in the middle of the street as I looked inside the pickup.

The rifle rack was empty. Otherwise, everything seemed normal, and the keys were dangling from the ignition. I felt the hood, and the warmth from the engine was still there, but could see no signs of my truck, the brothers, Tuyen, or the missing girl.

It didn't make sense—the Dunnigans, but no Tuyen?

It was obvious that Virgil was reading my mind as he circled around and joined me. "You check the school, and I'll stay here."

I thought about it and then looked up and down the deserted street. "Virgil, I can't . . ."

"You must find the girl."

"They're liable to shoot you."

He opened the driver-side door and pushed me into the Suburban before I could voice any further objections. He stood there looking down at me and smiled as he shut the door. He rested his giant hand on the knife at his belt. "I have been shot before."

**Tan Son Nhut, Vietnam: 1968**

I lay there on the floor of the personnel carrier and thought that it sure hurt a lot to be dead. I stared up through the open hatchway and watched the sickly lemon color of the sky as the sun fought to bring more heat to the Southeast Asian morning. I could hear helicopter support coming in from Tan Son Nhut and watched as the Huey gunships shot in and through the sky above.

The 7.65 × 17 slug had taken part of the clavicle and a lot of meat with it, and it was all I could do to stay aware and watch as

Baranski climbed through the opening of the APC. He continued to point the Type 64 at my face. My head was lodged against the bulkhead and the driver's station, with my left arm pinned behind me. I made a futile kick at him as he stood over me.

The CID man watched the helicopters fly overhead. "Re-gas, bypass, and haul ass. That'd be the Troop D gunships, and I'd say that means the end of Charlie's little Tet surprise." Baranski propped a foot up on the seat and studied me with an indifferent look on his face. "Damn, you can't hit shit with these little Chinese fuckers."

I choked out a response, figuring the more time I took, the more of a chance there was that somebody would show up. "You hit me."

"Yeah, but I was aiming between your eyes." He laughed. "You should have stayed at BHQ, dumb ass; it would have been a lot safer there."

I grimaced as another stab from my shoulder caught my breath in my throat. "So, it was your operation?"

He pulled the pack of Camels from his shirt pocket and bumped one, placing it between his lips. "It became mine." He redeposited the pack and pulled out the Zippo and lit up. "It was kind of a rag-tag operation, but it held promise." He inhaled deeply and looked down at me again. "I'm pulling in almost a hundred thousand dollars a month, and I was going to cut you in, but you were so fucking *gung-ho*."

"Hoang was your partner?"

He sniffed and cleared his throat before taking another long drag on the cigarette. "Yeah, and he's going to be hard to replace. The satchels were a hell of an operation; I could get anything—hashish, opium.... Whatever anyone wanted, I could get it, and even better, I could get it out and back to the land of the great PX. I'll have to get another pilot for this route, but that really shouldn't be that much of a problem." He studied me and laughed. "All the trouble started when that stupid bitch decided to tell you about the deal. Do you believe that? All this because of some fucking *putain*." He took another drag and considered me. "We can talk as long as you want, 'cause there's nobody coming. Charlie Troop is over at the *Ville* shooting prisoners right now." His eyes were uncaring, and he palmed the Chinese pistol as he spoke. "You see, Mr. Marine Investigator, nobody gives a shit."

I tried to readjust my position, but wedged in the walkway there wasn't anywhere to go. "What about Mendoza?"

"The beaner? What about him?"

It hurt just to breathe, but I had to keep talking. "Was he in on it?"

"Nah, I had him pretty much trained to look the other way. The only thing was I figured he'd get suspicious if I fragged you." He pulled the cigarette from his mouth and spit out a piece of tobacco from his tongue. "He was pretty torn up from the wreck, so I just walked over and put one in the back of his head. Put him out of my misery. Kind of like I'm going to do to you. I'm glad that I didn't kill you the first time. It's nice that I get to see you, see your expression when I shoot you in the face." The Type 64 came back up and leveled at my eyes. "Look at me, not a scratch. You know, they say that George Washington was like that; Patton, too; there'd be a battle with bullets zipping around all over the place and they'd never get touched." He smiled again, and I watched as his finger tightened on the trigger. "Like them, I guess I'm just fucking lucky that way."

The blast of the gun sounded like two, and the blood sprayed everywhere.

I lay there for a moment thinking that I shouldn't be thinking.

I blinked and looked up through the blood on Baranski's face, at his lips where the cigarette continued to hang, just before he toppled over and landed on top of me. He shuddered once and then lay still. I looked up at the one-eyed sergeant who was seated against the bulkhead and still holding the AK-47 with the thin trailing of smoke drifting from the barrel.

His voice had a singsong quality to it, just before his single eye closed again. "I guess your fucking luck just ran out, asshole."

There was no one at the school.

I pulled into the driveway and got out, taking the Maglite from the pocket in the door along with the handheld two-way radio. The batteries were weak in the flashlight, but it provided more illumination than the listless moon that was just rising. I listened to the soft tinging of the hardware against the flagpole and remembered the school on the Powder River that I'd attended. I walked up to the front door of the single-story, concrete-block building and saw that it was padlocked. I peered through the window and could see a couple of desks and a computer on a side table. Abandoned for summer, it looked like no one had been in the place in a couple of months.

I sighed and glanced around, hoping to see a Vietnamese girl somewhere in the high-plains night. I was disappointed.

I punched the button on the radio and looked up at the red cliffs that seemed to soak up the light of the moon. "Absaroka County Sheriff's Department, this is unit one. Is anybody out there?"

Static.

Damn cliffs.

I drove over the hill back to Bailey and parked the Suburban in front of the Dunnigans' old Ford. I climbed out with the flashlight in my hand again—this time, someone was sitting in the driver's seat. I pulled my .45 and shined the dimming flashlight into the cab; I recognized the profile and spoke through the open passenger-side window. "James?"

He turned to look at me as I trailed my sidearm below the window where he couldn't see it. "Hey, Walt."

I waited a second and then lowered the beam of the Maglite, but he didn't continue. "What're you doing here, James?"

He took a deep breath, pushed his straw hat back, and sipped from a tarnished flask. I could see the .30-30 lever-action propped up next to the door. "Oh, I was headin' back from the bar and come lookin' for that girl... the dead one."

I studied him and then rested an elbow on the door to strike a more conversational posture. "What's the Winchester for?"

He smiled and looked embarrassed. "This place, it kind of worries me.... I guess I'm gettin' scary."

"You mind if I take it?"

He studied the rifle, then me. "Sure, sure... nothin' to be afraid of if you're here."

I carefully reached in and pulled the Winchester through the window, threw the lever a couple of times to empty it, and then shuttled it and the loose rounds onto the floorboard of the Suburban. I locked the truck and watched James, who hadn't moved except to drink from the flask. "You find her?"

He took a breath to give himself time to think and then shook his head. "No, no, no..." He stared at the dash as we listened to the soft tick of the big-block cooling on my vehicle. He extended the flask toward me, and I could smell the trademark brandy. "Care for some?"

"No thanks." I shook my head. "James, have you seen anybody else around here?"

He brought the flask back to his lips and took a swallow, then brought a finger up and touched the shift knob on the old truck. "You know, most people don't believe the things I tell 'em...." He turned his head and looked at me. "So I just stop tellin' 'em." His eyes wavered a little, and I noticed he was looking past me and to the right—I turned and followed his gaze, but there was no one there. "Do you know you're bein' followed?"

I turned and looked again but still couldn't see anyone. "Now?"

"All the time." He took another sip from the flask, and his eyes returned to the dash. "They're with you all the time, or all the times I've ever seen you." I continued to study him, but he didn't move. ". . . Met a giant."

It took me a second to respond. "You did?"

"Yep, real big Indian fella."

"And where was that?"

He leaned forward and peered through the top of the windshield. I followed his gaze past the graveyard and above the rock shelf at the end of town. "Up there."

I pushed off with the Colt still camouflaged beside my leg. "Thanks, James."

"That big Indian, he brought me back down here, took my keys, and told me to stay in my truck." His look trailed up toward the union hall. "I offered him my saddle-gun, but he said he liked to work quiet." I nodded and turned to continue up the street, where the edge of the moon was just beginning to clear the cliffs. They looked black, the way blood does in moonlight. "Hey, Walt?"

I stopped and looked back at him through the reflection of the vent window. "Yep?"

"Is that big Indian a friend of yours?"

I thought about it. "Yes. He is."

He cast a glance up the street and then back to me. "Is he . . . ?"

I waited, but the drunken man who saw things that nobody else saw just continued studying me. "Is he what?"

He took another slug of the brandy and then turned to look back up the hill. "Is he dead, too?"

"I sure hope not." I started to grin, but it wouldn't take. "Stay in the truck, James."

He nodded. "I will."

I walked up the street with those feathers of anxiety scouring the insides of my lungs as I checked each dilapidated building. I still saw no sign of Virgil, Tuyen, or the girl. A ghost town and, except for James and me, deserted.

It was like the place was swallowing souls.

I saw a glimmer of something beside the collapsed wall of the saloon and eased myself down the wooden boardwalk far enough to see the nose of my truck. I took a breath and raised my Colt. Staying next to the crumbling wall, I slipped in behind the Bullet and saw that the doors were locked and the keys were gone.

I pulled the two-way from my belt and gave it another try. "Unit one, anybody copy?"

Static.

I looked up past the cemetery to the union hall, at the castellated cornices and second-story outcropping that gave it the appearance of a fortress standing on the hill. The still listless moon was at a full quarter, and I could see that the sicklelike point had just cleared the cliffs.

I started the climb, keeping the .45 in front of me. I was unconcerned about the rattlesnakes since the evening was cool and they'd likely be sleeping in the crevices of the stone outcroppings off to the right, attempting to glean the last bit of the day's warmth that was still held by the rocks.

I paused at the cemetery and laid a hand on the steel railing, looked up at the dark windows, and then peered at the path. In the darkness it would be difficult to see if anyone had passed. The steps appeared the same but, as I tipped my hat back for a better view, I could see the door to the union hall was open. I knew that I had closed it.

The sweat at the middle of my back had adhered my uniform shirt to my spine, and I shivered in the cooling breeze.

It was a steep climb, and I took a few deep inhales to steady my breathing. I stood at the doorway and looked down the shotgun hall, past what used to be offices and into the gloom of the back rooms. I could see the size 13 swirls my rubber-soled ropers had left in the heavy dust from my previous visit, and there was an obvious trail where I'd gone farther into the building and then doubled back to go up the stairs to the dance hall.

Barely visible inside my boot prints were a set of well-defined, high-arched, tiny footprints exactly tracing my tracks.

I stepped into the entryway and led with the .45. She had continued up, carefully placing her bare feet inside mine. I shifted my weight, clicked off my radio, and stared up the stairs, then climbed as quietly as I could. It was useless—I sounded like a collection of squeals and creaks, ascending.

I paused at the landing and looked at the dance hall floor. The wavering moonlight cast across the flat surface and illuminated our joined tracks like pools of liquid mercury. I eased myself further up the steps and took hold of the railing at the top. The old upright piano sat on the stage, alone.

Standing room only and nobody there.

The moon suddenly decided to take an interest, and the full force of its shine spread through the bay windows at the front of the hall, through the half-glass doorway that led to the balcony beyond, and across the dance floor in a blue light of growing rectangular proportions.

I stepped up onto the floor, my eyes following the tiny footprints that had continued in mine as they crossed the room, up the three steps to the right, and across the stage.

I trained the Colt from corner to corner and then approached the proscenium arch. She had stopped at the piano. I placed my empty hand on the lip of the elevated area and hoisted a boot onto the edge, effectively, if not gracefully, taking the stage.

There were no more footprints. It was as if she'd walked there and then not so simply had disappeared.

The cover was open, and I could see the dust on the hammers of the keys that I hadn't played and a new accumulation on the ones that I had. She hadn't touched the keys.

The bench was still under the piano. There were no fingerprints on it, no sign that she had sat there. I nudged it out a little bit, put the .45 next to me, and sat, half facing the dance floor. I extended a forefinger and touched an F, the offkey sound almost reverent in the empty hall. I thought "Moonglow" would be appropriate, but changed my mind, thinking that I should play "A Good Man Is Hard to Find" for Mai Kim's great-granddaughter.

I played an octave lower than it was written in an attempt to stay within the narrow confines of the soundboard. I'm not sure what I was expecting, but after playing a few stanzas, I heard a noise to my left. I picked up the Colt and turned with it extended to see that a small trapdoor had risen about four inches at center stage.

I stopped playing, and my breathing was the only sound in the room. The door in the floor slowly and silently shut.

I noticed that the footprints leading past the trapdoor were slightly smudged; she must have retraced them and retreated exactly upon them. I lowered my sidearm to my knee, turned back toward the piano, and placed my free hand back over the keyboard, plinking the F again as a starting point. I played the melody this time with one hand, and after a few seconds, the trapdoor rose again, allowing me a view of the small fingers that had pushed it.

I continued to play one-handed, then turned back, set

the .45 on the bench, and allowed my left to join my right. I thought about Vietnam, and about how I'd filled the empty evenings at the Boy-Howdy Beau-Coups Good Times Lounge with Fats Waller.

Like a snake charmer, I played the song that Mai Kim must have told her daughter about and about which she must have told her daughter in turn. I played a smooth and steady version that left off with a trilling finish. I sat there, unmoving, until I couldn't stand it any longer and turned.

She stood beside the trapdoor that was in the stage floor. She was tiny, and she wore a cheap slip dress that perversely made her look even more like a child. Her black hair was long and tangled, and it covered part of her face so that I could only see one of her dark eyes. She held a laptop close to her chest. Her thin arms crossed its lid, and she looked like a computer with a head and legs.

She didn't move, and I found a word sliding up my throat and filling my mouth. "Hello . . ."

She still didn't move, but her head inclined just a little. "Hi."

I smiled and steadied the .45 on my knee. She stepped back, and I raised the other hand in reassurance. "Wait, I'm not going to hurt you." She stood there, silent again. "I've been looking for you, and I think you've been looking for me."

Her weight shifted, but that was all. She looked like Mai Kim. "What's your name?"

"Her name is Ngo Loi Kim."

I snatched up the Colt and leveled it at Tuyen's half-hidden face as he stood there on the last step of the stairs with his own arm extended. In his hand was Saizarbitoria's Glock, and it was pointed directly at the girl. I'd neither seen nor heard him.

Ngo Loi Kim dove for the trapdoor and scratched for the inset handle, but when it wouldn't open she scrambled to the back wall and crouched against the floorboards. She held the computer like a shield in front of her and whimpered, terrified. I was off the piano bench and had taken a step toward the edge of the stage. "You're under arrest."

He took the last step from the darkness and, with the moonlight raising shadows across his legs, his voice seemed disembodied. "I'm willing to make you a deal."

"I don't deal. Drop the weapon."

"Try to shoot me, and I shoot her." He didn't move. "The girl for the laptop."

I stared down at him and could see his muscles straining the sleeve of his leather jacket. I figured the only thing to do was shoot. His weapon was pointed at her chest and chances were he'd hit her, but it was possible that my first shot would be on target and would do more damage than his responding fire.

I could feel the weight of the big Colt in my hand. What if I missed? What if he didn't? I was willing to take those types of chances with my own life, but not hers. I thought about who she was, and what she'd gone through—all to find me.

Talk. It was the only way.

"Ho Thi wasn't your granddaughter."

"No."

I swallowed and prepared myself for any opening that might present itself. "Did you kill her, or did Maynard?"

He looked at me. "He did."

I didn't believe him for a moment. Phillip Maynard hadn't been the type, but Tran Van Tuyen was. "Okay, let's say that's the truth. Then why kill him?"

His gun hand stayed steady, and he was focused on the whimpering girl at the wall. He'd had the better part of a week to get to know me, and he'd done his homework well—he knew that I wouldn't endanger her. "He committed suicide, as you said."

"You're lying."

He glanced at me. "One of the ranchers, Mr. Dunnigan..."

"You're still lying."

"I am to assume from this that the bent bottle caps didn't succeed in misdirecting you?"

"No."

"It was a habit Phillip Maynard informed me of." He actually smiled and finally took a breath. "Phillip was actually blackmailing me. He was supposed to retrieve the girls, and more importantly, the computer. He made a mess of it and killed Ho Thi. I suppose he thought that if he planted the girl near the culvert and threw the purse in with the Indian, there wouldn't be any questions. I assume he was counting on a preconceived prejudice."

"So you drugged him, just like Rene Paquet, and hung him?"

He didn't say anything. The unspoken truth lay there between us like a bad smell, and I started formulating a new plan in hopes that he'd become so agitated with me that he might change his aim. "Paquet wanted to save Ho Thi and get her out of whatever human-trafficking scheme you've got going, which is why she got picked up by the undercover detachment in L.A."

He studied me. "You know, I really am unfortunate to have arrived in your county, Sheriff."

"So you killed him and, consequently, the forty-two people in Compton." He took another breath but didn't move or say anything. "So, under the auspices of Children of the Dust, you retrieved Ho Thi and returned her to the brothel, but once there, she met the sole survivor of the Compton truck massacre." I nodded my head very slightly toward the young woman at the wall. "Ngo Loi Kim. She and Ho Thi were desperate, and I'm assuming Paquet was the one who had given them this laptop as an insurance policy in case something happened to him." His resolve didn't appear to be weakening, so I kept talking. "The wild card was the photograph of Ngo's great grandmother, sitting in the Boy-Howdy Beau-Coups Good Times Lounge with an unidentified Marine investigator who played Fats Waller, and once told her about a favorite fishing hole in the Bighorn Mountains of Wyoming, USA."

"You have an overactive imagination, Sheriff."

"It doesn't take any imagination at all, and you're still under arrest."

There was a long silence, where we both reviewed our options. "My offer still holds—the girl for the laptop." I was thinking about how I could prolong the conversation, but I was running fresh out of options and he confused my silence with my considering his offer. "You don't know what is in the computer, nor should you care. It is nothing in comparison with the life of this girl—the great granddaughter of a wartime friend—and you can save her." He took another step. "You didn't know I existed last week, and I can assure you that you'll never know I existed tomorrow."

"You can't possibly think you're going to escape."

"It is something at which I'm very good." He smiled again.

He wasn't going for any of it, and now was the time I would have to choose—fire or give him the computer for Ngo Loi. I took a deep breath, and the darkness shifted. It was as if the entire stairwell was growing behind Tuyen, and a face appeared almost a foot and a half above his.

Something was there.

Somebody.

Virgil.

Apparently, Tuyen was not the only one who had used my piano playing as a cover to ascend the steps, our conversation notwithstanding. My expression must have changed, because the lithe man's face suddenly stiffened and he spun.

I held my fire in fear of hitting the big Indian but jumped off the stage in an attempt to get to the two of them as I heard the muffled report of the 9 mm. They slammed into me, and I slid backwards on the dusty wooden floor.

The Glock fired again, but the bullet ricocheted into the wall, and I watched as Virgil lifted Tuyen, swung him through the air like an oil-pump jack, and dashed him against the floor. He had to be incredibly tough, because he held on to Virgil's arm and made the big Indian stagger. I scrambled to get at them just as the smaller man planted two powerful kicks in the giant's midriff.

Virgil grunted and then closed a hand on Tuyen. The 9 mm fired for the third time, and I heard the round go through the ceiling before the semiautomatic clattered on the hardwood surface. I threw myself forward just as Virgil swung Tuyen again, his legs striking me across the face.

It was silent for less than a second, and I was trying to push off the uneven surface of the broken plaster when Virgil let Tuyen go. It was like some modern dance crack-the-whip, and I saw Tuyen's body crash through the glass door at the far end of the room and through the railing on the second floor balcony. He froze like that and was a tableau of desperation. His hands grabbed at the broken and rotten wood, and it looked for a moment as if he might just make it, his fingers snapping and curling at the collapsed pieces of railing.

But he didn't and fell from view without a sound.

I scrambled forward and glanced back at the girl. She hadn't moved, and I gestured to her with my open hand. "Stay there!"

It was quiet except for Virgil, who was breathing raggedly

in the center of the room like some towering Windigo. I ran past him across the wide planks of the dance floor and stopped just short of the gaping doorway and collapsed balcony. I stared down at the moonlit hillside.

He had hit the rocks twice, first the ledge above and then the bigger one below. Somehow, he was still alive. At first, I thought he was trying to get up or roll over and escape, but that wasn't it.

I'd been right about where the rattlesnakes had been sleeping. Tuyen slapped at the flat level of the shelf around him to try to keep the snakes off, but there was nowhere for him or the snakes to go. He stopped screaming, he stopped moving, and the night was silent.

# EPILOGUE

Lucian studied his part of the file and then looked up from the faxed sheets. "You think this Dick Van Dyke character was the ringleader?"

Jesus.

Vic, Lucian, and I sat by Saizarbitoria's bed at Durant Memorial. The Basquo was missing a kidney but looked pretty good, considering, as he flipped through the entirety of what we now called the Tuyen File, passing it on sheet-by-sheet to all of us. Ned Tanen had forwarded most of the information from the Los Angeles County Sheriff's Department and, from the look on Santiago's face, he was having the same sickening response as I had had.

The report from the Immigration and Naturalization Service indicated that in the last few years as many as fifty thousand female illegal immigrants had been brought to the United States exclusively for use in the sex industry. Ho Thi Paquet and Ngo Loi Kim's story was horrific, but it wasn't exclusive.

"Children of the Dust was the front for the importation of the young women, and Trung Sisters Distributing distributed them into the brothels worldwide, as far as London. It's all in the report." I took a deep breath. "Ngo had a facility with computers and a tenuous connection to Wyoming, and Ho Thi had learned to drive, so..."

Vic looked up from her part of the report. "Ngo doesn't speak English?"

"No, so the e-mails she was sending were phonetic Vietnamese, which looked to us like a garbled mess."

Saizarbitoria raised his head and looked at me as he passed the last of the file to Lucian. "So, Phillip Maynard was drugged before he was hung after all?"

"Drugged like Paquet, according to the Yellowstone County coroner." I plucked at a loose straw in my hat. "Maynard was the advance man Tuyen sent from their Chicago branch. Henry translated, and Ngo filled in the rest of the story. The girls had gotten separated—Ho Thi ended up in Powder Junction and Ngo ran to Bailey. Tuyen came to finish the job, found Ho Thi, but couldn't find either the computer or Ngo. He killed Ho Thi when she wouldn't tell him where Ngo had gone. He needed a fall guy, and he needed some time. He had seen Virgil and knew that he lived in the culvert near Murphy Creek, so he planted her body there and threw her purse in the tunnel, but when it didn't look like I was going to bite, he sacrificed Maynard with the fake suicide." The Basquo folded his hands on the bed covers, and I played with my hat in an attempt to soften the unease between us. "Tuyen's wounds looked self-inflicted, and the bottle-cap thing just seemed too obvious—so I started thinking about who would gain from implicating the Dunnigans."

Saizarbitoria continued to study me as Marie pushed the door open with a tray that I assumed was lunch. "What about the quarters?"

We'd been warned against tiring him, so I plucked my hat from my bent knee, put it back on my head, and stood. "I asked Ned about that. He said that they would bring the girls in, some of them as young as ten, and lock them in a manufacturing building that had been cordoned off into little twelve-by-twelve rooms. Then they were..." I glanced at Marie. "*Trained*—and told they owed Trung Sisters twenty thousand dollars apiece for their transportation to the U.S. and that they would work off the debt and be released. They were given twenty dollars a week in quarters, so that they could eat and drink from the vending machines in the building."

The Basquo let out a long slow breath.

Vic handed the rest of the report to me as she and Lucian stood. "What happens to Ngo now?"

"The people from INS picked her up about an hour ago and flew her back to Los Angeles under a Temporary Protected Status. Under the Victims of Trafficking and Violence Protection Act, it looks like she's going to be granted a T-Visa and citizenship through adoption."

Saizarbitoria watched as his pregnant wife rolled a stand and tray table over to his bed and removed the stainless covering from his lunch—it looked ghastly. No wonder he was trying to bribe all of us into bringing him food from the Busy Bee. "Adopted by who?"

I stuffed the thick file under my arm. "If I were a betting man, I'd say the sheriff of Los Angeles County has two daughters and is about to acquire a third." I smiled at Marie as she seated herself as comfortably as she could in the corner chair and gestured for the staff to follow me as I crossed and opened the door. "We'll leave you to your lunch and your wife." I smiled at her again. "When, exactly, are you due?"

She rested her hands on the sides of her stomach. "November."

I ushered Vic and Lucian out—the old sheriff was having lunch with Isaac Bloomfield, but the rest of us were on our own. I began closing the door behind me.

"Hey, boss?"

I stopped and leaned back in. "Yep?"

Santiago looked down at the boiled meat, but I was pretty sure that wasn't what he was contemplating. "I . . ." He stopped, looked up, and then started to say something again.

"Don't worry about it, Sancho."

Vic rolled down the window of her eight-year-old unit in the parking lot of Durant Memorial. "I guess that leaves only one more mystery."

I opened the door of my truck and watched as Henry moved the bags of groceries to the center and climbed in on the other side; Dog was asleep in the back. "Not really. Mai Kim had given birth to Ngo Loi's grandmother three years before I ever got to Tan Son Nhut."

"I guess you're off the hook." She flared the canine tooth at me and started her truck. "You're fast, but not that fast." She slipped the vehicle into gear. "You do remember that you have a debate tonight."

I pulled out my pocket watch and checked the time. "Yep, but that should be over by eight."

"So?"

I tucked my watch back in my pocket and considered the fact that I was about to ask my deputy out on a date in front of Henry. It was enough to curdle my fortitude, but I figured it was time to get the thing out in the open. "I was wondering . . . ?"

She didn't say anything.

I glanced back at the Cheyenne Nation, who continued to watch us. "Henry has to tend bar and Cady and Michael have plans, since he's leaving tomorrow, so I was thinking . . ."

She studied me. I thought I should say something else, but then she started to speak and I stopped. "I'm washing my hair."

I stood there looking at her drive away, her vehicle barking the rear tires as she turned out of the parking lot. I tried to figure out what I'd done wrong. I knew I was out of practice, but the response seemed a little abrupt. I started the Bullet and put my seat belt on. Henry sat there without saying a word; Dog didn't speak either. "What?"

He turned his head to look out the windshield. "Nothing."

"What?"

I watched as he tried not to smile. "Just a small piece of advice." He turned and looked at me again. "Next time, try not to make it sound like you have nothing better to do."

**Tan Son Nhut, Vietnam: 1968**

I didn't have anything better to do, so I figured I might as well get drunk.

My right shoulder still hurt like a son-of-a-bitch, but I found that after a little practice, I could drink with my left hand. I'd been practicing steadily since being released from the base hospital two hours ago. I wasn't wheels-up till 1820 hours; the flight itself would be only twenty minutes back to BHQ, and then the provost marshal wanted a personal debriefing on my investigation. He wouldn't be happy that I was drunk, but he wasn't going to be happy with me anyway, so I figured what the hell. I stared at the empty piece of paper on the piano bench next to me and knocked back another whiskey. It was not my usual weapon of choice, but I was in a hurry. Things were just starting to pick up at the Boy-Howdy Beau-Coups Good Times Lounge, and the place was getting crowded, but nobody came near me.

If you're unlucky enough in life, there's a time when people will start associating you with death.

I had written three letters already, and I was getting depressed writing about dead people. Le Khang promised to deliver this one to a girl who knew someone near the village where Mai Kim's family supposedly lived. Would the letter actually get there? Would the family care? Did any of it really matter?

I picked up the bottle, refilled my glass, and struggled with the wave of regret, depression, anger, and disgust that continued to churn under the flood of alcohol. I thought that there should be somebody in the place that I should say good-bye to, but there wasn't anybody left.

Letter number one would go to San Antonio, Texas. Baranski had indeed shot Mendoza in the back of the head along Highway 1.

Letter number two would go to West Hamlin, West Virginia. The one-eyed sergeant's name had been George Seton, and he'd survived another four days after his two rounds of AK fire had taken most of Baranski's chest. Before he succumbed to the wounds he'd sustained during what they were now calling the Tet Offensive, he'd made a statement to the 377th Security Investigators that had exonerated me in the death of Baranski. I was probably going to end up getting a Bronze Star and a Purple Heart for my efforts in driving back the offensive; I figured that, and a dime, would get me a phone call.

Letter number three would go to the Airwing of ARVN to be delivered to Hoang's parents in Saigon. I attempted to put a brave and honorable face on why their son had bled to death in the back of a jeep on the way to Tan Son Nhut Air Force Base.

Letter number four was the one I hadn't written yet. I set the shot glass down and stared at the chipped keys of the piano. There was no other music in the Boy-Howdy Beau-Coups Good Times Lounge, because I had ripped the electric cord from the bar's jukebox and thrown it into the bamboo outside. I extended an index finger and hit an F, listening to the tone of it resonating through my life.

In Mai Kim's memory, I launched into a one-handed version of Fats Waller's "A Good Man Is Hard to Find." I'd made the bridge and was into the chorus in a dirgelike manner when I noticed that a short soldier was standing by the piano and was singing along.

*"A good man is hard to find, you always get the other kind. Just when you think he's your pal, you find him foolin' 'round some other gal. Then you rave, you even crave to see him laying in his grave . . ."*

I looked up at the squat but flashy-looking woman with the oversized lips; she couldn't sing very well, but she was loud. "Marine, you don't look like 285 pounds of jam, jive, and everything." She had an enormous smile. "I haven't heard Fats Waller in quite a while."

I looked down at my hand and noticed that I'd stopped playing. I swiped my utility hat off and saluted the two Special Forces men who accompanied her. She wore the beret and the uniform but no insignia for rank. She didn't salute me, so I figured she was the brass and started to stand, but she put out a hand and seated me back on the piano bench. We were just about eye to eye. "Are you Lieutenant Walt Longmire?"

"Ma'am?"

She shook her head and smiled again as she read my nametag. "You are Marine Inspector Walter Longmire from Durant, Wyoming?"

"Ma'am."

"I'm from Butte, Montana, myself." I didn't know what to say to that, so I said nothing. She pulled a piece of paper from her substantial breast pocket and tried to hand it to me. I sat there looking at her and it, so she picked up the untouched shot glass and rested the note on the piano. "It's from a friend of yours up north. He knew I was coming through Tan Son Nhut and I promised that I'd hand deliver it." She studied me for a moment more. "You are Walt Longmire?"

"Yes, ma'am."

She smiled, slugged my shot down, and daintily placed the now empty glass on top of the note. "You take care of yourself, Lieutenant." She placed a kiss on the top of my head, and I watched as she made for the open doorway.

An airman came up and looked at me as I picked up the shot glass and plucked the paper that was stuck to its bottom. It was typed in black letters and was obviously written by a two-fingered typist since the pressure was even on all the letters. It was from a mountainous site ten miles inside Laos; a station that wasn't supposed to even exist. Recon Team Wyoming was assuring me that he was fine and was inquiring as to how I'd made out in the war's most recent developments in his own special way. I read "Seen your ghost lately?"

The shot glass stayed steady in my hand as I remembered a professor of Shakespeare at USC who read to an uninterested class, "I have heard, but not believed, the spirits o' the dead men walk again."

The airman leaned forward and looked in my face. "How do you know her?"

I poured myself another shot. "Who?"

"Colonel Maggie."

"Who?"

"Martha Raye, Lieutenant. She was on the *Steve Allen Show,* she was a movie star…"

I slugged the shot down and set it back on the Bear's note, picked up the pen, and started on the letter to Mai Kim's family with a renewed vigor. I had to get out of Vietnam, it was getting as strange as Wyoming.

I dropped Henry at his T-Bird and Dog with Ruby and was late getting to the gym but changed my clothes and quickly climbed the steps to the second floor and the Universal machines. I made the corner at the landing and started the last leg when I heard a smattering of laughter that caused me to slow.

I stopped on the stairs. I could see Cady, who was seated at the leg press, and Vic's brother, who was standing in front of her with his back to me. Michael's T-shirt stretched across his broad young shoulders and read PHILADELPHIA HOMICIDE UNIT, OUR DAY BEGINS WHEN YOURS ENDS. They laughed again, and I listened as he attempted to motivate my daughter into finishing her workout. "Two more . . ."

I waited to see how the conflict would resolve itself and then fought against the wave of exhaustion that cemented my feet to the concrete steps and forced me to think about the scene that had unfolded only an hour ago. I caught my breath, more than a couple of emotions tearing at me like the mockingbirds had torn into Virgil's untouched groceries.

The bag I'd left at the beginning of the week had still been hanging off the Lone Bear Road guardrail.

I had sat with Dog at my side, placed the new grocery bags at my feet, and watched as the sporadic traffic dutifully slowed and swept into the opposite lane. Wyoming was an emergency-lane-change state, after all. I thought about this morning. I thought about Ngo Loi Kim, and how she wouldn't get out of my truck.

A three-way conversation had lasted for almost an hour with Henry as the translator, but it still seemed that there had been so much more to say and not enough time to say it. I tried to tell her about Mai Kim and about the war.

She had given me a letter. The words had been written in an unsteady hand and poorly. The word choices were simple and sentimental, and the guy who had written it had needed a lot more practice giving condolences. He'd gotten it.

I wondered what I'd have told that baby-faced Marine; and the things I wouldn't have. I wondered what he would have had to say to me. Would he approve of how we had turned out? Would he think I had done everything I could? Would he think I was a good man?

I hoped so and, as I'd read the tattered letter, fuzzy at the edges where it had been folded and refolded, I remembered how I had written Mai Kim's family that I had told her about a place on the other side of the world—about an unremarkable pass in a remarkable red rock wall where a number of unsavory characters had found a place through which they could herd stolen livestock, about the fat trout flipping their powerful tails through clear freezing water—about my home, a place where the snow-capped peaks stood guard.

"You did not really expect him to be here, did you?"

I looked up at Henry Standing Bear and then down at the plastic bag from the IGA that had twisted in the wind and cinched itself down to a braided strip. I could still see the outline of the untouched groceries—there were a few apples that the mockingbirds had broken through the plastic and gotten, a box of Chicken in a Biskit crackers, and a tin of smoked oysters.

The afternoon sun warmed us and a cooling breeze feathered down from the mountains as I looked at the entrance of the tunnel but could see no tracks in the shallow mud of Murphy Creek. "I guess it's like a wild birds' nest, once you touch it, they move on."

The Bear sat beside me on the guardrail and looked off toward the Bighorns. There were two clouds that hung over Cloud Peak like smoke signals. "Maybe so."

Virgil had sustained two gunshot wounds, but they hadn't done much damage—one had grazed his ribs and another had lodged in the meat of his calf. Henry had stayed with the giant until he'd been repaired and then through the following two days and nights. On the third day, the Cheyenne Nation said that he'd gone to take a shower as Virgil slept, but that when he returned, the big man was gone.

That was his story and, so far, he was sticking to it.

I pulled out the crackers from the old bag, then keyed open the oysters, drained the cottonseed oil, and spooned a few onto a Chicken in a Biskit. Under Dog's close observation, I handed it to the Bear. "Where do you think he went?"

He looked rather dubiously at my blue-collar hors d'oeuvres and then popped it in his mouth to keep from having to say anything.

I waited a little, fed Dog a cracker, then made one for myself and joined Henry in viewing the few snowfields left on the mountains. I could feel the sunshine on my face and squinted my eyes in the pleasure of warmth, just happy to be there. "You wouldn't tell me if you knew, would you?"

"Two more."

Michael's voice interrupted my daydreaming, and I was drawn back to the drama unfolding in the gym at the top of the stairwell. Cady looked up at him and smiled; so beautiful. "One more."

His voice, in turn, was kind but insistent. "No, two more."

I smiled at the jealousy I felt and the surge of unsettled anxiety at being replaced, then eased back down the steps. Michael only had another afternoon with her, and I had another month before she would return to Philadelphia. Anyway, he was probably motivating her better than I ever could. I stopped at the bottom of the stairs.

"One more . . ."

I stood there and listened to their laughter. The Bear had laughed at me for leaving the groceries, for wanting to solve all mysteries, but he had done so gently. Virgil White Buffalo, Crooked Staff, Crazy Dog Society was out there somewhere, and maybe Henry was right in not telling me exactly where.

He knew that our tracks were not that dissimilar. We'd both

run as far as we could from the war to the fringes of our separate societies, but Vietnam had overtaken us again: circumstance, two desperate girls, a very bad man, a battered photograph, and a faded letter had seen to that.

Maybe it was not so much that we were haunted, but how and when we chose to deal with these reverberations in our lives that would be the sign of our individuality. Perhaps the battle that I had chosen to fight in Vietnam had marked me. It was a legacy that had tied me to the dead more than the living. It was, as Ruby had said, my failing.

Their voices continued to echo down from above. "No, two more . . ."

**Craig Johnson's eleventh novel featuring Sheriff Walt Longmire is now available in Viking hardcover.**

**Read on for the first chapter of**

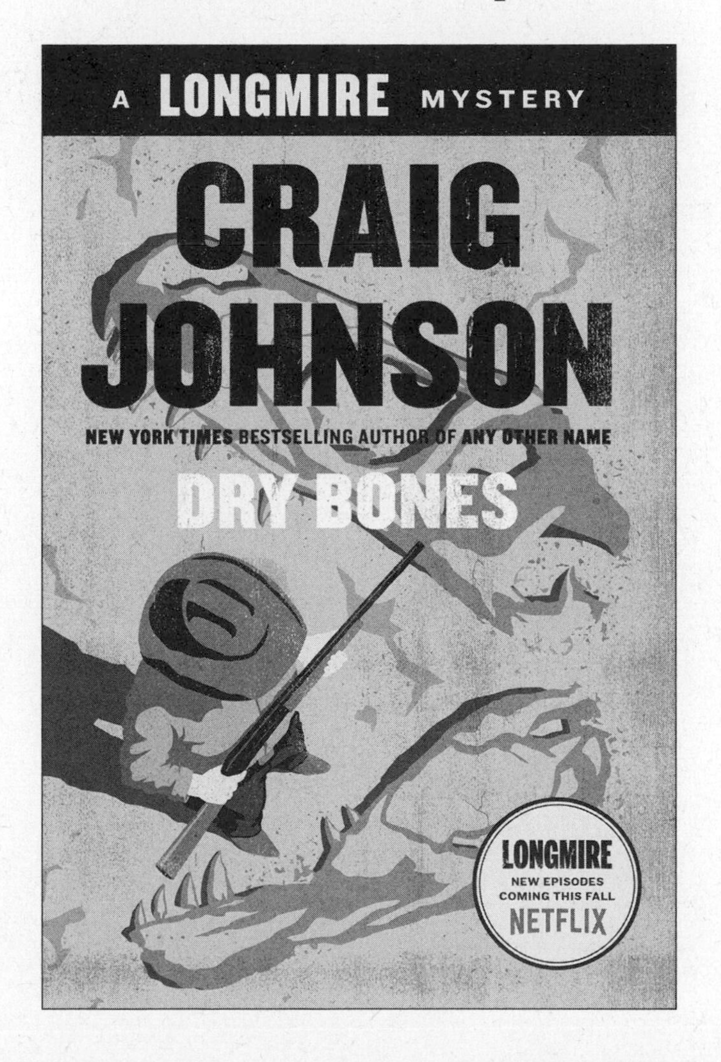

# 1

*She was close to thirty years old when she was killed.*

*A big girl, she liked to carouse with the boys at the local watering holes, which of course led to a lot of illegitimate children, but by all accounts, she was a pretty good single parent and could take care of herself and her brood. One night, though, a gang must have jumped her; they were all younger than she was, they had numbers, they might've even been family, and after they broke her leg and she was on the ground, it was pretty much over.*

*There was no funeral. They killed her and left what remained there by the water, where the sediment from the forgotten creek built up around her, layer after layer, compressing and compacting her to the point where the bones leeched away and were replaced by minerals.*

*It was as if she'd turned to stone just to keep from being forgotten.*

*It's interesting how her remains were found; her namesake, Jennifer Watt, was traveling with Dave Baumann, the director of the High Plains Dinosaur Museum, when they got a flat—not an unusual occurrence on the red roads the ranchers used for the more inaccessible areas of their ranches where the larger chunks of shale attacked sidewalls like tomahawks. The bigger rock is cheaper, but it's also the size of bricks and has lots of sharp edges, edges that like to make meals of anything less than ten-ply.*

*Dave had been trying to squeak another season out of the tires on the '67 Land Rover, but there they stood, staring at a right rear with a distinct lack of round, in the middle of the Lone Elk Ranch. While he fished the jack and spare from the hood and began the arduous task of replacing the tire, Jennifer unloaded Brody, her Tibetan mastiff, and went for a walk. Hoping to meet a friend on the place, she followed a ridge around a cornice, but the dog, who was 150 pounds with a heavy coat, began panting. Before long Jen decided that it might be a pretty good idea for the two of them to try and get to some shade, not an easy proposition out on the Powder River country; luckily, there was a rock overhang along the ridge with plenty enough room for her and the dog to get out of the late afternoon sun.*

*She wore her blonde hair in a ponytail that stuck through the adjustment strap of her Hole-in-the-Wall Bar ball cap, and, pulling the collapsible dog bowl from her pack, she slipped out a Nalgene bottle, took a swig, and then poured the mastiff a drink.*

*Jennifer looked out onto the grass that undulated like a gigantic, rolling sea. It was easy to imagine the Western Interior (Cretaceous) Seaway or the Niobraran Sea that had once covered this land, splitting the continent of North America into two landmasses, Laramidia to the west and Appalachia to the east. The great sea had stretched from Mexico to the Arctic and had been over two thousand feet deep. Jen settled under the rock and petted the dog, her green eyes scanning the landscape.*

*She pulled her video camera from her pack and panned the distance, seeing things out there on the high plains, things that didn't exist, at least not anymore—predatory marine reptiles like long-necked plesiosaurs and more alligator-like mosasaurs almost eighty feet long. Sharks such as* Squalicorax *swam through her imagination along with giant, shellfish-eating* Ptychodus mortoni.

*When she'd been six, her father had brought her to this country from Tucson, Arizona, and had dragged her along on his private excavations that helped support his rock shop on the old highway out near Lake DeSmet between Durant and Sheridan. She still remembered what she'd said one day as they'd gotten out of his battered pickup, her fingers climbing up his pant leg until she found the reassuring hand with gloves worn like saddle leather, the adjustment straps with the transparent red beads. "There's nothing out here, Daddy."*

*He surveyed the rolling hills that led from the Bighorn Mountains to the endless Powder River country, smiled as he pushed back his straw hat, and spoke gently to her. "There's everything here; you just have to know where to look."*

*Jennifer had learned to look and had never stopped; Dave Baumann's hands and hers were in the excavations that had led to the displays that crowded the High Plains Dinosaur Museum in Durant, and at twenty-six, she was still searching.*

*Truth be told, Jen liked dead things better than live ones—they were less trouble, the conversations being one-sided. A lot of investigators and paleontologists are more comfortable that way, able to accept the consensus of truth, disregarding the absolute as something that always carries the danger of being overturned by some new and extraordinary piece of evidence.*

*She lowered the camera, took another sip of water, and poured her dog more. Brody sighed and shook his massive head, and Jen leaned back under the rock overhang to try to decide what she was going to do with the old man's rock shop, a ramshackle affair near the lake that had started out as a trailer but through the years had evolved into a labyrinth of wooden fences lined with geodes, gems, quartz, and rock samples, most of them worthless.*

*He had died the year before, and she knew the land was more valuable than the structure itself, but she'd grown up there and loved the old place, as cluttered and tacky as it might be. She pulled the cap over her eyes and dozed until she became aware of a protracted growl in her dog's throat. She swatted at him, but he continued to rumble a warning until she finally lifted the bill of her cap to look at him. He was looking directly up. Jen's eyes followed to where a two-fingered talon stretched out of the rock ceiling down toward her, almost as if it were imploring. She grabbed the camera and began to film what would become one of the greatest paleontological discoveries in modern times.*

Victoria Moretti sipped the coffee from the chrome lid of my thermos, leaned forward, and, peering through the windshield, watched the man with an intensity that only her tarnished gold eyes could command. "Is that some weird-ass Wyoming fishing technique I don't know about?"

I could see that Omar was tossing something into the water from the banks of the man-made reservoir.

"What the hell is he doing?"

Ruby, my dispatcher, had received a call from him early in the morning and had bushwhacked Dog and me with it when we came in the door. I had filled up my thermos and in turn bushwhacked Vic before heading out to the ten-thousand-acre Lone Elk place to find out what was up.

Outdoor adventurer, outfitter, and big-game bon vivant, Omar Rhoades had contracts with all the big ranchers and sometimes used their property for extended hunting and fishing junkets. Usually he kept his spots secret, but this time he'd told Ruby where he was and that I might want to come out and meet him.

Most everything was in bloom in late May, and I breathed in the scents from the open windows of my truck. As I stared at the aspens and cottonwood, they all began stretching to the sky like those cypresses in Italy that looked like thumb smudges.

My undersheriff turned and looked at me some more. "I thought he was in China."

"Mongolia."

The Custer look-alike was dressed in a state-of-the-art fishing vest, waders, and his ever-present black cowboy hat with more flies stuck in it than Orvis has in its catalog. All in all, I estimated the total worth of his outfit at somewhere close to two thousand dollars, and he wasn't even carrying the fly rod, which was sticking out the rear of his custom-made SUV that dwarfed my three-quarter-ton.

I leaned forward and stared through the windshield. We watched as he drew something from one hand, carefully took aim, and tossed whatever it was onto the smooth surface of the water, black like an oil slick.

Vic turned to look at me as she reached back and scratched the fur behind Dog's ear. "Do you think he's finally lost it?"

I pulled the handle and climbed out of the truck, careful to keep the Saint Bernard/German shepherd/plains grizzly inside. "Let's go find out."

The beauty of Italian descent followed with my thermos as we glided our way through the morning dew in the buffalo grass. "You know, the landed gentry get like this when they spend too much time alone."

I whispered over my shoulder, "Like what?"

"Fucking nuts." She increased her pace and caught up with me. "He's not armed, is he?"

"If he were, I don't think he'd be throwing rocks." I stopped at the worn path surrounding the reservoir, curious, but still attempting to abide by the protocol of the high plains angler so as to not upset the fishing—if, in fact, that was what he was doing.

"Hey, Omar."

He started, just visibly, and spoke to us over his shoulder as he continued throwing pebbles into the water. "Walt. Vic."

"What are you doing?"

He glanced at us but then tossed another stone. "Trying to keep those snapping turtles off that body out there."

We tiptoed to the edge of the bank in an attempt to keep the water from seeping into our boots, and Vic and I joined Omar in his target practice, Vic showing her acumen by bouncing a flat stone off the shell of a small turtle that skittered and swam into the depths. "Any idea who it is?"

Omar leaned forward and lifted his Oakley Radarlock yellow-tinted shooting glasses to peer into the reflective surface of the water at the half-submerged body. "I'm thinking it's Danny."

I stared at the corpse, which was a good forty feet from the bank, and tried to figure out how we were going to retrieve it, in that we had no boat. "Himself?"

My undersheriff squinted. "How can you tell?"

"Not everybody has hair like that." Omar nailed a big turtle that had risen beside the body like a surfacing submarine and had gotten caught in the mass of silver locks that had fanned out from the body. "Danny always had nice hair."

Omar reached behind him and, pulling out a fancy, stainless steel thermos of his own, poured the tomato-red contents into a cut-glass double-old-fashioned tumbler. "Libation?"

She stared at him, one hand on her hip. "It's eight o'clock in the morning."

He shrugged and sipped. "Sun's over the yardarm somewhere."

Omar and I watched as Vic expertly skipped a pebble across the glossy surface of the water, the pellet deflecting off another turtle. "How many turtles are there in this damn thing, anyway?"

Omar grunted. "Danny and his brother Enic protect them; nobody is allowed to hurt them—they're sacred to the Crow and the Northern Cheyenne."

Vic shook her head and nailed another. "Is there any living thing that isn't sacred to the Crow and the Northern Cheyenne?"

I tossed a stone but missed. "Nope."

Omar sipped from his Bloody Mary. "They're a totem for fertility, protection, and patience." He turned to look at me. "How are your daughter and granddaughter?"

There was a silence as I formulated an answer, but before I could speak, Vic chimed in. "Excuse me, but did I miss a transition in the conversation here?"

I tapped my shoulder. "Cady's got a tattoo of a turtle—reminiscent of her willful youth at Berkeley." I glanced back at him. "Should be here the day after tomorrow."

He nodded. "Lookin' forward to meeting Lola."

I smiled and picked up my thermos. "Any ideas on how we get him out of there?" I glanced at the big-game hunter. "You've got your waders on."

He shook his head. "Oh, no. The bank drops off ten feet out, and the reservoir is about sixty feet deep—used to be a shale pit."

I nodded and drank some coffee as Omar refilled his glass and Vic tossed a rock, this time missing her shelled target but causing it to duck its head and silently retreat into the depths. "Can I assume that nine-thousand-dollar Oyster fly rod of yours will do the trick?"

Vic crouched at an inlet on the other side of the pond. "I'm trying to resist saying something about the ironic aspect of a guy who protects the turtles but then falls in his own pond and becomes snapper chow."

"We don't know it's him."

"Sure we do." She held up a paper bag. "I found his lunch, and it's got his name on it." She read, "Daddy-O."

"Topflight detecting, that's what that is." I watched as Omar flipped the fly rod back and forth, trailing the line in cyclical patterns, reflecting in the morning sunshine. "Think you can get him on the first try?"

He ignored my crass remark and flipped the fly forward, yanking it back to set the hook in what appeared to be the sleeve of a green canvas shirt. The outdoorsman carefully walked the banks and reeled in the body as we watched who we assumed was Danny Lone Elk spin slowly with his one arm extended like a superhero in flight, a trail of disappointed turtles in his wake.

As the body came alongside the bank, I reached in, grabbed it by the collar, and dragged the upper part of him onto the grass. "He weighs a ton."

"Lungs are probably full of water." Vic leaned over and

grabbed the other side of his collar and we both heaved the deadweight onto the bank, a forty-pound snapping turtle with a carapace the size of a washbasin attached to the dead man's left hand.

Vic dropped her side and backed away from the radially set iridescent eyes, the color not unlike her own. "What the fuck?"

The aquatic monster released the dead man's hand, hissed like a steam train, and extended its neck toward us, evidently not willing to give up its breakfast.

Vic drew her sidearm, but I pushed it away. "Don't. It doesn't mean any harm."

"The hell it doesn't; look at him." She considered. "I've shot people for less than that shit."

I kneeled down, and the beast stretched out its neck even further and struck at me with snakelike speed, the reach surprisingly far. "You know these things are seventy million years old?"

Vic reluctantly holstered her weapon. "This one in particular?"

"They appeared before the dinosaurs died out." I picked up a stick and extended the end toward the animal's open mouth. "See the little wiggly red thing at the end of its tongue?"

Vic raised her eyebrows. "What, that means he's popular with the ladies?"

"That's what he uses to ambush fish—they think it's a worm."

"That's disgusting."

I walked around it and raised its rear end, placing my hand underneath the plastron and lifting the creature, rather awkwardly, from the ground. Its head swiveled back, and it snapped with the sound of a small firecracker.

Both Omar and my undersheriff stepped back. "He's going to bite the shit out of you."

"No, they can't reach if you're holding them from the bottom." A stream of something dribbled down the length of my jeans onto my boot.

They studied me, Vic, of course, the first to speak. "Did that thing just piss on you?"

"I believe it did." I swung the big beast around, lowered it back into the water, and watched as the creature settled in the mud and looked back at me, apparently now in no great hurry to get away.

"I guess he likes you."

I shook the water from my hands and studied the round eyes that watched me warily. "Might be a female."

"Well, anytime you're through turtle diddling, we've got work to do." She approached the cadaver again and rolled the body over, looked at what remained of Danny Lone Elk's face, and immediately turned away. "Oh shit, his eyes are gone."

Omar kneeled by the dead man and turned his chin. "Critters always go for them first." He sighed. "Those turtles sure did a number on him." They both turned to look at me as I stared at the body. "Walt?"

It was a man I'd seen before, in my dreams.

"Walt?"

In the dreams, he also had no eyes.

"Walt."

The man's words came back, and it was almost as if he were standing beside me, repeating the mantra of warning I'd stowed away: *You will stand and see the good, but you will also stand and see the bad—the dead shall rise and the blind will see.*

"Walt."

I took a deep breath. "You're sure it's Danny?"

Omar nodded and looked back at the body. "His belt says Danny." He paused for a moment. "And I recognize what's left of him."

"Does he have a wallet or anything else on him, like a fishing license?"

Checking the pockets of the dead man, Omar shook his head. "Nothing, but he's on his own property. I don't carry my wallet with me when I'm fishing—always afraid I'll dunk it."

I glanced at Vic. "Did you check his lunch?"

"Might as well; I'm about to lose mine." She reached down, picked up the brown paper bag, and, rummaging through the sack, called out the items. "Daddy-O had one can of orange soda, one cheese sandwich, one bag of Lay's potato chips, an assortment of celery and carrot sticks, and . . ." She fumbled in the bag, finally pulling out a withered, handmade billfold. "One wallet."

"Is it Danny's?"

She held it up for us to look at. "Well, seeing as how it has DANNY engraved on the outside, I'd say yes." She opened it and studied the Wyoming driver's license and the face of the elderly Cheyenne man. "He liked putting his name on stuff, didn't he?"

Omar reached out and straightened the collar of the dead man's shirt. "He was a good old guy—let me bring clients out here whenever I wanted and even let me fly my helicopter into this place."

I glanced around. "Where is the ranch house from here?"

He ignored my question. "There's going to be trouble." He pointed. "The eyes—the medicine men will have to do something about this or Danny will wander the earth forever." He looked up, and I could see tears for his old friend. "Lost and blind."

I nodded, fishing my keys from my jeans so that we could load the man into the truck bed and take him to Doc Bloomfield and room 32, the Durant Memorial Hospital's ad hoc morgue. "I'll get in touch with the family, Henry, and the Cheyenne tribal elders." Walking back to my truck, I thought about my vision and what Virgil White Buffalo and the stranger had said—that stranger, the stranger with no eyes, who ended up being Danny Lone Elk.

The last time I'd seen Danny was at the Moose Lodge at the end of town. It had been a few years back, and he had still been drinking. I'd gotten a radio call that there was a disturbance, but by the time I'd gotten there, no one seemed to remember who had been involved in the altercation.

Asking why he was a Moose and not an Elk, I'd grabbed a Rainier for myself and joined him.

"They got a better bar down here."

He looked up at me and smiled. Lined with more wrinkles than a flophouse bed, the old man's face was cragged but still handsome and carried the wisdom of the ages. He reached over to squeeze my shoulder with a hand as large and spidery as a king crab.

Well into his cups, he spoke to me through clinched teeth;

Danny Lone Elk always talked as if what he had to say to you was a very important secret, and maybe it was. "You off duty, Sheriff?"

"End of watch. I came here looking for trouble, but there isn't any."

"Can I buy you a beer?"

I gestured with the full can. "Got one."

He closed one eye and looked at me. "You too good to drink with an Indian?"

"No. I—"

"'Cause you gotta have a reservation." He kept his eye on me like a spotlight, guffawed uproariously at his own joke, and then leaned in close. "You wanna know why they called you?" He gestured down the bar where a small contingency of men did their level best to ignore us. "You see that sharp-faced man with the ball cap? That fella in the cowboy hat beside him asked him what he was gonna do on his vacation and he said he was gonna go to Montana and go fishing. Well, cowboy hat told sharp-face he couldn't understand why he was going fishing in Montana 'cause there was nothing but a bunch of damned Indians up there." Danny sipped his beer and looked past me toward the men. "Then sharp-face asked cowboy hat what he was gonna do on his vacation and cowboy hat said he's goin' hunting down in Arizona and sharp-face said he couldn't understand why he was going hunting down in Arizona 'cause there was nothing but a bunch of damned Indians down there."

I nodded. "Was that all there was to it?"

"No." He grinned the secret smile again. "That was when I told them both to go to hell, 'cause there sure wasn't any Indians there."

His voice rose. "Bartender." He looked back at me, again smiling through the ill-fitting dentures. "I think that's when this guy called you."

The man approached somewhat warily. "Can I help you?"

He lip-pointed at sharp-face and cowboy hat. "Yeah; I think I better buy those guys down there a beer; I'm afraid I might've spooked 'em."

As the barkeep went about distributing the conciliatory beverages, Danny leaned in again. "I knew your daddy."

"Really?"

"Yeah, made the mistake of tryin' to get him to go to Indian church one time."

"Uh-oh."

"Yeah." He grinned again and nodded. "I was working down at Fort Keogh and lived out your way—had this wife that thought since your family lived so close we should go and invite them to go to church with us." He leaned in again. "Well, just my luck, your father answered the door, and boy did he give me an earful."

"I'm sorry; my mother was the religious one."

"He said he figured I was just tradin' one superstition for another."

I took a sip of my beer. "He wasn't a big one for churches."

"They still have that place out near Buffalo Creek?"

"I have it now—they've both passed."

He nodded. "I am sorry to hear that—they were good people." He was silent for a moment and looked down at his lap. "Do you ever see them?"

I turned and looked at him, thinking that I hadn't made myself clear. "They're dead."

He nodded again and then stared at the can in his hands. "Yeah, but do you ever see them?"

"Umm, I don't . . ."

"When I am alone, hunting or fishing . . ." He breathed a laugh. ". . . And that is the only time I'm alone, by the way . . ." He looked at me. ". . . I see my ancestors, the ones who have walked the Hanging Road to the Camp of the Dead. When I see them, they are far away but watching me like the eyes of the stars."

Not quite sure what to say to that, I nodded. "That's nice . . . that they're looking out for you."

"I don't know if that's what it is." He took out some antacids, shook a few of the chunky tablets into his hand, and washed them down with some beer. "Mmm, peppermint, my favorite." He started humming the theme to *Dragnet*, which was also the jingle for the pills. "Tum, tum, tum, tum . . ." Then he opened a prescription bottle that he took from the pocket of his shirt, shook out a few pills, and swallowed them, too. He looked at me blankly. "What was I talking about?"

"Family."

"Oh, right . . . I am old, and I know I am standing on the brink of the life nobody knows about, and I am anxious to go to my Father, *Ma-h ay oh*. To live again as men were intended to live, even on this world, but I fear for the remains of my family."

I knew that his ranch was vast and there had been talk of gas, oil, and fossil deposits, but I still couldn't understand Lone Elk's concerns. "You've got children, right? I'm sure your family will look after those things after you're gone, Danny."

It was a long time before he spoke again. "Maybe that's true, but I would take some things back if I could."

---

“I said . . .” My undersheriff raised an eyebrow and sighed, still holding her end of the now blanket-wrapped body. “Did you hear that?”

With Danny Lone Elk’s voice still resonating in my head, I turned and looked around, fully expecting to see the man and his ancestors. “Hear what?”

She glanced at Omar, and then they both looked at me. “A gunshot.”

I took a deep breath to clear my head and my ears. “Close?”

“What, you were having some kind of out-of-body experience?”

“No, I was just remembering when I had seen Danny last.” I thought about adding more, but I hadn’t shared my experiences in Custer Park with anyone. “Probably the hands who worked for Lone Elk, chasing off coyotes or plinking prairie dogs.” I looked around. “Where was the shot?”

Vic looked toward the ridge. “Not far.”

We hurried to get Danny loaded as quickly as we could, having decided to use Omar’s massive SUV since it had better cover for the body than the open bed of the Bullet and, of all things, a slide-out game rack.

He gestured toward the passenger side. “Get in.”

I glanced at my truck. “Maybe we’d better leave Danny in yours and take mine.”

He shook his head. “This thing’s faster—besides, it’s bulletproof.”

Ushering Vic into the front, I climbed in the back and

gaped at the leather and burl-wood interior. "Omar, what the heck is this thing?"

He fired up the engine, slapped the transmission in gear, and tore up the two-track toward the ridge, the three of us thrown back into the butter-soft bucket seats. "A Conquest, Knight XV—it's handcrafted out of Toronto."

As we flew across the prairie, I glanced up through the skylight. "What does something like this set you back?"

He shrugged. "Couple hundred thousand, I don't know—the accountant said I needed to spend some money fast, so I did."

When we made the top of the ridge, Omar wheeled the glossy black fortress to the left and stopped; we rolled down the windows to listen but didn't hear anything. Vic leaned forward in the passenger seat and pointed down the valley. "There are some vehicles parked at the fence down there through a few cattle guards—you want to go check it out?"

Spinning the wheel, Omar drove down the slope to a better-maintained road and started off toward the area Vic had indicated.

She turned to look at me. "So, you know the deceased?"

Thinking it best to keep the visions to myself, I told her about the Moose Lodge encounter. "I had a couple of beers with him one time a few years ago." I could feel her looking at the side of my face as I looked out the tinted windows. "There was a disturbance at the bar and when I got there it had settled down, so I had a beer with him. He was worried about some things, so we talked. It took a while for me to remember him."

She nodded, not buying a word of it. "What was he worried about?"

"Nothing, getting old, the land, family, the usual stuff."

"He should've worried about learning to swim."

I recognized Dave Baumann's weathered, light-blue Land Rover, emblazoned with the logo of the High Plains Dinosaur Museum, driving at high speed toward us. He slid to a stop alongside Omar's rolling fortress. A quarter of a mile away, I could see another gate where two flatbeds were parked nose to nose blocking the entrance, with some people milling about; beyond that was a working backhoe.

I rolled down the window and was about to speak when the paleontologist began yelling to the young blonde-haired woman in the passenger seat. "They're using a backhoe!"

I stared at Dave, an athletic-looking fellow with glasses, curly light-brown hair and beard, blue eyes, and an easy smile that made him popular with the young female scientists who sometimes came to intern at the private museum—they called him Dino-Dave.

"Excuse me?"

He took a deep breath to calm himself and continued. "They're digging up one of the most valuable sites in recent history with a backhoe."

"I'm no expert." I sighed and glanced at both Vic and Omar. "But that's probably not good."

"No."

"Who's in charge here?"

"I am." He studied me and revised his statement. "What do you mean?"

I had been involved in these kinds of conflicts where the university, the colleges, the museums, and the landowners quibbled about the exact location of digs, and I liked to get the full story before mobilizing the troops. "Is this official or something more loosely structured?"

"It's a straight-ahead deal; I paid thirty-seven thousand dollars last year for the fossil remains."

I opened the door. "I guess we'd better go over and take a look. Why don't the two of you jump in here with us, Dave?" They did as I requested, and I thrust a hand toward the blonde. "Walt Longmire."

She didn't take my hand or return my smile. "Jennifer Watt." She raised her small video camera and began filming through Omar's windshield.

I shrugged and sat opposite the two of them—the behemoth vehicle had limousine-style rear seating—feeling like I was in some sort of executive conference room. "Tell me about the deal."

Dave leaned forward as Omar drove south. "It was the standard arrangement with the landowner and the HPDM—that we would search for fossils, and anything we found, we would share the profits."

Vic turned and looked at him. "I thought the museum was a nonprofit?"

He nodded. "It is at the end of the fiscal year, but when we first unearthed the jawbone last August and we needed more time, I thought we'd better cement a deal with the landowner." He pointed toward the backhoe. "Just to make sure that exactly this type of thing didn't happen." He paused for a moment and pointedly sniffed the air. "What's that smell?"

Vic threw a chin toward me. "Oh, the sheriff here got pissed on."

It was about then that a round from some sort of small

arms fire caromed off the cab, leaving a narrow but nasty gash on the windshield, and Dave ducked. "My God, they're shooting at us again!"

I stared at the groove as Omar yelled back over his shoulder, "Ballistic armor glass."

He hit the gas and barreled down the makeshift two-track toward the roadblock as I turned back to Dave. "They shot at you before?"

"You're damn right they did!"

Another ricochet and Omar fishtailed to the side and gunned it again, in hopes that if we made it closer to the parked vehicles the shooter might be less inclined to fire. We stopped in front of the two flatbeds.

Vic drew her Glock, but I held out a hand, rose up, and got out the other side, just as an Indian cowboy charged up the hillside to slap what looked to be a bolt-action .22 from the hands of a teenage boy.

I walked around both trucks with my hands raised, quickly covering the twenty yards between us. "All right, I'm not sure whose property we're on, but we need to stop the shooting right now."

With one last, hard look toward the kid, the Indian cowboy turned as another, older man in a black flat-brim hat joined him. "Sorry about that, Sheriff . . ."

The teenager interrupted. "You told me to stand guard and not let anybody in!"

The Indian cowboy picked up the rifle and threw it to the older man with the black hat as Vic and Dave joined us. "I didn't mean for you to shoot the sheriff."

"What's going on here?"

He smiled a wide grin. "Protecting our investments." He slapped the teen in the back of the head, knocking off his straw hat, and gestured toward Dave. "You can shoot Dave if you want to . . ." The kid actually reached for the rifle on the older man's shoulder. "Leave your uncle alone; I was kidding." He then threw the bearded paleontologist a glance. "Kind of."

I looked at where the bucket of the big CASE backhoe was scraping away the side of the hill. "You need to stop excavating. Dave here says that you're going to do irreparable damage to the dig."

The Indian cowboy lifted a hand and whipped off his own hat, raising it in a wide wave, his dark hair swooping around his head like a flight of crows. The sound of the heavy equipment halted almost immediately. He turned back to look at us, his perfect teeth contrasting with the tan skin of his handsome face as he extended his hand. "Randy Lone Elk, Sheriff. I don't think we've met." He gestured toward the older man holding the rifle. "This is my Uncle Enic." He lip-pointed toward the teenager. "And the All-American sniper here is Taylor, my nephew."

I shook the hand and gestured toward Baumann. "Dave here is concerned about the integrity of his site."

"*His* site, huh?" He continued grinning. "Then he doesn't know exactly where *his* site is." He spread his arms and half turned, exemplifying the open country. "We are trying to draw some attention, and I guess it worked." He gestured toward Dave. "These guys are attempting to get this fossil out of here before anybody could find out, but we're renegotiating the deal." He looked at me and then at Omar's vehicle. "What the hell is that thing, anyway?"

I ignored the question. "Dave here tells me that you've been compensated to the tune of thirty-seven thousand dollars on this dig."

Randy Lone Elk pointed a finger at Baumann's chest. "That's bullshit, and even if it wasn't, thirty-seven thousand dollars is a joke, if not an insult."

The paleontologist spoke up. "It's a fair price for what we've uncovered so far, more than anyone has ever been compensated . . . And there's the profit sharing."

Randy laughed and returned his hat to his head with a tug, settling it hard on his forehead. "Sheriff, do you know what she's worth? One smaller than this in the Black Hills went for over eight million dollars twenty years ago."

I shook my head. "I don't even know what we're talking about."

Baumann looked a little embarrassed but then provided the much-needed information. "A Saurischia, suborder Theropoda, genus . . ."

"A *T. rex.*" The rancher began yelling again. "Maybe the largest and most complete ever found."

Baumann shook his head. "We don't know that until we get the rest of her."

Unable to contain his enthusiasm, Randy yelped, "We measured the exposed fossil bones, and Jen's a lot bigger than the one at the Field Museum in Chicago—probably the biggest in the world!"

I couldn't help but ask, "She?"

Baumann answered, "We can't tell what sex it is, but generally the larger ones are female."

Vic laughed. "Why Jen?"

Dave gestured toward the young woman still filming while leaning against the front of the SUV. "Jennifer was the one who found her, and usually you use either the Latin, or a place name, or the name of the person who discovered the specimen for its name." He continued to shake his head as he glanced back at Randy. "Anyway, it really doesn't matter. I already paid for the find, and I'm not paying again."

Randy approached him, sticking his nose inches from Dave's face. "Well, who the hell did you pay, 'cause it sure wasn't me."

"Your father—I paid Danny."

He took a deep breath and swung around to look at all of us, his fists planted at his hips. "Then I guess we'll have to wait for the old man to get back from fishing to find out about that."

A PENGUIN READERS GUIDE TO

# ANOTHER MAN'S MOCCASINS

Craig Johnson

# An Introduction to *Another Man's Moccasins*

"No matter what aspect of law enforcement with which you might be involved, there's always one job you dread," Walt Longmire says near the beginning of *Another Man's Moccasins*. "For the Western sheriff it's always been the body dump. . . . There you stand by some numbered roadway with a victim, no ID, no crime scene, no suspects, nothing" (p. 15). In this case, it is incongruously enough a young Vietnamese woman found murdered along a highway in Absaroka County, Wyoming. And Walt is baffled.

No suspects present themselves at first, but soon enough Walt is assailed by one. Poking through the brush, he is attacked by what at first appears to be a wild animal but turns out to be something slightly more ferocious—Virgil White Buffalo—a seven-foot-tall Crow Indian living in a culvert who appears to be in possession of the dead woman's purse. Despite the evidence and proximity to the crime scene, however, Virgil seems an unlikely suspect. To make matters more complicated, Walt discovers a hauntingly familiar photo in the victim's purse. It shows a woman who looks very much like someone he knew when he was serving in Vietnam. It also shows a man who resembles—and indeed is—a young Walt Longmire. This photo, in addition to the facts that the victim is Vietnamese, that Virgil White Buffalo is a Vietnam vet, and that a Vietnamese man, Tran Van Tuyen, shows up in a local bar, sets in motion a series of reveries in which Walt recalls his first murder case, when he was a Marine investigator in Vietnam. The novel moves deftly back and forth between these parallel time frames, as the past intrudes upon the present and the cases overlap in uncanny, and uncomfortable, ways.

Like all of Craig Johnson's novels, *Another Man's Moccasins* investigates not just a particular murder or murders, but the larger social issues that give rise to such crimes. In this case, it is primarily prostitution and human trafficking that set the wheels in motion. But on an even deeper level the novel explores the tensions between the worst and best aspects of human nature. Though the novel does not lend itself to easy moralizing, it clearly juxtaposes two value systems—one based on greed and selfishness, the other on loyalty and a deep sense of justice. Walt's own morality is built upon loyalty not only to the living but to the dead, and on his desire to be fair to everyone he encounters—even those who, like Virgil White Buffalo, have tried to harm him. Over the course of the novel, however, Walt is forced to ask himself whether or not he is in fact guilty of racial prejudice. That inner investigation provides a compelling counterpart to the outer search for the killer who is at work in Absaroka County. And with consummate skill, and a relentless nose for the truth, Walt finds the answers to both.

## A Conversation with Craig Johnson

*In an earlier interview you said injustice is the "burr under your saddle" that motivates you to write. What injustice prompted you to write* Another Man's Moccasins*?*

About 14,000 people, usually women and children, are trafficked into the United States for use in an industry that is third only to arms dealing and drugs as one of the most profitable global commodities. Prostitution is a multibillion-dollar industry in which women and children, desperate for a better life, are abducted and routinely raped, beaten, and sometimes killed. Their stories are so horrific that I didn't have to fictionalize them. I just needed to change the names to protect the innocent, as it were.

*Why did you choose to make the parallel story of Walt's investigation in Vietnam so prominent in this book?*

Déjà vu all over again. It seems as though a lot of the problems that confronted us in Vietnam continue to face us today, so that is surely a reason to have Vietnam play such an important role. And I figured those years were formative for Walt and explain a lot of the choices that he made and still makes. I wanted to carry the immediacy of those scenes within the novel, so I thought that if I could think of another crime that took place in the present that was connected to the one that Walt had solved in Vietnam in 1968, I'd be able to push that immediacy. The problem was how to do that without it seeming contrived.

*During the course of the novel, Walt references Shakespeare, Dante, Virgil, Tennessee Williams, and Harper Lee. He is also a fine pianist and serviceable chess player. Why is it important that Walt have this level of cultural sophistication? Is he a better detective because of it?*

I think what you're referring to are symptoms of an active mind. Unlike us, Walt doesn't like mysteries, and that's why he's so good at his job. Another factor is that the books are written in the first person. Would you want to spend three hundred pages in the head of a dullard? Walt may also have just a touch of the Renaissance in him, which reflects my belief that modern mystery readers expect a great deal more than what has been presented historically. They anticipate social conscience, full character development, history, and humor, just to name a few. These things would be difficult to convey in a character unaware of the world around them.

*Your vision of the West, and of human nature, is quite different from that of a writer like Cormac McCarthy. Do you see yourself ultimately as an optimist or an idealist?*

An idealist possibly, but an optimist, definitely. I guess I subscribe to what Abraham Lincoln used to refer to as "the better angels of our nature." After what I've seen, I feel compelled to have a strong belief in human beings, and that the survival of our species might be indebted to the fact that we are at our best when things are at their worst.

*Would you say that your novels present an ideal of community and of the values necessary for a healthy community? Do you think this ideal is achievable in the real world?*

I'm not sure if young women are left dead along the roadsides in what I would consider an ideal community, but I see what you're getting at. My beliefs are pretty simple along those lines: If we all look out for each other, we won't have to look out for ourselves. And yes, I do think it's achievable. There is chaos in the universe, and so many of our human conventions are designed to hold that in check, to provide order where there is none. I don't write to display that anarchical given, but I concern myself with the ways we defend ourselves against it with love, hope, and law. The negative aspects of our natures are easy enough to highlight, but the positive ones are more ephemeral and, inevitably, more enlightening.

*Virgil White Buffalo is a very compelling character in the novel, even though he utters only a few brief sentences. What drew you to make him part of the story?*

My ranch is near the Northern Cheyenne and Crow reservations, and I've said before that Western writers who choose to leave the Indians out of their work are doing themselves a great injustice. There are so many wonderful things to say about the Crow, about their intelligence, humor, and spirituality, but another thing you can say is that a few of them really took to carbohydrates. Suffice to say that when it came time to build my barn and I couldn't afford a tractor, I went and got my friend, Daryl Pretty-On-Top.

With Virgil, I was looking at Walt's and Henry's Vietnam experiences through a glass darkly—looking to see what they would've become without all the safety nets. Then the question became, how could this character survive, and what would society do with him?

*Has your relationship to the characters in the Walt Longmire mysteries changed over the course of four books? Has your writing process changed in any way?*

I think that one of the joys in writing or reading a series is the ability to get to know the characters over a longer arc than a single book can provide. The lifeblood of any series is the complexity of the characters, and I think you have to allow them to change and grow. Walt, Vic, and Henry have all changed over the course of four novels, and that allows them to surprise me, which in turn, might allow me to surprise the reader.

As to the process, I don't think it has changed particularly. I get up in the morning, make coffee, and start writing. To be a writer you have to write, and if you challenge yourself enough, you might even become a better one. I refer to it as the ditch-digging school of literature, and I've never heard of a ditchdigger who got a shovel in his hands and just didn't *feel the ditch* that day.

## Questions for Discussion

1. Why has Craig Johnson chosen to title the novel *Another Man's Moccasins*? In what ways does Walt Longmire show himself to be an empathetic person in the novel? At what moments is he able to feel, and to fully imagine, the pain of others?

2. When he first questions Tuyen, Walt wonders if he is guilty of racial profiling, and at various points he asks his fellow officers if they think he is in any way racist. What are Walt's racial attitudes? Does he let himself be guided, or misguided, by racial stereotypes as he attempts to solve the murders in *Another Man's Moccasins*?

3. The novel moves back and forth in time between Walt's drug and homicide investigations in Vietnam and the current case in Wyoming. What does the story of Vietnam add to the novel? In what ways do the plots of each story intertwine and overlap throughout the novel?

4. How have Walt's experiences in Vietnam prepared him for his job as sheriff in Absaroka County, Wyoming? In what ways has he changed since Vietnam?

5. Ruby tells Walt: "You do have one prejudice. . . . You don't care about the living as much as you do the dead" (p. 149). Why does she think that? To what degree, and in what way, might it be true? How do the dead influence the action of the novel?

6. As Walt picks up Virgil White Buffalo's file, he thinks "about the author of *The Aeneid* and Dante's supposed guide through hell. I studied the folder and hoped his travels had been more pleasant. They hadn't" (p. 131). What does placing Virgil White Buffalo's life in this broader historical and literary context reveal about the way Walt's mind works? In what ways are Walt and Virgil White Buffalo alike?

7. How is Walt able to solve the murders presented in the novel? What combination of intuition, experience, deductive reasoning, knowledge of human nature, and old-fashioned detective work enables him find his way to the truth?

8. Troubling social issues are typically at the heart of Craig Johnson's novels—in this case, human trafficking and prostitution. What more positive traits balance out the human propensity toward deceit, violence, and greed in the novel? Is *Another Man's Moccasins* ultimately an affirming, optimistic book, despite its tale of murder, war, and human exploitation?

For more information about or to order other Penguin Readers Guides, please e-mail the Penguin Marketing Department at reading@us.penguingroup.com or write to us at:

Penguin Books Marketing Dept.
Readers Guides
375 Hudson Street
New York, NY 10014-3657

Please allow 4–6 weeks for delivery.
To access Penguin Readers Guides online, visit the Penguin Group (USA) Inc. Web site at www.penguin.com.

# AVAILABLE NOW

*Any Other Name*

It's a chill high-plains winter when Walt's former boss asks him to take on the special case of a detective, dead by his own hand. Soon enough, Walt is elbow-deep in a cold case with a blood trail that hides a secret so dark, there are sure to be more bodies before Walt can untangle the mess.

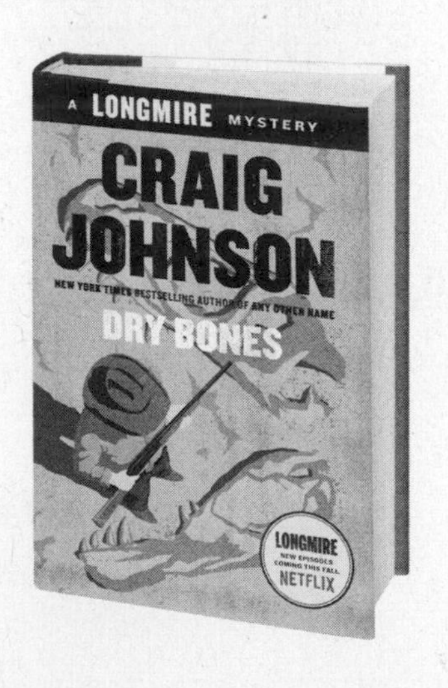


*Dry Bones*

When the most complete fossil of a T-rex ever found is discovered in Absaroka County, and the Cheyenne rancher who claims her is found face down in a turtle pond, it's up to Walt to investigate a 66 million-year-old cold case that is heating up fast.